£2

THE ALPINE JOURNAL 2009

Triglav (2864m), highest summit of the Julian Alps and Slovenia. One of a beautiful collection of aerial photographs by Matevz Lenarcic in his book, *The Alps: A Bird's Eye-View* (2009).

THE
ALPINE JOURNAL
2009

The Journal of the Alpine Club

A record of mountain adventure
and scientific observation

Edited by Stephen Goodwin

Production Editor: Bernard Newman
Assistant Editor: Paul Knott

Volume 114

Number 358

Supported by the
MOUNT EVEREST FOUNDATION

Published jointly by
THE ALPINE CLUB & THE ERNEST PRESS

THE ALPINE JOURNAL 2009
Volume 114 No 358

Address all editorial communication to the Hon Editor:
Stephen Goodwin, 1 Ivy Cottages, Edenhall, Penrith, CA11 8SN
email: sg@stephengoodwin.demon.co.uk
Address all sales and distribution communications to:
Cordée, 11 Jacknell Rd, Dodwells Bridge Ind Est, Hinckley, LE10 3BS

Back numbers:
Apply to the Alpine Club, 55 Charlotte Rd, London, EC2A 3QF or, for 1969 to date, apply to Cordée, as above.

First published in 2009 jointly by The Alpine Club & The Ernest Press
Typeset by Bernard Newman
Printed in Singapore by Kyodo Printing Company

A CIP catalogue record for this book is available from The British Library

ISBN 978 0 948153 94 5

Foreword

When Arne Naess returned to Norway after leading the 1964 Tirich Mir East expedition, a TV interviewer asked the philosophy professor why he had started climbing.

'I? No, I did not start,' Naess replied. 'You gave up!'

It was a playful theme that Naess, an AC honorary member who died in January 2009, aged 96, would return to over the years, pointing out that from early infancy climbing up was a positive experience, from chair legs and tables to trees and rocks. 'For me it is difficult to understand why grown-ups let such experiences go, and thus, with increasing routine, do not go on from trees to mountains'[1]

Watch any child climb a tree and you see the empathy between body and its natural environment that Naess proclaimed; hand and branch seem to communicate without the intermediary of the brain, the child flows up the tree like a high-speed vine. As climbers we experience those golden moments only fleetingly (very fleetingly in the editor's case) but yet with an intensity that hints at alchemy, the rock or ice speaking to the outreached arm.

The American academic and climber Jeff McCarthy calls it 'connection' and in an essay written especially for this *Alpine Journal* he traces the notion from John Muir through Yvon Chouinard to a growing number of present day climbers who he sees as a bellwether for a cultural shift in society's attitude to the natural world, and perhaps a little more hope for the planet. Surely Naess would smile an amused smile that his message, the Taoist injunction to 'think like a mountain', might be getting through.

Kazuya Hiraide and Kei Taniguchi certainly left little between their slender selves and the raw mountain on their impeccable alpine-style ascent of the south-east face of Kamet. Though the 2000m face has attracted a good deal of admiring attention, nobody had previously got a foothold on it. The Japanese pair took just a single sleeping bag and four day's food for what proved to be a seven-day climb.

Hiraide and Taniguchi's story is recorded in this volume along with those of the other five teams fêted at the 2009 *Piolets d'Or* ceremony in Chamonix, an event in which the Alpine Club found itself involved to a considerable degree. Guided by the new president of the *Groupe de Haute Montagne*, Christian Trommsdorff, the 17th Piolets rose from the ruins of an annual event that had collapsed amid anguish among mountaineers over the business of treating climbing as a kind of beauty contest. With the emphasis now on a celebration of alpinism rather than a 'best' climb, the Piolets has reinvented itself with *élan*. (Some of us would like to see the giving of prizes dropped altogether and take heart that it is an evolving story.)

1 A. Naess, Climbing and the Deep Ecology Movement, *The Trumpeter*, Vol. 21, 2005.

Alpine Club support for the Piolets was one of several developments last year, often on the initiative of our Hon Sec Francoise Call, which have seen the AC reaffirming its internationalism. It was good to renew the Club's links with Chamonix – President Paul Braithwaite being one of several gazing up at the town's unique skyline and recalling great routes – not only through the Piolets but also in July 2008 at an event hosted by Chamonix mayor Eric Fournier, *Rencontres aux Sommets*, celebrating the ascents of Everest and Annapurna, and attended by George Band, Maurice Herzog and Doug Scott. The Club was invited on the 150th anniversary ascents of both the Aletschhorn and the Bietschhorn (a Leslie Stephen first) and I had the enjoyable privilege of attending an Editors' Summit of fellow toilers on mountaineering journals and other media, generously hosted by the American Alpine Club within hailing distance of the crags, cracks and towers of Colorado and Utah. As the saying goes, 'All work and no play…'

Those visits to Chamonix and Colorado have both borne fruit for this journal, with accounts of not only the six Piolets climbs, but also – courtesy of another special piece for the *AJ* by Kelly Cordes – a résumé of the often unsung achievements of North America's young alpinists, a new generation of 'dirtbag' climbers in the making. AC members have been active too; there's an alpine-style first from Simon Yates on Mount Vancouver, Paul Knott in the Chinese Tien Shan, Mick Fowler running out of options as cold and altitude bite in the Garhwal, and plenty more.

Add together the air miles of all the above and it is inescapable that mountaineers must have among the biggest carbon footprints around. This is certainly troubling guide Rob Collister who asks when we are going to take our collective heads out of the sand and exercise restraint. Jeff McCarthy also touches on this dilemma, though he contends that our time in the mountains also make us ambassadors for their preservation. It's a justification I've heard before, but how long can it stand? This is also a journal that prods the conscience.

As always, producing this 114th volume of the *AJ* has been a collective effort. I must give particular thanks to Area Notes editor Paul Knott, to our assiduous proof-reader Margot Blyth, and to Bernard Newman who took on the task of production editor. And then there are the dozens of people who have contributed words or photos in any form. There would be no *AJ* without you. Many thanks to you all.

While this journal was at the printers, we learned of the death of Peter Hodgkiss whose Ernest Press has been joint publisher of the *Alpine Journal* since 1993. The classic appearance of the journal over those years has been down to countless hours of dedicated work by Peter. Elected to the AC in 1988, he remained passionately involved with the journal until his final days. I would like to personally dedicate this 2009 *AJ* to Peter, one of the great unsung servants of the Alpine Club.

Stephen Goodwin

Contents

SCIENCE

ARTS

HISTORY

AREA NOTES

Illustrations

Front cover: Ueli Steck on the summit ridge of Teng Kangpoche (6487m) (*Simon Anthamatten*)

Endpapers: Simon Pierse, *Morning Sun on Kangchenjunga*, 2005, watercolour, 24 x 64cm

Frontispiece & Rear Cover: Triglav (2864m), highest summit of the Julian Alps and Slovenia. One of a beautiful collection of aerial photographs by Matevz Lenarcic in his book, *The Alps: A Bird's Eye-View* (2009).

Obituaries

NOTES FOR CONTRIBUTORS

The *Alpine Journal* records all aspects of mountains and mountaineering, including expeditions, adventure, art, literature, geography, history, geology, medicine, ethics and the mountain environment.

Articles Contributions in English are invited. They should be sent to the Hon Editor, Stephen Goodwin, 1 Ivy Cottages, Edenhall, Penrith, Cumbria CA11 8SN (e-mail: sg@stephengoodwin.demon.co.uk). Articles should be sent on a disk with accompanying hard copy or as an e-mail attachment (in Microsoft Word) with hard copy sent separately by post. Length should not exceed 3000 words without prior approval of the editor **and may be edited or shortened at his discretion**. It is regretted that the *Alpine Journal* is unable to offer a fee for articles published, but authors receive a complimentary copy of the issue of the *Journal* in which their article appears.
Preferably, articles and book reviews should not have been published in substantially the same form by any other publication.
Maps These should be well researched, accurate, and show the most important place-names mentioned in the text. It is the author's responsibility to get their maps redrawn if necessary. If submitted electronically, maps should be originated as CMYK in a vectorised drawing package (Adobe Illustrator, Freehand or similar), and submitted as pdfs. (Any embedded images should be at 300dpi resolution at A4 size.) Hard copy should be scanned as a Photoshop compatible 300dpi tiff at A4 finished size. This can be arranged through the production editor if required.
Photographs Colour transparencies should be originals (not copies) in 35mm format or larger. Prints (any size) should be numbered (in pencil) on the back and accompanied by a separate list of captions (see below). Pre-scanned images should be CMYK, 300dpi tiffs or Maximum Quality jpegs at A4 final size. Images from digital cameras should be CMYK, 300dpi jpegs or tiffs at the maximum file size (quality) the camera can produce. All images (slides, prints and digital) should have unique names/serial numbers that correspond to a list of captions supplied with your article or as a word processing document or via email.
Captions should include subject matter, photographer's name, title and author of the article to which they refer.
Copyright It is the author's responsibility to obtain copyright clearance for text, photographs, digital images and maps, to pay any fees involved and to ensure that acknowledgements are in the form required by the copyright owner.
Summaries A brief summary, helpful to researchers, may be included with 'expedition' articles.
Biographies Authors are asked to provide a short biography, in about 60 words, listing the most noteworthy items in their climbing career and anything else they wish to mention.
Deadline Copy and photographs should reach the editor by 1 January of the year of publication.

Alpinism

Simon Pierse, *La Grivola,* 2006, watercolour, 72 x 53cm

MICK FOWLER

Vasuki Parbat

The Judgement Game

The cold was getting to be a concern. It was early on our fifth day on the face. Starting up a difficult pitch I took my mitt off to use an undercut for 20 seconds or so. On removing my fingers from the crack I was shocked to see a blister on my middle finger. I warmed it immediately but I swear it was a blister – a memorable, unwelcome and frightening new experience after more than 25 years climbing in the greater ranges. Stakes were rising in the judgement game.

It had all started about five years before when Harish Kapadia, extra helpful chap and acknowledged expert on everything to do with the Indian Himalaya, sent me a disturbing CD containing photos that he thought I might find 'interesting'. One in particular caught my attention – an eye-catchingly steep face on with a single buttress line cleaving the centre. For some years the image lurked invasively in my subconscious and by 2007 it had found its way onto my screen saver where it provided a sufficiently regular reminder to prompt Paul Ramsden and I to organise an attempt for post-monsoon 2008.

It was nine years since my last trip to India and I had a niggling concern that the country's much vaunted economic growth might have diluted the aspects of India that I have always found so attractive. I need not have feared. The Indian boardrooms might be stashed full of cash but the adhesive beard salesmen still paraded outside the Red Fort, the roads were still clogged with every method of transport imaginable, people still slept in the most remarkable places and the whole place still had a vibrant feeling of continuous activity and interest.

Much as I had previously managed to derive a degree of satisfaction from overcoming Indian bureaucratic challenges I was, perhaps naively, hoping that surging economic activity would have gone hand in hand with a reduction in the amount of red tape. That may or may not be true for India as a whole but I was soon to conclude that it is certainly not true as regards mountaineering in the recently created state of Uttarakhand – and in particular in the Gangotri region where Vasuki Parbat is situated. Once this was thought of as a bureaucratically straightforward area and it was possible to climb on a set of permits one could organise from one's home country. Now though it is necessary to obtain permits from the local Uttarakhand government and Forestry Commission, register and pay a daily rate to the Gangotri national park authorities, stick to a rule that says no more than 150 people can enter the park each day and deposit a 10,000 rupees rubbish bond. All of these hurdles can be overcome but tend to sport hidden catches to trip up the unwary.

Brejish, our Liaison Officer, was a Brahman with an endearing personality and a persuasive aura of confident authority. He proved a star at overcoming such difficulties. Banker's drafts were forced through at short notice, obstructive officials expertly overcome and rip-off merchants curtly dismissed. It was a credit to his efficiency that two days after leaving Delhi we were ready to leave the roadhead at Gangotri and the way seemed clear to base camp. What I regard as Key Stage 1 to any trip (overcoming bureaucracy) had been accomplished.

An hours walk beyond Gangotri a smart official with a side parting and fetching cardigan sat in a tin shack at the side of the track.

'Rubbish bond. 10,000 Rupees. Banker's draft only. And park fees.' Our paperwork clearly showed that we had already paid park fees but this was apparently irrelevant. But it was the rubbish bond that was the real sticking point. Mr Side Parting insisted that a banker's draft was necessary. The last bank was in Uttarkashi about six hours away. This didn't look good. Brejish battled firmly, exercising his mobile telephone (amazing where you get a signal nowadays) and harassing senior officials in various distant towns. And then for some delightfully inexplicable reason the problem disappeared as quickly as it has arisen, tea was offered, cash accepted and we were free to go on our way. In retrospect such encounters add to the Indian Himalayan experience. At the time though it is not always easy to see it that way.

Three days later we were approaching base camp and having our first good view of what we had come to climb. It didn't disappoint. Several buttresses soared up towards an overhanging headwall that appeared to be broken by a single possible line. The west face looked as impressive as it had in the photograph on Harish's CD. And it appeared that conditions were good – a plastering of snow and ice on the face but none on the approach to the base. Could this be too good to be true?

Forty-eight hours later only about 5cm of our tent poked out of the snow. Brejish dug a trench and stuck his head in.

'What are you going to do?' he asked, a twinge of concern audible in his voice.

Paul and I lay in our sleeping bags contemplating. It had been snowing for 36 hours and we had already delayed the start of our acclimatisation by a day. One day might not sound a lot but on a tight timescale it was pretty significant. We had allowed one week to get here, one week acclimatising, one week doing the route and one week getting home. On that time scale we had three days leeway. So one day lost was a cause for concern.

'Be fine tomorrow,' we chorused glumly.

Next morning the clouds had lifted just above base camp. Taking this as a sign that the weather might be clearing Premsingh, our cook, prepared an inspirational bowl of hot milk on cornflakes and we waded off to acclimatise. Our plan was to follow the tried and trusted method of somehow getting up high and then just lying there reading and popping headache

2. The west face of Vasuki Parbat (6792m), Garhwal Himalaya, attempted by Mick Fowler and Paul Ramsden. (*Mick Fowler*)

3. Ramsden eyes conditions at Vasuki Parbat base camp. It will snow for another 24 hours. (*Mick Fowler*)

4. Fowler searches for a bivvi at the close of Day 3. *(Paul Ramsden)*

tabs for a couple of days. Brejish and Premsingh stood outside their tent and waved goodbye until we had disappeared. This took a ridiculously long time and their arms must have been exhausted by the time we dropped out of sight down onto the Vasuki glacier.

Here the conditions were such that it reminded me of the Arwa glacier, perhaps only 20 miles away in a straight line. There, back in 1999, the surface crust was such that Steve Sustad and I were reduced to crawling on all fours pulling our sacks behind us. Here there was no crust but wading was so exhausting we resorted to one person breaking trail without a sack, the other following with his sack on and, after half an hour or so, the first person returning to his sack and bringing up the rear. The roles would then be reversed. Progressing in this manner was ridiculously slow and amaz-

5. Mick Fowler in his element. Pushing the route on Day 4. (*Paul Ramsden*)

ingly exhausting. It took just over two days to reach the foot of the face at a paltry 5100m. Here we lay in our tent trying unsuccessfully to convince ourselves that the seriously heavy breathing necessary to get to this height might be better for acclimatising than lying still at our target altitude of 5800m. We tried to go higher but the snow stayed uniformly appalling such that we only managed one night at about 5200m. That would have to do.

Back at base camp the weather seemed to be changing. Up to now we had been too hot in our sleeping bags. Now though it was suddenly cold, base layers were worn and we woke to find water bottles in the tent had frozen solid.

'Be nice and cool at 6800m,' commented Paul cheerfully; he being a man with a well exercised urge to climb in sub-zero spots such as Antarctica and Patagonia in winter.

I prodded my frozen water bottle doubtfully, noted the heavy build up of hoar frost inside the tent and packed some extra long johns.

'Winter is here now,' announced Premsingh helpfully whilst serving up yet more hot milk on soggy cornflakes.

And it certainly felt that way. The skies had cleared completely and the day had that cold, crisp feel reminiscent of the European Alps in fine winter weather.

Four days later we were below the steepest section and had cut a pleasingly level but narrow nose to tail ledge, hung the stove between us, put some snow in to melt for a brew and snuggled down to some reading.

In a world where weight is so important it sometimes surprises me that we cut our toothbrushes in half but still carry superfluous weight in the form of reading material. I never used to do this but five days stuck in a tiny mountain tent with Victor Saunders on Spantik in Pakistan in 1987 was the turning point. It snowed incessantly and we left the tent only to go to the toilet. Even the normally garrulous Victor ran out of things to say. We just lay there in a mind-numbing silence except for the patter of snow against

6.
Fowler with the 'alarm call' rock. Note the hole in the tent.
(*Paul Ramsden*)

the tent. Eventually I didn't even bother to put my contact lenses in and just sat there in a blur. The experience left a marked impression on us both and since then I have always carried reading material to sustain morale through periods of inactivity.

From our bivouac the walls above looked disturbingly challenging compared to how they had appeared through binoculars. The snow and ice that we had hoped would provide enjoyable mixed climbing could now be seen to be stuck loosely to near-vertical rock or blasted up under overhangs. A snow/ice traverse line leading to a tenuous vertical line near the edge of the buttress looked to offer the best possibility but the first section of the traverse was devoid of ice and looked far from straightforward.

Normally we alternate leads with both the leader and the second climbing with their sacks on. That is the style of climbing we most enjoy and it generally flows smoothly. It gives us both the opportunity to enjoy the climbing and, equally importantly, have a good rest and admire the view at stances. Here though it didn't take long before our usual routine took a knock. Paul's first pitch turned out to be challenging to the extent that he was soon forced to abandon his sack. Sack hauling is the anathema of our style of climbing, particularly on diagonal pitches. When it was my turn to climb, not only was I soon teetering badly in the face of a nasty pendulum but my efforts to control the sack were sadly lacking. In fact all I could do was unclip it and vaguely control its pendulum to where it promptly got stuck, after which Paul pulled as hard as he could while I pushed as hard as I could. Paul's sleeping mat parted company in the struggle and we were both exhausted by the time I reached the stance. I hate sack hauling.

Panting aside, the climbing position was now magnificent. Days away from anyone else; just the two of us half way up a huge unclimbed face with steep ground all around and wild drops below. Together we both savoured the position in between staring intensely at the little digital screens on our cameras and trying to zoom into our images of the face to pick out the best line up the technical ground ahead.

Out right still seemed best. The further right we traversed the more the ground fell away steeply below. Great squeaky white ice traverse pitches followed until a rock pinnacle on the crest provided a wild bivouac spot right on the edge of a huge overhanging wall forming the right side of the buttress. Although the pinnacle itself was vertical or overhanging on all sides its top had accumulated a knife-edge snow crest deep enough for us to simply chop the top off and pitch the tent. Inside it was easy to forget surroundings. We could have been on a grassy campsite; the only slight giveaway being the belay ropes snaking out of the entrance.

But much as I was cosy and slept soundly, the cold was becoming an issue. My feet had been intermittently numb during the day and although they looked pink and healthy when I peered at them in the evening I could feel the first stages of cold damage were present. Paul's feet too were cold, despite him wearing boots designed for much higher altitudes.

But it was the blistered finger incident first thing the next morning that really gave me food for thought. I'd only had the mitt off for seconds to use the undercut. I squawked about it to Paul who looked suitably subdued.

'My feet are cold,' he said forlornly. '8,000m rated boots too.'

From my point of view I was uncomfortably aware that I was already wearing my biggest mitts. I wondered whether it would be warmer to get two sets of inners into one shell but vaguely thought the extra tightness might have the wrong effect. And I concluded that this was not the place to experiment. I was going to have to make do with what I had and be careful. The pitch itself was fantastic; Scottish V right on the edge of a wildly exposed buttress and leading to an excellent small, flat belay ledge. But we could both increasingly feel that all was not well. The pitch had taken me 90 minutes to lead and we both knew we were slowing down and gasping (even) more than usual. My trademark 'rest the helmet against the ice' move was becoming more and more frequent. At that point though the elation of making upward progress in such a fantastic position was such that neither of us voiced any concerns.

It was difficult to pick out detail on the screens of our digital cameras but it seemed the best way ahead was to cross the rib to our left and traverse a hidden ice band left for 50m or so. After that it looked possible to easily gain access to a snow/ice slope and the end of the section we felt would contain the most technically difficult climbing.

It was not long before we had to conclude that small camera screens are not the best for detailed route-finding decisions. Firstly the traverse proved a lot more challenging and time consuming than we had expected but the real shock came on the second traversing pitch when it became clear that the ground we had expected to lead easily to the snow/ice slope was, in reality, near-vertical rock with powdery snow stuck at a remarkably steep angle. Out to the left a much longer route, exposed to falling ice in the afternoon sun, looked a vague possibility but my immediate reaction on seeing what was ahead was that we should retreat along the traverse and try to climb a short rock buttress which looked to give an alternative route to the snow/ice slope.

The trouble was it was getting late in the day. By the time we had reversed the traverse it was time to be looking for somewhere to spend the night. And where we were there was no possibility beyond a hanging or, at best, a sitting bivouac. It was this that prompted our first major dither. Normally I would vote strongly for staying at our highpoint but here I knew we were tiring and the cold was giving increasing cause for concern. Two abseils below us was the pinnacle bivouac site where we knew we could pitch the tent and enjoy a sound night's sleep. Paul was keen to descend, have a good rest and return fresh to our highpoint the following morning. I dithered. We had two 7.5mm ropes and the idea of tying them together, abseiling on a single rope and then starting the next day with a long jumar back up was enough to prompt me to hesitate. Surely it would be best to stay where we were? But the sun was low in the sky and I could feel the cold biting hard already. Cutting a reasonable bum ledge might not be possible and would, at best, take a long time. The pinnacle bivvi platform was ready and waiting. We discussed, traversed a bit in search of a possible ledge, failed to find one, discussed more ... and decided to retreat to the pinnacle bivouac. As I was abseiling over the difficult ground that we had fought our way up that day the balance of probabilities about our success began to change in my mind.

There was little conversation in the tent but an unspoken acceptance that we were weakening. The conversation lacked sparkle and our reactions were slowing. Our dream was slipping but we couldn't yet bring ourselves to discuss turning back. We were determined to push on while we judged it was even vaguely sensible to do so.

The alarm bleeped at 4am but our sluggishness was such that it was 9am before we were back at our highpoint. The alternative line we had chosen looked as if it would be straightforward rock climbing at sea level. It was Paul's lead. He took one glove off, touched the rock for a few seconds, commented, 'No way', and put the glove back on again. Meanwhile I rested my helmet against the slope and worked to warm a finger that had gone an unpleasant pasty white colour.

7. High pitch… Bivvi for nights 4 and 5. (*Mick Fowler*)

8. Paul Ramsden on the west face of Vasuki Parbat, Day 4. (*Mick Fowler*)

9. Fowler on Day 5. Scottish V, fantastic climbing, numbing cold. *(Paul Ramsden)*

We always work on the basis that one should continue unless there is no sensible alternative. That leaves plenty of scope for debate about what is 'sensible' but here, even our increasingly befuddled brains recognised that our problems were not going to decrease as we got higher. Try as we might to convince ourselves otherwise, we had to accept that if we tried to go higher the air wasn't going to contain any more oxygen, we weren't going to move any faster and it wasn't going to get any warmer. Frankly, it was clear that we were on the verge of taking on more risk than either of us was prepared to take. It was Paul who spoke first:

'What do you expect to happen if we get over this rock pitch?' he asked. We looked at each other and the decision was made.

Sometimes the mountain wins.

As if confirmation were needed, it was delivered in the form of a hurtling rock as we spent our sixth face night, bivouacked on the ledge we had cut for night two on the way up. A nasty hole in the tent and the disintegration of our hanging stove was not the most relaxing way to start the day. The message was clear. It was time to go home.

Summary: An account of an attempt by Mick Fowler and Paul Ramsden to make the first ascent of the west face of Vasuki Parbat (6792m), Garhwal Himalaya, India, September/October 2008.

Acknowledgements: Thanks to Berghaus, Black Diamond and First Ascent for their invaluable support. Also to the Mount Everest Foundation and British Mountaineering Council whose support is so vital to the health of British Greater Range mountaineering.

DEREK BUCKLE & MARTIN SCOTT

Temples and Mountains[1]

Climbing in the Garhwal Himalaya

Our destination was the Obra valley, a remote region of the Garhwal Himalaya characterised by a blend of steep granite walls and magnificent glaciated peaks rising to almost 6000m in height. It looked as though there was something here for everybody, but we had our eyes set on the rugged mountains that formed a broad cirque at the head of the glacier enclosing the upper reaches of the valley. With typical armchair enthusiasm we had greedily identified the highest of these peaks (5930m and 5760m) as our primary objectives.

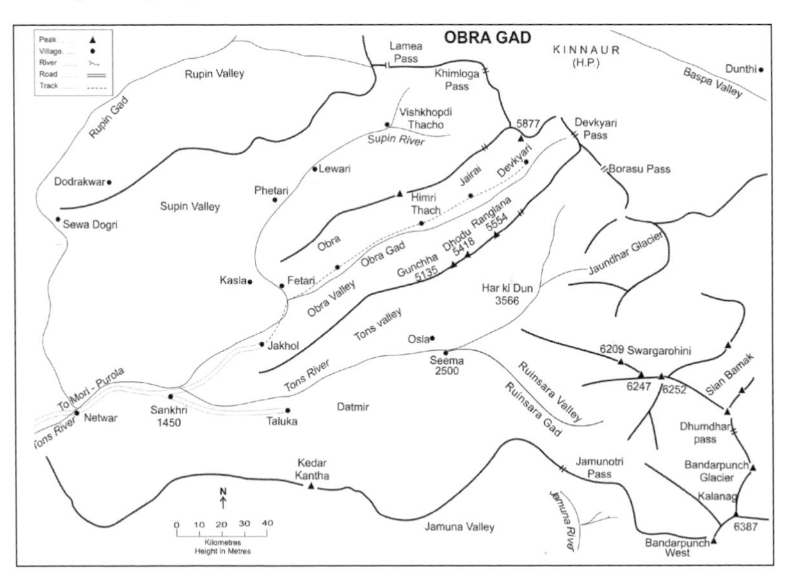

10. Obra Gad valley, Garhwal Himalaya, by kind permission of Harish Kapadia.

It transpired that this is the spectacularly beautiful grazing ground of Devkyari, an area almost unvisited and unknown except by a few shepherds and the local inhabitants of Jakhol who every 10 years make a pilgrimage here. This is the supposed birthplace of their village deity, Lord Someshwara Mahadev – the lord of *devas* (gods) and *pitars* (forefathers) and the provider of fearlessness. On account of this, there are regularly spaced *thaches*, or shrines, along the valley that culminate at the deity's birth place in a holy cave just short of the current terminal moraine. From here onwards frequent square-cut prayer stones lead towards the glacial

11. Looking south from Camp 2 over the Devkir glacier to Ranglana.
(Buckle & Scott coll.)

12. Prospecting the Devkir icefall, Peak 5760m behind. *(Buckle & Scott coll.)*

13. Sherpas Dawa and Dorje traversing under Devkir icefall, Peak 5760 behind. *(Buckle & Scott coll.)*

snout and a less obvious thach that is said to exist close to the glacier itself.

We had originally planned to return to the Nyenchen Tanglha range in Tibet in order to attempt some unclimbed mountains that we had seen from the summit of Beu-tse, a 6270m peak in the neighbourhood of Yangpachen to the northwest of Lhasa[2]. Sadly, a combination of world politics and the impending Beijing Olympics meant that permission was not forthcoming.

Fortunately, during an earlier visit to India during the spring[3], Martin had met with Harish Kapadia, an authority on the Indian Himalaya. It was his recommendation that we should visit the Obra valley, which he had visited in 2006 with Suman Dubey[4-7]. Their expedition had explored the middle valley in the region of the Jairai Rocks where they had unsuccessfully attempted the impressive Ranglana (5554m). They did, however, succeed on a nearby peak, Dhodu Ka Guncha (5130m)[5].

So, after flying to Delhi, we boarded the Shatabki Express to Dehra Dun. Then, after a night in the hill town of Mussoorie, we travelled in a 4x4, driving north towards the Garhwal Himalaya. Gradually the roads became narrower and bumpier until finally giving out at the village of Jakhol where we met our porters. It was immediately clear that any anticipated cathartic experience would be spoilt, at least on the walk-in, by the inclusion of numerous porters, morning tea in bed and other luxuries; conditions quite unknown on our earlier Tibetan expeditions.

We then had a beautiful three-day walk-in up the valley. Initially the scenery was almost Swiss-like with deep pine-clad valleys and distant peaks protruding high above the tree line. Further up we passed the very tempting granite slabs of the Jairai Rocks before reaching large, ancient terminal moraines. Finally the valley opened out to an extensive grassy plateau large enough to land a largish aircraft. It was here, at 4055m close to the Himri Thach temple, that we made our base camp.

Exploration of the Upper Obra valley

There was simply too much choice. Base camp, at a little over 1km from the snout of the Devkir Glacier, was surrounded by impressive, unclimbed peaks, all between 5000 and 6000m high. Moreover, we had not yet seen our primary objective, which formed part of the cirque at the head of the main glacier. It would have been all too easy to get sidetracked into attempting one of the many mountains that we could see. Nursing mild altitude headaches, and the customary lethargy associated with initial sojourns above 4000m, we temporarily suspended our ambitions to settle for a little local exploration.

14. Sherpa Dawa on the Devkir icefall. *(Buckle & Scott coll.)*

First we embarked on short forays up both the terminal moraine and then a side valley to the north in the hope of gaining a better perspective of our surroundings. Both afforded superb views of the north faces of Ranglana and Dhodu, but neither allowed sight of the upper glacial cirque. From the side valley the dominant glaciated Peak 5877m to the north-east of base camp was clearly visible.

From Camp 1 near the prominent 2km long left lateral moraine of the Devkir glacier it was possible to reach Camp 2 at the foot of the icefall and explore the obvious col almost due east across the glacier. We had hoped to attempt the peak to the right of this col, but after lengthy and strenuous post-holing culminating in bottomless snow our enthusiasm for this was rather diminished. Despite encroaching mist, this col did give extensive views into the steep-sided Maninda valley, which provides access to the valleys north of the Borasu Pass.

Steep and often overhanging sugar ice separated by deep crevasses prevented a direct route through the main Devkir icefall but it was possible to traverse rightwards into a prominent couloir that led steeply to a broad plateau at the head of the glacier. It was from here at Camp 3 that we had hoped to attempt our primary objectives. A quick survey of its icy south-east buttress was sufficient to eliminate Peak 5930m from our plans, but the fine, corniced western arête leading to Peak 5760m looked well within our

5. Toto Gronlund, Martin Scott and Bill Thurston ascending the couloir, bypassing the icefall en route to Camp 3. *(Buckle & Scott coll.)*

capabilities. Unfortunately, by the time that we were fully established at Camp 3 and in a position to attempt this peak the weather had deteriorated to zero visibility. Unconsolidated snow added to the difficulties and our attempt was short-lived. After spending an unpleasant night of wind-driven snow in whiteout conditions at Camp 3 we unanimously decided to retreat to base camp.

Back at base camp we looked around for an alternative peak that we could attempt in the limited time that was now left to us. The obvious choice was Peak 5165m that we believed was accessible via a side valley leading northwards from the camp. Following the steep valley bed we eventually emerged onto a snow-plastered rocky plateau that traversed upwards to an obvious col overlooking the Supin valley. From here a narrow south-westerly ridge led easily (Alpine PD) to the final mixed arête over which we scrambled to the rocky summit; there were lammergeiers circling and so it seemed appropriate to name it Lammergeier Peak. A magnificent panorama greeted us. Apart from the obvious Ranglana and Dhodu group above case camp, and the nearby peaks 5877m and 5489m, a particularly impressive 5889m mountain was visible to the north of the Supin valley. There are no recorded ascents of any of these mountains and the opportunities are endless.

With our time in the Obra valley nearing its end we returned to base camp to prepare for a three-day trek back to civilisation and then the Mus-

16. Toto Gronlund on the summit ridge of Lammergeier Peak (5165m) looking WSW to Peak 5405m. *(Buckle & Scott coll.)*

soorie express back to the fleshpots of Delhi.

Summary: In late September to the end of October 2008 Derek Buckle, Toto Gronlund, Martin Scott and Bill Thurston travelled to Jakhol in the Garhwal Himalaya where they trekked for three days up the Obra valley. From a base camp at 4055m they attempted Peak 5760m at the head of the Devkir cirque but were defeated by poor weather and conditions underfoot. Returning to base camp, Toto and Derek successfully climbed Peak 5165m overlooking the Supin valley at Alpine PD.

Acknowledgements: The expedition would like to thank the Mount Everest Foundation for generous sponsorship.

References

1. Derek R Buckle, *Obra Valley 5000m Peak Expedition 2008*, MEF Report
2. Derek Buckle & John Town, Climbing the Fish Village Mountain - An Account of the British Beu-tse Expedition, *Alpine Journal*, Vol 109 (2004), pp 36-45
3. Martin Scott, Himalayan Club 80th Anniversary, *AJ* Vol. 114 (2009), pp 396
4. Suman Dubey, *Harmony Magazine*, September 2006
5. Rajal Upadhyay, The Himalayan Newsletter, Vol. 5, July 2006 pp 2-3,
6. Gerry & Louise Wilson, *The Himalayan Journal*, Vol. 62 (2006), pp 199-206
7. Soli Mehta & Harish Kapadia, *Exploring the Hidden Himalaya*, 2007, ISBN 97881738720082

PAUL KNOTT

Adventure and Discovery in The Chinese Tien Shan

From the well-known summits of Pobeda (Tomur, 7439m) and Khan Tengri (6995m), the 6000m peaks of the Tien Shan extend eastward into Xinjiang as far as they do to the west into Kyrgyzstan. Yet for all this vast potential, the climbing history of the range within Xinjiang is succinct. The major summit Xuelian Feng ('Snow Lotus', 6627m), 60km east of the Inylchek glacier basins, received its first ascent only in 1990, when the last of four Japanese assaults reached the summit from the south-east. More recently, a group of Russian climbers explored and climbed in the area immediately south of Pobeda and nearby Military Topographers' Peak (6873m). Everything else beyond the Kyrgyz border appears untouched from a climbing perspective.

'I'll have you know, I am not suicidal,' Bruce exhorted. For me, this story begins here – Mt Tasman, New Zealand, January 2006. Much to Bruce's disgust, I had refused to continue towards the face. I found the constant stream of falling rock and ice and the sound of running water too much to ignore. Putting aside our conspicuous differences in risk appetite and temperament, Bruce Normand and I subsequently pursued our common interest in exploring the Chinese Tien Shan. Our initial research pointed to the north side of Xuelian Feng as an attractive target. Satellite-derived images and maps formed our only detailed information; in contemporary terms, we were exploring a blank on the map.

It seemed clear that we were destined to have an adventure, not a holiday, and this adventure started well before the trip itself. Our first difficult choice concerned the access route. The historic Xiate trail traverses the range from Aksu in the south to Ili in the north, and actually crosses the Muzart glacier close to Xuelian Feng. It used to be an important trade route, and in the 1940s the Uighur army used it to launch surprise attacks on the Chinese to the south. Subsequently, it fell into disrepair, though it is beginning to undergo a revival for trekking. Reports suggested that high river levels would prevent horses from following the trail from the south, although the Japanese parties on Xuelian had approached this way. Instead, we elected to start from the north via the smaller Xiate valley, and cross the 3582m Muzart pass.

We also had to get some sort of official permission. Given the restive history of the Ili region and the close proximity of the former Soviet border, we expected, and found, a well enforced set of bureaucratic and security checks on the approach to the Xiate valley. Through our agent, Kashgar-based Kong Baocun, we obtained a permit for Xuelian Feng. This seemed

17. View from Zhaosu Hotel, from left to right: Yanamax (6332m), Xuelian East (6400m+), Xuelian Feng (6627m), Baiyu Feng (6422m). *(Paul Knott)*

18 View from Hadamuzi base camp, (L–R): Xuelian North (6472m), Xuelian Feng (6627m) and Baiyu Feng (6422m). *(Paul Knott)*

straightforward, though it was not cheap and it made us dependent on Kong. The timing of our trip, in August 2008 during the Beijing Olympics, caused various concerns, not least of which was tight enforcement of China's visa regulations. The New Zealand team members, Guy McKinnon and I, trusted the bureaucracy to function and paid for our plane tickets. For a variety of reasons, in the weeks before we were to leave, Bruce's loosely assembled party of eight dwindled to four. Shortly before we departed, it became tragically clear that the four were now three, as news emerged of a solo climbing accident in Pakistan.

Despite these unsettling developments, Guy and I flew to the regional capital, Urumqi, and shortly afterwards we met Bruce, who arrived by sleeper bus from Kashgar. After some difficult exchanges with Kong, Bruce had thrashed out a compromise deal in which we paid only for the climbing permit, base camp staff (a translator plus a guide for the journey in) and insurance for the staff. Kong took every opportunity to deal dishonestly over the prices for these services. Fortunately, with the help of our translator David, we were able to arrange everything else independently, finding the local prices very reasonable. Unsettling developments continued, however, as we read news reports of bomb attacks on Xinjiang border posts, which we felt could compromise our permission to travel. We finished buying food and supplies, and set off overnight on the modern highway past the scenic Lake Sayram to Yining, capital of Ili Kazakh Autonomous Region. As we passed through the rich, cultivated land around Yining, we encountered the first of many checkpoints where we had to show our passports and permits. In the city itself, we had more paperwork to process, which took all afternoon and required intervention from Kong. In the evening, we continued on upgraded roads through the Ketmen range of limestone hills to the small county town of Zhaosu.

In the morning, our first view of the mountains lifted our spirits: a panorama from Yanamax (6332m) in the east to Khan Tengri in the west. A short drive, and several more checkpoints, one of which parted us from our passports, took us to the road end at Xiate Hot Springs (2380m). In all, our journey from Urumqi had taken us 1½ days including the overnight stop. Notwithstanding the onerous security checkpoints, we noticed that the authorities are developing the Xiate valley as a tourist centre. A new concrete bridge and hotel were under construction at the hot springs, and an upgrade of the access road was mostly complete. Beyond the hot springs, we had a further 22km to cover to base camp. For this, we relied on horses, and we knew this could be problematic given the lack of previous parties. The terrain was gentle through pasture and forest, but we made slow progress, as our horseman was ineffective at securing the loads and generally seemed inept. After a forced overnight stop due to high afternoon river levels, we continued on 8 August up the distinct trail over the barren Muzart pass (3582m) to reach our long-anticipated base camp.

Base camp was at Hadamuzi (3525m), a stunning, if exposed, alpine meadow clinging to the slopes south of the Muzart (Benzhaerte) glacier.

19 Guy McKinnon and Bruce Normand on Hanjaylak I (5424m). The peaks behind, from left to right, are Xuelian North East (6231m), Xuelian Feng (6627m) and Xuelian North (6472m). *(Paul Knott)*

In earlier times, this area housed a large military garrison to maintain and guard the trail, and artefacts from this habitation were clearly visible around the site. Immediately across the glacier was the imposing north face of Baiyu Feng (Aketasi Feng or 'White Jade', 6422m or 6438m) and the cirque formed by Xuelian North (6472m) and Xuelian Feng (6627m). These peaks were typical of those we saw in that they were apparently of granitic rock with steep walls on the north sides, long ridges, and sérac-threatened slopes on most aspects. As we arrived at the site, an afternoon squall caught us in what was to become a regular pattern. Cloud often built up in the north, and the pass channelled it in our direction.

We focused our reconnaissance on what we hoped would be accessible climbing near the head of the Muzart glacier. Some 12km of undulating moraine-covered glacier took us to what became a kind of advanced base camp on rivulet-covered white ice at 3950m. As we negotiated this glacier, we passed surprisingly dry-looking peaks, with slopes stripped of snow to remarkably high levels. It was also apparent that accessing routes could take some cunning, as most of the side glaciers contained broken icefalls. Disappointingly, the reconnaissance ended when we woke to a covering of several inches of wet snow. Snow continued to fall through the day, and we returned to base camp.

Our second reconnaissance was more productive, and took us through the crevassed area where the glacier curves south beneath Yanamax (6332m). The terrain that unfolded was awe-inspiring and grandiose, but frustrating from a climbing perspective. Tempting summit ridges always seemed inaccessible above icefalls, crumbling walls, and sérac barriers. We continued to the 4640m col between Yanamax and Xuelian East (6400m+), hoping to find a route to the snowy upper slopes of Yanamax. Disappointingly, a rocky ridge and fore-summit separated us from these slopes. The precipitous walls on the south side were out of the question. This left only a somewhat threatened slope rising under the west face, an option I had already rejected as too contrived and risky. Meanwhile, Bruce's child-like enthusiasm was unabated.

Back at the glacier camp, we looked again at a route to two of the 5000m peaks visible from the Xiate valley and its Hanjaylak summer pastures. These became our acclimatization objectives, but a prolonged dump of snow again disrupted our plans. This time, snow lay deep at base camp too. Information varies as to whether this pattern is typical. The nearby Inylchek glacier basins are known for unsettled summer weather, but some sources suggest it should be drier further east. Fortunately, our tarpaulin shelter held up well, and we sat in it making fry-ups. I was also glad of some escapist reading, appropriately entitled Absurdistan.

As soon as the weather cleared, we headed back to our glacier camp and up the side glacier to the north to position ourselves for the Hanjaylak peaks. We bypassed the icefall on the rocky moraine to the left. On 21 August, we finally set off for our first summit. A slope with a small area of fallen ice blocks led us to the south ridge of what we were to call Hanjaylak I (5424m, WGS84 GPS height). A detour to the left to avoid 'schrunds took us over packed wind deposits to the snowy summit. Here we lingered at length, photographing the panorama of unclimbed peaks around us.

The following morning, we walked in moonlight through the upper glacier bowl towards Hanjaylak II. Positioned second on the rope behind Bruce, I was beginning to wonder why we were approaching glacial relief on the right-hand side when suddenly, the crust gave way beneath me and I fell forward. For an age I felt and heard myself crashing through what seemed like layer on layer of aerated ice. Finally, I broke free of this honey-comb and felt a rush of air as I accelerated face first into a black abyss. Just as I became convinced I was in for serious injury, I felt the powerful elastic tug of the rope. Pulling myself upright, I found myself swinging uncomfort-ably in my minimalist Alpine harness. I looked around in the torch beam to see that I was in a sizeable icicle-encrusted cavern. I thought I must be deep under the surface, until I looked up to see my own hole a few metres above. When I reached out to the walls with my ice-axe, this only brought down more icicles from above. I prepared to prussik out, but knew from experience that pulling from the surface is usually easier, and anyway was nervous about the state of the belays. We had inherited our snow-stakes from Bruce's Pakistan trip, and they were of the bendy homemade variety cut from soft aluminium section.

After this incident, I returned to the tents, not only to recover some composure, but also feeling that things were not right. Bruce continued like a machine, and he and Guy summited Hanjaylak II (5380m, altimeter height) via slopes on the north-east side. Following this, we returned to our camp on the main glacier. During the rest day that followed, it became clear that Bruce was set on the route he had enthused about on Yanamax, and Guy was equally keen to follow. For me, several things were not right about this plan, and the risk simply too high. Unfortunately, there seemed no mileage in selling the merits of carrying through a project as a team, or in proposing the alternative Xuelian East (6400m+). Feeling a sense of social exclusion, I returned to base camp to await the outcome.

Guy and Bruce returned two days later. Their climb had not started well, as they had set off an avalanche that carried them, roped, far enough to create minor equipment damage. Drive unabated, they had continued by a different line, still on very poor snow, unconcerned about the séracs on the face above. After a camp at 5150m, they had followed the upper south-west ridge to reach the well-earned summit of Yanamax (6332m) on 25 August.

After this, even their risk appetite was compromised, besides which there was more snowfall and stormy weather. We descended a few days later, reaching the hot springs in one modest day with the assistance of Kazakh herders from the high pastures. Our return to Urumqi was trouble free, assisted by China's curious but surprisingly civilised sleeper buses. Guy and I spent several days in and around Urumqi, and found these enriching but thought provoking; in the new museum, I was struck by the portrayal of every era in the region's history as 'inalienably' connected with China.

Our exploratory trip leaves many unvisited, unseen glaciers and unclimbed summits for future parties. West of the deep Muzart valley is a 25km-long ridge containing numerous 6000m summits, culminating at its western end in what may be Chulebos ('Tiger', 6769m). South of this ridge are several individual 6000m peaks including Muzart (6571m) and peaks 6342m and 6050m. There are plenty of 5000m summits too, including some elegant-looking ones we saw and photographed. For these areas, the northern access we used would not be convenient, mainly because horses would not be able to negotiate the moraine-covered lower Muzart glacier. Instead, it may be worth investigating the access route from the south. We rejected this due to concerns about the Muzart river, which drains a large area and is described in one source as 'tempestuous'. Trekking parties come in spring or autumn, when the water is lower. The main problem appears to be a section of the river that runs against 150m-high bluffs. Climbers can negotiate these, but not horses. There are also major side streams to cross. Although the Japanese parties on Xuelian successfully passed through this valley to access their base camp, they branched east well below the Muzart glacier snout.

Based on our experience, these mountains offer much potential for future adventure. Their form is challenging, the weather is fickle, and snow and ice conditions unreliable. Added to the access issues, these things create a huge sense of uncertainty and discovery. As for my own sense of discovery, on this trip it was as much to do with diversity in the climbing community as it was with this alluring range of mountains.

Summary: An account of exploratory climbing in the Xinjiang Tien Shan, China, by Paul Knott, Guy McKinnon and Bruce Normand in August 2008. First ascents of Hanjaylak I (5424m), by all three members, and of Hanjaylak II (5380m) and Yanamax (6332m) by McKinnon and Normand.

20 Bruce Normand on Hanjaylak II (5380m) with Hanjaylak I (5424m) behind. *(Guy McKinnon)*

21. West face of Yanamax (6332m). *(Paul Knott)*

SIMON YATES

Short and Very Sweet

Alpine-style on Mount Vancouver's south-west ridge

Having climbed a significant new route on the west face of Mount Alverstone in 2005, Paul Schweizer and I were keen to return to the remote Wrangell St Elias Range on the Alaskan-Yukon border. We knew the routine, had seen some good-looking objectives, and the spring climbing season worked well around Paul's academic commitments. I booked flights to Whitehorse in the Yukon and we were on our way. Then the problems began. At a late stage of planning we discovered that our proposed route – the compelling west ridge of Mount Hubbard – had been siege climbed back in the 1970s. We needed another objective. Wrangell activist Jack Tackle suggested we look at Mount Vancouver. It was a good tip. Paul was soon drawn to the huge south-west ridge of Good Neighbor Peak – the southern summit of this large, complex mountain. Amazingly, it had not been climbed or even attempted. Or so we thought.

To climb the route we needed to be dropped off by ski-plane in a glacier basin to the south of the peak – nominally in Alaska. Since our previous visit some misinformed bureaucrat had decided to bring in a raft of regulations concerning bush pilots crossing the border. The Canadian operator we had used previously from Kluane Lake would not land us in the US, as he had in 2005. We had become unwitting victims of the US 'War on Terror'. Ideally, we now needed to fly in from Yakutat, but could not change our flights to Whitehorse from the UK without prohibitive cost. Our only other option was to cross the land border from the Yukon into Alaska and take the longer (and more expensive) flight in from Haines.

We left the UK on Friday 24 April and after a monumental day of travel arrived in Whitehorse in the middle of the night. A day's shopping and packing was all that was required in the Yukon capital before transferring to Skagway on the Alaskan coastline the following morning. Our pilot – Paul Swanstrom – kindly flew over from Haines to pick us up, saving the ferry journey across the fjord. He also brought news of impending good weather and said he would fly us into the mountains next day. By Monday lunch time we were on the glacier at the base of our route, somewhat jet-lagged, basking in spring sunshine from a clear blue sky. We set up our base camp and slept. Events seemed to be turning our way at last.

The following day was frantic. We examined the ridgeline through binoculars as the sun continued to shine. It all looked do-able with the exception of a headwall of rime flutings at the top, which were impossible to fathom from such distance. The forecast was good for the week, adding urgency to our actions. We sorted gear and food, agreed on a rack and

22. Mount St Elias, the Seward Glacier and Mount Logan from Mount Vancouver. *(Simon Yates)*

23. In profile, Mount Vancouver's south-west ridge, the line of Yates and Schweizer's ascent. *(Simon Yates)*

24. Paul Schweizer starting up Vancouver's south-west ridge. *(Simon Yates)*

finally packed. I spoke with my wife Jane on the satellite 'phone and told her to expect us to be on mountain for four or five days.

At 4am on Wednesday 29 April we were woken by the alarm and began our climb. A 30-minute walk across the glacier led to a broad couloir leading up to the ridge. We roped up to cross the tricky bergshrund and then soloed simultaneously, hoping to reach the ridge before the sun hit the walls above the fall line we were climbing. It was not to be, but we did manage to clear the narrowest section before the rays arrived and sporadic stone-fall began. The widening upper slopes soon turned into a flog as the heat melted snow underfoot and drew precious water from our skin. We rested on the col at the base of our ridge and marvelled at the panorama to the west – the vast Seward Glacier with Mount St Elias and Mount Logan on either side.

Some gentle trudging up the initial undulating section of the snowy ridge soon brought us to mixed ground. We roped up and would stay that way until the summit. Following the line of least resistance – generally to the left of the crest – we made steady progress. By late afternoon we began looking for a tent site, but the terrain offered none. As time passed we started to consider less than perfect options. Luckily we regained the ridge and late in the evening hacked out the first of what would be a succession of knife-edge snow ridge tent platforms.

Our second day brought more mixed climbing and long traversing sections on ice to outflank a steep buttress on its left side. Later we rejoined the ridge and excavated another dramatic campsite.

25. On the ridge towards the end of Day Three. Mount Cook (or Boundary Peak 182) beyond. *(Simon Yates)*

The morning began with an exciting horizontal section along the corniced ridge. I followed Paul to what he described as an Alaskan belay – he was sat astride the crest. We continued uneventfully before stopping mid-afternoon below an imposing rock tower. Getting around this was obviously going to be one of the key sections of the route. It was not something to start on late in the day.

Day four was pivotal. Having already done a long upward traversing section of ridge, a retreat in the event of a storm was already looking problematical. The steep east side of the ridge – the most direct way to reach the base camp by abseil – was a no-go, threatened by a band of séracs from above. The western aspect offered little more solace – relatively gentle slopes into a chaotic glacier, followed by a massive hike around a group of lesser peaks in order to be re-united with our duty-free. We approached the tower with some apprehension and traversed leftwards over hard ice. Paul led a tricky section of mixed climbing into a basin and let out a shriek of delight having discovered a thin ribbon of perfect ice, hidden from sight below, that led up a narrow gully to slopes above. I moved quickly up the gully knowing that our way off the mountain now lay up and over the top. Pitch followed pitch, first of ice and then of deepening snow with the rime headwall looming menacingly above. Late in the afternoon we reached a shoulder and dug our final tent platform. The weather was holding, but ominous lenticular cloud caps had formed over Logan and St Elias during the day.

26. Day 4, Paul Schweizer on mixed ground above the tower. *(Simon Yates)*

We regained the ridge crest in the morning. The exposure was sensational as we followed a cornice fracture line to below steep ice slopes that led up to the rime headwall. The feature was bizarre – a mass of strange, feathery, wind-blown formations, some massively overhung. However, there appeared to be weaknesses and we headed for the most obvious central one. It began as a couloir of very hard ice, which Paul struggled to lead under the weight of his rucksack. He belayed early and I ditched my sack before continuing above. The couloir entered an almost completely enclosed tube of ice and rime – it was more akin to caving than mountaineering – before opening out into a small basin. Above were two narrow, parallel runnels. I placed an ice-screw and set off. A superb series of moves led up the right-hand feature with a wild pull into the left one. Another basin led to a small wall, before a final pull brought the summit plateau. The central and north summits of Mount Vancouver lay in front of me. I let out a scream. Five days of climbing had led up to this point (probably 3000m in total) and somehow our route had saved the best until last. You dream, you plan, you save, you pack, travel, pack some more and finally climb in the hope of sublime moments like this. The miscommunication that followed, as I tried to haul my rucksack on one rope and bring up Paul on the other, hardly mattered. They arrived eventually. Paul's face filled with joy, as he came over the top to join me.

'I'll never do anything better,' he said simply. I had been thinking exactly the same since pulling onto the plateau. In Paul's opinion the route was harder and better than the Cassin Ridge on Denali that he did years ago.

We wandered around, soaking in the moment and the astonishing views for a few minutes, before making our way up onto a knoll of rime just above our finishing point to take summit photographs. Then pragmatism returned – it was time to begin our long descent.

After a few hundred metres of gently angled, but heavily crevassed snow slopes following the east ridge, we dropped to a col where we called it a day. That night the wind increased and we awoke to snow. We passed the day in our sleeping bags – the mountain hidden in cloud and the tent buffeted by wind. You need visibility to get off these big complex peaks and navigate back to base camp through complicated glacial terrain. Thankfully during the second night the storm blew itself out and allowed us to continue.

The day back to our base was a prolonged affair. We had hoped to descend by the Centennial Route, but the speed of our approach had meant that we were unable to go and look at it before starting the climb. As a result we continued down the east ridge rather than taking a spur off it to the south. The ridge ended in a hideous band of séracs, forcing us to regain height before starting a long series of abseils off its south side. We then crossed a glacier and climbed to a col, only to face a further two abseils to another glacier below. An icefall lay between base camp and us. We weaved our way through it until a deep crevasse barred the way. There was a way around, but it was going to involve a long walk back down the glacier. Instead we opted to jump. I belayed Paul as he made the dash and two-metre leap. Then, having hauled the rucksacks across, I took the jump. We arrived back at camp at 10pm having been on the go for a solid 14 hours.

I immediately made a 'phone call home. Jane was emotional, but very relieved at our return. She had contacted Paul in Haines and was preparing to instigate a search and rescue operation.

A storm moved in during the night, confining us to camp. I spoke with Paul in Haines and he told us to call when the weather improved. We were glad of the rest – our first since leaving the UK 12 days earlier.

On the fourth morning the cloud began to disperse and after a couple of satellite telephone calls Paul informed us he was on his way. We were still packing when he arrived. With perfect bad timing a bank of cloud began to drift up the glacier as we loaded the plane. We frantically dragged the remaining gear across the glacier and stowed it inside. Paul hastily started the engine and then gunned the machine for take-off, but nothing happened. One of the plane's skis was stuck in the snow. It was soon freed by digging, but the cloud was now upon us. We all got out of the plane and sat on the glacier, Paul Schweizer and I feeling stupid for not being ready earlier.

An hour later the cloud lifted sufficiently to fly. The plane accelerated slowly down the glacial basin, skipped a shallow crevasse and finally became airborne over the icefall. Then Paul Swanstrom made a steep turn back into the cirque. I assumed he was aborting the take-off, but he had other ideas, banking the plane into another tight turn after the skis made a brief contact with the snow. With the turn completed the plane began to

27. Paul Schweizer approaches the flutings guarding Vancouver's summit plateau. *(Simon Yates)*

28. Looking down through the flutings on the top pitch of Yates and Schweizer's route. *(Simon Yates)*

29. Paul Schweizer on the south summit (Good Neighbor Peak) with Mount Logan beyond. *(Simon Yates)*

increase speed and height as we headed once more back over the icefall. Paul had used the manoeuvre to gain altitude to clear a bank of cloud rising up the glacier below. It was an incredibly committing piece of flying that seemed to mirror our own efforts, a fitting finale to a very special climb.

Postscript: Two months after returning to the UK we were stunned to learn that 'our' south-west ridge had been climbed way back in 1968. A 10-strong expedition from the Osaka-Fu Mountaineering Association, Japan, tackled the ridge siege-style over 13 days in May-June. Masaru Shibata and Masaichi Kimura reached the summit of Good Neighbor Peak on 10 June. That same day three other team members perished in an avalanche. A brief report of the expedition appeared in the 1969 *American Alpine Journal.*

Summary: An account of the first alpine-style ascent of the south-west ridge of the south summit of Mount Vancouver (Good Neighbor Peak – 4850m), Yukon-Alaska border, by Simon Yates and Paul Schweizer, 29 April to 5 May 2009. Approximately 3000m of climbing with a 2450m vertical height gain, up to Grade V Scottish ice and mixed with an overall alpine ED grade.

Acknowledgements: Simon Yates and Paul Schweizer wish to thank the Mount Everest Foundation and the Mountaineering Council of Scotland for their financial support.

ANDY PARKIN

Solo Khumbu Solo, Part II

Following my Dawa Peak trip of 2007/2008 I decided to return to Nepal and the Khumbu region 12 months later. I thought I understood a little bit more about Himalayan winter soloing and wanted to carry on the idea of ever harder and technical climbing in austere surroundings. Of course the Khumbu area is not that wild; good paths, villages and lodges take the

30. Watercolour painted by Andy Parkin at 4000m looking up the Omaga valley, Kangtega on right. Parkin attempted the unnamed central flat-topped summit (6080m) via its central couloir and system of gullies.

sting out of the winter experience, but once on the mountain and alone it becomes something like the real thing. This time, thanks to the previous expedition, I at least had an idea of what I could climb. Familiarity lends an air of intimacy to an area, the imagination can run free and new routes appear everywhere. I had found my alternative winter playground and it was exciting.

After the chaos of Kathmandu with its power cuts (18 hours a day without electricity), arriving in Lukla was literally a breath of fresh air and once having engaged Pemba as porter we set off towards his village, en route for Phakding. At Pemba's home we had tea and I met his wife, all smiles now but just six months earlier she had lost their first child. A few days later she walked up to Khumjung to visit the clinic for a check up (a two or three day walk for a western trekker). Pemba had once been a novice monk, studying then leaving the order to marry and work as either porter or guide, and of course farming their land.

One cold and very frosty morning we walked into Pangboche, the village at the foot of Ama Dablam. The rising sun thawed out the terrace of the Everest View Lodge. It was perfect; around us peaks towered in every direction, Kangtega to the south of Ama Dablam while to the north Nuptse's broad face shone in the sun. I decided that this would do as my base and whilst eating negotiated cheaper rates as I planned to live here for a few weeks. Pemba left for Namche Bazar and I went up and over the Imja Khola river to contour round and explore the alpages above its southerly bank. There I discovered the abandoned settlement of Omaga and at the head of the valley a northern facet of Kangtega with other summits running north-east, tantalising stark north faces, all unclimbed. This was it – nirvana! It was a horribly cold and dark place (to be visited sparingly) so I spent time above the clouds in the sun at the base camp of Ama Dablam, a lovely place to acclimatise and paint. When food or paper ran low I moved back to Pangboche and the warmth of the lodge, sometimes teaching painting to the children there. Kharsang, a boy 10 years old, was good and I think he must still have his paintings hung on the walls.

Finally it was time to get on with the main business – that is of climbing – so I began carrying up to the base of the peak that dominated the head of the Omaga valley, a flat-topped mountain with no name but on one map it's given a height of 6080m. Its glowering north face is cut by a gully that promised some hard climbing. Being now January the sun shone a tiny bit more into the head of the valley; in fact it had melted the small amount of snow there leaving nothing to use for water. At 4700m I pitched my tent and set about scraping frost off the moss so I could make a drink. Next morning I carried the hardwear up to the foot of the snow couloir, the initial part of my proposed route, and brought down about 20kg of ice to melt.

After a few nights spent at 4700m and a brief rest in the village I was ready to go up again to begin the climb. It began as a classic couloir of good snow leading to a small flat col. Though the first night I spent here was comfortable, I didn't sleep. High up on the summit crest the wind howled, sending down spindrift and, worse, blocks of ice. A mind too alert and constantly revising the possibilities kept me awake 'till dawn. Up I went all the same – 'just to have a look', I kept repeating. Snow turned to névé and the névé turned to ice; things became precarious and the first crux of the day had me shedding the sack to climb a near-vertical corner with dabs of névé stuck on rock then dry tooling to finish. Up with the sack and on with climbing that took on an ever more serious feel as the gully steepened. An awesome wall of delicate ice had me hanging the bag on a sling again. 'This is real climbing,' I shouted in my head, not daring to say it aloud. I didn't want to break the silence. Of course the sack stuck fast so I went down to free it, prusiking back up on my 'oh so thin' Dyneema ropes. Once back at the belay I could take in the next section ... and it was horrible. Protecting myself with gear placed in the poor cracks, I had just enough confidence to force the exit onto the icefield above. As I did so it went dark, leaving me pinned to the hard black ice with nowhere to go and surrounded by sheer walls. I cast out to my right and in the beam of my headlamp there beckoned a small ledge with a bit of a roof to give shelter.

Tense seconds of a daring traverse landed me on the ledge but what a let-down it was, miniscule, sloping and with an enormous drop to one side. Nor was it that safe from anything dropping out of the sky. It was going to have to do though. Squirming into my sleeping bag, thrust into the rucksack as a sort of half hammock, was diabolically hard work. This done, I put the rope round my torso to hold me in position, glad of the down suit now as I couldn't properly get into the bag. I managed to brew up and eat as swirls of snow poured from above. All night lumps of ice came down, scattering fragments like shrapnel, some hitting me. Needless to say, sleep was impossible. It was a truly awful night. First light found me groggy and bad-tempered for I knew it was a no-goer. With the light came the realisation of where I had put myself. Above, a steep dark wall had a smear of ice that looked as if it would shatter under the first blow of an axe; the surrounding walls overhung. Out to the right lay my imagined escape route. Through binoculars a zigzag line had suggested itself, avoiding the worst. Now, close up, it looked suicidal. 'Forget that,' I thought. I turned my eyes to a vague line above. 'Even well belayed it would be hard to do,' I ruminated over a hot drink as a volley of ice blocks whirred past into the void. Four hundred or so metres above beckoned the wind-blasted summit, and potentially harder ground too. I had pulled the trigger too many times already. Dare I do it again? It was starting to look a bit sick and maybe there's more to life than roulette. What about some fun for a change?

The die was cast. Abseiling towards salvation I tried not to think of failure but reasoned that instinct had saved me again. Ice threads, nuts and pitons were all sacrificed as gravity drew me down and out of that now dismal place that just a few days earlier had been the focus of all my desires. Now I couldn't wait to get out of there. I staggered down the final snow slope and the hideous moraine before, just on nightfall, the tent appeared out of the gloom and drink, food and rest rounded out the day's experience. Next day I walked out to the village. Bent under a gigantic load, I meandered along the lower valley coming across snow leopard tracks and then a man! There he was, a bearded and bedraggled figure standing next to a small tent. His name was Dave; offering me a warm drink we talked a while. He was waiting for his two friends, out climbing on the icefalls that hung down the shaded walls of this now seemingly crowded valley. Talk of a coincidence! The local climbing Sherpas had told me there had never been an expedition into here before. I carried on down to where comforts of village life awaited me, resting the next day and fixing up a porter to help me back down to Lukla. Lachpa turned out to be a smiling rogue who liked his beer, but then again so do I and as we lost height the taste buds became active once again.

Back in Kathmandu a few days of easy living had me ready for the next phase of the journey. I had in mind to go to Barabise, a small town some 100km east of the capital on the highway to Tibet where Community

Action Nepal, the charity set up by Doug Scott, has established a school for deaf children. I wanted to teach an art programme there – an idea I had discussed with Ian Wall, CAN's representative in Nepal. Thanks to Ian I met up with the CAN's Nepalese staff and all agreed the project would be worth a go so one morning off we drove. I immediately recognised Barabise as a place we pass through when returning from Tibet, usually in the dark and with our minds set on the fleshpots of Kathmandu. Spanning the river at the north end of the town, a typical Himalayan footbridge gave access to terraces for the rice paddies. At their foot lay the CAN school in an idyllic setting, a true haven of peace after the bustle of the city.

31. Banana tree at Barabise, Nepal, February 2008. Parkin painted these with the children of the CAN school for the deaf outside the classroom.

I speak some words of Nepali and of course many people speak English. But neither language would suffice here where all of the 50 or so pupils are deaf. I could, however, communicate with images, as so many times before whilst travelling. I taught painting to 22 of the children, hoping they all would profit from my 'on sight' techniques, in the sense that eventually they could earn a living when out on the streets. In Nepal so many things are hand-painted, everything from rickshaws, trucks and buses to cinema signs, and of course there's also the selling of paintings to tourists. If it isn't practical it won't work in Nepal. Painting cannot be a regarded as a luxury when daily living is about survival.

In all this I was counting heavily on the fact that Nepalis can be amazingly talented. This proved to be true; as the weeks went by we did good work together and I took them out of the classroom to paint the bamboo and banana trees. The children were so keen and quick to seize my ideas; I think at least six of them could become artists. I certainly hope so as my stay at Barabise took more out of me than had the climbing! Some evenings, after eating the eternal dal bhat, I would feel so drained of energy it was as if the classroom were a stage demanding constant attention. I'm not sure I could do it all the time but I am definitely returning to follow up all we have begun. I got a lot out of it, and, as Doug says, it's good to put something back in. It was about time I did just that, and at the end of the day if it is all about Karma then perhaps the gods will continue to smile down on me as I climb.

KELLY CORDES

Young Guns of North America

A Dirtbag Renaissance

Last year an older friend of mine, a top alpinist in his day, bemoaned that today's young North American climbers aren't getting after it with the big alpine adventures. This wasn't the first time I'd heard that sentiment. My friend seemed to think that the days of unencumbered dirtbag climbers willing to scrape by, empty their piggy banks, and chase alpine-style windmills in the mountains, sans sponsorship and media circus, had passed. Of course, older people complaining about today's world are commonplace, and they're often right. I'm getting there myself at 40. But I think he's wrong. Mostly.

32.
Colin Haley psyched up before tackling the vertical and overhanging rime of the penultimate pitch of a new linkup up Cerro Torre in January 2007. Haley and Kelly Cordes linked the *Marsigny-Parkin* to the upper west face to the summit and down the *Compressor Route* in a 48-hour trip from the Niponino bivvi. Though previously attempted, the 1400m linkup (AI6 A2) via the upper west face had never been completed.
(Kelly Cordes)

I told another friend about this notion. 'I agree,' he said. 'You go to Yosemite and it's not like it was 40 years ago when everyone was getting after it; instead it's full of drunks talking about what they did or could do. Not to say that no one was getting drunk 40 years ago or that no one is getting after it today. But what I really think is happening, and very quickly, is that society is 'evolving' to where safety has become number one – or at least the illusion thereof.' As we talked, however, I wondered if

33. Colin Haley leading one of several natural, wind-formed tunnels high on the upper west face of Cerro Torre. *(Kelly Cordes)*

every generation says this. His knowledge of Yosemite 40 years ago comes from what he's read, from the legends. My friend here, Kyle Dempster, is only 25.

Old joke:

Q: How many climbers does it take to screw in a light bulb?

A: Ten. One to do it, and nine to stand around and say, 'Dude, I could totally do that.'

It's probably as true as ever. Maybe it just seems worse today due to un-

34. Maxime Turgeon new routing on the north face of Mt Bradley, Alaska, in 2005. Bringing gym and crag skills to the big faces, Turgeon and fellow Quebec climber L P Menard put up *The Spice Factory* (1,310m, 5.10R M7 WI5), in a 55-hour round-trip. *(L P Menard)*

precedented communication channels spewing a deluge of crap from marketing and PR departments and shameless self-promoters. I suspect most of us can think of plenty of supporting examples. Is real adventure climbing a dying thing over here? Maybe. But instead of focusing on the omnipresent examples of over-hyped bullshit, I wondered about the opposite.

I thought about my trip to El Chalten, Patagonia in December 2006 and January 2007, when I was there with young gun Colin Haley (then 22). First, I know that a couple of examples don't prove a larger point. But no definitive answer exists to this question, only perceptions. In the Chalten massif – admittedly a largely climbed-out arena of good rock – about half the climbers seemed to be on their first big trip, and most of them were getting after it as best they could (regrettably, there were slacklines and bongo drums present, but I digress). Two youngsters in particular stood out:

'The Montana Boys', as we all called Ben Smith and Justin Woods, had been best friends since childhood, growing up on the outskirts of Glacier National Park. They'd just quit their jobs and figured that before anything else came along they'd better go climbing in Patagonia. Not wanting to lose momentum, they bought airline tickets immediately – to Santiago, Chile. By the time they'd figured out that they were about a million miles too far north, it didn't matter. Interminable bus rides later, they got to Chalten and promptly hiked to the Niponino bivouac. Only they hiked the wrong

35. Josh Wharton on probably the world's biggest alpine rock route, the *Azeem Ridge* on Great Trango Tower (2250m, 5.11r/x A2 M6), done over four and a half days in 2004 with Kelly Cordes. *(Kelly Cordes)*

way around the lake, missing the well-trodden track and taking a heinously steep and loose scree field along the opposite shores of the mile-long lake.

'Yeah, we're too stupid ta buy a freakin' map,' Justin said when I met him. 'Too cheap, too,' added Ben. 'But we'll get there,' Justin said with a grin. I liked them immediately. My friends and I marvelled at their attitude – smiling the whole way, even while hunkered down in bivvi bags, no tent, in the tempest at Niponino. The winds blew sleet sideways. I suppose I also liked them because they reminded me of something I saw – or hoped I had, anyway – of myself when I started climbing, 15 years ago, also in Montana. It's the place I cut my teeth, along with trips to Alaska, and everything about it was about adventure. The boys and I talked a little about the climbing in Montana and the wild, remote, huge arena of wintertime ice and massive crumbling summertime rock faces that is Glacier National Park, but they never said much about their adventures. They just kept smiling and looking forward.

These guys, like all the climbers I met in Chalten, weren't the average Americans (most of the climbers I met while there were American). They went in search of the kind of adventure not found in shopping malls and on the Xbox ('pass the chips, will ya?'). The *New York Times* recently featured the American king of adventure climbing, Fred Beckey, now 86, who said: 'Man used to put himself on the line all the time. Nowadays we're protected by the police, fire, everything. There's not much adventure left.

36. Wharton relaxes at base camp after the Great Trango climb. *(Kelly Cordes)*

Unless you look for it.'

Over here, at least, indeed we have a continual, systematic dumbing-down of our culture into Brittany Spears, reality TV, and unapologetic materialism. And while times change and cultures shift, the sofa ornaments of the middle ground populace never did much anyway, whether in the era of reality TV or in decades past. Those were never the Shipton and Tilman types, or the Herman Buhls, Voytek Kurtykas, and Mugs Stumps of this world. It's always been a few outliers that expand our collective vision. And the more I think about it, I think we've still got a healthy crew of young outliers.

In terms of the exploration aspect of adventure, there isn't much that can be done about the fact that our mountains aren't multiplying. Heading into the mountains and exploring untouched peaks or massive virgin faces used to go hand-in-hand. Sure, exploratory climbing still exists, and a noble few embrace it, but it cannot be as total in its remoteness as the Shipton-Tilman days or even the 1980s. Furthermore, the drive to remove risk has certainly extended into climbing; witness the bouldering revolution, climbing gyms, and sport climbing. It's easy to say these examples represent a dumbing-down of adventure, but that's an inherently limited argument. Let's get real, people who can't imagine anything bolder than a bolt at their waist were never destined for the high-adventure pool to begin with. Before accessible and safe climbing, they were the people bound for the golf courses, or maybe tennis or gymnastics. And that's cool.

Adventure shifts in climbing more than it disappears, I think. For an example of finding potential adventure, would it really be a greater adventure to seek out one of the remaining untouched peaks on the Patagonian icecap – meaning ones smaller and easier, since that's what remains – than the first ascent of the Torre Traverse, one of the last great prizes of Patagonian climbing, as Colin Haley and Rolando Garibotti did in 2008? Given today's standards, cruising up some mountain by its easiest route might not be much of an adventure for competent climbers. The level of a challenge certainly relates to unknown outcomes. I'm not convinced that attempting a blank-looking section of a wall, one bordered by existing easy routes up the ridges on either side, necessarily entails less adventure than exploring a little-known area. It might just be a different kind of adventure.

When I first started working for the *American Alpine Journal*, I operated under the fantasy that we reported on all of the world's big new routes – or damn close to it. After nine years with the *Journal*, more than 15 alpine expeditions around the world and a life devoted to climbing (I know, it's pathetic that I'm not any better after all this time, but that's another issue), I realize that we miss plenty. Every year I learn of climbers I've never heard of doing big things, proud ascents from years past that went wholly unnoticed, and incredibly worthy climbs overshadowed in the media by louder climbs and louder climbers. And more than anything, despite our public and popular bemoaning of the 'damn kids these days', it's precisely the young guns that have mostly caught my eye.

37. '...like two high-school kids who'd just cut class.' Young Canadians Jason Kruk and Will Stanhope summiting on Desmochada, Patagonia, January 2008. *(Jason Kruk)*

For American climbers, Alaska costs exponentially less than a Himalayan expedition and offers similar challenges. It's where so many American alpinists cut their teeth, yesterday and today. In 2008, young American climbers – almost none of them 'names' – ventured off the well-worn Denali circuit and established impressive new routes in the Chugach and Revelation mountains, the Kichatna Spires, the Arrigetch Peaks and the Coast Mountains.

Youngsters like Alaskan Clint Helander, who last year established two new routes in the Revelation Mountains – not world-class climbs, but big adventures, followed by a two-day trek out across 21 miles of the Alaskan wilderness. This year they were heading back in, because there's plenty left in the Revelations. Ryan Johnson, of Alaska, and Sam Magro, of Montana (younger brother of Whit Magro, an unheralded hardman), visited the Mendenhall Towers in the storm-blasted Coast Mountains of Alaska and put up an impressive new route. Last week I got an email from Johnson asking about Pakistan info – he was saving money, living out of his car and couch surfing. Maybe the kids aren't all just into their bling-bling after all.

Or take Quebec climbers Maxime Turgeon and LP Menard who debuted in Alaska in 2005 with a bang. Still in their 20s, they'd been climbing just a

38. Will Stanhope following on the north face of Rafael Juarez. Kruk and Stanhope free climbed the Freddie Wilkinson route *Blood on The Tracks* (600m V 5.12) right to the summit in a single push. *(Jason Kruk)*

couple of years and it was their first trip to any of the bigger ranges. After racing up repeats in the Ruth Gorge, they saw the north face of Mt Bradley. I'd spent two months of my life in the Ruth and never seen the line – and I don't think it's that conditions were suddenly much better. It's just that they are that much better. They brought their gym and crag generation skills with them and fired a new route, *The Spice Factory* (1310m, 5.10R M7 WI5), in a 55-hour round-trip. The following year they ran up one of the last remaining unclimbed projects on Denali's south face, establishing the *Canadian Direct* (8,000ft/4,000ft new, 5.9 M6 AI4) in 58 hours.

Another fine example of recent dirtbags in Alaska also came in 2006, when Jed Brown and Colin Haley (then 23 and 21 years old) caught a one-way flight into the remote Hayes Range (lacking funds for the flight out, they hiked out, including a sketchy river crossing in a one-man pack raft) for the massive north face of Mt Moffit. Their lightweight ascent of the 2,300m *Entropy Wall* (5.9 A2 WI4+) received disappointingly scant attention. I joked with Haley that he needed to learn how to spray. Colin's subsequent world-class ascents have garnered more attention, but he still considers the route on Moffit his finest adventure and most committing route.

Haley, Dylan Johnson, and Josh Wharton – all in their 20s – teamed up for Pakistan this summer. Though largely overlooked in the mainstream climbing media, Johnson's epic new route on Siguniang last year, with Chad Kellogg, was, according to Haley, 'the best American achievement in the Himalaya last year.' Anyone familiar with the details would be hard-pressed to argue otherwise. Wharton is no longer obscure, and climbs high-end sport and bouldering as well as cutting-edge alpine routes, emerging into likely America's finest all-around active climber. His relative fame doesn't lessen his big-adventure accomplishments. He's put up likely the world's biggest alpine rock route, the Azeem Ridge on Great Trango Tower, in 2004 (2250m, 5.11r/x A2 M6), in 4 and a half days with a single 13kg pack, and led unbelievably bold pitches well beyond the point of easy retreat (I know, my trembling hands held the other end of the rope on the hardest parts). His adventures have seen him up new routes elsewhere in Pakistan, Alaska, Canada, Patagonia, and his back yard, the big and loose Black Canyon of the Gunnison in Colorado. But he's probably most proud of his and Brian McMahon's lightweight first ascent of the Flame, also in Pakistan, in 2002, back when he was an unknown. It was the summer after 9-11 and nobody was going to Pakistan. Thinking for themselves, Josh and Brian refused to succumb to the fear, and indeed the only dangerous part of the trip was the climbing. Wharton's summit lead – a 50m runout on 5.10+ to lasso the tiny summit pinnacle – surely ranks among the boldest summit leads in history. They returned to base camp, rested a day, and put up a new route on Shipton Spire in similar style. At the time, McMahon was 25, Wharton 22.

I first learned of young Canadians Jason Kruk and Will Stanhope (then 20 and 21) after their 2008 season in Patagonia. (In 2009, Stanhope ventured to a remote, practically unexplored valley in Argentina with gorgeous granite walls up to 800m tall.) Both 5.13+ sport climbers, the pair had a tremendous season and turned heads with their tactics. After jumaring on second during their first route, they then insisted on climbing all free on both lead and second. 'I guess it allows us to look at old routes with fresh eyes,' Stanhope later told me. 'And the possibilities are endless.' On one of their first free ascents, after falls they lowered, pulled the rope (if leading) and went at it again until free. Mucking around? Sure. As with any climbing. Just don't tell me that 5.9 A2 is somehow more real-deal than free at 5.12. It's part of the evolution, because it wasn't just enough to do the route, they wanted to free it. Just like, for the old explorers, it wasn't enough to stay away. Like for some of us now, all in our own way, so much of life just isn't enough. Adventure evolves with those so drawn, and to scoff at such refining only shows a stuck-in-the-past mind. There aren't so many blank spots on the map anymore, but there's plenty left to do. When I got Will's report for the *AAJ*, they included a summit photo where they literally looked like two high-school kids who'd just cut class. I could only laugh, shake my head, and give them 'mad respect,' as the young kids say.

One could argue that nothing represents true adventure more than soloing, and on that front, too, the youngsters are doing alright. In the *AAJ* 2008, we had a feature article from a climber who celebrated his 26th birthday earlier that year while making the first ascent – solo – of the east face of Cerro Escudo, in Torres del Paine. (An account of the same climb appears in the Piolets d'Or section of this *AJ*, page 68-72) Others had done some climbing on the face – routes or attempts depending on who's doing the talking – but Turner not only climbed the 1200m big wall face but continued along the ridge to the summit, another 300m of ascent. Turner climbed in extraordinarily better style than nearly any other big wall, a mix of true capsule style (that is, not the deal where you fix thousands of metres and then 'commit' to the wall) and alpine style. His route checked in at commitment grade VII – the first grade VII solo in the world – and 5.9 A4. He'd soloed three new wall routes on El Capitan, and the previous summer put up a new alpine route on Taulliraju, in Peru. As I write this, he's packing for a two-month solo expedition to Baffin Island.

39. Kruk following Stanhope on their variation (700m V+ 5.11+ A1) to *The Sound and The Fury*, a Freddie Wilkinson-Dave Sharratt route on Desmochada. *(Will Stanhope)*

My friend Kyle Dempster, the 25-year-old I mentioned up-top, calls himself 'part of the bouldering-sport-trad-bigwall-ice-alpine evolution'. He learned to climb 5.13 at a young age, put up a grade VI new wall in Baffin, soloed the Reticent Wall on El Cap, then spent a winter in Canada climbing WI6 and M10, then went to Alaska and made the true first ascent of the north face of the Mini-Moonflower – not a huge face, at 2,300 vertical feet, but a difficult new route to most of us at M7 AI6, and topping out and doing so faster than the big dogs with existing no-summit routes on the face (with a partner you've never heard of, either – and surely you've heard of the other climbers whose north face routes come close to the top: Cool-Parnell and Koch-Prezelj). That was just a warm-up for his Pakistan trip. Last July, solo and on a shoestring budget, negotiating as he went, he made his way to the Hispar region where his porters dropped him at the junction of the Hispar and Khani Basa glaciers. He had no cook, guide, or partners, and spent the next seven weeks completely alone. After six gear carries of 8 or 9 miles each way, he set off on his objective: the unclimbed west face of Tahu Rutum

40.
Kyle Dempster's solo route on the previously unclimbed west face of Tahu Rutum (6651m) in Pakistan's Hispar region. After 24 days on the 1350m wall, he retreated from high on the summit ridge and, refreshingly, still called it just 'an attempt'.
(Kyle Dempster)

(6651m, sometimes spelled Ratum). He didn't have an altimeter and the maps aren't exact, but the face rises c1350m from base to summit. Climbing in capsule style, through a storm, and extending himself nearly too far for 24 days on the wall, he retreated from high on the summit ridge – and, refreshingly, no 'moving the goalposts', he called it an attempt. I only knew about it from my personal contact with Kyle – not a word made it to the mainstream climbing media. I recruited a report from him, and we ran his harrowing account in the 'Far' department in the first issue of our e-zine/newsletter site, *The Alpine Briefs* (**alpinebriefs.wordpress.com**). Kyle lives with his parents in Salt Lake City to save money, works odd jobs (including his 'morally disgusting' work hanging Christmas lights on rich people's houses all December, and then taking them down in January), and sold his car to save for his coming summer's adventures. Damn kids these days!

I realize these examples, possibly isolated exceptions, don't prove an overall theory. Depending on what we count as 'climbers', no doubt the proportion of climbers chasing adventure is lower than back when it was all about adventure. I suppose my point is that, though we can't say for sure if it's any better or worse than those good-old-knickerbocker days, when climbers were all real men and our parents all walked uphill both ways to school for 10km each way through deep snow, I actually think we're doing pretty well.

41. Dempster's aerial view down Tahu Rutum's west face. *(Kyle Dempster)*

Last year while working on the 2008 *AAJ*, I heard about a 2006 new route on the north face of Mt Siyeh, in Glacier National Park, Montana, by a couple of low-key hardmen, my friends Chris Gibisch and Ryan Hokanson. Forget Yosemite (aside from rock quality), the north face of Siyeh is bigger than El Cap. It gains 3,500 vertical feet from base to summit – and a pile of choss the whole way. Depending on how you measure, it's the first or second biggest technical rock face in Glacier, making it the first or second biggest in the Lower 48. Steeped in lore, the massive face had one known route, an epic over three days (completed on the fourth try) by old-school badasses Jim Kanzler and Terry Kennedy, unrepeated for 25 years. When I heard about Chris and Ryan's climb, I contacted them. They'd set off light, got shut down up high, endured horrific rock and a frigid unplanned bivvi – 'a night of agony' – and escaped off to the north-east ridge and scrambled to the summit for the face's third ascent.

Third ascent, I asked? Who did the second? Turns out that the Kanzler-Kennedy line up the plum central rib was repeated in 2005, in typical no-fanfare Montana style by Ben Smith and Justin Woods - the 'Montana Boys' I'd met in Chalten. They'd said nothing of it.

I emailed Justin. He and Ben had started up one day without bivvi gear,

42. Kyle Dempster: 'At approximately 6500m I reached the steep snow and ice ridgeline leading to the summit...and I had had enough. It was snowing with 40 mph winds, the Earth had rotated the expanse of the Karakoram into complete darkness, and my headlamp was near dead. I was dehydrated and malnourished, but stoked on my effort. The decision was easy. I bailed.' *(Kyle Dempster)*

got slowed by still-unmelted snow from the previous week's storm up high, got benighted, shivered on a ledge until daybreak, then finished the route. 'Interesting climb,' Justin wrote. 'Can't say I'd recommend doing it. But on the other hand, I've been thinking of going back. Guess when the memory fades you can talk yourself into just about anything.'

Last August I returned to Montana for a couple of weeks. I met up with Justin and we put his short-memory to use. From a bivvi below the face, we climbed a 3,000-foot new route (3,000 feet on the face, plus 500 feet of ridge scrambling to summit), all-free in 11 hours – the first one day ascent of likely the biggest face in the Lower 48. Not much to spray about, though, because it wasn't 'hard', just a good adventure.

What? Mt. Siyeh? Where's that? Justin Woods? Never heard of him.

Exactly.

And the route wasn't 'hard'?

Exactly.

Perhaps the difference is perception, which often comes from presentation. We do indeed live in an age of unparalleled bullshit. But sometimes there's a backlash, too. I caught word of a valley in South America with 800m–1000m untouched walls, where an Argentine climber had pioneered some routes. Rumour had it he'd been keeping it low key, but I tracked him down and asked for a report on his explorations and climbs there. Here's where I add that the *AAJ* is a non-profit publication that has never broken even and tries to avoid the hype. I can count on one hand the number of people who've not wanted their info in the *AAJ*, while I know of scores who've deliberately avoided mainstream publication. When I asked this Argentine fellow for an *AAJ* report, he politely declined. 'I'm not interested in advertising myself or the place,' he said.

Just because we don't hear about it – or just because it's drowned out sometimes – doesn't mean it isn't happening.

Piolets d'Or 2009

April 2009 saw the return of the *Piolets d'Or* after a year's absence during which its principal organisers, the French *Group de Haute Montagne*, wrestled with the contradictions inherent in awards for alpinism. Does the new, less overtly commercial, format meet the objections of those who baulk at the notion of winners and losers in mountaineering or is the *Piolets d'Or* still, as Marko Prezelj famously charged, a circus for climbers addicted to Miss Fame? It is a question for later in this section of the *AJ*.

First, for the climbing is always more interesting than the controversy, we feature accounts from the six teams whose achievements were celebrated in Chamonix at the 17th edition of the *Piolets d'Or*.

43. Ueli Steck on the summit ridge of Teng Kangpoche. *(Simon Anthamatten)*

44. The Benoist – Glairon-Rappaz line on the south face of Nuptse.

ARE YOU EXPERIENCED?

PATRICE GLAIRON-RAPPAZ

11 October 2008: Here I am again at the base of the south face of Nuptse. From the snow slope just below the bergschrund, I see the superb line of gullies that highlight the bottom of the wall for more than 300 metres before fading into the unknown. Images run through my mind. Two years have passed since my first attempt in the autumn of 2006. As in my memories, the south face of Nuptse is majestic, gigantic, impressive …

The wall rises for more than 2000 metres and huge bastions of rock cut across the face, like rose petals, flowing outward, mesmerizing. You feel reduced to nothing in front of this wall, a wall that confronts you face-to-face with yourself. You have to tame this beast that at first seems ferocious. But deep inside I know that it is possible to subdue it. It will take time, careful reflection and, without a doubt, audacity, though such an undertaking requires humility. Even though we feel ready, we know we must form a strong and tightly knit partnership to have a chance. I am happy that I am here with Stéphane. It may be the most important thing for me and I do not think it would be possible otherwise.

7pm, 15 October: After a frugal meal, we shoulder our heavy packs and leave advanced base camp. There is a full moon and we decide to take advantage of it by climbing all night, trying to get to a bivvi site at 6500m the following day, the same place where I bivvied in 2006[1]. The cold is intense and the south-west wind that has been blowing since we got to base camp is hammering the face. We exchange glances; we understand each other, no need for words. We have never before experienced such brutal conditions on a climb. The tip of Stéphane's nose becomes frozen and our feet and fingertips are seriously damaged by this night of hell. After many

1. Rappaz made a solo attempt on the face in October 2006, reaching this 6500m high point.

45. Patrice Glairon-Rappaz on the lower third of the climb. *(Stéphane Benoist)*

46. Patrice at the top of the steep gully at around 6450m. *(Stéphane Benoist)*

47. Patrice at the first bivouac, 6500m *(Stéphane Benoist)*

pitches of gully climbing we gain the 50-60 degree snow slopes at 6100m. Dawn illuminates the sky and the eventual sunlight feels great. However the night-long conditions have tested us and now we are moving slowly.

A barrier of steep gullies blocks our access to a snow slope that in two pitches leads to the bivouac. Stéphane emerges exhausted from a sustained pitch of 5/5+ at 6450m. Around noon (16th) we arrive at the spot where I had slept in 2006. The sun is warm and ironically, we're almost hot. Our first 'Ginat' is behind us but a second waits above[2].

Exhausted and dehydrated, we chop out a platform and set up the tent. I sense that something is wrong with me; I'm trembling, drained, and have stomach pains. We drink much-needed water before settling into our shelter.

18 October: Despite the cold, we sleep well and I think I'm going to be able to continue. But I haven't completely recovered and we decide to spend the day resting at our bivvi. My condition deteriorates. I have no more energy. Stéphane spends the entire day looking for a bag of clothing that I Ieft here two years ago. He finally finds it and digs it out.

19 October: The second night at the bivvi really tests me. Sick and in bad shape, when morning finally arrives I have only one pressing desire – to go back down and recover. There is no other choice. Fifteen 70m rappels later we are on the glacier. We painstakingly pick our way down the chaos of the glacier to base camp.

This first attempt was harsh to say the least. But on the bright side, the two nights at 6500m were great for our acclimatization and we cached

2. A comparison with the ED2 Ginat route on the north face of Les Droites, Mt Blanc range.

48. 'Pitch after pitch of technical climbing – superb.' *(Stéphane Benoist)*

sleeping bags, parkas and stoves, allowing us to go much lighter on our next attempt. I had told myself exactly this after descending two years ago but bad weather never permitted another chance.

Days pass and the violent winds up high do not relent, keeping us from venturing back onto the face. At least we regain feeling in our fingers. A sort of lethargy sets in and thoughts of bailing start to creep through our heads. The tension is palpable and the air is heavy – not between us of course, but within both of us as we question ourselves and grow withdrawn. The expedition is coming to an end … and the end justifies the means. A small weather window appears for the following days.

27 October: It's minus 17°C and cloudy when the alarm goes off at 2am at advanced base camp. An unforecast storm has descended on Khumbu during the night and our courage is waning. But we go for it anyway, digging deep inside ourselves in order to avoid becoming discouraged and setting ourselves up for failure. The beast is lying in wait; it senses we are vulnerable and wants to deliver the final blow right away. But the avalanches it pours down on us, even though they frighten us, do not discourage us. We use our combined experience and tenacity to get over the bergschrund and climb the couloir as snow sloughs over us. Stéphane arrives out of breath at the belay that I set up out of reach of the avalanches, feeling slightly unnerved by the situation we are living through. He admits that he doubted we would make it.

The avalanches ease as we climb up through the cold and wind to bivvi, as planned, at 6500m where the tent, sleeping bags, and stoves are waiting for us. Fine weather returns and the winds die down. Maybe the beast had relinquished its throne? I think we've earned some respite.

28 October: An amazing day! Pitch after pitch of technical climbing. The climbing is superb and the ambiance insane. We bivvi at 6800m after an incredible sunset.

29 October: While climbing out of the summit couloir at around 7100m

after two final difficult mixed pitches, I say to myself that success has become possible[3]. But don't try to sell the skin of the beast before you have killed it.

At 7500m the cold becomes intense, darkness descends, and the wind picks up again. The sunset is dramatic and during the small breaks we take every 15 steps to catch our breath I savour this privileged view. I have a sensation of being detached from time. Only the present matters, we are completely focused on our movements, we have to use the minimum amount of energy possible to advance and achieve our goal. Stéphane is a few minutes ahead of me and at around 7pm I join him on the summit ridge. I am groggy and freezing cold, but profoundly happy. We don't have time to fully appreciate this moment; we need to descend before we freeze on the spot. We snap a few photos, glance into Everest's Western Cwm, then start down-climbing, paying careful attention to our extremities to keep them from freezing. Only critical things matter, it's survival. I sense the animal instinct within me functioning, almost on autopilot. We are on the edge and I believe that at this moment we may have gone beyond our limits.

49. Stéphane Benoist *(Patrice Glairon-Rappaz)*

After several hours where everything could have been lost, we are back in our tent, finally in shelter. We immediately examine our feet – signs of frostbite are visible. How bad is it? We don't know yet.

30 October: It's 3am and the wind is gusting hard, keeping us tent-bound. I quickly fall asleep. I no longer have the energy to dream. Around 8am the sun illuminates our tent and it is time to descend. V-thread after v-thread, we arrive, 20 rappels later, at the bergschrund as night falls. With the help of our cook, who has come up to meet us, we break down ABC and immediately continue to base camp.

From the trail, I take one last look at the face. Tears fall down my cheeks and my eyes tremble with emotion. A page has been turned. For my part, today I see our success on Nuptse as the culmination of a journey by Stéphane and myself and I am a happy man, a 'satisfied' alpinist. Trying to do something even greater wouldn't make any sense to me. But I know that the beast is still in me, sleeping. Will it re-awake one day?

Summary: An account of a new route, alpine-style, on the south face of Nuptse by French climbers Stéphane Benoist and Patrice Glairon-Rappaz, 27-30 October 2008. *Are You Experienced*, 2000m, M5, ice 90 degrees. The pair reached the summit ridge at c7700m but were unable to continue to the actual summit (7864m).

CHECKMATE

UELI STECK

50. North face of Teng Kangpoche showing line and camps of first ascent by Ueli Steck and Simon Anthamatten.

I have a small set of equipment at my disposal: 14 normal pitons, three Camelots, six nuts, five ice-screws and eight quickdraws. Each of the pitches is an adventure in itself; but that is exactly what we are looking for in the mountains. With this minimal equipment I have to protect difficult rock and mixed passages. Meanwhile Simon has to belay for up to 45 minutes in the cold and then jumar up with a backpack weighing 25kg, moving as fast as possible in order to catch up on the time I have 'wasted' leading the pitch.

Such was our first attempt to climb the north face of Teng Kangpoche (6487m) in the Khumbu region of Nepal, a face attempted by many well-known alpinists without success. We began the climb on 10 April 2008 and reached almost 6000 metres. Then the weather changed – half a day earlier than forecast – and grew worse and worse. All of a sudden the wind and snowfall increased and spindrifts turned to avalanches. Below us lay a 1600-metre steep wall. We were quite exposed and the situation was getting uncomfortable. What to do was clear and simple. We had to retreat; abseiling off as fast as possible, however with avalanches falling over us, we frequently had to wait before being able to move on. We were close to our limits. The cold was hard to bear yet we had always to maintain concentration. At 8pm on 11 April we made it back to our base camp.

This first attempt had cost us a lot of energy. We knew that we had to change our strategy if we were to summit Teng Kangpoche. We recovered at base camp, eating well and checking the weather forecast. After a two-day 'holiday' in Namche Bazar, fuelling up on 'yaksteak', we returned to base camp highly motivated and ready to go for it once more.

We started out from base camp at 8am on 21 April after a sumptuous breakfast and a last good coffee from my great coffee machine. Our plan was to conserve as much as energy as possible over the first two days so as to have sufficient reserves for the upper part of the wall. This easier pace meant we would be longer on the climb; on the other hand we should become less exhausted. We were each going to climb exactly the same pitches as on our first attempt. In this way we would know what to expect and so should be faster and more efficient. Once again, the second climber would have to carry the heavy backpack.

That first day we reached a small platform at c5200m with enough space

51& 52. Simon Anthamatten on the north face of Teng Kangpoche. *(Ueli Steck)*

to erect our single skin tent. We had climbed about 1000m from base camp. This proved to be the only place to camp on the whole of the 2000m face. It was an incredible luxury, as we were to appreciate over the following days. After having had something to eat I still had some work to do. It was 4.15pm and the first pitch after the platform was waiting for me.

I seemed to remember that it was going to be an easy pitch, but far from it. I had to give my

utmost. After 50m the crack system I was following came to an end. Now I had to go over a ledged zone without adequate handholds to gain the next crack, some 3 metres further up, where we had placed a belay piton on the previous attempt. But the slabby move defied me. I climbed with my crampons and tried to get a purchase with my ice tools on tiny edges of only a few millimetres. Then the inevitable happened; I twisted an axe, it slipped off and I fell. Simon was watching very carefully and held the fall. I had dropped about 5 metres and was pretty angry with myself. Now I had to

& 54.
e as hard as
›ne.' Ueli Steck on
› north face of Teng
ıngpoche.
imon Anthamatten)

start all over again. It was no easier but this time I concentrated fully and completed the passage without further mishap. I banged in a second piton and fixed our rope. Simon was already in the tent as I abseiled. Tomorrow morning we would just climb up at the rope and start into the next pitch.

22 April: After a more or less comfortable night, the day started early at 5.30am. We breakfasted, put on our frozen shoes, packed and jumared up the first 60 metres. Here our day definitively started. Simon belayed me. The climbing was still steep and technically very demanding. On the third pitch I had to use pitons on the first 8 metres before resuming free climbing. After 240 metres it was Simon's turn. He shouldered the light backpack with all the climbing gear and I took over the big heavy one with our supplies.

Leading for the next 120 metres, Simon also had a fight on his hands. And as on our first try, he needed a lot of time for the last pitch. I was glad to be sitting at the belay; it was a nice pitch to be following as a second! An overhang prevented me from see what Simon was doing. For long periods he didn't seem to be moving, just once in a while I had to pay out a little bit of rope. I sat at the belay for more than an hour. However, I didn't have a

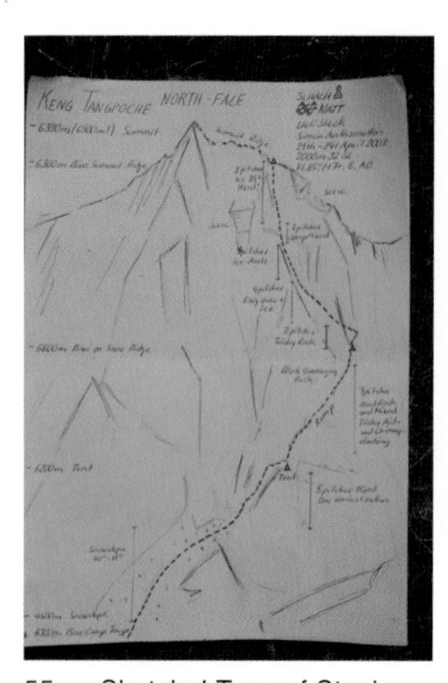

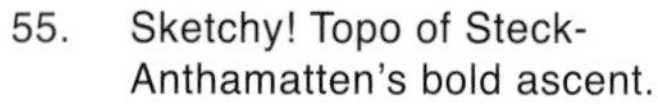
55. Sketchy! Topo of Steck-Anthamatten's bold ascent.

56. Sweet moment: Simon Anthamatten (left) and Ueli Steck on the summit of Teng Kangpoche.

problem with the fact that Simon was probably struggling with a very difficult situation. He is a strong climber and this time we were in no hurry.

It was about 3pm when we reached a tiny bivvi spot at 5600m. We built a balcony of snow and ice, about 60cm wide and 4 metres long. As the temperature fell, we melted snow for drinks and prepared for the night. We lay on our balcony in our sleeping bags and bivouac bags, belayed with webbing on the upper part of our bodies. To be honest, you do not really sleep on such nights. It was dreadful, and the wind howled terribly.

Luckily I was not cold; however I was worried about the prospect of a cold night to come. We wanted to move from now on with only our light backpacks. This would mean we would leave the sleeping bags here at 5600m and climb with our bivouac bags and PrimaLoft trousers. But what about the nights? I did not like the thought of being up at 6000m without a sleeping bag. I started to calculate the weights: bivouac sack of 300g plus trousers of approximately 450g makes a total of 750g. Our Phantom 0° sleeping bags weighed 1150g. The forecast was for hardly any snow during the following days, or just a few flakes. If we left the bivvi sacks and insulated trousers behind and instead took our sleeping bags we would be carrying an additional 400g each but at least we would spend a more or less comfortable night …

23 April: The alarm rang at 4.30am. At last the night was over. Once more the business of snow melting. Breakfast was meagre: Simon ate a Bounty and I had a muesli bar. I told Simon about my night thoughts. He also does not like to freeze. So we packed the sleeping bags into our 30-litre backpacks, which still seemed small and quite light, and set out on a long day's climbing.

It was my turn to lead. Once more we encountered steep and very difficult rock-climbing before entering an ice funnel leading to a big icefield. In the funnel we climbed together, linked by a 40m rope and always with a running belay, so-called 'simul climbing'. We moved fast as we were well acclimatized and our equipment was light to carry. At the icefield my belaying equipment ran out and Simon took over the lead. Another 120m of rock lay ahead of us.

We reached the point at 6000m where we had been forced to retreat. This time we were luckier and the weather was OK. Simon continued up the fragile rock and then one more ice pitch before we changed again. We had been climbing for 10 hours and it had started to snow. We became slower. The ice was as hard as stone and kept splintering. It required a great deal of strength-sapping aggression to plant the tool into the ice. This time I really wanted to get up there. It was our very last chance. And this thought gave me the necessary energy. Hit by hit we moved up to the summit edge. My calves were burning from standing on the front points of my crampons. Again and again I needed a rest, hanging fully on my ice tools to relieve my feet.

The cloud lifted and it stopped snowing. I looked up and I saw that the edge was only about 30m above me. I belayed myself one last time on an ice-screw and let Simon go through. At 6.30pm we stood on the summit ridge. We had just climbed the north face of Teng Kangpoche. What a feeling! To complete the ascent we had still to go over the ridge to the summit. But this would have to wait until tomorrow. We settled into our last bivouac, glad of our decision to carry that extra bit of weight up to 6300m.

24 April: We walked up the snow crest to the summit. It was 7.15am and the rest of the day would be spent abseiling. Late in the evening we arrived back in base camp and celebrated our success with a beer. Checkmate!

Summary: An account of the first ascent of the north face of Teng Kangpoche (6487m), Khumbu region, Nepal, by the Swiss Ueli Steck and Simon Anthamatten, 21-24 April 2008. *Checkmate*, 2000m, VI, M7+ or M6 A0, 85 degrees.

57.
Sanctuary of base camp. Steck and Anthamatten's 'home' beneath Teng Kangpoche.

SAMURAI DIRECT

KAZUYA HIRADE & KEI TANIGUCHI

Kamet (7756m) is the second highest mountain in the Garhwal Himalaya, India, after Nanda Devi. It was first climbed in 1931 by Frank Smythe's British expedition via the Purbi (East) Kamet glacier, Meade's col and the north-east ridge. It was then the highest summit ever climbed.

Our objective was the formidable south-east face that rises almost 2000m from the head of the Purbi Kamet glacier. Though in view of every party that has repeated Smythe's original route, the only known 'attempt' on the face was by John Varco and the late Sue Nott in 2005, and this was abandoned without setting foot on it due to bad weather.

We first tied on a rope together in 2004 in the Karakoram when we climbed a spur on the north-west face of Spantik (7027m) and the west face of Laila Peak (6200m) near the Gondokoro La. Next year we climbed variations on the east ridge of Muztagh Ata (7546m) in Xinjiang and a partial new route on the north face/north-west ridge of Shivling (6543m) in the Garhwal.

Naturally we thought that once we had climbed the face of a 6000m peak it would be possible for us to attempt a face on a higher mountain. After examining many photographs, we decided on a line up the obvious discontinuous couloir that cuts the centre of the south-east face of Kamet. In the meantime we each bagged two 8000m peaks: Manaslu and Everest for Taniguchi and Gasherbrum II and Broad Peak for Hiraide. Now we thought we were ready to attempt a face at high altitude.

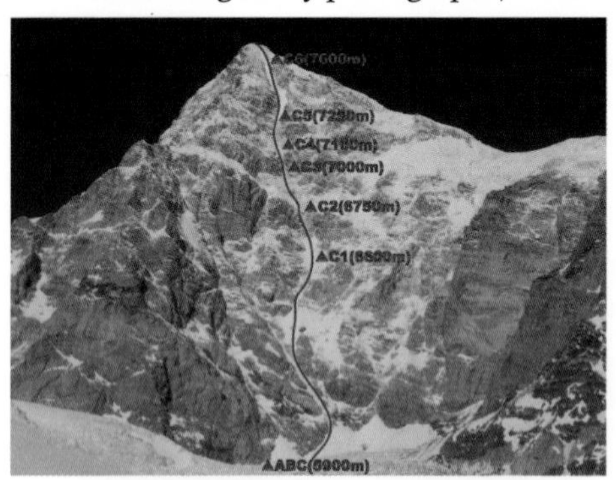

58. The south-east face of Kamet with route and bivouacs marked by Kazuya Hiraide.

We established our base camp at 4700m at the confluence of the Raikana and the Purbi Kamet glaciers on 1 September. Acclimatization was done in two stages. On 4th-7th we made a roundtrip to the foot of the face at 5750m and determined that avalanche danger was not too serious in the couloir. On 10th-16th we climbed the normal route to 7200m above Meade's col, reconnoitreing and caching food and fuel at 6600m for our descent.

As we could not afford to refer to expensive weather forecasts regularly we instead received the daily forecast for Joshimath via our satellite phone[1]. We deduced that it would be fine on Kamet when the wind blew from the south-west in Joshimath and there would be bad weather when it

1. Asked at the Piolet d'Or ceremony about the apparent change in Japanese mountaineering from siege style to alpine style, Kei Taniguchi said that for her and Giri-Giri Boys it was a matter of necessity. 'We are not rich. We cannot make the big expeditions. We just do it the simple way.' Taniguchi was the first woman to be awarded a golden ice-axe.

blew from the north / north-east. Thus we remained in base camp and let the snowstorms of mid-September pass through. Meanwhile our friends on nearby Kalanka were forced to sit out storms for three days at their bivouac high on the north face.

We reduced our gear and provisions to the minimum, preparing food and fuel for four days and taking just one sleeping bag, which we shared. In fact it took us seven days to climb the route though we never worried about our provisions.

Finally the weather cleared on 25 September. We departed from base camp and plodded through deep snow on the glacier. It took twice the time of our earlier foray to break trail in the fresh snow which was more than a metre deep at our glacier camps. Fortunately we found our cache had remained dry under the deep snow though the tent was half broken. We established advance base at 5900m at the foot of the face on the 28th.

The climbing began next day under a clear blue sky. Crossing the bergschrund and up a left-slanting gully, we simul-climbed most of the lower section of the face and roped up at the upper snow patch. We reckoned the route would have three cruxes. Our first day ended at the base of the first crux at 6600m as planned. It took us one hour and a half to dig out a small ledge.

On the 30th we climbed mixed terrain of loose rock and ice. The south-facing wall caught full sunshine in the morning and this released frequent spindrifts and falling stones. This continued even in the night. We bivouacked at 6750m on a tiny snow ridge that felt a little bit better than the previous night.

Next day we reached the second crux. From our reconnaissance we had assumed this to be the hardest section of the whole route; and it proved harder than our estimate, up loose, mixed terrain. We were already at 7000m and the altitude was sapping us. We couldn't complete the section in a day and had to bivouac at 7000m, only halfway up the section. It was already midnight when we crawled into our small refuge to sleep.

After a short, cold night, we were welcomed by a clear sky. Only two pitches of mixed climbing remained to finish the second crux. Then, above two pitches of snow slopes, the enormous third crux confronted us. It was much bigger than we expected. We decided to bivouac early at 7100m and rest in preparation for the next day. We had to massage our chilled toes.

On 3 October we completed the third crux. It consisted of one pitch of rock and ice and three pitches of ice before entering the 'banana couloir' at 7250m. We were intent on climbing the couloir next day, however we couldn't reach the summit and made our sixth bivouac on the snow ridge at 7600m. Only 150m remained to the top.

A vivid red sky to the east greeted us on our seventh day, 5 October. We were grateful to have been favored with such a long (eight days) spell of fine weather. We emerged easily onto the final snow slopes and veered right of the ridge above our bivouac. At 10am we reached the summit and looked out over a fantastic 360-degree panorama of the mountains of the

59. Kei Taniguchi and Kazuya Hirade.

Garhwal Himalaya.

We descended to the cache at 6600m that day and regained our base camp before dawn on 8 October. Our adventure was complete and we left base camp two days later. It was time to go home.

Summary: An account of the first ascent of the south-east face of Kamet (7756m) in the Garhwal Himalaya, India by Kazuya Hiraide and Kei Taniguchi, 26 September – 7 October 2008. *Samurai Direct* 1800m M5+ AI5.

BUSHIDO

Yusuke Sato

Kalanka (6931m) is one of the peaks that comprise the outer rim of the Nanda Devi sanctuary and lies just to the east of Changabang in the Indian Garhwal. The first ascent of the mountain was made by Ikuo Tanabe's four-member Kamiichi-Hosokai expedition from Japan in 1975. They approached the Rishi Ganga gorge, crossed over Shipton's Col to gain the col and climbed the west ridge. The summit was reached by Noriaki Ikeda, Tsuneo Kouma, Kazumasa Inoue and Tanabe on 3 June. Two years later a 14-member Czechoslovak expedition, led by Frantisek Grunt climbed the right side of the face to the col between Changabang and Kalanka and

60. The north faces of Kalanka (left) and Changabang showing the Japanese line.

repeated the west ridge. Jozef Raconcaj and Ladislav Jon reached the summit on 20 September.

Over the last decade, the north face direct had been attempted several times by some of the world's strongest climbers and yet still remained unclimbed when we three Giri-Giri Boys, Fumitaka Ichimura, Kazuaki

Amano and myself, approached the mountain at the end of August 2008. In 2001 Americans, Carlos Buhler and Jack Roberts made the first unsuccessful attempt on the elegant central (north) spur. Two years later another American team, the late Sue Nott and John Varco, climbed the lower part of the spur, then used a portaledge to fix ropes through the vertical to overhanging central barrier (M6), completing all the technical difficulties and bivouacking at 6,550m before being forced down by storm. Buhler returned in 2004 with Sandy Allan and John Lyall but the attempt failed at around 6,000m. In 2007 Nick Bullock and Kenton Cool tried another tack, climbing the big snow and ice slopes of the north-east face left of the spur, only to be defeated on the crest of the east ridge at more than 6,300m.

61. Yusuke Sato on the long traversing pitch, Day 2.

62. Steep mixed terrain on Kalanka's north face.

We arrived at our base camp at 4500m on the Bagini glacier on 1 September. As we couldn't find any suitable slopes in the vicinity of base camp, we had to acclimatize on an unnamed 5800m peak to the south of Saf Minal. Even after our acclimatization period I remained worried about my condition. I had suffered various symptoms of high altitude sickness on the upper slopes and was unsure of my strength. But I had to overcome my uneasiness if we were to achieve our goal of the north face.

We left base camp each with a 30kg sack and reached ABC at 5100m on 14 September. The face still looked severe though I felt we were not being totally

63. *(Above)* 'Hotel Kalanka' at 6600m where the trio sat out three days of storms.

64. 'Climbing became a struggle in minimum visibility.' Kazuaki Amano follows on Day 3.

refused. Next day we began by a roundabout route to the left as the lower slabs were covered by unstable snow. We climbed cautiously on mixed terrain with poor protection. Unable to find any natural bivvi platform, we dug a tiny ledge on a snow spur at 6000m at the late hour of 9pm.

On the 16th we made a long, almost horizontal traverse to the right, below the upper rock walls, to gain the crest of the central spur and the direct line to the summit. For much of the day we were simul climbing and there was no time for rest or to eat or drink. The night was spent sitting on a tiny 50cm ledge at 6100m. Next day we were on steep mixed terrain (M5+) that we thought the crux of our route. It began snowing and the climbing became a struggle in minimum visibility. At nightfall we dug a ledge for our small tent at 6550m and fell asleep at 1am on 18th.

Three hours later we were awake again but snowfall prevented us leaving the tent until 8:30am. After one and a half pitches we found a better terrace at 6600m and there set up our small tent. We called it 'Hotel Kalanka' and we were to be locked in here for three long days as snowstorms battered the face. I lay in a damp sleeping bag and ate only tiny amounts of mashed potatoes – just 20g a day as 'brunch'. We had brought food and fuel for only five days. Altitude, low temperatures, exhaustion and lack of food weakened us but somehow we held up.

65. Fumitaka Ichimura.

66. Kazuaki Amano.

67. Yusuke Sato.

On the evening of the 21st we saw a small patch of blue sky and thought that maybe tomorrow, we would be able to resume our climbing. Next day – our eighth on the face – we woke before dawn but the snow was still falling and once again forced us back into damp sleeping bags. However the snowfall grew lighter and at 9am we launched our summit bid.

Only 300m remained between our 'hotel' and the summit, but after four hours of struggle in deep snow up a gully we had gained only 150m. We realized how weakened we were after three days' confinement. We had to reduce our gear to speed up our climbing. With only a thermos and a waist bag, we pushed on up the last 150m of the face and reached the summit at 6pm.

We rappelled in a hurry using headtorches and reached the tent at 6600m at 10pm to spend our fourth night at 'Hotel Kalanka' without any food. We descended to advance base next day and ate and drank our fill. Twenty-four hours later we picked out the light in our base camp through the mist and darkness. We had been 11 days on the mountain with just five days of food and it would be another three days before we were sufficiently recovered to go and bring down advanced base.

Summary: An account of the first ascent of *Bushido*, (1800m, M5+), the direct, central spur on the north face of Kalanka (6931m), Garhwal Himalaya, India, alpine style by Fumitaka Ichimura, Kazuaki Amano and Yusuke Sato, 14-24 September 2008.

TASTE THE PAINE

DAVE TURNER

Sitting upstairs at Café Andino in the Peruvian town of Huaraz, sipping Americanos and browsing climbing mags, I came across an article about Cerro Escudo. In 1994/5 three Americans had climbed a route up the east face of this colossal peak in the Torres del Paine; two other lines nearly reached the summit ridge but no one had climbed the steep eastern and northern aspects all the way to the summit. Seeing the pictures of the Americans in Gore-Tex suits and plastic boots, battling up this wall amid legendary Patagonian storms, I was hooked.

January 2007 saw me at the foot of Cerro Escudo on a reconnaissance trip. I scoped out a potential line to the left of the American route; steep, beautiful grey and golden granite, and more than 1200m high. Ten months later I was back.

From the beginning I was against the idea of hiring horses or porters, finding it more rewarding to bring in everything alone. The approach was a 24-mile round trip from where the minibus drops you off. I covered this 11 times, carrying gear, food, and fuel, for a total of more than 260 miles. But soon I was established at the base of the route, with a nice camp out on the middle of the glacier.

The climb started with a 150m slab that went pretty easily, mostly 5.6 and A2+, which brought me to a large, sloping snow ledge. Above that, the next 1000-plus metres would prove steep and very difficult. Most days, I would be lucky to climb a single long pitch, clean it, and prepare the rack and ropes for next day. On average the 65-70m leads took five to eight hours and often wind and snow forced me back to the portaledge. I had chosen to make this ascent starting in December, a bit earlier than most big climbs in the park, so I would experience snow rather than rain. I would stay dryer, but it also was a lot colder. The trade-off seemed good as the vast majority of the climb was on direct aid and it doesn't make such a big difference if it is cold.

I usually moved my portaledge camp every two pitches rather than fix long strings of rope to the ground, or between widely spaced portaledge camps. Camp-moving was the most nerve-wracking part of the ascent. I had so much equipment and weight, it would take me the better part of a day. I used a Cliff Cabana ledge with a custom double-wall, triple-pole system and anchored this to three different points at all times. The updrafts on the wall were so severe they would lift even the haulbags, and I tied those down too. About half of my anchors used no bolts.

Four pitches of difficult and increasingly steep climbing brought me to the only natural ledge above the big snow ramp. The weather was quite unstable. At about 5pm I decided to move everything up to the three-foot by eight-foot ledge. All went well while I hauled the bags, but by the time I started to break down the portaledge below, the storm was building at an uncomfortable pace. I sat in the portaledge for five minutes, debating

68. The 1200m east face of Cerro Escudo showing routes and significant ascents: **1.** South-east couloir attempt (Banbolini-Jover 1996) halted 200m below ridge. **2.** *Taste The Paine* (VII 5.9 A4+ Turner 2008) continued to summit. **3.** *The Dream* (VII 5.10 A4+ Breemer-Jarrett-Santelices 1995) descending from ridge. **4.** *Via de los Invalidos* (6c A3 German Alpine Club 1994). **5.** *Et Si Le Soleil Ne Revenait Pas* (VI 5.10 A4 Nicolet-Zeiacker 1997). **6.** North Ridge (5.10 A2 Gore-Perkins 1992) 12 pitches of mixed climbing followed by 12 pitches on the north ridge, with a high point near the top of *The Dream*. *(Dave Turner)*

whether to move it. I had only two hours before nightfall, which at that season and latitude is 11.30pm. I went for it - and paid a price.

Almost as soon as I lowered out the kit on the haul line, it started to snow and the wind picked up. Even jumaring was difficult. At the ledge I fought to set up the Cabana; it's the biggest portaledge made and like a giant sail. Then came the crux – putting on the double rainflys. An expedition fly doesn't simply pull over the ledge like a tent fly. You have to open the fly and insert the ledge through the open door. If you don't get it just right, it won't fit together. Halfway through this stage, I heard an approaching gust that sounded to be ripping open the fabric of time. I had one second to grab the corner of the ledge and then I was airborne. The updraft picked up the portaledge and pulled me up with it until my feet were an honest two metres above the rock ledge. My daisies snapped up tight against the anchor, and the portaledge and I rode the wild wind for more than five seconds.

69. Cerro Escudo, showing Turner's east face and ridge route to the summit. *(Dave Turner)*

During the next two and a half days, 3m of snow fell as Patagonia tried its best to remove me from the wall. Having made it through this I was content that my bivvi system was sufficient for even the worst storms.

Pitch after pitch of long, thin cracks and seams presented themselves at just the right times. As one started to blank out, another was usually not far away. Mostly I would pendulum across just before I would have to drill. But, of course, sometimes rivets were needed; a time-consuming and mentally draining task, the dirty deed of big-wall climbing. Since most of the steep established routes I'd done on El Cap and other walls had 100 to 200 holes, I carried more than 200 rivets. But in the end I drilled only 80 lead holes on the climb. In 25 pitches, I averaged only three to four holes per pitch. Nothing really blank stood in my way – a miracle, actually.

Day eight on the wall underlined the loneliness of a long distance solo:

Wiping ice from my goggles, I could barely make out the glacier far below. I stepped higher in my aider, gaining a few inches onto the poor hook placement. 'Don't blow it now,' I thought. Just a little higher and ... pop! The hook went and I went with it. Gold and grey rock accelerated in front of my eyes as I involuntarily headed back toward the belay. I heard the reassuring but somewhat scary sound of nylon ripping apart as a screamer clipped to a beak ripped open. The beak popped and I kept falling, now swinging wildly. Another screamer activated on the next beak placement, and then I rattled to a halt.

My belay anchor was just below. I debated ducking into the portaledge for a minute or two, to let a snow flurry pass and collect myself. Obviously it was going to be a long day. Instead I reached to the back of my harness for a jumar to go back up and finish the pitch. As I clipped the jumar to the rope, I noticed a squishy feeling inside my left glove. When I took it off, blood poured out. Apparently the hook had ripped open my knuckles when it sheared from the edge above. But the bleeding soon stopped, and I knew I could take care of it later; inside the portaledge I had pain meds and stitching materials, and later that night I could play doctor.

I started back up to finish the pitch, but after one move with the jumar the beak that had held my fall decided it had had enough, and I crashed down against the portaledge. Shocked, I glanced over to the belay anchor, half expecting to find a partner to whom I could yell, 'Did you see that?' But I was alone.

Once I had two pitches fixed above my highest hanging camp, I considered my summit strategy. I loaded my alpine pack with ice tools, crampons, butane stove, bivvi sack and other gear. On day 33, I made my way up the two fixed ropes, intending to fix one last hard aid pitch, which would get me to an easier ramp leading to the long summit ridge. Reaching the ramp at 11am, I reckoned enough time remained to climb its two pitches and get a peek at the ridge. Soon I was sitting astride a notch, one leg draped over the east side of the massif, and the other over the west. A huge vertical tower blocked my view ahead. It was still early, around 1pm, and I thought, 'Why not just go for it?' I had not brought food, or water but I was excited and the weather seemed to be holding. I tied a 70m lead line onto my back, clipped some pro to my harness, and started free soloing.

On the ridge, the rock turned from beautiful, solid granite to loose, fractured metamorphic rock. Occasionally I self-belayed short sections with a loop of rope clipped to protection. I climbed up or around a seemingly endless series of towers and gendarmes, until eventually there was nothing higher, and my dream had come true. No, I made it come true.

I found a small trickle of water in the back of a crack to sip from. Almost as quickly as I had fallen into the magical summit mindspace, I returned to the reality of getting down. By 11pm I was back in the ledge, stuffing my face with chocolate and hot drinks, with the iPod on full blast. The party didn't last long, but I remember waking up the next day with chocolate all over my face.

Remarkably the weather was still holding and with 1000m vertical metres to descend with 250lbs of gear, I started moving early. Eighteen hours later I was headed down the last rope on the last set of rappels. By this time the ropes were in bad condition, with numerous core shots and severe abrasions. About 60m above the glacier, one of the damaged sections passed through my specialized rappel system (a Gri-Gri feeding a double-karabinered ATC extended from the harness), and suddenly the rope seemed to break.

The damaged rope hit the overheated ATC, the sheath either broke or burned, and I plunged the scariest two metres of my life. As the sheath stripped its way down the core, I started to smell burning nylon; the hot ATC was now beginning to burn through the core strands. I desperately reached to the back of my harness for my knife to cut away the heavy bags, but couldn't find it. So I just watched as the ATC burned its way into the core, until finally the device cooled sufficiently and stopped melting nylon. But now I was stuck. So much of the sheath had bunched below the ATC that I couldn't budge it. Eventually I found my knife and cut my belay loop from my harness, freeing myself from the ATC. I dropped a bit onto the Grigri, which was now clipped to my two tie-in points, and I pulled the handle as fast as I could and slid down the slab until my feet hit the glacier. I let out the biggest monkey call ever, and it echoed through the Valle del Silencio. Soon a few other climbers who had been watching me for weeks started to flash their headlamps and holler from their high camp above the other side of the glacier. What a moment!

70. Alone on the wall. *(Dave Turner)*

Unfortunately, that rope's core was so damaged it would have been stupid to go back up to retrieve my ropes; other climbers and park guards talked me out of trying. I have been beating myself up over leaving this junk on the mountain; it was the one flaw in an otherwise perfect ascent. Many people believe the weather will remove the ropes, but I have a few rounds of drinks waiting for the next team (or soloist) who, when making the second ascent, cuts these ropes from the wall and piles them at the base for me to carry out.

Summary: An account of a first ascent to the summit of Cerro Escudo, Torres del Paine, southern Patagonia, Chile, solo by Dave Turner, December 2007-January 2008. *Taste The Paine*, VII 5.9 A4+. Turner spent 34 days on the 1200m wall, climbing it in 25 pitches, followed by the summit ridge with difficulties to 5.9.

Acknowledgements: Turner thanks the American Alpine Club and Cascade Designs/MSR for generous support of this expedition through a Lyman Spitzer Cutting Edge Award.

PACHINKO ON DENALI

KATSUTAKA YOKOYAMA

'Giri-Giri' is not a word of great meaning. It is only a parody of sexy Japanese girls on a TV show. Generally speaking, Giri-Giri means 'at the very limit of something' in Japanese. We have no money, little experience and are immature in our climbing technique. But we always are seeking to be 'on the edge' in the mountains. Why do we like Alaska? The reason is simple. It has many attractive faces and offers low budget expeditions from Japan.

71. Bear Tooth, Buckskin glacier, Alaska, showing the line of the Japanese route, *Climbing is Believing* (AK 6, 5.10a M7R A1+, 1250m) on the north-east face.

For us Giri-Giri Boys, April 2008 was our fourth consecutive season in Alaska. There were five of us: Tatsuro Yamada, Yuto Inoue, Fumitaka 'Itchy' Ichimura, Yusuke Sato. Although sometimes in different combinations, we had climbed together in Alaska, Andes and Himalaya.

Our ascents in Alaska over the previous years were as follows:

2005: First ascent of *Shi-Shi* (Alaska grade 4) on the west face of Mt Huntington and the third ascent of the Denali Diamond (AK6) by Ichimura and Yokoyama.

2006: First ascent of *Before The Dawn* (AK5) on the north face of Broken Tooth and the third ascent of *Deprivation* (AK6) on the north buttress of Mt Hunter by Ichimura-Yokoyama.

2007: First ascents of *Season of The Sun* (AK5) on the south-east face of Mt. Bradley, *Memorial Gate* (AK5) on the north face of Mt Church, and *The Ladder Tube* (AK5) on the north face of Mt Johnson, all by Yamada, Ichimura and Sato.

Five firsts and two early repeats of Alaska grade 6 routes in only three years seemed to be good going given our limited experience. So what next? Our goal for 2008 was easy to imagine. We would try an *enchaînement* of great routes in a single alpine-style push in the same manner as our usual winter climbing in Japan.

The idea dawned on Mt Huntington in 2005 when we climbed a new line on the west face. Although not so difficult, it was important for us

The line of the eight-day *enchaînement* on Denali by Fumitaka Ichimura, Yusuke Sato and Katsutaka Yokoyama. Dates are shown month/day.
Top to bottom:
72. The *Isis Face*; 73. *Ramp Route* and *Slovak Direct*; 74. *Ramp Route*, descended; 75. *Slovak Direct*.
(These and previous page courtesy of Tamotsu Nakamura, *Japanese Alpine News*)

that we found the line by ourselves, not out of the guidebook. It was the same on the Denali Diamond. We followed the line of dièdres and ice runnels and only learnt the name of the route when we returned to Talkeetna. We climbed Broken Tooth in 2006 and three routes in the Ruth glacier in 2007 in the same way.

Climbers should find and climb their lines freely following their intuitions. It's easy to say but sometimes difficult to put the principle into practice. In 2006, no ascents had been made that season on Hunter's north buttress before our arrival. Local climbers kept saying 'conditions are bad this year'. However it didn't seem so bad as we climbed *Deprivation*.

It was only our second season in Alaska, so we didn't know how the regular conditions on the buttress should be.

After summiting Mt Hunter, we descended the west ridge. At the landing point, a climber asked us why we had descended that way. Most climbers seem to think it better to rappel the route from the top of the buttress. However for us it was natural to continue to the summit and to descend the ridge. The most impressive part of our experience on Mt Hunter was the difficult down-climb of the ridge, not the ascent of the buttress or the summit itself.

Of course it was not new, but our approach to the climb had made it fully satisfying. I think the true value of climbing doesn't exist in technical difficulties and grades but in commitment to the mountains. We modern climbers have highly developed gear, good technique and detailed information. But I ask myself, 'Are we facing the mountain with the same enthusiasm as great pioneers?'

Bear Tooth

On 7 April 2008, Sato, Ichimura and I flew in to the Buckskin glacier. Our goal was the east face of Bear Tooth on which we had been driven back in 2006. It appeared much drier than previously and instead we decided to try an obvious dièdre in the centre of the north-east face. Despite some climbers having paid attention to the line, we knew it was still unclimbed.

On 13 April we climbed the east gully and two more pitches on the north-east face before being halted by snowfall. It continued for three days. We resumed climbing five days later. The first pitch was on delicate thin ice/snow in a steep dièdre with the crux for the lower section coming on the third pitch; partially overhanging, it required some aid climbing. We made a comfortable bivouac on the snowfield, clearly seen from the glacier.

Next day, the upper portion of the face was still steep, however solid rock and stable ice allowed us good progress. The crux here was pitch 10, tackled with delicate hookings and run-outs. Above that came entertaining climbing on verglas, corners and icicles. It was never boring!

A big cornice barred the way on the final section. We out-flanked this on the left (pitch 16) from where a right slanting crack (5.10a) emerged onto snow slopes leading to the summit. We bivouacked after reaching the top and next day descended to the col between Moose's Tooth, then down the east gully. We named the route *Climbing is Believing*. However the adventure there is unfinished and we will try again for the east face of Bear Tooth very soon.

Denali

Pachinko is our name for the game of climbing more than one route in a single push. It began in the Japanese mountains in the 1960s as training for bigger walls, especially for the Alps. The idea was to climb up and down several routes continuously. But it was not mere training, you face much more of the mountain. We decided to play *Pachinko* in the big mountains of Alaska. Local climbers equally said this was crazy but to us their word 'crazy' sounded like praise for our bold plan.

After Bear Tooth, we spent some lazy days at the landing point on the south-east fork of Kahiltna glacier and acclimatized on the west buttress of Denali. The weather was still unstable. We assumed 10 days for our *enchaînement*, starting with the Isis Face, descending the *Ramp Route* and finally climbing the *Slovak Direct* on the south face of Denali. We could hardly expect 10 days of good weather in Alaska and so hesitated no longer.

On 11 May, we flew to the west fork of the Ruth glacier. The Isis Face appeared bigger than we imagined but did not look so difficult. We completed the route in three days of simul climbing, including sitting out snowfall for 24 hours in an ice cave. It is a beautiful line in a superb location. The only mishap was that I lost my sunglasses – a serious loss in the fierce Alaskan sunshine.

We followed the south buttress northwards and began to descend the *Ramp Route*. It was the most worrying part of our plan because of crevasses and avalanches. The route is rated Alaska Grade 3 and only 55 degrees but the seriousness exceeded that of other routes, especially when slowed by our heavy packs. We still had six days of food and fuel when we got to the bottom of the south face on the 14th. It seemed enough for our climb on the Slovak Direct. Although the route was technically difficult, we would climb it pitch by pitch. Our only anxieties were bad weather, objective danger and maybe our own carelessness.

The wall steepened as we climbed higher. Alternating the lead meant the leader enjoyed excellent climbing on stable ice while his followers laboured up, jumaring with heavy packs. We found a peg left by the first ascensionists. Although they employed a heavy style with fixed-ropes, they had the satisfaction of touching unknown terrain. We had to console ourselves with climbing in better style.

76. Denali trio (l to r) Sato, Ichimura and Yokoyama.

My eyes were getting worse and on the second day I had to give up leading after two pitches and followed the rest of the way as third man. We were already at the crux of the route so far and retreat would be impossible if we pushed further. We discussed the situation and finally decided to continue climbing. Itchy led a WI6 pitch with only two ice-screws and Yusuke smoothly led a 5.9 X rock pitch. Their fine leading was decisive in our success and we slipped above the crux before sunset.

Next day (17th) the steepness of the wall relented and we continued to the juncture with the Cassin Ridge. Here we found new footprints on a snow patch, detouring around rock and continuing to the upper slopes. We thought the prints might be Tatsuro and Yuto's. They might have completed the traverse of Kahiltna Peaks, reaching here by the Cassin Ridge and continuing towards the summit. Determined to follow them, we gasped our way toward the summit, reaching it on the 18th in a whiteout.

I think of climbing as painting our thought on a big canvas called 'mountain'. Our eight days on Denali had created a piece of work requiring all our strength. Tatsuro and Yuto never returned from the Cassin. Maybe they found a more attractive line on the ridge and almost succeeded on it before their disappearance. Five months later, I was walking down a glacier below Kangtega in Nepal, looking back at the north face I had just attempted. There were many reasons for defeat. But to tell the truth, I feared the wall. Tatsuro and Yuto had planned to be with me and their absence undoubtedly affected me. I felt uneasiness about my climbing on Kangtega and about Itchy and Yusuke on Kalanka's north face. They had departed for India a month earlier.

Perhaps my feeling below Kangtega is a proof that I am maturing. I had climbed rather rashly in these years. As a climber, I cannot avoid thinking about the death of friends or myself. From the loss of Tatsuro and Yuto I had learnt not only fear but also the importance of inquiring into one's philosophy and dreams on the mountain. I'm always happy when thinking 'what next?' for my climbing but I nonetheless have complex issues to work through. It is surely the same for my friends of the Giri-Giri Boys.

Summary: An account of an eight-day *enchaînement* on Denali by Fumitaka Ichimura, Yusuke Sato and Katsutaka Yokoyama, 11-18 May 2008; *Isis Face* (Alaska grade 6: M4 5.8 A1, 2200m) to the south buttress, descend by *Ramp Route* (AK 3: 2800m), re-ascent by the *Slovak Direct* (AK 6: 5.9, 2700m). The trio also made a first ascent, *Climbing is Believing* (AK 6, 5.10a M7R A1+, 1250m) on the north-east face of Bear Tooth.

'...AND ALL MUST HAVE PRIZES'

STEPHEN GOODWIN

'Everyone has won and all must have prizes.' So said the Dodo to Alice at the end of the Caucus Race. Something of this Wonderland spirit touches the reborn *Piolets d'Or*. When Doug Scott accepted the invitation to be president of the jury for the 17th edition of the French alpinism awards, his first instinct was that all six of the nominated teams should receive a golden ice-axe. In essence, the Scott view on competition is that while we compete to be first to climb particular routes, the idea of a competition for the title 'best climber', or even a 'best climb', is anathema. However, in the end representatives of only three teams stepped up to receive a shiny axe. Hard choices had been made.

The 2009 *Piolets d'Or* was undoubtedly a success in the sense of a festival of alpinism and a showcase for the town of Chamonix. Over four days in May (22-25) mountaineers young and not so young, from across the globe, debated, partied, gossiped endlessly, and even managed to fit in a bit of climbing – champions of the free-climbing ethic happily clipping bolts on the Chamonix and Aosta valley crags. 'When in Rome... How could it fail with a line-up including Walter Bonatti, Peter Habeler, Scott, Jim Donini, Japan's Giri-Giri Boys and Simon Anthamatten; reliving their adventures before audiences in the Salle Docteur Michel Payot in the Hotel Majestic, and then reliving their youth boogying to a blues band at the *Bistrot des Sports* until 4am? The *Strictly Come Dancing* award would probably go to Donini for his table-top twist. For most of the time then, the so-called 'coveted axes, seemed little more than a pretext to be there.

Guided by the new president of the *Groupe de Haute Montagne*, Christian Trommsdorff, the 17th Piolets rose from the ruins of an event that had collapsed due mainly to a deep dislike among mountaineers of the idea of picking winners in alpinism. An attempt to meet these concerns in time to hold a 2008 PdO failed and for most of that year there seemed little prospect of its revival. Undoubtedly there were other complicating factors, money being one. But perhaps that is now history.

Early in 2009 Trommsdorff and his friends, as he put it: 'saw an opportunity to relaunch the Piolets as a climbers' festival celebrating the pure amateur spirit of alpinism. The 'opportunity' was a coherence, or coming together, of what the GHM wants to promote in terms of climbing 'by fair means' and a deep respect for nature and what Chamonix wants to promote as an alpine resort.'

Trommsdorff emphasises the need to revive an amateur spirit – in the French sense of the word of doing things for love rather than the British notion of a bumbler – and for a sharing within the community of alpinists. 'When you go climbing somewhere, say the Rockies, you should be able to connect with people there who you don't necessarily know, but who share the same spirit; to learn what they're doing, or maybe to climb together.'

The involvement of the municipality of Chamonix Mont-Blanc and later Courmayeur, just through the tunnel in Italy, provided the GHM with the resources necessary to lay on a major festival with little reliance on commercial sponsorship. Suddenly the *Piolets* had cash to provide not only travel and hotels for its stars, but also venues and vital administrative backup. The mayors of both resorts, Eric Fournier (Chamonix) and Fabrizia Derriard (Courmayeur) were much in evidence, both the embodiment of chic New politics, not at all aldermanic. Past *Piolets* budgets have been around €30,000; Trommsdorff reckoned 2009's was a basic €80,000; add in the municipal infrastructure and the time of council officers and volunteers, and it was at least €120,000. Also in the organising group were publishers Nivéales and the magazines *Montagnes* and *Vertical*.

An important element for the new team in gaining acceptance among sceptical climbers was the endorsement of the *American Alpine Journal*, which became involved in the selection of the climbs, and the appointment of Doug Scott as president of the jury. To a lesser extent the Alpine Club also became a player in the event. The award of the golden axes was preceded by the presentation of the first of the AC's 'Spirit of Mountaineering' commendations to six climbers who had attempted to rescue Iñaki Ochoa de Olza on Annapurna in May 2008.

A total of 57 first ascents from 2008 were considered of which six were put before a jury, presided over by Doug Scott and comprising 8000m specialist Dodo Kopold of Slovakia, Jim Donini, outgoing president of the AAC, Peter Habeler, Im Duck Young, a Korean mountain journalist, and Dario Rodriguez, editor of *Desnivel*, Spain's premier mountain publication. Their criteria included: style of ascent, spirit of exploration, level of commitment and self-sufficiency, suitability of the route in the light of objective dangers, efficiency and sparing use of resources, respect for fellow climbers, porters and local people.

With at least one member of five of the teams present at Chamonix – the exception was the solo climber Dave Turner – the hour of judgement was approached with some unease. We had heard all their stories, each was impressive in its own way and the images the climbers had brought back of alpinism at its most committing were breathtaking. It seemed churlish to start setting one on a pedestal above another. This had been the thrust of Marko Prezelj's protest in 2007 when he condemned the *Piolet d'Or* from its own platform:

> *'It is not possible to judge another person's climb objectively. Each ascent contains untold stories, influenced by expectations and illusions that develop long before setting foot on the mountain ... Comparing different climbs is not possible without some kind of personal involvement, and even then it's difficult. Last year (2006) I climbed in Alaska, Patagonia and Tibet. I cannot decide which expedition was the most ... the "most what?" in fact.'*

With two golden ice-axes in his trophy cabinet, Prezelj was wide open to the charge of hypocrisy, but his fundamental argument is a hard one to rebut. In their hearts, the 2009 jury surely must have known this, but having accepted their role, they now had to deliver. For me, a note of sadness crept in at this point. Only the day before, there had been such a sense of shared enjoyment and fraternity as we'd climbed and joked together at Arnad, a sport crag in the Aosta valley. Maybe that is a little misty eyed. But so it seemed; and now we waited, slightly awkward and embarrassed I thought, to hear the jury's verdict. And for all one might say that it is the quality of the climb that is being saluted, look at how these things are trumpeted on publicity blurb put out by the sponsors, of winning climbers, or on their own websites – 'Joe Soap, winner of the prestigious *Piolet d'Or*, etc, etc...' Business is business.

Doug began his address with words that, to me at least, caught this sense of discomfort: 'This should be the most important part [of the festival]. But is it? The greatest thing is that these six climbs have created the spirit that has surrounded us in this great week.' The *Piolets d'Or* had been reinvented and there had been 'many winners, – Christian Trommsdorff and his fellow organisers, Chamonix and Courmayeur, and climbing itself. 'Rather like the great religions which occasionally need to be brought back to basics, climbing needs an occasion like the *Piolets d'Or* as a reminder of what is best in climbing at a time of commercialism and dumbing down with bolts.'

The jury had been unanimous in all its decisions, said Scott as he set about eliminating three of the nominated climbs: The Denali enchaînement had been 'an incredible *tour de force* but it was not original. 'It didn't go anywhere new.' Because of his use of bolts, Dave Turner's 34 days solo on the east face of Cerro Escudo 'lacked that bit of commitment'. And the French ascent of the south face of Nuptse failed because although Glairon-Rappaz and Benoist topped out on the face, they did not reached the summit. The

Nuptse climb had given the jury their biggest headache, Doug said, adding that the climbers had turned back for very good reasons. 'They wanted to come back with their fingers and toes.' However the dismissal of such an impressive alpine-style route on what seemed akin to a legal technicality will reinforce the view that reform of the *Piolets d'Or* must go deeper still.

Golden ice-axes were presented to: Kazuya Hiraide and Kei Taniguchi for their first ascent of the south-east face of Kamet, to Kazuki Amano, Fumitaka Ichimura and Yusuke Sato for their alpine-style ascent of the north face of Kalanka, and to Simon Anthamatten and Ueli Steck for their first ascent of the much-tried north face of Teng Kangpoche. As if this were climbing's Oscars, there was also a 'lifetime achievement' award for Walter Bonatti. The 69-year alpinist *par exellence* was given an affectionate reception in both Chamonix and Courmayeur, where he was the focus of the Piolets' Italian festivities.

77. Piolet People 2009

Scott declared: 'There are no winners and no losers. The honoured are ambassadors of an art, a passion.' Ideally there should be no winners and losers, however, while there is a jury delivering a verdict on who will receive a golden axe and who will not, it is a hard claim to stand up. Although it wasn't explicit at the presentation, a subsequent press release categorised the awards as follows: the Kamet climb embodied the 'spirit of exploration', the Kalanka axe was for 'commitment', while the Swiss pair were honoured for the 'technical difficulty, of their Teng Kangpoche ascent. The jury's approach was that all the nominated climbs that met the event's exacting criteria would be honoured, and there were, reportedly, six axes in the cupboard just in case. Is it conceivable also that if one year no climb measured up fully there would be no final award? The fact is that at the moment when Doug got up to speak, the audience, and presumably the nominees, thought that all six climbs were in with a chance. But disappointment for some was inevitable when climbs had been shortlisted which actually fell short of criteria – fell short of the summit of Nuptse for example.

Christian Trommsdorff and all concerned with the 2009 *Piolets d'Or* can take pleasure and credit at having created a great festival of alpinism – some 300 people filled the hall for the final event – but I hope they will give further thought to removing the invidious business of choosing between feats of alpinism each unique. In the end, surely all that climbers desire, like any practitioner of a craft, art or profession, is the respect of their peers for what has been achieved? Honours or baubles are mere chaff by comparison.

CLIMBING ETHICS

ALPINE STYLE VS COMMERCIAL EXPEDITIONS

The opening night of the Piolets d'Or included a discussion on Climbing Ethics. Here, mountain guide **Victor Saunders** *expands on his contribution to that spirited debate.*

There are those who think commercial expeditions are unethical, that commercial expeditions should use alpine-style tactics, and that maybe they should not exist at all. I will show that this view is mistaken and that the ethical issue is in fact irrelevant; but before dealing with the so-called ethical issue, I wish to set aside the usual diversions that get mixed up in this discussion. There are three that I commonly hear:

First: Commercial expeditions bring too many people to the same mountain, by the same route. Well, to these people I say, if you have a romantic desire to find raw nature, go away and do new routes on unclimbed mountains. Let the wonderful climbs that have been nominated for this year's Piolets d'Or inspire you. It is not intelligent to do the normal route on Mont Blanc in August and complain that you are not alone.

Second: The environmental thing. Commercial expeditions typically go back to the same site year after year, and so it is in the operator's interest to keep camps clean and tidy for the next visit. Amateur expeditions rely solely on the good moral values of the climbers, because there are no other controls on them. By far the worst garbage I have seen in the mountains was left by a recent European amateur expedition with sponsorship. It included half burned Karrimats and lead-acid car batteries (see photos).

78.
No reputable commercial outfit could return to any campsite it left in such a state. Garbage left by a European 'amateur' expedition below Shishapangma.
(Victor Saunders)

This was nothing less than a desecration of one of the most beautiful bases under an 8000m mountain. No self-respecting commercial expedition would leave this kind of mess behind. Let us just agree that this kind of thing is completely unacceptable to all types of expeditions, amateur, sponsored and commercial.

Third: This diversion is surprising. I hear climbers say that commercial trips are dangerous. This seems to me to be a really strange one. Between

1970 and 1982, British expeditions trying new routes on 8000m peaks were losing climbers at a rate that would not be acceptable in the commercial world. No commercial enterprise would survive the litigation. On the other hand, there is no doubt that alpine-style climbing at high altitude is extremely dangerous; we just prefer to use the euphemisms 'serious' and 'committing'. We need to be honest about this. We need to accept that 'serious' and 'committing' are the very qualities we are somewhat romantically attached to in alpine-style climbing.

Let us set aside these diversions then and move on. For 'ethics' read 'rules of the game'. All climbing is just a game; it is governed by rules. The fact that people 'cheat' and/or get accused of 'cheating', proves the case that it is all about rules. Whether we follow the rules or break them is up to us. There is only one meta-rule here; do not lie if you have not followed the rules. That is almost the only really unforgivable sin in climbing.

As the game evolves so do the rules. The first recorded climbs had no recognized rules, though Moses did return with a nice set of commandments. The common ancestor of modern climbing is the first ascent of Mont Blanc, but it is not till almost 100 years later that we begin to see the idea of 'fair means' expressed by Alfred Mummery. By 1913 the great Paul Preuss was writing that all artificial aids are unethical in the game of rock climbing. Meanwhile, at the end of the 1800s bouldering had been invented by Oscar Eckenstein, its grading and rules to be redefined in the 1950s by John Gill. The use of pitons, bolts (invented in 1927), ice-screws, crampon heel-spurs, bottled oxygen, fixed ropes, porters, fixed camps and chalk have all been circumscribed by rules.

All of this reflects the evolution of climbing into differing and quite separate activities. We started with the same common ancestor, and now climbing has evolved into many species, each with its own rules. If you are bouldering, the rules for a hammerless ascent of The Nose are not relevant. On the other hand, it would be plain silly to say that because you have been bouldering, you are now no longer allowed to climb The Nose.

The corollary is, there is no contradiction in climbing with lightweight alpine-style rules on one expedition and guiding clients on a commercial trip with fixed ropes and camps the next. To say there is an ethical contradiction between alpine-style climbing and commercial expeditions is exactly equivalent to saying that a boulderer is not allowed to climb any other style; it's not that logical. If you have agreed with me so far, you will agree that the criticism of the ethics of commercial expeditions, by climbers following alternative rules is ultimately just an irrelevance.

And finally I must diverge from the strict tramlines of my argument to add something that is not predicated on the rules of the games. I believe in tolerance: we should keep to as light a footprint as possible and interfere with the other games as little as possible. If we accept these constraints and that one game does not negate another, we should tolerate other styles of climbing, even if we do not follow or delight in them. This would be a mark of the respect we owe to other climbers and to ourselves.

THE SPIRIT OF MOUNTAINEERING: ANNAPURNA 2008

The first 'Spirit of Mountaineering' Commendations of the Alpine Club were presented at the closing ceremony of the 17th Piolets d'Or to six climbers for their attempt to rescue the Spanish alpinist Iñaki Ochoa de Olza from 7400m on the east ridge of Annapurna in May 2008.

Three of the climbers were present in Chamonix for the ceremony: Simon Anthamatten (Swiss), Don Bowie (Canadian), and Horia Colibasanu (Romanian). The other three recipients are: Alexy Bolotov (Russian), Ueli Steck (Swiss) and Denis Urubko (Kazakh).

Introduced by the AC in 2007 on the initiative of Norman Croucher, the commendation acknowledges and thanks persons who, 'in the true Spirit of Mountaineering, have shown unselfish devotion to help a fellow climber in the mountains, and in doing so have sacrificed their own objective or put their personal safety at risk'.

The commendations were presented jointly by Norman and AC President Paul Braithwaite. In support was Iñaki Ochoa's brother Pablo, who praised the six as 'a great bunch of men' to whom the Ochoa family owed a great debt. 'They are great examples to the rest of us,' he said. 'They had a real hard time, no romanticism in it at all. Lots of snow, no

79. At Annapurna base camp: left to right, Horia Colibasanu, Iñaki Ochoa de Olza, Ueli Steck, Simon Anthamatten.

food, no proper gear and terrible conditions.'

Iñaki Ochoa, aged 40 and from Pamplona, was an experienced alpinist who worked as a high altitude cameraman and guide. A veteran of 30 Himalayan expeditions, he had climbed 12 of the 14 eight thousand metre peaks including a new route on Shishapangma, solo, in 2005. Only Annapurna (8091m) and Kangchenjunga (8586m) remained.

80. Iñaki Ochoa de Olza at Annapurna base camp, May 2008.

81. Horia Colibasanu.

82. Don Bowie.

With Ochoa on Annapurna's east ridge were Colibasanu, 31, his partner on K2, Manaslu and Dhaulagiri, and Bolotov, 45, who had been with a Russian team also on the mountain. According to Colibasanu, a dentist by profession, the Spaniard 'had a stroke' as he entered the tent at camp 4 after the pair of them had retreated from about 7850m. 'We got close to the east summit. But there was a misunderstanding over the rope; we had run out.'

Bolotov pushed on; however a delicate section lay ahead which Ochoa, whose hands were frostbitten, did not want to descend without a rope. 'Iñaki was not feeling too good and so I went back with him. After the stroke he was half paralyzed and it was really hard to move him.'

Via satellite 'phone, Colibasanu contacted Ochoa's family in Spain and they in turn set in motion an extraordinary international rescue effort during which some 14 climbers attempted to reach the scene. Most usefully placed were the Swiss pair Ueli Steck, 31, and Simon Anthamatten, 24, who after their stunning warm-up with the first ascent of Teng Kangpoche's north face (pages 56-61), were now waiting out the weather at 6000m below Annapurna's south face.

'We'd had a little weather window and been up to 6500m, still on the glacier, and left our high altitude equipment there,' Anthamatten recalled. 'And we'd been back at our base camp two or three days, waiting and waiting. Then about 9pm one night (19 May) we had a call from Horia on the sat' phone, saying they had a problem. We didn't think for one minute of our climb. It was: "What can we do? What can we take? How will we manage? Where is food? Will we take a GPS?" A big problem was that we had no high altitude boots or down things; they were stashed below the face.'

Climbing through the night, with just a brief rest at the others' camp 1 (5600m), the pair reached camp 2 (6200m) at noon and called a halt. Steck said: 'It was warm and the snow was soft. The 45-degree slope over the glacier up to camp 3 looked dangerous for avalanches. The Spanish people at base camp disliked our decision. Sure, they wanted us up there as fast as possible. But we had to think also about our own security.'

At 6am next morning, the Swiss resumed their ascent, freezing in their inadequate clothing and Phantom Lite boots as they broke trail through fresh snow chest high. Via base camp, they learnt that Bolotov had returned from the summit and was at camp 4. Though weary, the Russian was persuaded to continue his descent. It is the 3km ridge and steep wall to be negotiated to camp 3 that made Ochoa's position so strung out and vulnerable. When Bolotov and the Swiss met at camp 3, they discovered that the Russian had the same foot size, 45, as Steck and the pair exchanged boots. Steck, at least, now had high altitude footwear suitable to the task ahead, plus Bolotov's mittens.

By now, as the Swiss pair learnt from base camp, Denis Urubko, 34, and Don Bowie, 38, were also on their way up the mountain with medicines and bottled oxygen. Urubko ('arguably the strongest climber on the planet' according to Bowie, himself no slouch above 8000m) had just summited Makalu and returned to Kathmandu, from where he had flown to Pokhara by helicopter with Sergei Bogomolov, the Russian leader, who was pulling out all the stops for Ochoa. Bowie was already in Pokhara and agreed immediately to join the rescue, despite having split with Ochoa and Colibasanu days earlier after a disagreement over climbing tactics. After their small helicopter was twice forced back by cloud, a larger one attempted to land Urubko and Bowie at about 5400m, however in the end had to set them down at about 3800m. 'Denis and I bailed out in our big boots and in less than an hour we were at base camp,' said Bowie. By 10pm the same day they were at camp 2 where they met Bolotov on his descent.

At 4.30am, when Urubko and Bowie started up the face, Bolotov went up with them. By now the concern was not just for Ochoa but also for Colibasanu, who had already been five days at 7400m or above, and increasingly for the under-equipped Swiss. It was a rescue chain.

At camp 3, during the night of 21 May, Anthamatten started to throw up and show the first signs of high altitude sickness. Camp 3, at 6800m, was the highest the 26-year old Zermatt guide had ever been. 'We had prepared for this expedition for a year and now we were on this rescue. It was like a crazy dream,' he said. Having decided Anthamatten would remain at camp 3, the Swiss then sought, via base camp, to persuade Colibasanu to leave Ochoa and begin the descent. But Colibasanu and the base camp team would have none of it. Conscious of the danger of the long ridge in poor visibility, Steck decided to take the GPS along, but he had never used one before and had to be instructed by Anthamatten.

Steck left camp 3 at 5am and eight hours later gained the ridge from where he could talk directly to Colibanasu. Steck said he could not break trail all the way along the ridge alone and urged Colibasanu to start towards him to make a track. 'We knew that if Horia went just 10m along

83. Steck in deep snow early on the dash to try and save Ochoa.
(Simon Anthamatten)

the traverse he would not go back,' Anthamatten said. The Swiss are convinced that the trick saved Colibasanu's life. The Romanian acknowledges that he could barely walk when eventually he met Steck on the traverse, nor could he operate the familiar stove that the Swiss handed him to boil water. To Steck's relief, Colibasanu confessed it would be impossible to return to 7400m. Fuelled by an energy bar, a Dexamethasone tablet and a caffeine tablet the Swiss had given him, he continued down to camp 3.

'Ueli and Simon were really risking their lives for us,' said Colibasanu. 'I was really pushing them. I think at altitude you don't have too much imagination. You can just keep to your goal, to get to the summit or to save someone, and when things change it is difficult to assimilate the changes. You cannot think through this new situation.'

At 4pm on 22 May after 11 hours of climbing and with snow falling, Steck reached camp 4. It was a mess, better not detailed here. Ochoa was semi-conscious, lying in his sleeping bag, wearing his down suit. As instructed earlier over the phone from Switzerland by Dr Oswald Oelz, the high altitude medicine specialist, Steck gave Ochoa a Dexamethasone injection directly into his thigh. He also melted snow for water, but the Spaniard kept throwing up. Next morning, as Ochoa's condition worsened, Steck again called Oelz and administered another injection, but in reality it was days too late to hope this would bring recovery.

Ochoa died around midday on the 23th and Steck placed him in a crevasse near the tent. Advised from Bern of bad weather, Steck had to endure a second night at camp 4, with the temperature falling to minus 25°C before beginning the long descent. Overnight snow had blanketed the track and in poor visibility Steck made constant use of the GPS, until after 2.5hrs negotiating the ridge, he heard the voices of Urubko and Bowie advancing towards him.

Many other people were involved in various capacities in the attempt to rescue Iñaki Ochoa, but only the six commended met the Spirit of Mountaineering's declared criteria of having sacrificed their own objective or put their personal safety at risk in order to help a fellow climber. Helicopter pilots and professional rescuers, for all their bravery, along with base camp teams etc, are outside its scope as envisioned by Norman Croucher and the Spirit of Mountaineering committee.

Recapping on the origin of the commendation, Norman told the Piolets audience how appalled he had been to read reports (not entirely accurate) of summit-fixated climbers stepping past those who had fallen sick or injured by the wayside, particularly on Everest. The death of David Sharp in 2006 had lead to a rash of newspaper headlines to the effect that the spirit of the Good Samaritan was dead among mountaineers – clearly a painful idea to Norman but one with which a climber standing beside him at Chamonix, Don Bowie, might have agreed.

84. Steck's face at Camp 4 reveals the strain of a supreme physical and mental effort to try and save Ochoa.

In 2007, Bowie was ignored by a succession of climbers as he struggled down K2 without a rope, without crampons (stolen at 8000m!) and dragging a broken leg. In the end he had to threaten to embed his ice-axe into somebody's leg before he was begrudgingly handed the length of 'manky hemp rope' that enabled him to descend to Camp 1 and comparative safety. However Bowie is good evidence that the Samaritan is not dead. Despite his differences with Ochoa and Colibasanu, he climbed to 7400m to offer whatever help he could. Taken together with Steck and Anthamatten's instant response, the fortitude of Bolotov and Urubko, and Colibasanu's loyalty to his partner, it is a heartening, if tragic, story.

Compiled by **Stephen Goodwin**, mainly from interviews with the three Annapurna climbers present in Chamonix to receive the Commendations.

Journeys

85. Simon Pierse, *Kabru and Kangchenjunga From Sanga Choling, Sikkim,* 2003, watercolour and gouache, 79 x 109cm.

TAMOTSU NAKAMURA

Travels Beneath Blue Skies

Our autumn 2008 expedition to the Tibetan marches again proved that Tom Nakamura is a man of 'Blue Sky'. We spent 40 days journeying through the Gorge Country of south-east Tibet and the mountains of Sichuan. Throughout, the Gods blessed us with the finest weather, except for a couple of days in Sichuan.

Our objectives were two-fold; exploration of Dungri Garpo (6090m) in deep Gorge Country and the unveiling of a little-known peak of 6079m called Ren Zhong Feng, south of Minya Konka in Sichuan.

No one has accessed the Dungri Garpo massif from the west and so there are no photographs. The name and height of the peak 'Dungri Garpo' are seen only on the 1:2,500,000 Map of Mountain Peaks on the Qinghai-Xizang (Tibet) Plateau published in China. A huge mountain range named as Nu Shan, the watershed of which is shared by the Mekong and Salween rivers, runs from north to south forming three mountain massifs in the heart of the deep gorge country of the Hengduan Mountains. From the north these are Dungri Garpo, Damyon and the Meili Snow Mountains. Dungri Garpo's main peak (6090m) stands at E98°20' and N29°17'. According to local villagers, 'Dungri' means Tibetan conch horn. North of the main peak is an unnamed 6070m peak; south lie Jiamutongnan (5925m), several 5700m-5800m rock peaks and Longgequji Puzhong (c6000m) which is close to the main summit of Damyon (6324m). (For Damyon see 'Further Travels in Eastern Tibet', *AJ* 2008, 161-171)

There are 250 unclimbed 6000m peaks in Nyenchen Tanglha East and Kangri Garpo ranges of East Tibet, but only a few 6000m peaks remain virgin in Sichuan's West Highlands. They are:

Yangmolong (6060m) east of Batang. Japanese climbers attempted the south face in 1991 and the north face in 2003; an AC team of Dave Wynne-Jones, Steve Hunt, Dick Isherwood and Peter Rowat attempted the steep north spur in 2007 but were turned back at 5400m.

Xiannairi (6032m), Gongga Xueshan, Daocheng County, was attempted by a Japanese team in 1989. Currently the Daocheng County local government will issue no climbing permit, citing environmental protection.

Nyambo Konka (6114m), Minya Konka massif, and a couple of satellite peaks in the massif.

Peak 6079m - tentatively named as Ren Zhong Feng - south of Minya

86.
Dungri Garpo (6090m) west face seen from a point at 4700m in the Hong Qu valley.

87.
Dungri Garpo's east and north faces seen from the Markam pass on Sichuan-Tibet Highway.

88.
Unnamed 6070m peak north of Dungri Garpo, its face seen from the Markham pass.
(Photos: Tamotsu Nakamura)

89. Opposite page: East of the Himalaya.
(Map provided by Tamotsu Nakamura)

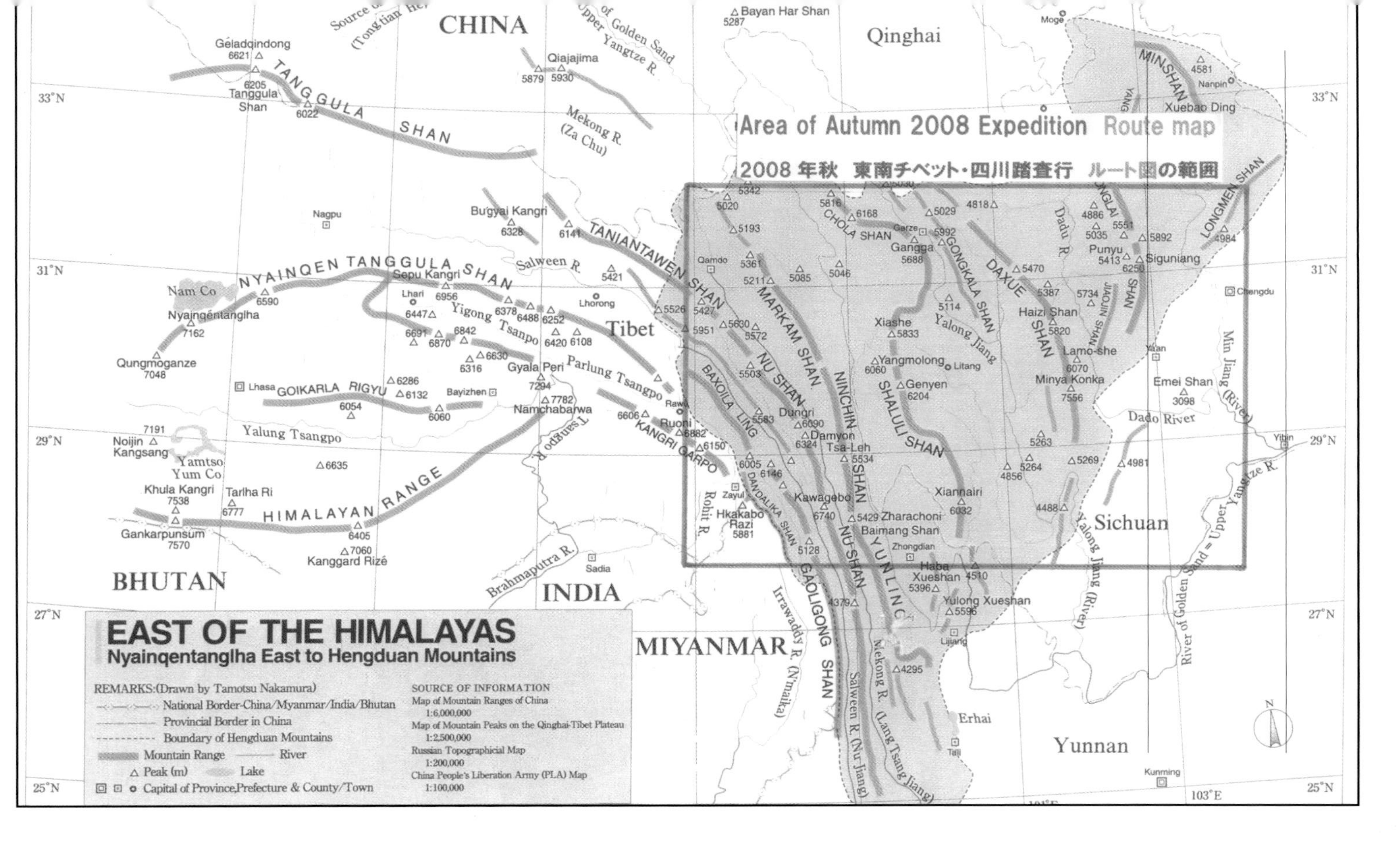

Area of Autumn 2008 Expedition Route map
2008 年秋 東南チベット・四川踏査行 ルート図の範囲
EAST OF THE HIMALAYAS
Nyainqentanglha East to Hengduan Mountains
REMARKS:(Drawn by Tamotsu Nakamura)
National Border-China/Myanmar/India/Bhutan
Provincial Border in China
Boundary of Hengduan Mountains
Mountain Range
River
Peak (m)
Lake
Capital of Province,Prefecture & County/Town
SOURCE OF INFORMATION
Map of Mountain Ranges of China 1:6,000,000
Map of Mountain Peaks on the Qinghai-Tibet Plateau 1:2,500,000
Russian Topographicial Map 1:200,000
China People's Liberation Army (PLA) Map 1:100,000
CHINA
Qinghai
Tibet
Sichuan
Yunnan
BHUTAN
INDIA
MIYANMAR
33°N
31°N
29°N
27°N
25°N
103°E
TANGGULA SHAN
NYAINQEN TANGGULA SHAN
TANIANTAWEN SHAN
GOIKARLA RIGYU
HIMALAYAN RANGE
KANGRI GARPO
BAXOILA LING
NU SHAN
MARKAM SHAN
NINCHIN SHAN
SHALULI SHAN
CHOLA SHAN
GONGKALA SHAN
DAXUE SHAN
JIAOJIN SHAN
LONGMEN SHAN
MINSHAN
DANDALIKA SHAN
GAOLIGONG SHAN
YUNLING
Géladqindong 6621
6205 Tanggula Shan
6022
Qiajajima 5879 5930
Bayan Har Shan 5287
Source of (Tongtian He)
of Golden Sand Upper Yangtze R.
Mekong R. (Za Chu)
Bugyai Kangri 6328
6141
Salween R.
5421
Nagpu
Nam Co
Nyainqêntanglha 7162
6590
Qungmoganze 7048
Sepu Kangri 6956
Lhari
6447
6691 6870 6842
6378 6488 6252
6420 6108
Yigong Tsanpo
Lhorong
Parlung Tsangpo
6630 6316
Gyala Peri 7294
Namchabarwa 7782
Lhasa
6286 6132
Bayizhen
6054
6060
Yalung Tsangpo
6635
Noijin Kangsang 7191
Yamtso Yum Co
Khula Kangri 7538
Tarlha Ri 6777
Gankarpunsum 7570
6405
7060 Kanggard Rizé
Tsangpo R.
Brahmaputra R.
Sadia
Rawu
6606 Ruoni 6882 6150
Rohit R.
Zayul
Hkakabo Razi 5881
Qamdo
5342 5020 5193 5361 5211 5085 5046
5526 5427 5951 5630 5572 5503 5583
Dungri 6090
Damyon 6324
Tsa-Leh 5534
6005 6146
Kawagebo 6740
5429 Zharachoni
Baimang Shan
5128
4379
Zhongdian
Haba Xueshan 5396
4510
Yulong Xueshan 5596
Lijiang
4295
Erhai
Tali
Irrawaddy R. (N'maika)
Salween R. (Nu-Jiang)
Mekong R. (Lang Tsang Jiang)
5816 6168
Garze
5029 5992
Gangga 5688
4818
5114
Xiashe 5833
Yalong Jiang
Yangmolong 6060
Litang
Genyen 6204
Xiannairi 6032
5470 5387
Haizi Shan 5820
5734
Lamo-she 6070
Minya Konka 7556
5263 5264 4856 5269 4488
Dadu R.
4886 5035 5551 5892
Punyu 5413
6250 Siguniang
4984
YANG
Xuebao Ding
4581
Nanpin
Moge
Chengdu
Ya'an
Emei Shan 3098
Dado River
4981
Min Jiang (River)
Yibin
Upper Yangtze R.
River of Golden Sand = Upper Yangtze R.
Yalong Jiang (River)
Kunming
N

90. Longgequji Puzhong (c6000m), west face, above the headwaters of Tso Bong Qu.(*Tamotsu Nakamura*)

91. An invitation to climb? Jiamu-tongnan 5925m, south face, seen from the Tso Bong Qu valley. (*Tamotsu Naka-mura*)

Konka and the object of our 2008 reconnaissance. Located at E101°25' N29°18', this peak also appears on the 1:2,500,000 Map of Mountain Peaks on the Qinghai-Xizang (Tibet) Plateau. However there is no record of any exploration of Ren Zhong Feng and no photographs are available.

The first, Dungri Garpo stage of the expedition ran from 23 October to 17 November, during which we drove 2,270km, starting and finishing at Shangri La, Yunnan. Our group for this stage comprised three Japanese; myself, the 73-year old leader, Tsuyoshi Nagai (76) and Tadao Shintani (63), together with Chinese crew, Chen Xiao Hong (37 guide), Zhou Lu Liu (40 assistant guide), Jin Xuan (31 interpreter and the only woman), Ge Ding (51 cook), Jiang Chu (53 driver), Gan Ma (32 driver). From 3 to 8 November we travelled by horse caravan along the Hong Qu to Dungri

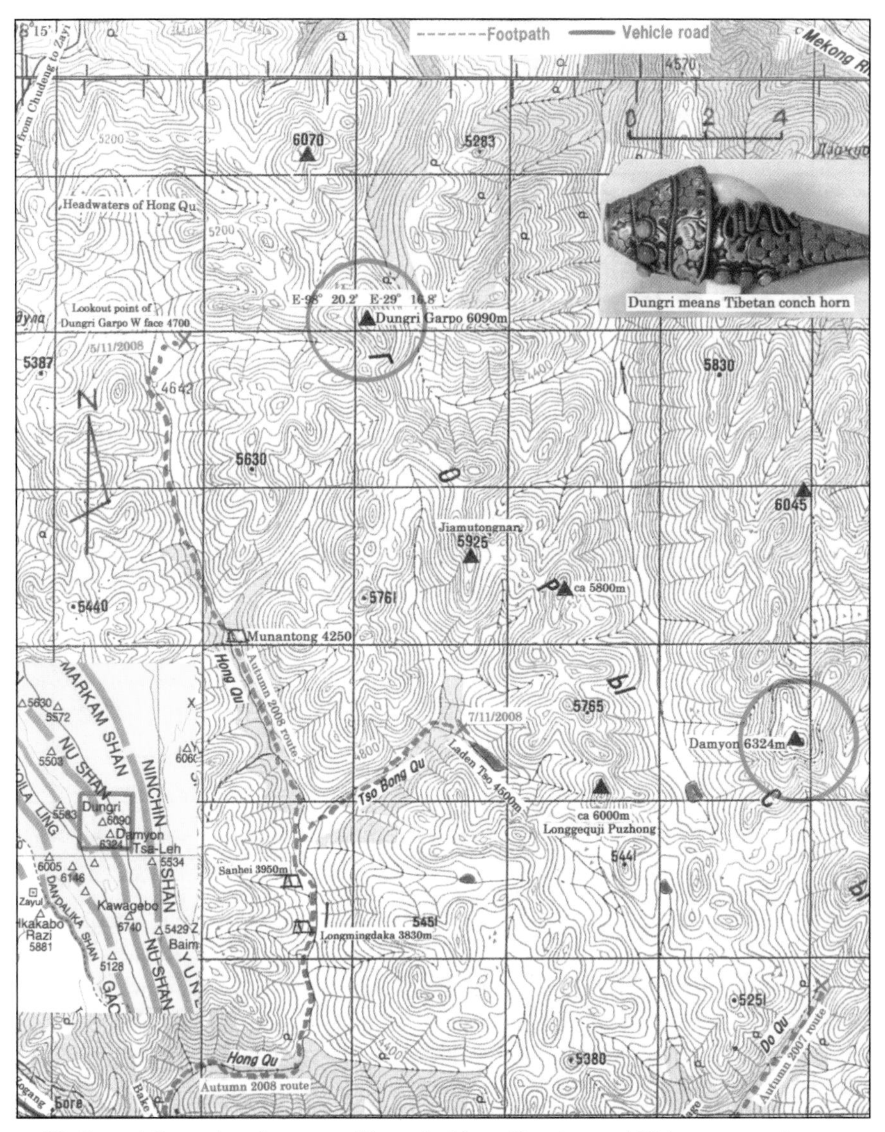

92. Dungri Garpo location map. *(Compiled from Russian and Chinese maps by Tamotsu Nakamura)*

Garpo and neighbouring peaks with camps at Longmingdaka (3830m), Munamtong (4250m) and Sanhei (3950m). On 13 November we trekked on horseback from Shangri La to Kongga Xueshan (4170m).

The second, Peak 6079m stage was from 19 - 29 Nov. during which we drove 1730km, starting and finishing at Chengdu, plus a horse trek to Xiaqiangla, Daxue Shan (4170m) on the 25th. There were four of us, myself, Tadao Shintani and Chinese Zhang Jiyue (45) and Jian Li Hong (29).

93. Litang Plateau and north face of 5838m peak, Sichuan. (*Tamotsu Nakamura*)

94. Map: Autumn 2008 Expedition route. *(Compiled by Tamotsu Nakamura)*

HIGHLIGHTS

Dungri Garpo stage

An early problem arose in Yangjing (Tibetan name Yakalo) on the way from Deqen (gateway to the Meili Snow Mountains) to Markam, a junction of the Sichuan-Tibet and Yunnan-Tibet highways. Yanjing is reputed for its 800-year old salt wells and hot springs, and is a developing resort. But the road north of Yanjing, along the Mekong is notorious for dangerous landslides and we were forced to stay four days at Yangjing due to rock fall.

Availing ourselves of this unplanned free time, we visited Yangjing Church. Yangjing is the only Christian village inside Tibet. Father Maurice Tornay, a Swiss missionary, was pastor here before he was driven out and later ruthlessly shot to death by warrior lamas in 1949 while crossing a high pass on the Mekong-Yu Qu divide on his way to Lhasa. When I first came to Yangjing in 1993, the church was in an ordinary Tibetan house, but in 15 years it has been reconstructed with large buildings. A couple of bells were donated from Japan in 1974. At present there are 200 Tibetan followers and religious services and events are regular.

Our preliminary plan, based on a Russian topographical map of

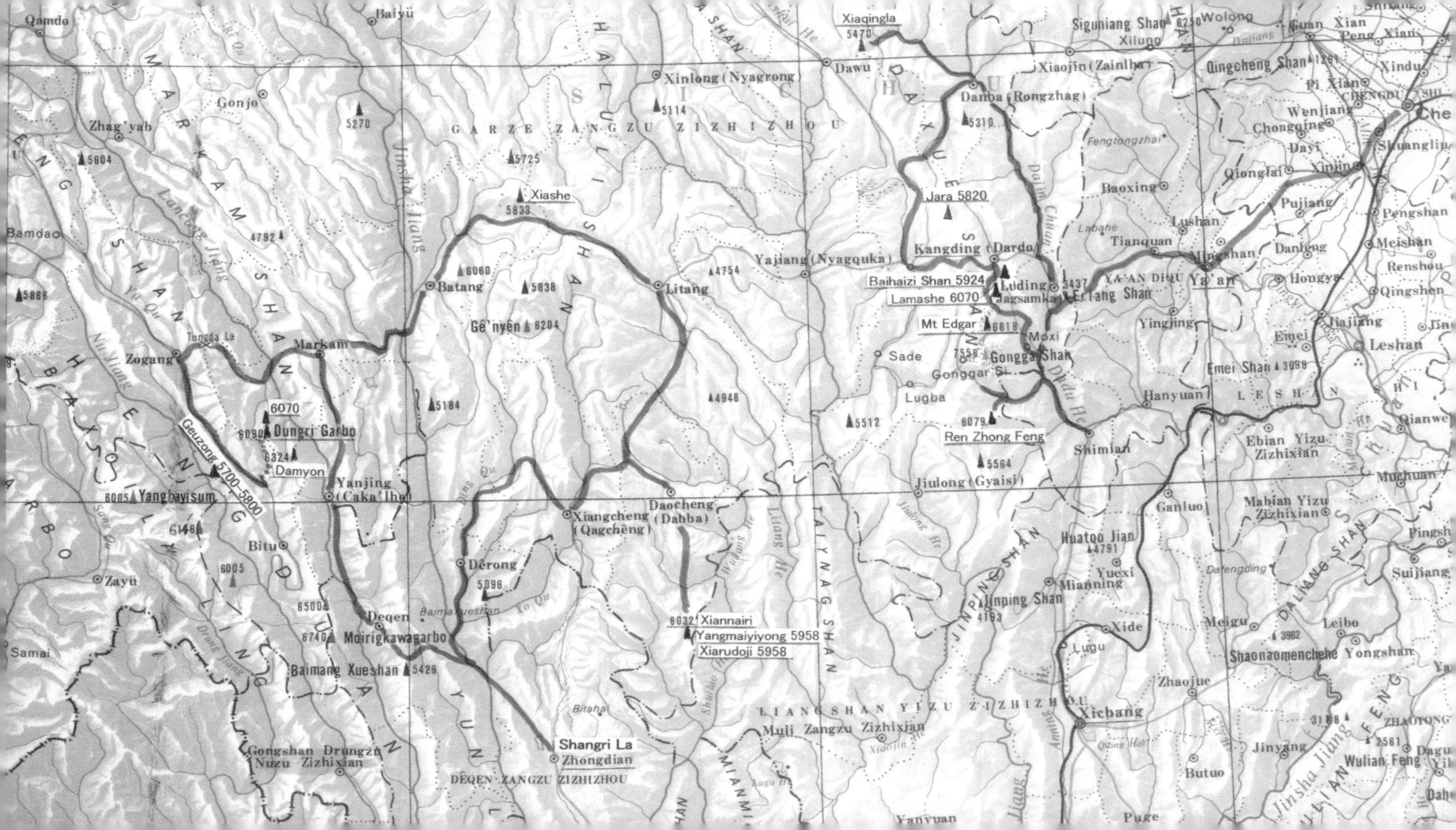

Qamdo
Baiyü
Xiaqingla 5470
Siguniang Shan 6250
Wolong
Guan Xian
Peng Xian
Xilung
Xiaojin (Zainlha)
Qingcheng Shan
Xindu
Dawu
Xinlong (Nyagrong)
Danba (Rongzhag)
Pi Xian
CHENGDU
Wenjiang
Chongqing
Dayi
Shuanglin
Gonjo
Zhag'yab
5270
5114
5310
5725
5604
GARZE ZANGZU ZIZHIZHOU
HALULI SHAN
DAXUE SHAN
MARKAM SHAN
Fengtongzhai
Dajin Chuan
Baoxing
Qionglai
Xinjin
Pujiang
Pengshan
Jara 5820
Xiashe
5833
Lancang Jiang
Jinsha Jiang
Bamdao
4792
Labahe
Lushan
Tianquan
Mingshan
Danleng
Meishan
Kangding (Dardo)
Yajiang (Nyagquka)
4754
6060
Batang
5838
Litang
Baihaizi Shan 5924
Luding
3437
YA'AN DIQU
Ya'an
Erlang Shan
Renshou
Hongya
Qingshen
Lamashe 6070
Jagsamka
5866
Ya Qu
Gê'nyên 6204
Mt Edgar 6618
Moxi
Yingjing
Jiajiang
Emei
Leshan
Tungda La
Zogang
Markam
Sade
7556
Gongga Shan
Gonggar Si
Emei Shan 3099
Lugba
Hanyuan
LESHAN
Nu Jiang
6070
5184
4948
5512
6079
Dadu He
Ren Zhong Feng
Qianwei
6090
Dungri Garbo
Shimian
Ebian Yizu Zizhixian
6324
Geuzong 5700–5800
Damyon
Yanjing (Caka'lho)
5564
Jiulong (Gyaisi)
Muchuan
Yangbayisum
6005
Ding Qu
Xiangcheng (Qagchêng)
Daocheng (Dabba)
Ganluo
Mabian Yizu Zizhixian
6146
Jiulong He
Litang He
TAIYNAG SHAN
Huatoo Jian
4791
Pingsh
Bitu
Dêrong
Wujiang He
JINPING SHAN
Yuexi
Dafengding
DALIANG SHAN
Suijiang
Zayü
6005
5096
Mianning
6500
Deqen
Baima Xueshan
Xo Qu
6032
Xiannairi
Jinping Shan
4193
Meigu
Leibo
Samai
6740
Moirigkawagarbo
Yangmaiyiyong 5958
Xiarudoji 5958
Xide
Lugu
3962
Shaonaomenchehe
Yongshan
Drung Jiang
Baimang Xueshan
5429
YUN
Zhaojue
Bitahai
LIANGSHAN YIZU ZIZHIZHOU
Shuiluo He
Anning He
Xichang
Qiong Hai
Muli Zangzu Zizhixian
3188
ZHAOTONG
Shangri La
Zhongdian
Xiaojin He
2561
Gongshan Drungzu Nuzu Zizhixian
Jinyang
Wulian Feng
Jinsha Jiang
Dagu
DÊQEN ZANGZU ZIZHIZHOU
MIANMI
Lugu Hu
Butuo
Yanyuan
Puge
Sang Qu

95. Ren Zhong Feng (6079m massif) east face south, seen from near Ren Zhong lake, Sichuan. (*Tamotsu Nakamura*)

96. Unveiling of Ren Zhong Feng, east face. (*Tamotsu Nakamura*)

1:200,000, was to approach Dungri Garpo from the north. We had in mind two possible routes, starting with a horse caravan from Chudeng village south of the Jo Ba La on the Sichuan-Tibet Highway:

1. To reconnoitre Dungri Garpo from two passes of 5300-5400m on the Mekong-Yu Qu divide tracing an old trade path from Chudeng to Zayi (Dayul) in the Yu Qu basin. Early explorers such as a Pundit A-K crossed these high passes and in the winter of 1950 George Patterson also followed this route.

2. To enter a tributary of the Mekong river from Chudeng to access to the north face of Damyon and the east face of Dungri Garpo.

97. Tibetan nomads on the Litang Plateau. (*Tamotsu Nakamura*)

However a chief of Chudeng village told us that there was no trail to Damyon from the village and that the high passes to Zayi has already been closed by snow too deep for horses. He advised us that the only possible approach would be up the Hong Qu valley, a tributary of Yu Qu. So we turned westwards along the Sichuan-Tibet Highway and entered the valley of the Yu Qu, largest tributary of the Salween, mystery river of Tibet.

98. Street barber at Jomei, Yu Qu valley, Gorge Country. (*Tamotsu Nakamura*)

On 1 November we arrived at Bake village (3320m) that would be our base for exploring Dungri Garpo from its western side. The following day we made a one-day reconnaissance of the peaks west of the Yu Qu. In fine weather, we got good views of unclimbed 5700-5800m peaks in the Geuzong, Minyabaigen and Bumubaideng massifs on the Yu Qu-Salween divide.

On 3 November we started up the Hong Qu valley with a caravan of 10 horses and five muleteers. The Hong Qu flows north to south and has a total length of 50km. Its valley is a deep curving S shape from Bake to a point 7km upstream and then it becomes wider with conifer trees, but the view is restricted. Dungri Garpo was veiled till the final moment. At intervals there are summer pastures with temporary cottages.

After two days we camped at Munantong (4250m). From here the trail

99. Xiaqiangla (5470m) rises beyond Hulu Hai lake, Dang Ling, Sichuan. (*Tamotsu Nakamura*)

100. 'Mountain of the Beautiful Goddess' – Xiaqiangla's east face. (*Tamotsu Nakamura*)

was hidden under snow 50cm to one metre deep in which the horses struggled. We forded streams several times. The horses gasped and sometimes fell down. My colleague was buried under his fallen horse and injured. However our caravan leader was very helpful and cooperated so that we might have at least a glimpse of Dungri Garpo.

On 5 November, a six hour trek from Munantong took us to a very cold and windy point at 4700m near the snow-covered headwaters of the Hong Qu. From there we got our first - and only - look at the west face of stunning Dungri Garpo and its summit ridge with steep buttress and hanging glacier. We were unable to see the unnamed 6070m peak that lies north of Dungri Garpo.

On the return journey we entered another branch valley leading northeast called Tso Bong Qu. This is a wide and beautiful valley; its headwaters on the Mekong and Yu Qu watershed are surrounded by towering rocky peaks of 5700-5900m and a c6000m peak called Longgequji Puzhong. These should attract climbers, Jiamutongnan (5925m), in particular, seems outstanding.

101. Stone towers and Tibetan houses near Danba, Sichuan (*Tamotsu Nakamura*)

On our drive from Bake, we were able to photograph the north and east faces of the Dungri Garpo massif, including unnamed 6070m, in the early morning at a high pass (4362m) on the Sichuan-Tibet Highway between Markam and the Mekong river. Excellent pictures of the Damyon massif were taken en route from Yanging to Markam and also from Jo Ba La west of the Mekong.

After Dungri Garpo we drove in a long loop from Gorge Country westwards over the River of Golden Sand (upper Yangzte) to the Litang Plateau then south to Daocheng and Xiangchen counties, which are the heart of the west Sichuan highlands, before returning to Shangri La. Thanks to fine weather, we were able to photograph peaks on the Shaluli Shan range such as Xiashe (5833m), Peak 5838m on the Litang Plateau, Genyen (6204m), and the three famous holy peaks of Kongga Xueshan - Xiannairi (6032m), Yangmaiyong (5958m) and Xiarudoji (5958m). The fascinating scenery combined with autumn leaves and Tibetan houses in Xiangcheng County was most alluring. Kongga Xueshan was closed to sightseers in 2007 for conservation reasons, but when we entered Daocheng County it was again open to visitors. In closing this part I would like to emphasise that Miss Jin Xuan is a pretty and excellent interpreter. She was very helpful to the team.

102. The imposing east face of Mt Edgar (6618m E-Gongga) in the Minya Konka massif, Sichuan. (*Tamotsu Nakamura*)

Sichuan stage

It had long been my ambition to unveil the 6079m peak that lies south of Minya Konka. Tentatively named Ren Zhong Feng, it is located south of the Tianwan river that flows into the Dadu, one of major tributaries of the Yangtze. The peak rises at the head of the Gang Gou valley north of Ren Zhong lake, hence its name. Access is very easy but only a few climbers have hitherto paid any attention to the peak. One who has is John Harlin III, editor of the *American Alpine Journal*.

Our base for exploring peak 6079m was Caoke hot spring, reached in a day's drive from Chengdu. At the wheel of the 4x4 was Zhang Jiyue, my friend of 18 years from Sichuan Earth Expeditions based in Chengdu. Caoke hot spring (1400m) has a good hotel and stands on the Tianwan river that divides the Minya Konka massif, to the north, from peak 6079m. Arriving on 19 November, we found the valley misty and the mountains draped in cloud.

On 21 November we went up to a point at 3240m in Gang Gou (dry valley) north of 6079m peak and south of Ren Zhong lake (2930m) a tributary of the Tianwan. Thick cloud blanketed the peak, though even had it been fine we would have been unable to see the whole of the peak from Gang Gou. On 23 November we hurried up the valley again to Ren Zhong lake. The valley is so deep that the peak is only visible from one or two points. However, we were lucky to avail ourselves of a narrow chance while going up to the lake. The photos thus taken must be of great value. I have written that there was no photo of this 6079m peak. Actually there is one of the north-west face of the massif taken from far away, from a high pass west of Minya Konka by Pedro Detjen, publisher of my book *Die Alpen Tibets*. But the peak in question remained unidentified until I confirmed it in autumn 2008.

Turning from the mountain peaks, we were surprised at the scale and terrific pace of the construction of dams and hydroelectric power stations in the Dadu basin, both on the main river and its tributaries. The Chinese government policy is to accelerate this West Development Drive – its slogan is 'sending electricity of the West to the East' - but with it goes widespread environmental destruction. The Dadu River is on the route of the Long March. A museum has been newly refurbished at a place where the Red Army crossed the river and marched toward their goal in 1935. The borderland is changing very fast; towns and villages are abuzz with development.

On 24 November we moved northward along the Dadu river to reconnoitre Xiaqiangla (5470m) in the Daxue Shan range from Dang Ling village, 68km north-west of Danba. The Danba area is called 'Valley of Beauties' in praise of its beautiful women. It is also noted for its unique Gyalong culture and architecture with its historic stone towers (or defence towers) drawing many visitors. The Danba County local government has reportedly applied for UNESCO World Cultural Heritage recognition in respect of the towers.

On 25 November, a one-day horse trek took us from Dang Ling to Hulu Hai, a lake at 4170m lying east of Xiaqiangla. The peak, a sharp pyramid whose name translates to 'Mountain of Beautiful Goddess', and glacier lake draw not only climbers but sightseeing tourists. The local government is keen to encourage tourism development. With perfect weather for photography on our last two days, Jiyue kindly took a long route from Danba to Chengdu via Ja-ra (5820m) (Haizi Shan), Kangding, Laoyuling hot spring, the Xuemenkan pass between Lamo-she (6070m)/Baihaizi Shan (5924m) and the Minya Konka massif. Thanks to Jiyue's arrangements many remarkable pictures have been added to my photo library. Among others, the photos of the east face Mt Edgar (E-Gongga) (6618m) are fantastic, as the weather is almost always bad in this area of the Minya Konka massif.

Summary: An account of a reconnaissance of Dungri Garpo (6090m) in deep Gorge Country, south-east Tibet, and the unveiling of a little-known peak of 6079m called Ren Zhong Feng, south of Minya Konka in Sichuan. In November 2009, Danes Kristoffer Szilas and Martin Ploug made the first ascent of Ren Zhong Feng. (*Danish Route*, 1300m, TD WI4 M4).

HYWEL LLOYD

High Adventure in Mongolia

'We plan some mountaineering in the Altai; would you like to come?' ... 'Where?' ... 'Mongolia' ... 'Well – it sounds fun'. This is how Ingram and I joined an expedition being organised by old friends, Jon Mellor and David Hamilton, for the summer of 2008.

The Altai mountains rise in the centre of Asia, starting in Russia and running from north-west to south-east through the western end of Mongolia and finishing in China. The whole range is roughly the height and extent of the Alps with snow summits rising to 4500m. To say that they are unfrequented compared to the Alps is an understatement. Access to both the Russian and Chinese sectors is difficult but access to the Mongolian Altai seemed more practicable. Alpine Club members had been before, notably in 1992 when Lindsay Griffin had had an horrific accident (AJ 1993, 125-9); also a good sketch map by Józef Nyka with additions by Ed Webster became available in 1993. Otherwise maps were difficult to obtain; the best seemed to be 1:100,000 Russian military maps but one had to decipher the Russian text.

David had made contact with a local travel company called 'Nomads'. They were brilliant, providing us with local leaders, vehicles, drivers, and permits into the military border area. Language was a problem, spelling of place names was somewhat random and we were very reliant on our interpreter.

103. The route taken by trucks and then camels from the town of Ölgii at the western end of Mongolia, to base camp in the Tavan Bogd National Park.

104. Snow peaks of the Altai mountains in Mongolia and China to the south-east of Khüiten 4374m. *(Hywel Lloyd)*

The plan was to fly to Ulaanbaatar, the capital in the centre of Mongolia; take a local flight to Ölgii (Ulgii), a town in the western end of Mongolia; drive in jeeps for two days, trek in towards the high Altai for six days (about 120km, and thus get fit); place a base camp by the Potanina glacier at 3160m; scale a couple of lower peaks; place a camp high on the glacier at 3660m; climb the highest peak, Khüiten (Huiten, 4374m); names and heights varied depending on sources and translations. Finally, we trek out by a shorter route back. And this is exactly what we did. It took nearly four weeks; the August weather was broadly good but it did have its moments when the strong north winds from Siberia took over.

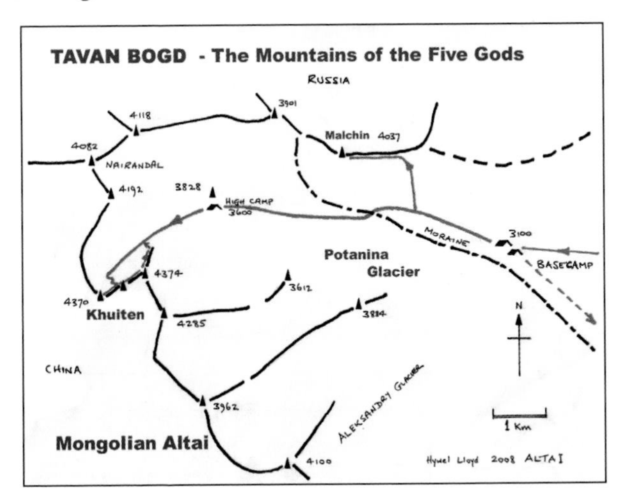

105. Location of the 2008 AC party's base camp alongside the Potanina glacier and routes up Khüiten (4374m) and Malchin (4037m). This is in the Tavan Bogd – the Mountains of the Five Gods (or Saints) in the Mongolian Altai mountains.

106. David Hamilton trying out his Bactrian chat-up lines. *(Hywel Lloyd)*

107. Kazakh woman cooking for us on her *ger* stove with mutton drying on the rack. *(Hywel Lloyd)*

108. Young Kazakh nomad girl with elegant toy camel made by her mother. *(John Fairley)*

Mongolia is nearly the size of mainland Europe; population 2.5 million people – 1million in Ulaanbaatar and 1.5 million nomadic herdsmen and coal or mineral miners spread thinly across this vast country. It has more than 36 million head of cattle and sheep. Apparently, there are only 100km of metalled roads outside Ulaanbaatar and town centres. The main roads are dirt and very poorly maintained; 4-wheel drive is necessary; side roads defy trade-descriptions norms. And the history? We had all heard of Chinggis Khaan (Genghis Khan to us) and his Mongolian warriors who conquered an empire from Beijing to northern India in 1206 AD. Later Mongolia was absorbed into Manchu China. In 1924 Outer Mongolia became independent but closely allied to Russia. Inner Mongolia remains Chinese. In 1990 Mongolia cast off Soviet-style communist rule to become a democracy and survive on its own; finances were very tough for 10 years – not helped by droughts and fierce winters taking a toll of the sheep and cattle. So the Mongolians are very tough people.

We arrived in Ulaanbaatar, a party of 14 AC members and friends (all 65 years or more except our youngster, David). We met up with the Nomads organisation and visited the sights, all rather Russian, generally a bit drab. Interestingly, even in town nearly every dwelling had a ger tent outside (like a yurt). Then great fun at the Mongolian Circus where David was enticed into the ring to join the jugglers, and more fun at the Mongolian National Song and Dance Academy, where the performance contained various styles of ornate national dress and typical instruments such as the two-string horse-head fiddle. Both evenings were extremely cheerful and colourful.

Nomads took us into nearby mountains to limberup. These were the Tsetsegun Ulul where we walked to the highest top, Bogd Khaan Uul, 2256m, (this language is impossible!). The lower slopes were very wooded, mainly pines, but the tops were clear and reminded us of the Dartmoor granite tors, except that they were bedecked with prayer flags and blue bunting. As we descended, we were met by the first 'secret weapon' that Nomads produced for us. It was an ex-army command truck built in 1976 by Magirus-Deutz with a Benz 9 litre engine and serious ground-clearance. More importantly, it was kitted out as a mobile cookhouse with an excellent experienced driver, Chuka. The previous summer it had been the cook-truck for the Paris-Peking car rally. Being an engineer, I was given a conducted tour of the underneath of the truck; all very impressive, this machine would prove to be able to go anywhere.

After fireworks at midnight to herald the start of the Beijing Olympics, it was time to move on. A small turbo-prop Fokker flew us 1500km to Ölgii, rather like a wild-west frontier town with the essentials to match. At the small 'supermarket' we stocked up with beer and vodka. Next we fitted ourselves and our gear into three Ütz-Furgon vans. These ubiquitous Chinese/Russian utility vehicles are like a Ford Transit 8-seater body on top of a 4-wheel low-ratio drive Land-Rover chassis, and they too would go almost anywhere.

109. Preparing to set out from camp at 3600m on the Potanina glacier after new snow during the night. *(Hywel Lloyd)*

With Duré, the local Nomad's leader and interpreter, our convoy of cook-truck and three vans set off across arid, desert-like open country with views of hills and higher snow-clad mountains around. The river valleys were verdant with flowers and trees but the passes were rocky and windblown. For two days we travelled with the scenery becoming more like the Lake District. After crossing rickety wooden bridges, visiting a *balbal*, a religious Turkic granite man said to be c600 AD, and checking in at a military post, we gained the shores of Lake Khoton Nuur by the Zagastain river.

Now we trekked on foot along a chain of lakes into the main Altai. In each valley we saw little clusters of three to four *gers* with an extended Kazakh nomad family, tending a herd of perhaps 1000 animals, mainly goats. All were very friendly and we were often invited in and offered the local delicacy, dried yohurt that could break one's teeth. Inside, every *ger* was very neat and colourful with a central stove and chimney for heating and cooking by dung. No electricity, but some *gers* did have a battery-operated satellite dish television. *Gers* are moved three times during the year to find the best pasture. The scenery was magnificent, with lots of flowers and many birds seen including kites and an eagle.

We met Mr Azamat who supplied Nomads' second 'secret weapon' – camels. Mr Azamat owned four Bactrian camels (two humps) and had friends who provided three more. Well trained and brilliantly led, this magnificent seven each carried more than 200kg without problems over terrain that became more steep and rugged as we progressed. We walked 20km per day, equipment on the camel train, and camped by water at night. Food was supplemented with fish (like trout) caught in the rivers. Local children often visited us; they rode stout Mongolian horses bareback, expert riders from the age of three. Eventually, we left the lakes and valleys and climbed over a high pass (as rugged as the descent from Snowdon down the PYG track) from where we had our first proper view of our goal, the high, snowy summits. Down a valley we were shown probably 100 petroglyph images of deer, hunters and dogs carved on rock slabs, reputedly from 1200 years ago.

Thus we reached another road into the area and entered the new National Park, Tavan Bogd (The Mountains of the Five Gods). Next day we established base camp alongside the Potanina glacier at 3100m. A small foray up to a ridge on the Mongolian-Russian border and we stood at about 3800m with one foot in each country (but no visa).

First big day was to climb Malchin (Malczin), 'The Herdsman' 4037m, also on the border. The route was up the east ridge with flanks of loose boulders and scree. As we gained height the north (Russian) side became a large snow 'Half-dome' partly separated from the main Mongolian summit. This north side descended into a glacier running many km into Russia. The final slope was a couloir to a rocky summit complete with a steel pole and new Mongolian flag.

Next, we set up a camp of four tents high on the Potanina glacier at 3600m to gain access to the highest peak, Khüiten (Huiten), 'The Cold Mountain' (4374m). The night was one of continuous ferocious storms and we feared that we might lose a tent, but all survived. At dawn, after awaiting a break in the weather, we set off to climb Khüiten. Reportedly, the north-east ridge is the usual route but as it appeared loaded with wind-slab we opted for a route near the north west-ridge. With a wind blowing direct from Siberia, conditions felt 'arctic' as we traversed into the north cwm to gain the west side of the north face; fortunately the wind dropped as we climbed the face. Several large séracs and crevasses were skirted and we had sustained steep cramponing on ice but no real difficulties. We considered that this route was probably around PD+ in standard.

I was seconding David and as we emerged at the top of the face I could see three summits along a crest of 500 metres. 'So, which is the highest?' ... 'Don't know. We'll have to climb all three'. So we did. Our GPS gave the heights at around 4400m with only 7m difference between the highest and the lowest summit. The crest was easy and is partly on the border between China and Mongolia – thus eight of us climbed Khüiten and visited China, without a visa. The views were absolutely stunning: Siberia to the north and countless sharp snowy peaks in Mongolia to the south-east and in China to the south.

Our rope descended by the ascent route. The second rope led by John Fairley decided to descend by the north-east ridge but encountered worrying wind-slab on steep ground and then had to negotiate an awkward bergschrund. Khüiten is a worthy alternative to Mont Blanc but, as far as we could tell, probably fewer than 100 climbers gain its summit in a typical year.

110. On top of Khüiten 4374m with north summit (and Siberia) behind; Mike Esten, Ingram Lloyd, Michael Turner-Caine, David Hamilton. *(Hywel Lloyd)*

That night there were more storms and even more snow, so the next day we abandoned our plan to ascend Nairandal (4180m) and descended to base camp, now also very snowy, where the large mess tent had been blown down, but all was well.

Coming out to the roadhead was a novel experience; I had never ridden before but the offer to use a Mongolian horse was too good to miss. The journey took five hours by a magnificent route following a large glacial river with gorges. The Mongolians could not believe that a grown man had never ridden a horse before but I think I acquitted myself well. My sturdy mount had a fine silver-trimmed saddle, a family heirloom, and insisted on trotting a lot so when I dismounted my knees were killing me; but it was definitely well worth it.

For the final evening with the local Tuva nomads a party was laid on in a *ger*. We ate goat that had been cooked in a milk churn converted into a large pressure cooker (but the meat was still pretty tough). It happened to be Ingram's birthday so the celebrations continued into the dusk. Next morning we had to say farewell to the families who had been so welcoming, hospitable and helpful, and start our journey back the world we knew. As we bade the children goodbye, we wondered what changes they will see in their lives.

Summary: An account of a four-week expedition to the Mongolian Altai in summer 2008 with ascents of Malchin (Malczin, 4037m) and Khüiten (Huiten, 4374m). Party: AC members, Stuart Beare, Mike Esten, John and Lizbet Fairley, Barbara Grigor-Taylor, David Hamilton, Hywel and Ingram Lloyd, Jon Mellor. Friends, Sue Esten, Rowena Mellor, Michael Turner-Caine, Anna Vaudrey, Cheryl Wells.

ELIZABETH 'LIZZIE' HAWKER

Running a Dream

We had a dream. And sometimes, just sometimes, dreams come true. Our dream was to make a journey from the wilderness of the mountain heights to the chaos of a city. We planned first to climb the stunningly beautiful Himalayan mountain of Ama Dablam, which at an altitude of 6837m was the highest any of us had been to, and to then follow this with an attempt at the record running back from Everest Base Camp to Kathmandu. A journey of some 188 miles (302km) with around 10,000m ascent and 15,000m descent, the previous record was set in 2000 by a Nepali,

111. Running in the shadow of Ama Dablam. (*Daz Stonier*)

Kumar Limbu, who had completed it in 3 days, 7 hours and 10 minutes. At the time of his run, Kumar was working as a climbing Sherpa with Doug Scott's Community Action Treks.

At 09:52 on Sunday 28 October 2007 we arrived in the dusty heat of the Sports Stadium of Kathmandu. Weary, footsore and grimy, we were greeted with smiles and garlands, and warmly welcomed by our friends, the press and the president of the Nepal Olympic Association. Our mission had been accomplished. A new record had been set. I cast my mind back over the previous 3 days, 2 hours and 36 minutes to another world. Arriv-

112. A pre-run warm-up: Lizzy Hawker high on Ama Dablam. (*Victor Saunders*)

ing to the chaotic heat of the streets of Kathmandu it felt a very long way from our start in the silence and peace of dawn at Everest Base Camp. It was an incredible contrast. And it had been an incredible adventure.

Om Mani Padme Hum. The omnipresent Buddhist mantra ingrained itself from the very beginning into our experience of Nepal. Carved into stone and spun on prayer wheels along every path we travelled, it represents the path of the practice of generosity, pure ethics, tolerance, patience, perseverance, concentration and wisdom. It was in this spirit that we needed to trek, climb and run together. The mountains of the Himalaya were home to us for a month. Their incredible beauty and inspiration were food for the soul.

In the chill of a minus-10°C autumnal Himalayan dawn, clad in fleece and duvet jackets, we touched the flag of the first Thai Everest expedition just as the first tents were stirring. We logged our GPS position, started our watches, and set off to scramble across the glacial moraine. It was an incredibly beautiful morning with clear skies above, early cloud filling the Khumbu valley below and sun hitting the summits of Nuptse, Pumori, Thamserku and Cholatse. We were lucky. I relished those early hours, emerging out of the shadows of the majestic summits into the early morning sunshine, with warmth on our limbs and moving fast over terrain usually taken at a snail's pace. In these early miles above 4500m there was delightful and easy running, although I felt for Mark and Spyke who still suffered bronchial coughs – a legacy of their exertions on Ama Dablam whose summit Mark and I had reached just a few days earlier. We startled the groups of trekkers, who were moving slowly upwards as though walking on the moon, receiving a mixture of doubt, intrigue and amazement.

Welcome refreshment awaited us at Dughla lodge, where our new friend Mr T (Tashi Tsering) had copious amounts of milky tea waiting for us as promised. Further down the trail the traffic started to increase considerably, with yaks, porters and tourists to dodge. For me, all too soon we had left the high mountains. Beyond Namche Bazar, where Victor Saunders awaited us with a welcome hug, hot tea and pastries, we were back to the hill country and the thicker air of lower altitudes. By nightfall we had passed the trail to the large village of Lukhla and its small airstrip. Having lost the crowds we were back to the 'real' Nepal, with simple lodges and sharing the trail only with the local porters carrying huge loads of everyday necessities. Until Jubing Bridge we followed the drainage of the Dudh Kosi, but from there we had to cross the grain of the land with five passes in quick succession. A beautiful but demanding night's running with steep ascents and rocky descents slowing our progress.

113. The Beginning of a Journey: Mark Hartell, Lizzy Hawker and Stephen Pyke at Everest Base Camp. (*Mark Hartell*)

We were as self-sufficient as possible, aiming to run non-stop, carrying just a little extra clothing, food and water and using the lodges along route to supplement our supplies and take advantage of copious amounts of tea, tsampa porridge and chapattis as we needed. Running through the hill country off the normal tourist track gave us a special, if fleeting, contact with the Nepalese people and their culture.

The rollercoaster of ascents and descents continued. The second nightfall was rapidly encroaching as we reached Shivalaya beyond the Deurali Pass. It was here that we decided to take the 'safe' route via Jiri and the road to Karatichap since earlier reconnaissance of the route had proved that the maps were unreliable and the paths hard to find. It was also here that Mark made the reluctant decision to quit at Jiri, his reserves drained. Thirty-six hours in and less than half the distance had been covered. However, what should have been a simple jaunt between Shivalaya and the road-head at Jiri proved a problematic epic in the dark as we repeatedly lost the old trail and had to resort to map and compass. We finally arrived in Jiri, but by then Spyke too had had enough. Mentally and physically I wanted to continue but with the current political situation and as a single woman it wasn't a safe option to run alone. Dejected and surrounded by a howling pack of stray dogs we attempted to contact our support and call the attempt off. The deserted town offered no shelter, but by some miracle we landed upon a hayloft and buried ourselves in the hay. A few cold hours later, stiff and dejected I awoke to a new dawn.

A few hours of sleep had given Spyke a different perspective on life. With renewed vigour we decided to continue together. Could the record still be possible? We snatched a few cups of tea at the roadside, stuffed some battered bread in our sacks and left Mark to catch a bus to Muldi. All being well, there he would meet our friends who were waiting to support us over the remaining miles. I had no idea if we could make it, but it was good to be on the move, and good to be trying. Some miles went fast, some went slow. Valuable hours were lost as some of our short cuts led us astray and demanded energy-sapping bushwhacking to make our way back on route. Finally by 7pm on Saturday evening we had arrived in the small town of Muldi. From running alone for so many hours it was strange suddenly to see so many welcoming faces. Not only our friends but also the local youth club were there to cheer us on our way. From here the route followed the road and our friends were able to support us. They took it in turns to run a mile or two with us, providing inane chatter to help pass the lonely night hours. Sunday dawned and we were on the final descent into Kathmandu. The roadside got busier, noisier and smellier as we reached the city outskirts. By 8am we were fighting our way through the gridlock of traffic to reach the national stadium. Miraculously a police motorcycle escort appeared out of nowhere and after an endless last few miles we reached the gates of the stadium. Spyke and I had set a new record. However, our success was truly a team effort and Mark's invaluable support after his reluctant withdrawal made all the difference.

114. The Final Miles – police escort as 'Spyke' and Lizzy approach Kathmandu. (*Mark Hartell*)

Whilst modern communications have replaced the need for human messengers to carry news from Everest, the route from Base Camp to Kathmandu remains of historic importance. Our objective was simple: to set a new record for this historic run. The style and ethics of the attempt, however, were just as important to us. We made our record attempt in the spirit of peace and friendship, with a style and approach to show respect for the local environment, peoples and culture. As a team we wanted to use this run to show our respect for the Nepalese people and for the steps being taken to ensure a peaceful future for the country. We hope that publicity gained from our run will help to support recovery in the tourist industry by highlighting how wonderful Nepal is – its people, mountains and culture.

Our journey was an incredible endurance challenge amid some of the most awe-inspiring and beautiful mountains we may ever have the fortune to experience. It truly needed us to run with our hearts and our souls as well as our head and our legs. The entire journey from the lowlands to the summit heights of the mountains and back at a run was an incredible exploration – physically, mentally and spiritually. It was a privilege to have the opportunity of such an exceptional adventure and experience. 'Success' on the mountain or on the run, was not what mattered. As in life itself it is the journey not the destination.

Summary: An account of a record-breaking run from Everest Base Camp to Kathmandu in October 2007. Team members, Mark Hartell, Stephen 'Spyke' Pyke and Elizabeth 'Lizzy' Hawker, three established UK ultra runners who have competed internationally, and between them hold a number of records in mountain, ultra and endurance races.

115. The End of a Journey – 'Spyke and Lizzy' breast the tape in Kathmandu Stadium (*Mark Hartell*)

Acknowledgements: Thanks to our respective sponsors. As a member of The North Face Global Athlete Team I was very grateful for the support of The North Face in enabling me to be part of the project so that my dream could become a reality.

Footnote: Through their run, Lizzy, Mark and Spyke raised £4,403 for Community Action Nepal. The charity's main focus is to work with local people and village communities through sustainable health and education projects. Find out more at **www.canepal.org.uk** All donations would be gratefully received.

Alps

116. Simon Pierce, *Gran Paradiso, cloud passing over*, 2006, watercolour, 51 x 67.5cm

DAVE WYNNE-JONES

4000m

Climbing The Highest Mountains of The Alps

At the outset I must make a distinction between climbing the '4000m peaks' and climbing the highest mountains of the Alps. There is a curious list of eighty-two '4000m peaks' produced by the Club 4000 based on a UIAA source but with a suggestion that the expanded list may rise to 120 or more. Many of these are not mountains. Some, such as the Aiguilles de Diable on Mont Blanc du Tacul, are no more than gendarmes on a ridge. Others like the Grande Rocheuse or Aiguille de Jardin on the Jardin Ridge of the Aiguille Verte could be classified as subsidiary tops by a Munroist, but the more far-fetched like Mont Brouillard or Pic Luigi Amedeo are truly hard to find on the bulk of Mont Blanc upon which they feature as insignificant excrescences. When I walked past the Balmenhorn I had decided that certain '4000m peaks' were unworthy of the name. The Diable and Jardin Ridges are fine routes in their own right and do not need any spurious claim to 4000m peak status. With all due respect to Karl Blodig and others, there is a quality of obsession that can blind one to the realities of climbing mountains. Indeed, if Blodig were alive today he would probably be agonising over the fact that his total only reached 76. I chose not to let that happen. Instead I found myself climbing with companions who had adopted the list of fifty-two 4000m independent mountains compiled by Robin Collomb. The irony is that I never set out to do any such thing.

My first 4000m mountain was Mont Blanc, often the case, I believe: go to Chamonix often enough and the biggest beast on the block becomes an inevitable target. In 1981, fit and acclimatised after three weeks of climbing, three of us halved the guidebook time from the Goûter refuge to the summit, at least in part because we were travelling so light we had to move fast just to keep warm. Freezing for hours on the summit, waiting for dawn, had little attraction; neither did forcing our way back against the queues of later climbers. On impulse we headed off down indistinct snow slopes on what we believed to be the traverse to the Aiguille du Midi. It wasn't, and all three of us very nearly disappeared into the biggest hidden crevasse I have ever seen before we got back on track. After that, we didn't have an appetite for Mont Maudit or Mont Blanc du Tacul. Our final summit of that trip was also 4000m but chosen only because it had been seen to dominate the Vallée Blanche from most of the routes we had previously climbed. The Dent du Géant turned out to be the only Alpine route I have done encased in a duvet jacket and our hands still froze to the fixed ropes – ethics don't survive when survival is at stake. These were not auspicious beginnings, but I wasn't aware of having made a beginning at all.

117. Dent de Géant – 'turned out be the only Alpine route I have done encased in a duvet jacket'. *(Dave Wynne-Jones)*

The following year found me bivouacking on the Moine ridge of the Aiguille Verte by a complete error of judgement, while in 1983 an ill-fated excursion to the Ecrins included a traverse of the Barre des Ecrins before loose rock and poor snow conditions sent us scuttling back to Chamonix. For the rest of the decade, despite repeated visits to Chamonix, the nearest I came to another 4000m summit was in 1986 when Rick Ayres and I finished the Frontier ridge of Mont Maudit by traversing off to descend to the Vallée Blanche without ever reaching the summit. No, 4000m peaks were not really on the agenda, not only because of my various climbing partners' priorities but also because of my own focus on routes in general, rather than peaks, and Rébuffat's 100 best routes in particular.

All that changed in 1990. I'd been climbing with Denis Mitchell and we both had a yen for pastures new. His ex-wife, the much-married Marian, Elmes as she was then, Parsons as she is now, was a fellow member of the Chester Mountaineering Club who had recently joined the Alpine Club. It was she who encouraged us to attend an AC meet based in Randa. Mountaineering around Zermatt is virtually impossible without climbing 4000m mountains; the place is stiff with them and our first season included the Zinalrothorn, Alphubel-Täschhorn-Dom traverse, and Bishorn-Weisshorn traverse. When Denis went home I teamed up with Charlie Kenwright for the Ober Gabelhorn and Dave Penlington for the Fletschhorn-Lagginhorn traverse. These were all cracking routes and dispelled any lingering doubts I might have had about these big mountains being boring snow plods. No doubt, the voie normale on the Lagginhorn is a tedious loose slog in ascent, so why do it when the fine ridges of the Fletschhorn-Lagginhorn traverse are there for the taking?

The following year the AC meet was again in Randa. Now a member, I was teamed up with Dick Murton for the Lenzspitze – Nadelhorn traverse, even though I'd passed out on reaching the Mischabel hut the afternoon before with what must have been a mixture of altitude and heat exhaustion. This was followed by the Dent Blanche via the loose cliffs of the infrequently climbed Wandflue, then the Dent d'Hérens when steep, delicate ice-climbing on the ascent of the north-west face was followed by a race back down through moving séracs to regain the relative safety of the Tiefmattengletscher. After Dick went back to work, unsettled weather set in so I joined Mike Pinney and Jeff Harris for an ascent of the Lauteraarhorn following a marathon walk-in from the Grimsel Pass. Mike had correctly read the local weather patterns to find a fine option.

One of the advantages of the AC meets was the fertility of ideas growing amongst the group as to alternatives when conditions were less than ideal. Another was the sense of others looking out for you. I can recall several tense evenings as the shadows lengthened with still no sign of an expected team's return, yet no real disaster until Rick Eastwood's death in 2007.

Of course any visit to Zermatt is overshadowed by the presence of the Matterhorn but I had no interest in joining the queues on the Hörnli: at least one AC team had taken 20 hours on the route! That was before Mike Pinney approached me with a cunning plan. This involved taking two days to traverse over the Theodule Pass, descend below the south face of the Matterhorn, then back up around the Tête du Lion to access the Carrel bivouac hut, climb the Italian ridge and traverse the mountain back to Zermatt.

Rising for the climb, we were disappointed to find a lightning storm lighting up the darkness over Monte Rosa and heading in our direction. We delayed for a day but with minimal supplies were forced to scrounge stale bread and discarded scraps that sparsely littered the shelves of the hut. Later that day the weather cleared up enough for us to scout the route as far as the crest of the ridge. It was very different from the guidebook description so was time well spent. Returning, we found Daphne Pritchard and Dick Sykes had arrived. Dick thoughtfully demolished half a kilo of cheese, later ensuring that not a soul in the hut got any sleep as he shared his terrifying dreams with us. That night Mike and I were first out of the hut and, despite someone stealing my head-torch, managed a rapid ascent of the superb Italian ridge. I particularly remember leaning way out backwards to grasp the icy rungs of the precariously placed Echelle Jordan. We didn't linger on the summit as the crowds were already forming characteristic bottlenecks on the Hörnli. In descent however, it was possible to take alternative lines with the advantage of height to identify them and we skipped around the bouchons to reach the Hörnli hut in just seven hours from the Carrel.

That was Mike's last route of the season but I was taking full advantage of the long summer break that teaching affords. Another advantage of the AC meets at that time was the involvement of families that guaranteed social support for climbing couples and an exciting extended family for the children. I had brought my family out with me so, with time to do the reading for the terms ahead on rest days, there was nothing to draw me home. I was also realising that long traverses were not only very enjoyable but didn't half total up some summits. I joined Bob Elmes and Mike Pearson for the Nadelgrat traverse from the Dürrenhorn to the Nadelhorn, and on the descent recovered a pair of gaiters from the guardian at the Mischabel hut that I'd left there weeks before: he opened the store door on a roomful of abandoned kit and told me to find them.

Mike and Bob then became enthusiastic about the Rochefort-Grandes Jorasses traverse, so we all adjourned to Chamonix. Unfortunately, after traversing the Rochefort arête over the Dôme to the Aiguille de Rochefort, the weather closed in and we were left with no choice but to reverse the route to the Torino hut whereupon the weather promptly cleared up. With a logic only mountaineers can aspire to, we descended to the valley by moonlight and spent much of the next day asleep. Unfortunately that moonlight had worked an unexpected effect on at least one of the traverse addicts who hatched the lunatic plan of traversing from the Aiguille du Midi over Mont Blanc, the Aiguille de Bionnassay and the Dômes de Miage by the light of the full moon that same night.

As the sun set, we left the ice cave on the Midi arête. Crossing towards Mont Blanc du Tacul, we found the snow reassuringly crunchy. Impatient with the tug of the rope, I was tempted to solo the route. Tyndall writes of the delights of 'going alone' and what was a little more lunacy in the mixture? We agreed to wait for each other at the Vallot hut. Toiling up the initial slopes of Mont Blanc du Tacul I regretted leaving my ski pole behind, then suddenly there was a ski pole at the side of the track. It's impossible to regard such things as anything less than good omens, though I was soon to wonder about that as I ran across the barely wedged ice blocks that bridged a giant crevasse.

My head-torch was only necessary when the way led into shadows, as Mont Blanc du Tacul, then Mont Maudit were gained. Reaching the summit of Mont Blanc itself, I had enough in reserve to make the enjoyable scramble out to Mont Blanc de Courmayeur for the views down into a moonlit Val Veni, before descending the Bosses ridge. There, stepping carefully along the narrow crest, I still found moments to pause and gaze at the silvered ridges and cloud-filled valleys spreading like ripples outwards over the map of Europe while distant head-torches found their way out of the Refuge les Grands Mulets far below.

At the Vallot hut the fug and squalor was something of a shock after the cold purity of moonlight, but I duly waited, warming up, until Mike and Bob arrived. We decided it was worth going on over the Bionnassay to the Dômes de Miage but I'd had enough of the hut so left while they were still resting. The notorious east arête of the Bionnassay was as thin as its reputation suggests, but I confidently tackled it à cheval until a sudden sense of foreboding stopped me in mid-shuffle. Carefully leaning out, I

118.
Denis Mitchell on the summit ridge of the Aiguille Blanche de Peuterey.
(Dave Wynne-Jones)

became aware that the arête that I was cheerfully straddling was holed right through at several points. I inched gingerly back to safe ground, climbed back up to the Dôme du Goûter and joined Mike and Bob to descend the voie normale – end of season!

Having skied for years, in 1990 I took my first hesitant steps, or rather turns, ski-touring, and realised that making ascents on ski would be one way of removing the more obstinately glacial of these mountains from the catalogue of drudgery. Not only do you move a lot faster with the kick-glide of the ski ascent, but routes that took hours to ascend can be descended in a matter of minutes on ski, with a great deal more fun to be had on the way.

Thus, in 1992, began a series of Easter ski-mountaineering trips that accelerated my tally of summits. On the first, bad weather in the Oberland drove our small team round to Saas Fee where Denis and I climbed the Weissmies, mostly on ski, in blowing spindrift and arctic temperatures. Switching to the Britannia hut, we climbed the Strahlhorn and Allalinhorn entirely on ski and skied to the shoulder of the Rimpfischhorn for the short climb up a couloir and rib to the summit. Then of course there were the challenges of speed and control in the descents. Leslie Stephen is prob-

119.
Jeff Harris tackling the mixed summit ridge of the Gross Fiescherhorn in ski-touring boots. *(Dave Wynne-Jones)*

ably the first to rhapsodise about the Alps in winter but this trip fairly confirmed my impressions that these mountains look just stunning in their winter raiment without the black ice and stonefall that can turn them ugly in summer.

That said, there was plenty of snow when Denis and I arrived at the AC meet in Chamonix that summer and the Whymper couloir on the Aiguille Verte was our first route of the season, closely followed by the north-west face of the Aiguille de Bionnassay. Climbing such routes one is aware of little beyond the pool of light cast by the head-torch for all those hours of climbing in the dark. It is the descents that offer moments when the mountains suddenly impress upon us their magnificent otherness, at least on the Bionnassay where the scary arête had become a broad thoroughfare linking the mountain to the Dôme de Goûter. On the Aiguille Verte it was a more hurried affair as we raced the sun to descend the south-facing Whymper couloir without avalanche.

Thinking to capitalise on the conditions, Denis was keen to go for the Aiguille Blanche de Peuterey. Crossing the lower Frêney glacier from the Monzino hut, I had my first inkling of the seriousness of what we were taking on. If you can tiptoe in big boots and crampons, we did, with bated breath, through the poised séracs. The Schneider couloir proved nearly as worrying, with no snow but rounded gritty ledges sloping in all the wrong directions. Beyond the Brèche des Dames Anglaises, the flanks of the ridge were a frustratingly loose collection of rubble ribs; sustained unpleasantness until we gained the rocky summit ridge above Pointe Gugliermina. On reaching snow we plumbed the depths again, postholing to all of the summits, just in case we missed the highest, then down to the Col de Peuterey. The plan had been to complete the Peuterey arête but the Grand Pilier d'Angle ahead looked to be just black ice, raked with stonefall. Temperatures had obviously risen. We made a game attempt to get up it but the bombardment of rock and ice turned us around. It was too late in the day to set out on the abseils down the Rochers Gruber so we bivouacked at the col.

Waking stiff and cold, we soon warmed up on the abseils, often running backwards and forwards across the rock at the rope's end looking for the next abseil point. Descending the Frêney glacier, we were fortunate that huge avalanches from the Frêney face had largely filled in the crevasses so that we had much more confidence to leap from their raised upper edges to the lower ones, safe in the knowledge that if we missed we were not going to disappear into the bowels of the glacier. When we finally regained the valley and campsite I was absolutely convinced it had been the only route on a 4000m mountain that I had thoroughly disliked. It would have left a lingering bad aftertaste to go home after that experience so I convinced Denis to tackle a TD+ rock route in the Aiguilles Rouges. It went perfectly and we departed well satisfied.

The next AC meet in 1993 was in Grindelwald. It was there, on the Jungfrau, that I had my only fall on any 4000m peak. Moving together in descent from the summit cloud cap, I slipped somewhere between belay posts on the ridge down to the Rottalsattel and slid off into the blowing snow. A combination of self-arrest and the rope coming tight stopped the slip and I was soon able to carefully move on. Below the cloud it was another world and when Ralph Atkinson reached me at the saddle he was unaware that anything untoward had happened. We had a much better day on the morrow when the Mönch provided superb views for the length of its elegant ESE arête. On the Schreckhorn, the peak held no terrors for Mike Pinney or me as we turned in a guidebook time for this classic route. As the weather turned unsettled Andrea Stimson and I headed for Zermatt for a walk in the snow – the traverse from Nordend to the Breithorn, the longest and finest of my alpine traverses.

Andrea had been suffering from the trauma of dealing with the deaths of two members of her expedition to Peru. She wanted some climbing in her comfort zone and the AC meet looked to be a good prospect. The weather had got her down as much as me so she jumped at the chance to decamp to Zermatt. On the first day we gained the Silbersattel from the Monte Rosa hut and climbed out along the fine snow ridge to the summit of Nordend, then back to gain the Dufourspitze from the saddle. Unfortunately the indicated route was a concave ice slope in a tremendously exposed position. We worked our way back along the flank of Dufourspitze until we found technical, ice-filled grooves and cracks that led up in a couple of pitches to the summit ridge, but I'd been travelling light again. Too light in an icy wind, and on the summit I reeled with incipient hypothermia. Despite a big hug from Andrea it was still hard work getting to the Signalkuppe for the night. Next day we traversed all the way to the Mezzalama hut, descending the Lisjoch to climb Pyramide Vincent before taking in Liskamm and Castor en route. The final day we climbed back up to Pollux then down to the Rossi e Volante bivouac hut, up the Roccia Nera and over all the summits of the Breithorn.

120. Mont Blanc from near the Vallot hut. *(Dave Wynne-Jones)*

That was my last big summer season. Easter 1995 I climbed the Gran Paradiso, having the dubious distinction of carrying my skis up and down in the vain hope that conditions would become skiable. Moving round to the Oberland, I made solo ski ascents of the Aletschhorn and Finsteraarhorn. In 1996 I managed an ascent of the Grand Combin during a brief summer visit to Chamonix with Pam Caswell in which we were stormed off Les Droites within 50m of the summit. From then on it was the odd flying visit to the Alps, mostly in winter. Over the next few years, I only made ski ascents of the Gross Grünhorn and Gross Fiescherhorn, but managed to climb in Tanzania, Kenya, Jordan, Morocco, Peru, the Caucasus, Alaska, Hindu Kush, Picos de Europa, Ecuador, the Pyrenees and Iran. My interests had shifted and proved that while climbing the 4000m mountains had been a great way to get a handle on the Alps, it had never been an obsession.

Then in 2002 I turned 50. I had been harassed out of my job into early retirement and had put my head back together by taking an MA in creative writing. Now it was time to set some priorities, settle some unfinished business, and, with only three 4000m peaks left to climb, this was an obvious target. That summer Yvonne Holland and I climbed Piz Bernina amongst several other peaks in an early season raid on the range before moving on to Courmayeur and failing in poor conditions on the Grandes Jorasses. Through the tunnel to Chamonix, we set off for the Couvercle hut but were caught by a nasty electric storm on the via ferrata that led up from the Mer de Glace to the hut. Yvonne went back. I went on. Arriving at the hut I asked the guardian what conditions were like on Les Droites. 'I don't know. No one has climbed it yet this season.' That night I left very early.

Before dawn I was at the foot of the initial couloir on the voie normale. I spent an hour, as the light strengthened, trying to overcome the bergschrund and get established in the couloir above the soft snow of its upper lip. Teetering over from the lower lip of the bergschrund, I tunnelled into the upper lip like a cornice, before back and footing my way up the shifting snow until at last I got some purchase with my axe. From then on it was straightforward: a steep snow couloir, a broad mixed ridge. No tracks, but there was a certain logic to the line that could not have been entirely down to my memory of 1996, unearthing slings from the snow just where they were needed. It felt just like swimming, that last 50m, up and along the snowed-up crest, with latterly the chance of a long swallow dive down the north face into the Argentière basin, before I gained the rock perch at the summit. There is an intensity about soloing that whets the appetite but it was my last alpine route that year. Later that summer I was to climb Pik Lenin, again soloing on summit day, and in November to make the first ascent of the south face of Pokharkan in Nepal. Opportunism was distracting me from my unfinished business.

In the next five years I climbed and skied in Kyrgyzstan, the Yukon, Xinjiang and Sechuan but only once returned to the Alps when I made my third ascent of Mont Blanc, with Adele Long. After heavy snowfall it was the only route in condition as guided parties had broken trail on the first fine day following the snow. For me it was an opportunity for the first time to take photos of the summit in daylight.

Then in 2007 there was an AC meet in Courmayeur. Gethin Howells, a youngster of half my age who had been with me and Adele on the AC ski-mountaineering expedition to Kyrgyzstan that year, joined me to warm up on the north face of the Tour Ronde and, with Martin Ghillie, on the Rochefort Arête. This is the only other 4000m-route that I have completed twice, largely because I didn't get any good pictures the first time. We had dearly wanted to make the traverse of the Rochefort and Grandes Jorasses but the word from those who had been on the summit ridge of the Grandes Jorasses was that there was a lot of ice so I didn't fancy the crux rock-climbing around Pointe Young in those conditions. Instead, Gethin and I set out from the Boccalette hut on the voie normale. It was a weekend and the weather was good so we didn't have the route to ourselves. This meant some delays on the rocks of the Rocher du Reposoir but I could often find an alternative line when there was a hold-up and we made good time. When we summited I think Gethin was more emotional than I was, especially when I told the guide who had more or less kept pace with us all the way that this was my last 4000m mountain. 'Oh, but you have done so well,' he replied. The nuances of language that can put us in our place!

Climbing these mountains has been a way of getting to grips with the Alps, and I shall be always grateful for the experience of these high wild peaks and the friendship of those people who shared that experience both on and off the mountains. Mike Pinney and Jeff Harris also completed in 2007 with the Aiguille Blanche de Peuterey that had eluded them for

121. Job done – Dave Wynne-Jones (right) and Gethin Howells on Dave's final 4000m summit (Grandes Jorasses) with the first (Mont Blanc) in the background. *(Dave Wynne-Jones)*

years, although since they were helicoptered off after being hit by stonefall on the re-ascent of Pic Eccles, Jeff's daughter, Jenny, did wonder whether it counted. Thankfully that was the only accident to those I climbed with and I put that down in no small measure to the good sense and wealth of pooled experience that characterised AC meets. Other friends are still on the 4000m trail.

So what now? Put simply, I go on climbing. There are enough routes to do on these and other mountains both in the Alps and elsewhere to keep me occupied for several lifetimes. There is something I noticed in the Dolomites last year, though: I'd had enough of the hustle of relentless commercialism after just three weeks. Perhaps that is why I have been increasingly drawn to more remote mountains. In 2007 I not only finished my 4000m summits but also made eight first ascents in Kyrgyzstan, India and China. There is no doubt that you can get a lot more climbing done in a month in the Alps than in the same time spent in the greater ranges but there is something very special about climbing where no one has climbed before, where you have not only the route but even the range to yourselves. It's all a question of balance.

Finally I make no apologies for the roll-call of climbing partners in this account, most of whom were AC members. It is our partners who make our climbing possible.

STEPHEN GOODWIN

Who Cares About 'The Playground of Europe'?

The source of the Soca comes as a surprise. All day we've been on or by this river, walking, rafting, even swimming it, and always it is in a hurry, foaming over shingle beds and carving in bow waves round boulders. Yet here at its cave mouth the karst spring of the Soca is still, a night-blue well, its surface so devoid of ripple that beyond a margin of limestone pebbles its depth is difficult to gauge. I linger, then turn and scramble out of the cave bed, traverse out of the ravine and follow the zigzag path down

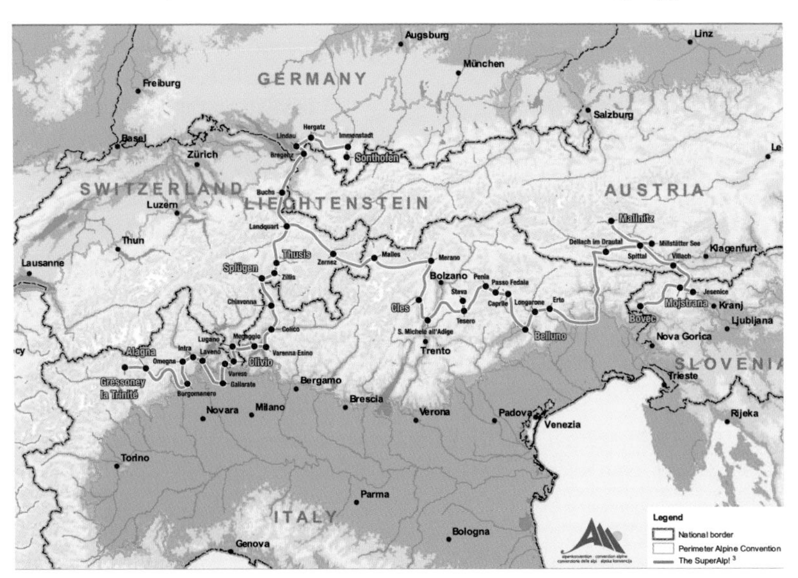

122. The 10-day route for the Alpine Convention's SuperAlp![3] starting in Bovec, Slovenia, on 19 June 2009 and finishing at Gressoney la Trinité on 28 June.

the wooded hillside. Apparently at other times the water of the *Izviru Soca* surges up in such volume that the cave is unapproachable.

This was day one of the Alpine Convention's SuperAlp![3] and a winding 10-day journey from the Triglav National Park to the shadow of Monte Rosa had begun heavy with symbolism. But I can see this is going take some explaining. (See above for the route.)

The Alpine Convention is an international treaty between the eight countries of the Alps and the European Community. Its aim is to promote

123. The source of the Soča in a cave bottom. A photo similar to this, taken closer, appeared on the cover of the Alpine Convention's 'State of the Alps' report on water and completely mystified me until I peered into this karst well. *(Stephen Goodwin)*

the sustainable development of the Alps – the largest single ecosystem in Europe apart from the Mediterranean – through cross-border co-operation. There is no great bureaucracy – a staff of five at the headquarters in Innsbruck and three in a branch across the Brenner Pass at Bolzano running on an annual budget of €800,000, drawn from the member countries. An extra five staff in Chambéry, financed by the French government to the tune of an additional €400,000, dealing with protected natural areas, was integrated into the Convention's Permanent Secretariat in 2006.

In case you're wondering, the eight Alpine countries are Italy, Austria, France, Switzerland, Germany, Slovenia, Monaco and Liechtenstein. The 'mountainous' parts of them covered by the Convention – including valleys and towns therein – totals 190,568 sq km along a 1,200km arc. Within this are 5,954 municipalities, 14 million people, 30,000 animal species from brown bears and bearded vultures to salamanders, and 13,000 plant species, edelweiss, gentian, saxifrage, you name it.

These statistics were not high in our minds as we rafted down the Soca from Bovec beneath a clear blue sky, though we did wonder whether the wooded hillside on our left might have harboured bears. Slovenia is the brown bear stronghold of the Alps; in fact it is something of a bear 'bank', with withdrawals for reintroduction projects elsewhere.

Musings on the bear would be interrupted by the noise of churning water as Soca twisted between boulders or down rapids; we'd ready our paddles and wait for instructions from our skipper, bikini-ed Betty from Budapest. 'Right back, left forward, go, go…'With none of the seven of us in the raft sharing the native tongue of another, and no one, except Betty of course, having a word of Hungarian, there tended to be a momentary delay between the command and its execution as each of the crew, except me, did a quick translation from accented English. Fortunately the Soca,

124.
Memorials to man-made tragedy: Above: headstones for the 1,910 victims, some never found, others beyond identification, in the Vajont dam disaster, Italy, 1963.

125. Below: a symbolic 'mud' cannon stands on the hillside above the site of the mine tailings dam at Stava, Italy, that burst in 1985, killing 268 people.
(Stephen Goodwin)

along the 14km we rafted, is a forgiving stream. Only Stefano, a photographer from the Aosta valley, fell overboard, and he was soon recovered, once his designated rescuer, Lei Wang from *China Pictorial*, Beijing, had stopped laughing.

(A bunch of journalists out on a 'jolly', I hear the cynics say. Well, 'Up to a point Lord Copper'. But there's always a purpose. And why not enjoy your work along the way?)

Our alpine odyssey had begun on the Soca for several reasons. One, Slovenia holds the presidency of the Alpine Convention (it rotates, EC style); two, the Soca, or the Isonzo as the Italians know it before it flows into the Gulf of Trieste, is very much a border river and a reminder of what happens when neighbours choose conflict instead of co-operation. The mountainsides we rafted beneath were a bloody battleground in 1915-17, the Soca/Isonzo Front. And three, the theme of SuperAlp![3] was 'water'. From the *Izviru Soca* we would, over the coming days, stand on the banks of the Drava, a tributary of the Danube, the broad and free Tagliamento, the tightly channelled Piave and Adige, the infant Rhine and the glaciated headwaters of the Po. We would visit projects to re-wild rivers by releasing them from canalised banks, Swiss mountain villages that had resisted inundation by dam builders and two in Italy where the greed and arrogance of dam builders had resulted in horrendous loss of life.

On the eve of our journey, the Convention published its second experts' report on the 'State of the Alps' entitled *Water and Water Management Issues* (the first, in 2007, focused on transport). Couched in the language of scientists, and taking care not to tread on sensitive political toes, it none the less makes clear that alpine communities will have to face up to big changes. The warming of the Alps – running at twice the global average –

with milder, wetter winters and hotter, drier summers, is expected to bring more rockfall, floods and droughts. The Alps may be the 'water towers of Europe' but with the flow from those towers increasingly unpredictable, the Convention report underlines the need for cooperation between communities and states in restraining consumption and guarding against damaging floods and drought. A stern finger is pointed at the ski industry's mania for snow cannons, particularly at lower altitude resorts that should be looking for alternative ways of generating tourism income. Ironically while snow cannons were a mark of shame a decade ago and barely mentioned by resorts, now they are regarded as a key selling point. You could hardly have a starker demonstration of global warming than the north face of Triglav, on our horizon late on day one. One hundred years ago a glacier stretched right across the lower face, today you have to strain to pick out the remaining patch. Most of the melt has occurred over the last 30 years.

126. Tranquility in the centre of Splügen, an architecturally rich old Swiss village that fought off proposals to submerge all of this beneath a giant reservoir. *(Stephen Goodwin)*

The 'State of the Alps' reports with their wealth of detail – rather like House of Common's select committee reports – are intended to assist the multifarious bodies whose decisions shape all the human aspects of the Alps, from whether peaks remain unsullied by cablecars or heli-skiers to how to ameliorate crowded transport corridors like the Brenner or the Aosta valley. It's about the high Alps we enjoy as mountaineers, the rail and road links we use for access and the valley towns we descend to for a glass or two and a hot shower. And that's why the Alpine Club should care about the work of the Alpine Convention.

In the spirit of the Convention's commitment to sustainability, our journey along the alpine arc was done as much as possible on public transport, though for some out-of-the-way riversides we had to resort to the SuperAlp![3] minivan. (SuperAlp![3], incidentally is the title the Convention has given to this annual public relations exercise, and 2009 was its third year.) My calculation is that we travelled on 29 trains, 17 buses, two ferries (lakes Como and Maggiore), two electric cars, two cable cars (over the Passo dei Salati linking the Alagna and Gressoney valleys), two electric bikes, one mountain bike and of course the raft on the emerald Soca. And we hiked a stretch of the Via Spluga, an ancient trade route

127. Grossglockner (3798m), highest mountain and symbol of Austria and centre of one of the biggest national parks in Europe, the High Tauern National Park. *(Matevž Lenarčič).* This photo plus 127, 130 and 131 appear in Lenarčič's inspirational book, *The Alps: A Bird's Eye View* (2009).

linking the upper Rhine valley with Chiavenna in Italy.

Our rather erratic-looking course is explained by the Convention's need to fly the flag in areas that have given it support and where projects are underway that exemplify its work. Visibility is crucial. The awkward truth is that of those almost 6,000 municipalities in its patch, most have either never heard of the Alpine Convention or have no idea of what it does. And too often even when communities are aware of the Convention it is regarded with suspicion, as another of those interfering outside bodies that wants to preserve nature at the expense of local business, be it mines, ski-lift operators or farmers.

One of the most heartening stops on our tour – and instructive in the role that can be played by mountaineering associations – was the dog leg up to the village Mallnitz at the southern end of the railway tunnel beneath the crest of the Hohe Tauern in Austria. Mallnitz is the province of Carinthia's gateway to Hohe Tauern National Park, a sprawling mass of 3000m peaks – more than 300 of them – receding glaciers and relatively unspoilt high valleys. And Mallnitz has a claim to fame in mountaineering that will be a cause of celebration in 2012. On the Tauern crest, just east in the line of the tunnel, stands Ankogel (3250m) which has the curious distinction of being the 'oldest glacier peak' in Austria, in that it was the earliest moderately difficult glaciated peak to be climbed - way back in 1762, twenty-four years

128. The 800m-high south face of the Marmolada (3343m) and the Cimon della Pala (3184m) viewed from the south-west. *(Matevž Lenarčič)*

before the first ascent of Mont Blanc.

Mallnitz is thus a worthy member of the family of 27 'Mountaineering Villages', an initiative of the Austrian Alpine Association (ÖAV), putting into practice ideas of sustainable Alpine tourism. The basic deal is that these small mountain villages – populations no more than 2,500 – don't go in for any gross developments, instead preserving their natural and cultural

assets, and in return they get help with marketing, training and appropriate infrastructure. (Regrettably I heard bolted *klettergartens* mentioned in this last category. Surely not!)

Other villages in the family include Vent in the Ötztal, Ginzling in the Zillertal and Kals at the southern foot of the Grossglockner. For several of the villages the project is an attempt to reverse decline and depopulation due to being overshadowed by big

ski resorts. All of the villages have alpine huts in the ranges around them

129.
Routes ancient and modern: heading out of the Rheinwald, Switzerland, on the medieval cobbles of the Via Spluga, the hairpins of the modern road beyond,

130. . .and close to the Splügen Pass (2115m), the border with Italy. *(Stephen Goodwin*

and it is this tradition of mountaineering that is seen as the anchor to the whole enterprise.

The Mountaineering Villages initiative owes a lot to two men – Peter Hasslacher of the ÖAV and Marco Onida, Secretary General of the Alpine Convention – who have seen their ideals come together. By giving its support and acting as a facilitator, the Convention has helped Hasslacher secure funding of €800,000 – half from the EC and half from Austrian environment ministry. Onida described it as a 'solidarity project'. The need for protection of the natural environment in conjunction with culture was felt as a shared value, both by those who lived in the Alps and those who visited, he said. 'The history of Alpinism is a history of men and women who changed the destiny of the mountain villages. That in 2009, villages united by this common history cooperate in order to pursue new forms of tourism, despite the challenges that this might sometimes imply, is of great significance.'

For Hasslacher it was one more step on his ongoing campaign for the welfare of the Austrian Alps. When I first met Peter Hasslacher, in 1983 at the ÖAV's Innsbruck headquarters, he was battling a proposal by Tyrol's water and electricity utilities to draw water from every glacier stream on the south flank of the Grossglockner and Grossvenediger ranges and collect it in a gigantic reservoir near Kals. The scheme would have killed stone dead the embryonic Hohe Tauern national park – at least within Tryol province, the wildest of the park's ranges. It looked like a David v Goliath struggle at the time; but as anyone who has ski-toured or climbed here since, perhaps descending by the foaming glacier-fed cascades of Umbaltal, will appreciate, David prevailed. Today the park covers 1,900 sq km, straddling the provinces of Salzburg, Carinthia and Tyrol. Big utilities were not the only threat; many in the local communities, particularly farmers, viewed the park with hostility, fearing its preservationist ethos; 25 years later fears have allayed and there are nearby villages wanting to come within its border.

Winning over public opinion and persuading people that the Alpine Convention is about development as well as conservation is an important part of Marco Onida's work. But the visceral attachment of farmers to the landscape can also make them allies. On the bank of Drava at Dellach im Drautal, Carinthia, were heard how a farmer had turned over fields to a re-wilding project in order to recreate the Drava of his childhood. (Of course, he wanted a parcel of land away from the river in return.) The man had learnt to swim in a river that could flood over shingle banks into lagoons, since when canalisation had made it deeper and fast flowing. That the upper Drau/Drava had been liberated hereabouts was obvious from the pools and silt on the track after days of heavy rain. We picked our way along to a point overlooking ponds dug by local schoolchildren, firemen and other volunteers amid a jungly floodplain forest. Willow and tamarisk is colonising the gravel banks while the yellow-bellied toad and the wolf spider are returning to the swamp.

Such were the stories we heard as we stepped off the trains and buses of SuperAlp's watery itinerary. The rain that had swollen the Drava had turned the Iller into a surging grey beast when we arrived in Immenstadt im Allgäu, Bavaria. Meanwhile the eastern foothills of the Alps near Vienna were experiencing the heaviest rains for 50 years. 'Flukatastrophe' shouted the *Kronen Zeitung*; 10,000 soldiers had been mobilised against the flood. However the highlight in the Allgäu was not the area's latest efforts to contain the Iller but its commitment to sustainable tourism. We travelled the 10km up-valley from Immenstadt to Sonthofen in a soaking *peleton* of electric bikes, just as the town hopes its tourists (and residents) will get about when not hiking up into the hills.

Next day in Switzerland I used an electric bike (solar charged of course) to good effect on the steep track from Thusis to the gorge of the Viamala on the upper Rhein, cruising up as younger comrades with ordinary mountain bikes had to dismount exhausted and push. As usual, Onida had several points to make: another demonstration of eco-transport, drawing

131. The Altesch glacier, biggest glacier in the Alps; an outstanding example of the formation of the Alps and the study of eco-systems, including the 'dying' of glaciers due to climate change.
(Matevž Lenarčič)

attention to the scenic hiking route through the Alps from Thusis to Chiavenna which provides green tourist euros for villages along the 65km cultural trail (W M Turner painted on the Viamala) and telling the story of Splügen, that 70 years ago fought off an

attempt to dam its valley. Villagers, whose ancient houses would have vanished beneath the reservoir, resisted all manner of pressure and inducement and, crucially, were able to use their very Swiss right to vote 'no'. Thwarted in the Rheinwald, the hydropower developers simply looked over the crest of the Alps into Italy and built their dam in Valle di Lei.

In Italy we saw what happens when man thinks he can master Nature

132.
Monte Rosa – Dufourspitze (4634m), Switzerland's highest peak, flanked by (left) Lyskamm and (right) Zumsteinspitze and Signalkuppe.
(Matevž Lenarčič)

– saw it in the vast mounds of rock and soil that slid from Monte Toc on 9 October 1963 to fill the Vajont Dam, and in the 1,910 identical headstones at Longarone – one for each of those who perished as a wave 170m high swept over the dam and down the valley. Early warnings of the instability were ignored and even when the mountainside was visibly slipping there was no attempt to alert the population. Renato Migotti, who showed us round the special cemetery, was one of the few survivors, 16 years old at the time, dug out from beneath the mud. As president of the survivors' association, Migotti tells the Vajont story as a warning to geologists, engineers and their corporate employers. 'Unfortunately we did not learn that much,' adds Migotti, and particularly he is thinking of Stava, 22 years later.

Stava lies at 1250m in a small valley above the Val di Fiemme in Trentino – less than 100km west of Vajont as the crow flies. Here we were met by another man heading a group keeping alive an 'active memory' of a man-made disaster. Graziano Lucchi was living away from Stava on 19 July 1985 when a tailings dam at a fluorite mine on Mt Prestavèl collapsed, spewing mud down the hillside at 90kph and killing 268 people. The tailings dams had been built on sloping, marshy ground and surveys had pointed up their chronic instability. Jail sentences for multiple manslaughter were handed down, but legal proceedings dragged on and nobody actually served time behind bars.

'Water was the main cause for the tragedy, but water can't be blamed,' said Lucchi. 'It was all man's fault. People have used water carelessly, without the slightest respect for it or for the mountain where it flows from.'

The autonomous province of Trentino is a declared supporter of the

goals of the Alpine Convention and as a part of the Alps where drought could become a particular problem it takes seriously the need to restrain water consumption. Trentino and neighbouring Bolzano produce most of Europe's apples, a thirsty crop, but persuading farmers to switch from 'diffuse rain' – whirling sprays – to less wasteful forms of irrigation isn't proving easy. Trentino too is engaged on river re-naturalisation projects, such as on the Brenta. And as winters warm it has embarked on a 'gradual conversion' of its tourism economy away from its 50 percent dependency on skiing. Lorenzo Dellai, the provincial governor, said Trentino could not give up snowmaking altogether, however it would focus on improving larger existing resorts and had 'given up' on developing smaller areas, particularly at lower altitudes.

The urgency for those lower resorts to find alternatives to ski incomes was underlined on the last day of SuperAlp![3] when we visited the Angelo Mosso scientific institute that stands at 2900m, just below the ridge dividing Alagna and Gressoney valleys, south of Monte Rosa. An outpost of the

University of Turin, it was built in 1907 and was the scene of early research into physiological effects of altitude. Prof Ardito Desio made use of the institute in preparing for the Italy's successful ascent of K2 in 1954. In June 2000 the building was struck by lightning and completely gutted by fire; re-building, even with the aid of cable cars and helicopters, took longer than it had in Mosso's day when all materials had to be carried up from the valley. Re-opened in 2007, the institute is now largely devoted to public education with a museum and displays on snow crystal and avalanches.

The institute's main role today for the scientists – who keep a room in the attic - is in the collection of meteorological and snow cover data, a valuable record that goes back to 1907. Interestingly, winter snow depth has remained pretty constant above the 1900m contour, though with increased temperatures the snow tends to be wetter. However, as researcher Michele Freppaz explained, the most noticeable change has been in the 1000m to 1600m 'middle' level where precipitation increasingly falls as rain. The impact is felt not merely by skiers as lower runs disappear but by forest and valley eco-systems. In some places trees are dying because they no longer have the insulation of a reliable snow blanket in winter.

Should we care? As the hack pack bounced down the Gressoney valley, off-road on mountain bikes for the very last transport mode of the trip, the Alps seemed every bit the carefree 'playground' suggested by Leslie Stephen's memorable book title. Gressoney and Alagna were keen to show off their efforts towards 'soft' tourism but the mountain villages need a corresponding response from their visitors – climbers, hikers, skiers, whoever – to be convinced that sustainable development is the way to go. They might also look to those who enjoy the snow and ice to join the lobby for big cuts in carbon emissions.

For the last couple of days SuperAlp![3] was joined by Annibale Salsa, president of the Club Alpino Italiano, and of course we had already seen the mutual support for the Convention of the ÖAV. Marco Onida, himself no mean mountaineer, sees the alpine associations as natural 'ambassadors' for the Convention's objectives. 'The fact that the UK Alpine Club is not from a member state of the Convention should not constitute a reason not to play a role; after all, we have 14 million residents in the Alps but some 120 million tourists,' says Onida.

'Alpine clubs from third states could be ambassadors for messages such as sustainable tourism and mobility, nature conservation and so on. Moreover, the UK is the cradle of Alpinism, as everyone knows. If in an ideal world all the ministers of the Alpine states received letters from presidents or members of Alpine clubs such as AC, this would give the Alps more political visibility. Maybe I am too idealistic, but I do believe that building an 'Alpine public opinion' – and it is public opinion that shapes policies – necessarily requires the involvement of all those who, one way or another, travel to the Alps, live in the Alps or care for the Alps. This includes for sure members of the Alpine Club.'

Surveys

133. Simon Pierse, *La Grivola, first light, morning stars, 2008-9,* watercolour, 53 x 71cm.

ROGER PAYNE

Sublime Sikkim

Alpine Peaks Emerge From The Mist

The good thing about discovering you are wrong about something is that you get a chance for a new start. Prior to my first visit to Sikkim in October 2004, my impression was that it was difficult and costly to climb there. Having now made five visits to the former Himalayan kingdom in north-east India, I can say with certainty that this need not be the case.

My first view of the mountains of Sikkim was in the spring of 2004 with Julie-Ann Clyma during an ascent of Chomolhari on the Tibet-Bhutan border. With the remarkable backdrop of Kangchenjunga, the Sikkim-Tibet border peaks looked interesting and tantalizingly accessible from the Tibetan plateau.

Since that first view, I have discovered that Sikkim has countless rock walls, winter icefalls in high forests and mountain valleys, many interesting unclimbed 5000m and some unclimbed 6000m peaks, a clutch of virgin 7000m peaks, and the world's longest un-climbed high-altitude ridge. A very welcome recent addition is regulations for 'Alpine Peaks' that allow small teams to easily obtain permission in Sikkim and at modest cost. We had an input into this improvement of access for climbing, which is welcome evidence of a state government that is open-minded and committed to sustainable development in mountain regions. This example was mentioned as a model of good practice at the 2009 annual congress of the Adventure Tour Operators Association of India (ATOAI) held on 16-18 January 2009 in Dehradun, Uttarakhand.

Back in the mist, and the zenith of alpine climbing

The relatively easy to cross passes between Sikkim and Tibet are strategically important. Hence, they became the eastern gateway to the Tibetan plateau and the route taken by Francis Younghusband for the historic 'Lhasa Mission' of 1904 and all the early expeditions to the north side of Everest.

Later, during the period of the Sino-Indian border conflicts, these passes closed and became major points of tension between India and China. Hence, both sides of the border became heavily militarised. The military presence remains on the border; however, the Natu La (4310m), one of the main mountain passes between Sikkim and Tibet, is now open for limited local trade and may eventually open for tourism.

On the other side of this compact and diverse state is the world's third highest mountain. In two remarkable journeys in 1848 and 1849, the legen-

134. Looking east from camp on Brumkhangshe to Pauhunri and peaks on the Sikkim-Tibet border, 2007. (*Roger Payne*)

135. Brumkhangshe (5635m), one of the two Alpine Peaks in North Sikkim. (*Roger Payne*)

dary naturalist Sir Joseph Hooker climbed several 5000m peaks, attempted some 6000m peaks, and almost completed a circuit of Kangchenjunga. John Claude White, the Political Officer to Sikkim and later Bhutan (1887-1908), travelled widely. White was a very able administrator and a farsighted conservationist. He introduced protected status to vast areas of Himalaya forest, and created a remarkable personal collection of photographs of his travels on the north-east frontier and in Tibet. In 1899 Douglas Freshfield's famous expedition around Kangchenjunga included Vittorio Sella, who took some inspirational photographs, including the striking peak of

136. Chombu's east face – 'high in objective danger' – and the upper Rula Kang glacier. (*Roger Payne*)

Siniolchu, once vaunted as the most beautiful mountain in the world.

The most prolific early climber was Dr Alexander Kellas, who made several visits to Sikkim in the period 1907-21. He climbed many peaks, mostly with local companions, and in 1910 made 10 ascents including Chomoyummo (6829m) and Pauhunri (7128m). Kellas wrote several important papers on the effects of altitude, but sadly, wrote very little about his extensive climbing experiences. Kellas wondered if Everest could be climbed without supplementary oxygen, and because of his experience and knowledge, was selected as a member of the first Everest expedition in 1921. Tragically, after crossing from Sikkim to the Tibetan plateau he became seriously unwell and died of a heart attack. He was buried at Kampa Dzong looking towards the mountains of North Sikkim.

Marco Pallis, Freddy Spencer Chapman, Paul Bauer, G O Dyrenfurth, C R Cook, John Hunt, and Eric Shipton were all among the climbers of what could be called the 'golden age' of mountain exploration in Sikkim. This period started with Hooker in 1848, and was arguably at its zenith in the 1930s on the peaks around the Zemu glacier in north-west Sikkim. Continuing the lightweight alpine-style approach that had been established, in 1936 Bauer, Adi Göttner, Karl Wien and Günther Hep made the first ascent of Siniolchu (6887m) and Simvo (6812m). The 'golden age' perhaps ended in 1939 with the ascents of Tent Peak (7365m) and Nepal Peak (7180m) by the Swiss-German party of E Grob, H Paidar and L Schmaderer. When Himalayan mountaineering resumed after the interruption of the World War II, the spotlight was on a different style of mountaineering and the 8000m peaks. In the case of Kangchenjunga, the focus was on

137. Chumangkang and Chomoyummo from Chombu's north-east ridge. An Indian attempt on the border peak of Chomoyummo (6829m) in 2004 ended in an avalanche tragedy. (*Roger Payne*)

the Nepal side of the mountain.

Despite a long history of mountain exploration, Sikkim lacks a reliable up to date record of first ascents. Climbs have been made but not clearly recorded, some ascents have been claimed but may not have been climbed, and some summits have been climbed but not recorded at all. I have even had the strange experience of reading in a Sikkim newspaper about a 'first' ascent of a mountain that I had already climbed myself (and that as a third ascent). Given this unusual and somewhat confusing background (and all that is recorded in the *Himalayan Journal* and elsewhere) this article is not an attempt to get the historical record clear and correct, but highlights selected achievements and some of the excellent climbing opportunities that exist in Sikkim.

Above the mists

Unlike some of the world's highest mountains, Kangchenjunga is easily visible from the lowlands and populated areas. It is an amazing sight from hill towns like Pelling and Darjeeling. Given its dominant size and shape, and magnificent appearance in early morning and evening light, it is hardly surprising that it has long been an object of worship and an inspiration to climbers. The remarkable first ascent in 1955 was from the Nepal side of the mountain. However, the Sikkim side had already seen two determined attempts on the northeast spur in 1929 and '31 by strong groups led by Paul Bauer. This dangerous and difficult route was eventually completed in 1977 by an Indian Army expedition led by the redoubtable Col Narinder ('Bull') Kumar, which was the second expedition to succeed on Kangchenjunga.

The ongoing history of climbing on Kangchenjunga has mostly been on the Nepal side of the mountain. This includes the remarkable alpine-style ascent of the south summit by the south ridge (which marks the border between Nepal and Sikkim) in 1991 by Andrej Stremfelj and Marko Prezelj. That same year the State Government of Sikkim classified the main, south and west summits of Kangchenjunga as sacred, and banned the 'scaling of the sacred peaks'. This has been taken to mean that all climbing attempts on the Sikkim side of Kangchenjunga are prohibited. However, it may be possible to obtain permission from the Sikkim authorities to climb Kangchenjunga if the sacred peak restriction is respected, and the summits remain un-trodden. If so, this would open up the possibility of a traverse of the formidable unclimbed east-southeast ridge, which includes Zemu Peak (7780m). This is, without doubt, one of the major high-altitude mountaineering challenges.

In the West

South along the border from Kangchenjunga is Talung (7349m) and at least three 7000m summits in the Kabru group. In 1883 William Woodman Graham claimed an ascent of Kabru, but later this was dismissed and it was thought he was on some other mountain. Kabru North (7338m) was climbed in 1935 (C R Cooke and G. Schoberth) and Talung from its Nepal side in 1964 (F. Lindner and T Nindra). Kabru Dome (6600m) and the North and South summits of Kabru are classified as sacred. However, this has not prevented recent ascents by Indian and foreign groups (although it is not clear if the groups concerned had the permission of the authorities in Sikkim).

Further south again is Rathong (6679m) and Koktang (6147m). Both offer interesting opportunities for alpine-style first ascents (and which Sagar Rai, Julie-Ann and I explored in autumn 2006, climbing some adjacent 5000m summits). According to the Alpine Club's on-line Himalayan Index, Koktang has been climbed twice (via the SW face in 1982 and via the NE face and north ridge in 1991), and Rathong has had two ascents (in 1964 and 1987 via the West Rathong glacier and icefall).

Koktang has a long, corniced summit ridge and, according to the great chronicler of Himalayan ascents Harish Kapadia, 'the true high point, lying at the northernmost end, remains to be climbed'. In 2006, having climbed quite a bit of new ground, we made some progress on the northwest-north ridge of Koktang, but deep cold snow and unstable cornices stopped us. This route would probably be a more reasonable undertaking in the pre-monsoon spring period.

The steep mixed south face of Rathong looks interesting, but has some sérac hazards. Its south-east ridge is a technical challenge which Julie-Ann and I tried in 2006 but ran out of weather and time. In November 2008, I returned with Owen Samuel for a second attempt. We reached around 6300m, but were deterred from continuing along the exposed crest of the ridge by very strong winds and low temperatures.

Near the snout of the Rathong glacier is the mountain base camp for the Himalayan Mountaineering Institute in Darjeeling. Groups from HMI

138. Frey Peak (5830m), one of the permitted Alpine Peaks of West Sikkim. (*Roger Payne*)

139. On Frontier Peak, 2006. (*Roger Payne*)

140. Right: on the north-west ridge of Koktang. (*Roger Payne*)

141. Koktang north face. According to Harish Kapadia, the true high point of this 6147m peak still remains to be climbed. (*Roger Payne*)

Darjeeling train on the glaciers and peaks thereabouts, including the technical Frey Peak (5830m) that has had numerous ascents with the aid of fixed ropes. It is one of the peaks designated by the Government of Sikkim as an Alpine Peak, and on which other technical climbs would be possible. In 2004 two Spanish climbers (Alain Anders and Garo Azuke) were active in this area and climbed two technical routes on peaks they referred to as Tieng Kg (c6000m) and Phori (5837m) (see *American Alpine Journal*, 2004, Vol 46, p385).

Running parallel and to the east of the above peaks is the route of Sikkim's most popular trek: a five-day journey from the historic village of Yuksom to the Gocha La (Heaven's Gate). The other well-known trek in Sikkim is to 'Green Lake' on the Zemu glacier in north-west Sikkim. Although not actually green or much of a lake, the views of glaciers and high peaks are spectacular. Of historical note in this area are the journeys of Kekoo Naoroji in 1958. Naoroji, a former president of the Himalayan Club, made an excellent photographic record of his pioneering lightweight treks. Today, there is the enticing challenge of linking the Gocha La and Green Lake treks in a continuous journey via the Zemu Gap, which would be an interesting and adventurous journey around the south-east flank of Kangchenjunga. The crossing of the Zemu Gap developed some notoriety after a visit in 1938 by W H Tilman, and was attempted as a south to north crossing in spring 2008 by Adrian O'Connor, Colin Knowles and Jerzy Wieczorek.

Back to the west, as you rise above the dense forests above Yuksom and head towards the Gocha La, there are excellent views of Kangchenjunga, and to the east a group of fine looking alpine-scale peaks. The first of real note is the technical looking Narsing (5825m, first ascent Kellas, 1921) that is another sacred peak. Just north of this is Lama Lamani (c5700m),

142. On Koktang, 2006, with Rathong in the background. Both peaks offer opportunities for alpine-style first ascents. (*Roger Payne*)

Jopuno (5936m, first ascent Sikkim Amateur Mountaineering Association [SAMA], 2002) and Tinchenkang (6010m, first ascent Indo-British Army expedition 1998); the latter two being Alpine Peaks, for which it is easy to obtain permission.

In spring 2005, with Sagar Rai and Kunzang Bhutia (friends in SAMA who had climbed Jopuno in 2002) we made the first ascent of Lama Lamani, then made the third ascent (and first alpine-style) of Tinchenkang. Jopuno had its second ascent in spring 2008, and the first by its west ridge. The ridge was climbed in a day from a camp at c4200m by an American team of Josh Smith, Jason Halladay, Sam Gardner and Sarah Demay. These peaks offer good alpine-style ascents of around AD to D standard, and are destined to become classic climbs of the eastern Himalaya.

Further north again is the dramatic peak of Pandim (6691m), which attracted the attention of the early explorers, and more recently has had some confusingly reported attempts. Pandim has a superb looking technical west

143. Narsing (5825m), climbed by Alexander Kellas in 1921 and today designated a sacred summit. (*Roger Payne*)

ridge, but is another sacred summit. It is actually a group of summits, so perhaps in the future it may be possible to climb one of the lower peaks.

In West Sikkim, as in other areas of Sikkim, Indian mountaineers have been very active. Instructors from the mountaineering institutes, military groups, and members of the Himalayan Club and SAMA have all made important climbs. Some ascents have been accurately documented in the *Himalayan Journal* and elsewhere, others less well recorded, and some not recorded for security reasons. If Sikkim ever has a definitive guidebook of climbs, it will have been the outcome of some very diligent research.

Along the border, North and East

North of Kangchenjunga is Jongsang (7459m, first ascent by its north ridge in 1930 by G O Dyrenfurth's international expedition to Kangchenjunga), which is at the junction of the borders between Nepal, Tibet and Sikkim. The Sikkim-Tibet border runs to the east following the watershed over high peaks and passes to Pauhunri (7125m, first ascent in 1910 by Kellas) in Sikkim's north-east corner. Just south of Pauhunri are two virgin 7000m summits, then a ridge of un-named 6000m summits. Further south again, the peaks become lower and lead to the historic passes of Natu La (4310m, between Gangtok and Yatung in Tibet) and Jelep La (4374m, between Kalimpong and Yatung).

Permission to access the peaks and passes along the Sikkim-Tibet border has been extremely limited since the start of the Sino-Indian border conflict of 1962. However, you can pick almost any mountain along the Sikkim-Tibet border and find an interesting climbing objective. In September 2004, a strong team organised by the Indian Mountaineering Foundation (IMF) in New Delhi attempted the border peak of Chomoyummo (6829m). The leader was the highly respected and hugely experienced Dr P M Das, a vice president of the IMF, and included experienced instructors from the Sonam Gyatso Mountaineering Institute in Gangtok. The attempt ended in tragedy when Das and four others were killed in an avalanche.

At some stage access to the peaks on the Sikkim-Tibet border will become easier, which could launch a new 'golden age' of first ascents and new routes in this part of the Himalaya. Meanwhile, just away from the border is a ring of peaks that are easier to access, and offer very interesting climbing potential from the valleys of Lachung and Lachen.

Within the border

During World War II, British climbers were able to take leave in the region of Lachung and Lachen, and members of the Himalayan Club, including Trevor Braham, explored the area. It is a fascinating journey up from the steep, forested slopes of the Lachung valley, to reach open plains typical of the Tibetan plateau around Yume Samdong (4624m), and then cross the Sebu La (5352m) down to the open part of the Lachen valley, to then descend back south to steep valleys and forests. Such was the interest in making this journey that the Himalayan Club built huts either side of the Sebu La (both of which are now in ruins).

After 1962, apart from military expeditions, this area was closed. Then in 1976 Harish Kapadia and Zerksis Boga obtained permission to do the Sebu La trek. Twenty years later in 1996, an expedition led by Doug Scott (including Lindsay Griffin, Julian Freeman-Attwood, Skip Novak, Mark Bowen, Paul Crowther, Michael Clark, Col Balwant Sandhu and Suman Dubery) obtained permission for Gurudongmar (6715m) and Chombu (6362m).

Gurudongmar and the other peaks in the Kangchengo group have steep southern aspects; they are approached more easily from the north and have shorter ascents. While returning from the 1936 Everest expedition by crossing the Naku La (5270m), Shipton, Warren, Kempson and Wigram, in less than perfect weather, made what they thought to be the first ascent of Gurudongmar. Having read their account, it seems that they reached the lower west summit of Gurudongmar (6630m), which would make the first ascent of the main peak in 1980 (Assam Rifles led by Norbu Sherpa). However, to confuse matters, some Sikkim mountaineers think of the lower west summit as being the main summit (presumably because it was climbed first) and think of the higher summit as Gurudongmar East.

Chombu is described by Doug Scott as 'the Matterhorn or the Shivling–like peak of Sikkim'. It was explored in the 1940s and 1950s by members of the Himalayan Club. Apparently, there was an attempt in 1961, but according to Harish Kapadia, 'A definite ascent of this peak is yet to be established.'

A large part of Scott's article 'Exploration and Climbs in Northeast Sikkim' (*HJ*, 1997, Vol 53, pp53-66) is about the difficulty, high cost, and

44. Padim (6691m) attracted the attention of early explorers - a 'superb-looking' technical west ridge but a sacred summit. (*Roger Payne*)

uncertainty they experienced in connection with obtaining permission for the peaks. The team members were enterprising in their explorations, in what was then considered a high security area, but somewhat thwarted by bad weather and heavy snow on their efforts to climb Gurudongmar and Chombu. As an indication of how things have changed since 1996, the expedition's base camp at Yume Samdong (4624m) is now a very popular day trip by jeep from Lachung. While on a trip to the area in October 2007, in one day during a public holiday, 93 tourist jeeps and one motorcycle registered with the last police post to drive up to Yume Samdong (or 'Zero Point' as it is usually called locally).

Above Yumtang in the Lachung valley members of SAMA and groups from the Sonam Gyatso Mountaineering Institute have made a number of ascents. In the winter of 2004, the Lachung valley was also the scene of modern icefall climbing. Richard Durnan and friends from Colorado, Canada and Austria climbed many easy-to-access routes up to 180m long and up to WI5 and M5 in difficulty (see *AAJ*, 2004, Vol 46, p384,). As Durnan says: 'There is great potential for further development of ice climbing in this area.'

We first tried to visit North Sikkim in 2006 to attempt Gurudongmar (6715m), but could not get all the necessary clearances. However, in the autumn of 2007 we got permission for Brumkhangshe (5635m), which is one of the two Alpine Peaks in North Sikkim (the other being Lama Wangden (5868m) in the Lachen valley). We had such an enjoyable trip climbing three summits and exploring three glaciers that in autumn 2008 I returned with a larger group.

On both these trips we used a roadside base camp near the police post at

Shiv Mandir (marked as 3905m on the Swiss map 'Sikkim Himalaya'). In 2007, Julie-Ann and I climbed the north ridge of Brumkhangshe and what we called Brumkhangshe North (c5450m). The former is a very good snow climb with some avalanche considerations; the latter is easier angled with a short mixed step. In 2008, our group (Claire and Simon Humphris, Owen Samuel and Tom Midttun) repeated the north summit, and climbed a rocky summit above the glacier, which we called Ta (horse) Peak (c5300m) because to reach the summit required some 'a cheval' technique.

In 2007, Julie-Ann and I explored the Rula Kang glacier and took a close look at Chombu. We found the east face high in objective danger, and the northern aspects under too much 'interesting' snow (the north ridge of Chombu could be a good route in the pre-monsoon season, and the west face may offer an interesting challenge from the Lachen valley). Immediately east of Chombu's north-east ridge is what we called 'Eagle Peak' (c5540), which has a very good mixed south-west ridge and from the summit awesome views of the peaks in the Kangchengyao group. Of the other peaks around the Rula Kang glacier instructors from the Sonam Gyatso Mountaineering Institute have climbed Pheling (c5500m), an easy snow climb that we repeated in 2007. This peak is just south along the ridge from Chombu 'East' (5745m) which Doug Scott and team climbed in 1996 (crux of V with limited protection).

In 2008, we turned our attentions to the western branch of the Rula Kang glacier. Samuel and Midttun made the first ascent of a rocky peak we called Changma (bride) Peak (c5000) just above our camp. Then next day (with C and S Humphris and me) made the first ascent of Marpo (red) Peak (c5400m), which is a shapely peak of red rock to the south east of Chombu.

Into the light

There is a growing realization in India that the considerable potential for adventure travel and mountain tourism is being restrained by outdated regulations and bureaucracy. I hope that the interested organizations and government departments can work together and make better use of the potential for adventure tourism to support sustainable development, to learn from experience and best practice in other regions, and remove unnecessary obstacles to adventure tourism. It will not be easy to achieve this, but there are grounds for optimism.

The future for mountaineering and climbing in Sikkim looks very promising. The State Government has made it easier for foreign visitors to get access to some interesting peaks that are away from the borders. Meanwhile, the border areas are becoming less sensitive, and hopefully in the future tourism and mountain recreation can resume. The tourism service providers in the capital Gangtok are very friendly and reliable, and are being supported by the Ministry of Tourism and the Sikkim Amateur Mountaineering Association. Together, they are expanding their capacity to provide services to international tourists and mountain recreationists, and at the same time promoting sustainable development in mountain

145. Rathong south face and south-west ridge. (*Roger Payne*)

regions. Hence, climbers and mountaineers in Sikkim are developing their skills and knowledge, helping with local guide training, and giving opportunities to young people in Sikkim to enjoy climbing and mountaineering. With limited resources, SAMA has been doing an excellent job.

For so long enveloped in the mists of border tensions and access restrictions, happily, the sublime mountains of Sikkim are now very definitely emerging from those mists, and the future looks bright.

The Alpine Peaks of Sikkim:
West Sikkim: Frey Peak 5830m (Chaunrikiang valley)
Tinchenkang 6010m (Thansing valley)
Jopuno 5936m (Thansing valley)
North Sikkim: Lama Wangden 5868m (Lachen)
Brumkhangse 5635m (Yumthang)

Regulations for the Alpine Peaks are published in the Sikkim Government Gazetteer, No 83, 29 March 2006 (go to **http://sikkim.gov.in/asp/Miscc/sikkim_govtgazettes/GAZ/GAZ2006/gaz2006.pdf** and scroll to page 90).

Reports of Julie-Ann Clyma's and Roger Payne's trips to Sikkim can be found at **www.rogerpayne.info/climbing.htm** (these contain contact details for Sikkim Holidays, Treks and Expeditions and the Sikkim Amateur Mountaineering Association).

Acknowledgements: Clyma and Payne would like to thank all the organisations that supported those trips and helped make them possible, including: The Government of Sikkim, Sikkim Amateur Mountaineering Association, Sikkim Holidays (**www.sikkim-holidays.com**), British Mountaineering Council, Mount Everest Foundation, UK Sport, Beal, Julbo, Lyon Equipment, MACPAC, Petzl Charlet, The Mountain Boot Company.

Selected bibliography:

Bajpai, GS (1999), *China's Shadow over Sikkim*, Lancer Publishers, New Delhi

Chapman, F Spencer (1945), *Memoirs of a Mountaineer*, The Reprint Society, London

Data-Ray, Sunanda K (1984), *Smash and Grab*, Vikas Publishing, New Delhi

Freshfield, Douglas W (1903), *Round Kangchenjunga*, 2000 edition by Pilgrims Book House, New Delhi

Kapadia, Harish (2001), *Across Peaks & Passes in Darjeeling and Sikkim*, Indus Publishing Co, New Delhi

Meyer, K and PD (2005), *In the Shadow of the Himalayas, a Photographic Record by John Claude White 1882-1908*, Mapin Publishing, Ahmedabad

Naoroji, Kekoo (2003), *Himalayan Vignettes, the Garhwal and Sikkim Treks*, Mapin Publishing, Ahmedabad

Pierse, Simon (2005), *Kangchenjunga, Imaging a Himalayan Mountain*, University of Wales, Aberystwyth

Shan, Zheng (2001), *A History of Development of Tibet*, Foreign Language Press, Beijing

Wangchuk, P and Zulca, M (2007), *Khangchendzonga, Sacred Summit*, Little Kingdom, Gangtok

White, J Claude (1909), *Sikhim and Bhutan, Twenty-One Years on the North-east Frontier 1887-1908*, 2005 edition by Pilgrims Book House, New Delhi

Younghusband, Francis (1910), *India & Tibet*, 1998 edition by Book Faith India, New Delhi

146.
Yume Samdong. A sign of changed times. In 1996 Yume Samdong was the base camp for Doug Scott's Sikkim expedition. Today it is popular picnic spot for jeep-borne day-trippers from Lachung. (*Roger Payne*)

EVELIO ECHEVARRÍA

Cordillera Huaytapallana, Peru

When I first saw the name Cordillera Huaytapallana of Peru I was thrilled. In Quichua, *huayta* means 'flowers' and *pallana*, 'the place to collect'. I conjured in my mind a mountaineer's paradise: natural gardens of tropical flowers with a noble background of those fluted ice peaks that are typical of Peru. What more could be desired? I was already acquainted with other paradises of that kind, such as the eastern Andes of Colombia and the Venezuelan Andes. In both, there exists a rich tropical high-altitude flora above which rise fine rock and ice peaks. In anticipation of exploring the mountains of Peru again, I collected together all the photos and maps of the Cordillera Huaytapallana I could find. They enabled me to establish the existence of the white peaks I had imagined; but as for high mountain flower gardens, that was another story…

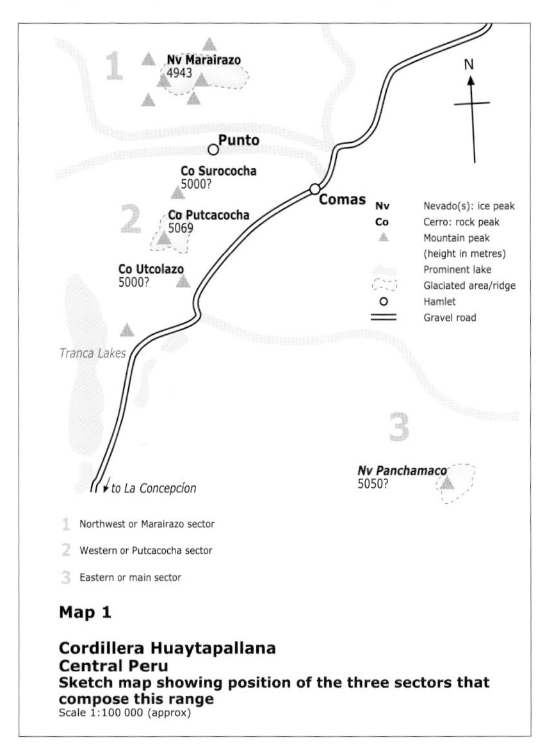

Map 1

Cordillera Huaytapallana
Central Peru
Sketch map showing position of the three sectors that compose this range
Scale 1:100 000 (approx)

148. Cordillera Huaytapallana: south end of the range, with Laguna Carhuacocha. *(Evelio Echevarría)*

At long last, in the Peruvian mountaineering season of 2003 I was able to pay my first visit to several high valleys in the Huaytapallana. I was both surprised and disappointed: no flowers could be seen anywhere. In a few hidden corners of semi-frozen ground, the petals of the tiny 'forget-me-not' could be found. But that was all.

I demanded from local shepherds, well acquainted with their own valleys, an explanation and they gave it to me: on the Day of Santiago (Saint James) shepherdesses roam over the higher valleys to collect any flowers they are able to find to adorn their hats and caps. Hence the very misleading but also very literal, name of Huaytapallana, 'the place to collect flowers'. A part of my dreams collapsed. But there remained the ice peaks.

The Cordillera Huaytapallana of central Peru is purely an ice range. Although it has between 4800m and 5100m peaks of good granite rock, its main characteristic is its display of wholly white peaks, ranging between 4900m and the 5572m of Nevado Huaytapallana (or Lasontay), the highest point in the system. It is a little-known range. Climbers at present do not visit it, and this is partly because there exist no monographs about its mountaineering aspects.

The Cordillera Huaytapallana is located north (and not east, as misleading alpine guides assert) of the Andean city of Huancayo (height, 3271m; population, 310,000). On its north, south and west flanks there are extensive bunch-grass slopes that reach almost to the ice level (4800m). On the eastern side is found what Peruvians call la selva (the jungle). This region is a heavily forested piedmont and is constantly under mist and fog. Mountaineers will not find any access to the Huaytapallana from that flank.

Access

From Lima, at sea level, there is an easy bus ride to Huancayo and from there one can reach the range in any vehicle via a gravel road often in bad condition. The road reaches the 4595m high pass at a crossing called Virgen de las Nieves ('Our Lady of the Snows'). There is a basic restaurant in this place. From it, vehicles can descend south to the towns of la selva or they can head for the upper valleys of the south and west sides of the range, following gravel vehicular roads.

Several Huancayo tour companies transport, mostly at weekends, local hikers to these high valleys, a journey of two to four hours and as many for the return, within the same day (some 18 Euros for a hired vehicle). Thus one can reach large and locally fairly well-known lakes at the head of the valleys: Laguna Lasontay, which yields access to the basin with the highest peaks in the south-west side of the range, and Lagunas Carhuacocha and Cocha Grande, at the southern end, accessible from Virgen de las Nieves. Around the last two, one can repeat what is locally known as la caminata ('the hard

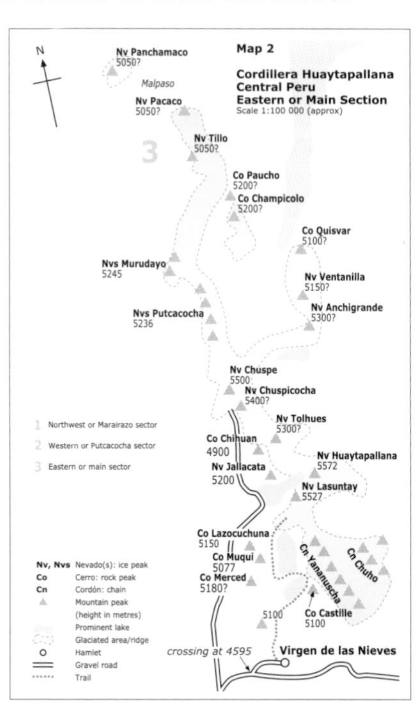

149. Map of Eastern section of Cordillera Huaytapallana, Central Peru. *Redrawn by Gary Haley.*

march'). It goes over a well marked trail all the way to the glaciers above the big lake of Cocha Grande. Hikers usually return to Huancayo the same day, a 16-hour-long effort. The mountaineering season runs from mid-May to early September, the theoretically dry Peruvian winter, and the local climate is usually cold.

The Ice

The Cordillera Huaytapallana is divided into three groups of rock and ice peaks, separated from each other by extensive undulating grass slopes, as well as depressions occupied by hamlets of little importance (see sketch-maps):

Sector 1
North-west or Marairazo sector: 5 ice peaks, 4800m to 4943m, already charted. Unexplored by mountaineers.

Sector 2
Western or Putcacocha sector: 5 ice peaks, 4850m to 5059m, already charted. The German scientist Olaf Hartmann ascended peaks believed to be 5100m high in this area. Incomplete charting.
(Access to these two sectors is by rural bus, Huancayo–La Concepción–Comas.)

Sector 3
Eastern or main sector: some 30 peaks, 4850m to the 5572m of Nevado Huaytapallana or Lasontay, already charted. Approximate length of the glaciated area is 18km, north to south, and some 6km at its widest part. Access to this sector is the easiest in the entire range and offers a number of other heights that do not appear in the Carta Nacional 1:100 000 of the Instituto Geográfico Nacional of Peru.

It is not known what the northern end of this eastern or main sector can offer. Olaf Hartmann described the granitic rock peaks of Runatullo in the ill-charted north end of the Huaytapallana. These are blanks on the map, at least from the point of view of the alpinist.

A scrutiny of the aforementioned Carta Nacional 1:100 000, which is not only the most detailed but also the official map of Peru, shows a total of some 70-80 peaks of importance (4800-5572m) of which some 20 to 25 peaks may already have been climbed, sometimes more than once (and Nevado Huaytapallana or Lasontay, 5572m, the highest, perhaps five or six times). The main unclimbed heights are either the handsome Nevado Chuspicocha (c5400m) or the unnamed 'Peak 5' of the American 1953 report. On the official map of the area there remain numerous peaks north of the big Nevado Chuspe (c5500m), as well as on the corniced ridge of the northern half of the Cordón (chain) Yanauscha (c5300m). Moreover, we do not know what the massifs of Runatullo and Marairazo have to offer, nor the very glaciated massifs of Chuho and Huaracayo (c5300m), east of

150. The main peaks of the west-central section: (left) Nevado Chuspe (c5500m) and (right) unclimbed Nevado Chuspicocha (c5400m). *(Evelio Echevarría)*

the Yanauscha chain, which were pointed out by the American expedition of 1953.

As for new routes, they simply abound. Every mountain peak already ascended will offer several. Furthermore we know nothing about the eastern flank of the range, constantly under clouds, which falls into la selva.

Climbing

This began in 1953, when three Europeans made the first ascent of Nevado Huaytapallana or Lasontay (5572m), highest point in the range (and not the smaller Jallacata, c5200m, as some misleading alpine guidebooks declare). Also in 1953 the ambitious American expedition of Frederick L Dunn took place, which traversed the southern half of the Yanauscha chain (5200m-5315m) and the rocky groups of Merced and Castillo (5100m?). Subsequently, Peruvian parties made some occasional ascents, unfortunately leaving rather vague information about them. Foreign visiting parties have been few. Incidentally, the only British mountaineers to have been active in the Huaytapallana were M Owen and D Porter, members of the 1962 Anglo-Italian expedition which made the first ascent of a peak placed at 5600m and variously called 'Andorno' and 'Lasontay Norte'[1].

It is a pity that the quite accurate national Pre-Carta of 1966 (1:100 000) was not used by all parties that visited this range before the mid-1970s. The heights they quoted were, on average, somewhat too high. Exact figures, at least for eight named peaks, finally appeared in 1983, with the Carta Nacional, 1:100 000.

One mountaineer who left precise and detailed reports of his enterprises was the German geophysicist Olaf Hartmann from Göttingen. Between 1962 and 1970, alone or accompanied, he achieved a number of good exploratory climbs. Furthermore, he was the onwly mountaineer known to have climbed in all three sectors that compose the Huaytapallana.

And briefly, my own experiences in this district: in early June 2003, alone, since no companions or guides could be found in Huancayo, I climbed Cerro Chihuán (4900m), a first ascent, Cerro Lazocuchuna (5150m), an easy ascent, and Cerro Muqui (5077m), a possible first or second ascent (perhaps visited by the 1953 Dunn party). And in late June 2007, in bitterly cold weather, I made a repeat ascent of Cerro Muqui.

Today this range is almost completely forgotten. It seems to have been left to what local entrepreneurs call 'turismo de aventura', which in this case draws its clients from among the people of the city of Huancayo itself.

Baptisms

Since this is a matter of some 40, 50 or more unclimbed and mostly unnamed summits, the task of filling in blanks on the map will fall on visiting mountaineers. New names will have to conform to the rules set by the Instituto Geográfico Nacional of Peru, which are:

- For new names, only the vernacular or regional language may be used or, failing that, Castillan Spanish.
- New names should be either descriptive (eg 'White Tower') or have a local application (eg to an alp, moor, stream, etc).
- New names should not duplicate others already existing in Peruvian toponyms.

I would like to close this brief monograph with two quotations, written in 1953 by Frederick L Dunn, that tell much about the Huaytapallana.

On the top of Cerro Castillo:

... the highest (17,500') and nicest of the rock peaks climbed. We were rewarded with glimpses of several large mixed ice and rock peaks on the rim of another bowl valley. We decided that these peaks of about 18,200' each were Chuoc and Huaracayo. They looked very inviting, but so did numbers of other shadowy shapes rising in ranks beyond them. On no day did we get a clear view of the country to the east[2].

On top of 'peak 6' or Yanauscha:

... This was our highest summit and it was certainly a pleasure, though not very difficult. Yanauscha lake, seen through the swirling mists, was very impressive, but because of the summit cornice we only permitted ourselves the luxury of a view of the far shore of the lake. We looked along the line of peaks between us and Lasontay; we saw a three mile ridge rising at four points to heights considerably higher than 18,000'. There were some notable cornice profiles and some fine flutings. We were not tempted to follow the ridge further to peak 5![3]

Summary: The Cordillera Huaytapallana of central Peru is primarily an ice range. It offers a quantity of first ascents, plenty of new routes, some good rock climbs and also the opportunity to work on much needed mapping of the higher terrain. There is no skiing (the ice is too crevassed), no archæology, fishing or animal life (much less flowers, in this range that is called 'the place to collect flowers'). Locally, there are no resources, guides, porters, pack or saddle animals to be found. Mountaineering in this area is a wholly uncomplicated endeavour. The key is to have a vehicle take you over there, march and start to climb.

Bibliography

Short Reports: The following short mountaineering notes have appeared for the Huaytapallana area:
In *Revista Peruana de Andinismo y Glaciología*:
No 3 (1958), 65. No 5 (1961), 31 and 98-99. No 6 (1963), 51. No 8 (1968), 11 and 126. No 9 (1970), 8. No 10 (1973), 21
In *American Alpine Journal*:
Vol 15 (1966), 172 and 176. Vol 16 (1969), 441. Vol 18 (1971), 405-6

Publications (mountaineering only): Frederick L Dunn, 'Some mountaineering in Peru' in *Harvard Mountaineering Bulletin* 12, 30-44, 1955.
Evelio Echevarría, 'A survey of Andean ascents' in *American Alpine Journal* 36, 176-7, 1962.
Evelio Echevarría, 'A survey of Andean ascents, 1961-1970' in *American Alpine Journal* 87, 376-8, 1973.
Piero Ghiglione, 'Esplorazione del 1953 nelle Ande del sur Peru' in *Rivista Mensile* 73, 82-88, Club Alpino Italiano, 1954.
Arnold Heim, *Wünderland Peru*, 80-87. Bern: Huberverlag, 1948.

Maps
Frederick L Dunn, sketch map of southern end of the range, in op cit, p40
Instituto Geográfico Nacional of Peru, '*Carta Nacional*' 1:100 000, *hoja* (sheet) 24-m, '*Jauja*', 1983.

References:
1. Short note in *Revista Peruana de Andinismo y Glaciología* 6 (1963), 51.
2. Dunn, op cit, 43.
3. Dunn, op cit, 44.

Commentary

151. Simon Pierce, *Above Val Ferret (i),* 2007, watercolour, 15.5 x 20cm *(Alpine Club collection)*

JIM CURRAN

Reflections on K2, 2008

As the editor of the journal put it to me, 'In the silly season of August, two media stories are more or less guaranteed – first, "Exams (GCSEs and 'A' levels) are getting easier"; second, "Climbers die on K2" '. Sometimes Mont Blanc or the Eiger are substituted, but you get the drift.

In 2008 there was a media feeding frenzy as a multiple tragedy played out on K2. It was fed by daily, even hourly news reports from base camp as satellite phones, emails and blogs poured their news and views into cyberspace and were quoted or misquoted worldwide. As a so-called 'expert' on K2, having written a history of the mountain, I had to field phone calls from all over the world. For three weeks the phone rang every day, then (to my relief) stopped as suddenly as it had started as the spotlight moved on to the imminent collapse of civilisation, the American elections, England's cricketers etc.

What to make of all this, as the story slowly unravelled? Twenty two years ago I was at K2 base camp when the last act of a grim season was played out. As the shocking fragments of a hugely complex story emerged I could only send one brief message to the outside world via a Pakistan Army helicopter. On my return to the UK I was horrified by the speculation and ill-informed criticisms that had already been voiced. If modern communications had been around, I can't imagine the confusion that would have ensued. Or rather, I can, because that is exactly what happened in 2008.

Now on the receiving end of the news, I was at pains to point out that the story was still unfolding and it would be quite wrong to speculate, or worse, judge. This, of course, was not what was wanted. I was reminded of a story Brian Hall told me in 1986. Asked what he thought had happened to the seven climbers missing high on K2, he surmised that there might have been a major avalanche or sérac collapse. That night on The News, it was reported that there had indeed been an avalanche. 'Hey, I was right,' thought Brian, before it dawned on him that this was his own reconstructed comment.

K2 in 1986, Everest in 1996, K2 again in 1997 and now another huge disaster – is it inevitable that with ever-increasing commercial expeditions to the 8000 metre peaks that this will continue? Each of the above disasters contained variations on similar themes – fixed ropes not in place, deals done in different languages, broken promises, avalanche, storm etc. But there is one common factor that seems to be to be painfully self-evident: far too many people in the wrong place at the wrong time. On 1 August 2008 on K2 *twenty-two* climbers set out from the Shoulder, all intent on climbing the Bottleneck (how appropriate that name has become). From articles in *The Observer* magazine by Ed Douglas and in *Rock and Ice* by Freddie Wilkinson, which meticulously pieced together the fragmentary stories, there were problems with fixed ropes (which should have been avoidable) and at least two big sérac falls above the Bottleneck (which were unavoidable). Lack of fixed rope caused delays, and when the sérac falls occurred, many were stranded above the Bottleneck with no fixed ropes. It seems that there was a wide spectrum of experiences on the mountain. No 'complete passengers', as have been ferried up Everest, but probably not enough experienced climbers to cope with the events unfolding. Unforgiving old men like me would suggest that to reach the summit of K2 only climbers of vast experience should be there.

Russell Brice, who has led more commercial trips to the north side of Everest than anyone else, has compiled statistics to show that nowadays K2 is easily the most dangerous of the 14 eight thousanders with a jaw-dropping ratio of 20.29% deaths per 294 ascents. Everest now drops to 10th place (4.53%) and Cho Oyu is at 14th with less than one. These numbers do not take into account the 2008 disaster. Talking at length to Russell at the 2008 Kendal Mountain Film Festival, I was impressed at how, on the north side of Everest, he left almost nothing to chance, as his long safety record proves. He made a point of telling me that he left spare ropes at vulnerable places that could quickly replace absent or damaged ones if necessary.

Given the seemingly inevitable growth of expeditions to K2, perhaps the pertinent question is, can there be any way out of an apparent spiralling of disasters stretched away as far as we can see? Some obvious if unlikely solutions are:

Ban all climbing on K2. (This won't happen). Only one expedition a year to the Abruzzi. (This won't happen). Devise time-slots over the summer for each expedition. Hard, if not impossible to police but could ease the traffic jams near the top of the mountain.

Investigate the possibility of avoiding the Bottleneck and the hanging séracs altogether. Unlikely, yes, but remember Fritz Wiessner very nearly did just that in 1939, climbing hard mixed ground almost to the summit snow-slopes. If this could be linked to the 'Basque' route to the left of the Abruzzi (suggested by many to be an easier and safer route), it might be possible to avoid the Bottleneck and the dangerous traverse under the sérac altogether. It would require some selfless effort to climb and fix the upper slopes but surely it is a possibility worth exploring? Although many of us hate these high-altitude *via ferratas*, if you are going to have them, then make sure they do the job properly. It will of course devalue the mountain, but in a way this is already happening. If the death toll on K2 can be reduced then it would be worthwhile.

A final impractical solution is to advise would-be K2 summiteers to be aware of history. Look at the list of those who have failed on K2 and lived to tell the tale. Houston, Bonatti, Scott, Bonington, Whillans, Boardman and Tasker are just a few of the great climbers who have given the mountain best. There is no disgrace in joining their company. Which would you prefer – a reputation for shrewd judgement or your name hammered out on a saucepan lid and hung with all the others at the Gilkey Memorial? Think about it.

ROB COLLISTER

Where Are We Flying To?

I suppose I have always been a traveller. I don't remember much about it but my third birthday was celebrated on the Warwick Castle, of the Union Castle line, during a three-week voyage from Southampton to Mombasa. My father was a teacher in the colonial service working at schools in Kenya, Tanzania and, briefly, Egypt. Over the next 11 years that journey became almost routine for our family, varied only by the need to go round the Cape of Good Hope for a while after the Suez crisis and, on one occasion, to Trieste and across Europe by train. Flying only entered the equation when we were evacuated from Suez at 12 hours' notice, losing everything except what we could carry as hand baggage. We flew from Egypt to Malta in a flying boat and my chief recollection is of being violently sick into a paper bag.

In East Africa there were overnight train journeys from Nairobi to Mombasa and from Dodoma to Dar-es-Salaam, but otherwise travel meant long, hot, dusty car journeys on corrugated dirt roads through the seemingly endless African bush, bare legs sticking sweatily to plastic seats, or the occasional epic mud-bath during the Rains. Later, as a student, my first two climbing trips to the Himalaya in the late sixties both required a gruelling overland drive through eastern Europe, Turkey, Iran and Afghanistan to reach Pakistan. A few years on, after travelling around India by bus and train, my wife, Netti, and I came home overland by public transport, which was unforgettable if arduous. Working for the British Antarctic Survey in the early seventies involved three months on the RRS Bransfield on her maiden voyage making a leisurely progression south before being dropped off for a year 'on the ice'. Travel took time.

It was not until 1973 that a climbing trip to India seemed a feasible proposition by air. Prices had come down and the weight restriction was somehow evaded by buying most of our food locally and wearing big boots and duvets with pockets stuffed with karabiners and pitons, onto the plane. Air travel rapidly became the norm for expeditions to the greater ranges, but travelling to the Alps remained, for me at any rate, a matter of sharing costs in a car or an uncomfortable coach journey – until the easyJet revolution of the nineties. Suddenly, a flight to Geneva was not only ridiculously cheap but skis and climbing gear were carried free (not any more) and flights could be changed for only a small penalty fee. Looking back, it is hard to realize that it is only in the last 15 years that we have come to take cut-price air travel so much for granted. Before that, it was definitely an expensive luxury.

All at once, many of the tensions created by enjoying my job as an alpine guide and yet valuing and often missing wife, family and home, were eased. I could come home more often and Netti could more easily join me for a week or two. For a few years I was making up to six flights to the Alps in a year as well as at least one, sometimes two or even three long-haul flights to more distant destinations. Unfortunately, this satisfactory state of affairs did not last – for me, anyway.

Over the last 10 years it has become increasingly apparent to everyone except George W Bush and his cronies in the oil industry, that global warming is a reality. It has also become clear that of all the elements of our profligate western lifestyle that contribute to global warming, air travel is the least defensible. Flying undoubtedly enhanced my quality of life for a while and, indeed, made my job as a guide possible. But it was having the opposite effect on other people, especially in the poorest parts of the world and sooner or later was going to rebound on us in the affluent west as well. For years, I continued to fly but felt increasingly uneasy about it and limited myself to one long-haul flight a year. I began to investigate trains to the Alps and discovered it was easier than I had expected and not prohibitively expensive, either. By booking well in advance it is possible to travel from North Wales to the Rhone Valley in Switzerland for not much more than £200. While this does not compare with 50p with Ryanair, it does not break the bank, either. The journey time from door to door is about 14 hours, only three or four hours longer than if I flew from Liverpool. After an initial hiccup when I found myself in the suburbs of Paris with 20 minutes to go, I discovered that using the Metro to travel from the Gare du Nord to the Gare du Lyon is not difficult. In fact, it is far quicker as well as far cheaper than taking a taxi.

So far, so good. At least I was doing something towards reducing my carbon footprint. But what about long-haul flights? Was I prepared to give up opportunities to work in the Himalaya or the Andes, Canada or Kenya? Could I call myself an international mountain guide if I never travelled outside Europe, someone asked? And what about my desire for personal adventures and wilderness journeys? Was I ready to give up visiting the sort of genuinely remote, wild places that have been the setting for many of my most memorable moments and profound experiences? My concerns did not seem to resonate much with either colleagues or clients, even though every conversation seemed to lead, sooner or later, to climate change. Responses varied from, 'The world is doomed. We might as well live for the day' and 'It's up to the government to take a lead. Nothing I can do will make any difference' to 'What's the point of Britain acting when the US refuses to budge and China and India are industrializing as fast and as cheaply as they can?' There seemed to be a mass inertia that was self-fulfilling – if nobody else was doing anything, surely it was OK to carry on as we were ...

In the end, I compromised. I decided to forego guiding outside Europe, albeit persuading myself that since Turkey had applied for membership of the EU it must be inside Europe. But I kept the door open for the occasional personal trip. My stance was that China and India would most certainly not move until they see Western governments taking global warming seriously. Those governments, including our own, would make token gestures like subsidising wind farms but do nothing really effective until they see that there is an electoral advantage in it. In a democracy no government will ever disturb the status quo until enough concerned people want it to. In other words, it is up to us as individuals to change our lifestyles before we can expect anything to happen.

When I flew to Vancouver in May 2007, I had not made a long-haul flight for three years and I relished the West Coast wilderness, both on ski and in a sea kayak, all the more for a period of abstinence. In the wider scheme of things, attitudes towards air travel seemed to be changing, if very slowly. Lonely Planet came out with a new slogan 'Fly less, stay longer', which seemed an admirable sentiment, and Eurostar trains were always packed. On the other hand, Climber magazine saw no harm in a series of articles on weekend alpinism and skiing magazines continued to promote heli-skiing *ad nauseam*. On a personal level, however, it seemed to be working out. I had dramatically reduced my air miles yet I could still earn my living as a guide in the Alps and from time to time venture further afield without feeling too guilty.

Then I was offered work in Antarctica and all too easily my resolve weakened. It was 35 years since I had spent an extraordinary and now unrepeatable year with a dog-team on the Antarctic Peninsula and I had come to accept that I would not be returning to the frozen continent. Now, faced with temptation, all my good intentions dissolved. Throwing ethical qualms to the winds, I accepted and took the long series of flights from London to Madrid, to Santiago, down the length of Chile to Punta Arenas and eventually across Drake's Passage and down the Antarctic Peninsula to Patriot Hills on the edge of the Ellsworth Mountains. At 80 degrees it was the furthest south I have been. Although my job was low-key and we made only one short journey away from the base, I loved the clarity of the light, the sense of almost infinite emptiness stretching away and the endless subtleties of colour, texture and shape to be found in a wind-blasted landscape of blue ice and sastrugi. The camaraderie of life on the base took me back to my time with BAS (British Antarctic Survey) and I was impressed by the rigorous environmental policy insisted on by ALE (Antarctic Logistics and Expeditions) to minimize pollution. I was glad to be there – until our departure was delayed by high winds and I found myself reading George Monbiot's *Heat*, a Penguin paperback I had picked up at Euston station.

Monbiot's book is not light reading. It is too detailed and painstakingly researched for that. But it is compelling, nonetheless, and convincing. His basic thesis is that the UK government's self-imposed target of reducing carbon emissions by 50% by 2030 is not nearly enough to keep the level of global warming below the critical 2 degrees threshold; nor is there the faintest chance of even that being achieved as government policies stand at present. He believes our emissions need to be cut by no less than 90% if we are to avoid global catastrophe. The good news is that he also believes, and endeavours to demonstrate, that this is, in fact, achievable, if the political will is there. However, that will is dependent entirely on us, on pressure from the electorate. Only when enough people begin to really change their habits and lifestyles and show that they mean business will the government step in with the legislation to make meaningful change possible on a wider scale – by introducing a carbon rationing system, for instance, by tightening up on building regulations, by radically changing the structure of public transport and by reversing current plans to build 4000 kilometres of new roads and to double the capacity of our airports by 2030. It is actually an optimistic book if, and only if, enough individuals are prepared to change the way they live and set the ball rolling. On the other hand, 'If the biosphere is wrecked it will be done by nice, well-meaning, cosmopolitan people who accept the case for cutting emissions, but who won't change by one iota the way they live.'

Surprisingly, and encouragingly, Monbiot's 90% reduction in carbon can be achieved in most aspects of our lives and most areas of the economy by the creative use of existing materials, techniques and technology. Only when it comes to travel are we going to have to accept drastic change. There is simply no alternative to using our cars less and regarding air travel as, at best, an occasional luxury. 'We might buy eco-friendly washing-up liquid and washable nappies, but we cancel out any carbon savings we might have made ten thousand-fold whenever we step into an aeroplane.' If we do not change the way in which we travel, hundreds of millions will be facing starvation, drought or drowning within our lifetimes – millions are already – our grandchildren will curse us for our folly, and the future not just of the human species but most other species also will be in jeopardy. Monbiot does not pull his punches. But nor do you get the impression that he is exaggerating or scare-mongering. He never relies on a single source or a single set of statistics, usually opts for the more optimistic figures, yet inexorably builds up his case to present us with an irrefutable, if unpalatable truth – we must stop flying. 'It means the end of shopping trips to New York, parties in Ibiza, second homes in Tuscany and, most painfully for me, political meetings in Porto Alegre – unless you believe that these activities are worth the sacrifice of the biosphere and the lives of the poor.' It also means the end of autumn sport-climbing in Sardinia, Mallorca or Greece, wintersports in Canada or the US, trekking holidays in Patagonia or the Himalaya, and expeditions to Greenland or the Antarctic ... Monbiot concludes his chapter on air travel with the words, 'Long distance travel, high speed and the curtailment of climate change are not compatible. If you fly, you destroy other people's lives.'

Lying in my sleeping-bag 10,000 miles away from home, I read that sentence and could only cringe. My absurdly brief visit to Antarctica was clearly nothing but a selfish extravagance I had no right to indulge. It was not as if I was blissfully unaware of the issues: I simply chose to ignore them. I shall not be wearing a hair shirt as penance but I shall definitely not be returning to Antarctica. And if I were to never fly again, would it really be such a hardship? We can reach anywhere in Europe by boat, train or bus and we live in a marvellously varied and still beautiful country that I, for one, have yet to properly explore. As I write, Al Gore, speaking in Bali, has been describing climate change as 'A challenge to our moral imagination'. As outdoor people we are used to accepting a challenge. Will we accept this one? Or, at least, take our collective head out of the sand, acknowledge that there is a global crisis to which we are all contributing, and exercise just a little restraint in planning our deeds of derring-do?

JEFFREY MATHES McCARTHY

A Wild Way of Seeing

The little plane jumps off the dirt strip like a yo-yo on a blue-sky string, and I'm heading into the Brooks Range, Alaska. Airborne is a light, expectant world, with the ropes, the food, and the tents stuffed in the tail. It's expedition time. We're aiming to climb a couple of peaks, and stoked as a Fairbanks furnace to spend three weeks in the range. That's three weeks surrounded by unruly mammals, floating the Hulahula River, exploring rough drainages and climbing unnamed peaks. So this is a climbing trip, yes, but not the usual white knuckles, dawn starts, too scared to take pictures excursion. This one's about wilderness. After all, the Cessna is rattling along above the Arctic National Wildlife Refuge where wolf and grizzly, wolverine and caribou have danced the same dance for ten thousand generations. You've probably heard that the great threat to the Refuge is the oil *under* all these beings, and while our trip is organized around mountains, down deep it expresses a desire to witness this wild threatened place.

In flight, the Refuge's grand tapestry unfolds beneath me and on south past the horizon. Russets and tans, reds and ochres, a weave of lichen and watercourse, alder and rain, sustaining the Porcupine caribou herd and the other birds, fish and beasts that live here. Beyond are the mountains, insisting on attention to serrated summits and shining glaciers – bleak and nameless and mesmerizing as any flame to a moth like me. From that glorious perspective the plan to develop this landscape – to drill for money – seems a singular insanity.

But, the bug in my eco-sensitivity soup is oil dependence. We all use oil. I took a taxi, a rental car, and three airplanes to get to this fourth airplane full of synthetic climbing gear and white gas ... and now I'm protesting the oil companies' greed. Can you be a climber and an environmentalist? That's the opening question I chew. I recognize the paradox as our plane startles a fox, then rouses a blizzard of snow geese. Would we do better just to stay home? Or is there something worthy about these wilderness voyages ... some way to forge a sharp, green identity from the raw material of our urban selves?

But first, are you bored with Nature Talk? The familiar admonitions about stewardship and consciousness and sustainability have begun to make us all drowsy. Thus when I say 'environmentalist' your eyes start skimming forward because you presume I'm en route to some high ground of moral fervour. But wait; this isn't preaching and hectoring from some finger-wagging vegetarian. This isn't even the usual rhetoric of Green good intentions; that is vague, just where I want to be specific. I've thrown beer bottles, trod the desert's cryptobiotic dirt, killed animals and eaten them –

52. 'This is where the mountains live.' Aerial view somewhere over the Alaska Range. (*Colin Monteath / Mountain Camera Picture Library*)

not proud of it, but there's no green halo over my desk. I am, in sum, your basic modern man, but in my basic modern life of consuming and wasting there runs, I think, a surprising thread of environmental redemption. You see, for the last two decades, what I've mostly done is climbed, and I'm starting to believe it's climbing that has made me care about the natural world.

Until lately I've experienced climbing as un-political, engaged only with weather and stone and the occasional landowner's fence. But when I think about it, climbers have been in the middle of environmental battles for a long time. In fact, you could say that North America's leading climbers have been motivated by ecological causes for more than a century, and that far from being apolitical, climbing has a powerful environmental heritage. Consider John Muir, David Brower, Yvon Chouinard and even Henry David Thoreau – they went to the mountains, and then they devoted themselves to environmental causes. Look at it, Thoreau and Muir invented what we know as environmentalism, Brower created modern environmental action and Chouinard shaped the prototype for the green corporation. All this from climbers.

So back to arctic adventure. Once the plane stopped bouncing in sickening gusts, and left us by the Hulahula, we were climbers in a wilderness. No guidebooks, no other parties, no support beyond the gear we could float on the river or carry on our backs. That's a pretty pure relationship, isn't it? I've always defined my own environmentalism by my presence in the wild. I care about wild nature and I demonstrate that with regular journeys to wilderness. The landscape of activism and petitions and board meetings is a nice place to visit, but I've never wanted to live there. So there I was in the cold wind with gathering clouds, a silty river, grizzly tracks and a big smile.

On the tundra I had a place to survey the wild and draw some conclusions about mountain climbing and environmentalism. It's easy for me to love Nature with a capital 'N' when it's a splitter granite crack or a view over my fruity drink. That loving gets harder when it's a grizzly that just might shred my tent, or a crevasse that swallows someone attached to me. But that same stress makes some climbers emerge from the mountains as serious environmentalists. Wilderness climbing is surely about paying close attention to the rock or the ice or the scree, and in that attention we internalise some lens that reshapes our perceptions afterwards. In contrast, a trip to the local crag is too easy. I have come to believe that intense experience in wild land reorganizes our brains. Wild climbing, then, gives us a wild way of seeing.

The upper river was shallow and cold. 'Shallow' as in jump out and drag the raft over braid after gravel braid, and 'cold' as in lose feeling in your fingers from the splashing, and cringe when feeling came and went to frosted toes in rubber boots. We dragged as much as floated those first days, but every frothing corner brought us deeper water until the dominant feeling was momentum. My eyes lifted from reading the river and all around was the green brown tartan of the country. Antlers on the bank, birds rising from the eddies, and twice a flash of fur where a wolf or a fox ducked to cover. At first brush, this arctic river seems a lonely spot. Named a century ago by Hawaiian whalers, the Hulahula winds through the biggest, wildest stretch of country on the continent. No sign of human visitors, no planes overhead, not even a cairn or a trail. The paths here are made by caribou, and then by the predators who pursue the caribou, and then by the scavengers who follow the predators. That blood balance makes brushstrokes against the canvas of water moving, willow thriving, and wind-packed snow. Soon, though, the big country welcomes you, and in the river's splash and rattle, and in the breeze's nipping chill, some kind of home is readied for the dodging, wheedling mind.

It's day four, and I'm following a game trail that contours up big hills. Finally I'm away from the river sound, that sandpaper white noise that shapes your days and scratches even your dreams. Behind me come three other backpacks, dark rectangles against the green-brown land and the grey shoelace of river. There's some rain from drooping mist, and the mosquitoes are inspired by our visit. This day matches terrain to map, and delivers a tidy pass that transfers our damp selves from broad river drainage to tight glacial valley. This is where the mountains live.

When you walk on a glacier, think good thoughts. It's a turnpike of ice, and you can follow it to many exits. But it's also a breathing thing, marching downhill, carrying stones in its bosom, birthing creeks in its

153. '...a time of absorption in organic patterns carved by the river and by glacial ice...' Denali National Park, view from Polychrome Overlook on the trail to Wonder Lake. (*Dick Sale / Mountain Camera Picture Library*)

loins. Little wonder medieval Europeans sketched glaciers as dangerous dragons. They can for sure reach out and take the unlucky with them. So think good thoughts for the glacier gods, and they'll steer you away from sérac teeth and deliver you across flimsy snowbridges that cover the deep blue jaws of crevasses.

The Esetuk Glacier greets visitors with rubble, a grey tongue of stones atop even greyer silt. The bullet-hard ground sparked our crampons and lead us on towards pure blue ice. Here it was all water runnels. Glaciers everywhere follow this pattern and I'm fascinated by this intermediate realm where live water flows across frozen water. The forces in play boggle me, as tons of glacier creak along millimetre by millimetre while bright splashes dance downhill or, in the warmer hours, roaring torrents firehose trenches wider than any sidewalk, then plunge into the glacier's darkness. Those holes rumble and sigh.

After the realm of polished ice and running water we reached snow. The Esetuk broadened, turned pillowy and white, and the road before us undulated into a tumbled snow-mass, taut with black cracks. We walked south, backs to the Arctic Ocean, faces to the peaks. This morning was blue sky clear, so the view sparkled from boots to summits. We snaked towards the middle of the glacier, two rope teams, ice-axes squeaking, and wound steadily upwards, one foot then the next, feeling for dead spots under snowbridges, listening for different tones to our footsteps, watching for the hollow that indicates a hole. A few clouds gathered in the north, conspirators in dark cloth. I hurried now, impatient with the thought of weather denying the summit. This mountain hurry is a subtle thing, barely obvious from the outside, but inside me the breath comes faster, the pack chafes, the snow grabs the boots.

Then it was afternoon. Clouds jostled in a sky gone grey. The glacier steepened and took a moody colouring. A headwall to climb. Here at the base the Esetuk compressed, and bunched its skirt into pleats and folds. Pecking along through complex terrain I zigged across hollow bridges and zagged over gaps. The wind came up. In flat light I misread a fold in front of me, and there came the ill portent of darkness beneath a step where white snow had been.

Gravity. . . crevasse. . . falling is a lonely country – there's no one else there, and you don't speak the language. Thump went my heart, thump went the snow around me, and what had been white was black. I was dropping through and moving forward in the air, and beneath my boots was all space, but my forward motion carried my hip onto snow that itself collapsed but sustained me for a moment, and I felt myself surfing an unwelcome wave. Here was slow-motion crumbling, and my pack lodged briefly to my left, and my right crampon points met solid snow in front, and my whole tumbling, levitating, Mr Magoo self teetered there in space – ice crystals spinning into blue depths, a breath of deep cold from below, bag pulling sideways, some rope, and my axe ever hopeful in reaching – and then momentum, pick into far snow, and a new balance stomached onto

154. 'Beyond are the mountains, insisting attention...' Chugach Range, Alaska. (*Doug Mathews / Mountain Camera Picture Library*)

firm ground.

Tugak Peak means 'Walrus Tusk' and we climbed it in the building wind. The clouds had sailed onto us to become a regatta of shifting winds and hail. This was not the first ascent I'd hoped for, but it was a powerful experience in the sky. The north ridge was a bright ribbon against a dark coat of clouds, and it stitched us in three long pitches to the jumbled stones of the summit blocks. A short rope-length to go. Awkward stones frozen in improbable postures above a great space, and then the top. No more up, but big views of unnamed peaks in unlikely drainages. We four huddled into quick photos, and a soft broom of snow whisked at us, urging us down.

On some trips the summit is the point. You take a steep line to the top of Mount Washington or the Grand or even El Cap and you pause at the peak ... until, with the first step down, thoughts swing to hot meals, to music, to the soft furniture of civilized life. My thoughts do anyway. Maybe yours are more reflective. But wilderness trips are different. There's a thrill beyond the summit and beyond the technical challenges that usually engage me. These trips cast me back to an era when the summit was just one part of a longer journey that included trail-breaking and navigation, other carnivores, uncertain passes and a suspense that animated those approaches like ghosts in the woodwork. Ghosts don't come out for cairned paths or National Park trails. Here in the Brooks Range I was engrossed in that thrill, and by charting uncertain ways over untracked terrain I was exploring the haunted house itself.

How is this way of seeing particularly *wild*? Well, in wilderness I experience the world differently than when I'm climbing at Smith Rock or Little Cottonwood. The difference isn't in the motions I make, or the heights I feel, it's in the texture of my perception.

Texture? What does that mean?

It means that climbing at the crag is like being in the city for me because my mind is occupied with a route's name, its grade and who is waiting to get on it next. It means my experience is formed by other people's ideas. Alternatively, in wilderness I'm not comparing my efforts to the description in the guide, or the person who just bled all over the crimpers. I'm just climbing and everything's on, and I'm tuned to all the input of stone and shade and snow. That broad awareness makes the natural world somehow denser, less a field for human titillation, and much more its own tightly woven soul.

John Muir wrote of mountaineering as a way to fuller living.

'Climb the mountains and get their good tidings. Nature's peace will flow into you as sunshine flows into trees. The winds will blow their own freshness into you, and the storms their energy, while cares will drop off like Autumn leaves.'

For Muir, being in the mountains affirms the best parts of being human, and any weather is good for climbing because climbing is about wildness itself, not just summits. Having said all that, I'm not sure freshness blew into us on the long descent from Tugak Peak, and I know cares didn't 'drop off' when we had to wade the swollen creek to get back to dinner. But, there was a pulse of energy throughout because the adventure wasn't done, the climb hadn't ended anything. We were still two days from our raft and deep in the process of living in a landscape and following its script of wind and cloudburst, trail and flow. That extended immersion gave us the mountains' good tidings, and opened us to the language of wilderness.

Our high camp gave us remarkable views north to the Arctic Ocean and its quilt of bright white pack ice. Beyond sight to the west squatted Prudhoe Bay and the massive thrumming installation there pumping oil – beyond sight, but very much in the picture, given the oil companies' plan to drill this same view. Drilling in this Arctic National Wildlife Refuge reenacts the formative tension in American environmental history between those who see wilderness as a resource to develop, and those who see wilderness as an inherent good with no need to pay its way in pieces of silver. It's a conflict as familiar as bears and dogs.

This archetypal American struggle can be summed up as Conservation versus Preservation and appeared in the 1890s when the United States began to designate the exact places we climb today as National Parks or Forest Reserves. Interestingly, it was the storm of conflict over use in these new areas that John Muir's power as an environmentalist first sailed. Muir came back from the mountains with the message that they were holy places, and that wilds like Yosemite and Hetch Hetchy were vulnerable realms to be defended for the sake of humanity's spiritual and physical well-being.

And these places do feel holy, like temples or cathedrals, but I notice my devotions are always accompanied by industrial products that are probably polluting some one else's sacred spot. There are two gallons of gas in camp, and if I lose them in a rapid, or they leak back into these grey stones I'd better hope caribou crap burns. So, I ask the breeze, is a climber automatically a conservationist, or is there something that prods me to preservation?

Here in the Refuge, the Preservationist stance is that caribou and wilderness are more important to the national health than oil. The oil companies respond that oil-rigs can stand beside happy caribou, and so they restate the Conservationist ethic that champions the 'wise-use' of resources for a country that needs the material, the jobs, the money. Preservationists from John Muir on reject these utilitarian values and advocate a natural world unaltered by humanity. Conservationists from Gifford Pinchot in the 1890s to the Forest Service today say Preservation is unrealistic and unsustainable in modern life.

That Arctic wind told me which side I'm on – there's some sternness about mountain experience, some rectitude of gravity and stone that sculpts a person into an effective representative for the environment. That's a pretty bold thesis, and there are a lot of us who never get deeper than our bumper stickers. That's why it's transformative for me to take a wilderness climbing trip – not Yosemite or Red Rocks, but deep wilderness. Out here I live Preservation. In this wild drainage the climb is more than a series of super-topo'd moves; it's the assembly of a thousand and one perceptions about landscape, weather, animals and ice. Somehow that broader net of interpretation brings me closer to Muir in both experience and attitude. So even though I'm burning gas to get there, being immersed in wilderness is my ticket to environmentalism.

Twenty days of wild country is a very good dose. All the forms are curved, all the colours blend, and the eye rests for days on only things that grow. It is this wildness that saves climbing from hypocrisy. Yes, we use the same oil we protest, and yes we admire the same wild we're busy using. But these lonely ridges and these untrodden glaciers occasion a new way of knowing the self – that frail dynamo at the heart of our world's environmental problems and environmental solutions. This is not Nature Talk in shibboleths or platitudes; this wild way of seeing is the means to a fuller identity acknowledging both human needs and natural limitations. In wilderness climbing the body encounters a world simultaneously beyond its control and hauntingly familiar. At the same time, the senses adapt into a context shaped solely by natural forces. What wilderness means for the body is a new – I might say dialectical – experience of the natural world as both independent of and unified with human being. What wilderness means for the mind is knowing itself as part of pervasive natural patterns, and not as a separate thought-box outside of nature. It's like learning some principle by experience instead of rote, knowing the golden mean from the pattern of seeds on a sunflower instead of learning it for a geometry quiz – where the first is alive, the second is an abstraction.

Galen Rowell wrote: 'At the heart of the climbing experience is a constant state of optimistic expectation.' I felt that optimism on the lichen-painted tundra, and I know it's recognizable too in the uncertain joy of new routes. David Brower made sure his environmental message was a positive one: 'If you are against a dam, you are for a river.' And maybe that optimism is the complement to a climber's grit that makes someone like Muir or Brower, or Chouinard a powerful force – even against the big walls of a society fixed in its views. So, I've decided we climbers are no more hypocritical about the environment than the next person, we're just better equipped to see there's another way. We can campaign and we can sign and we can participate, and all of it will be energized by not only what we've seen but by how we've seen it.

My group floated the Hulahula through spray and ice, across gravel and into rock walls, over wave trains and under clouds, then made camp by a tundra landing strip marked by caribou antlers. There the mosquitoes were glad to see us, and I found myself stemming between this world of alder and bear and caribou, and the sound of the plane with its promise of beer and news and cotton clothes.

If you've arranged bush planes you know that *schedule* means they'll get you when they get you. So better than sitting and waiting, I decided to head up the last sizeable peak before the Beaufort Sea. I wanted to travel light so I left camp with a litre of water and two trekking poles for what turned out to be a 4,000-foot jog. Nothing remarkable to report about the climbing – hardly Steve House on Nanga Parbat – but a shaping episode to conclude this arctic voyage.

The tundra was boggy, and balancing twixt topsy tussocks gave way to splashing in bug spawning pools … steadily upwards. The insects motivated a good pace and after an hour the tents looked like bright aspirin tabs against a green cloth. All around me was tundra lichen and puddles, a Pollock painting of bear sign and caribou antlers mingled with wolf tracks and sheep pellets and the honking of birds.

One ear I kept always open for a plane's whine.

Before much longer my stomach growled, and that reminded me of bears, so I sang out, breathing hard, attending to the wind, the smells that came my way, and the chatter of little birds. Solo trips in bear country are about as smart as nose-bleeds in shark pools, but I needed some altitude. Soon enough I was on rock and scrambling past mountain sheep trails to jump a craggy ridge which I climbed to the tippy-top. Not a fifth-class move on the whole thing, but the wild thrill was my companion since that setting demanded attention. Do you see? This solo scramble in the big wild was intense for me because climbing's fascination is the engulfing process, the loss of self to the necessity of grip and balance and hope.

We flew out the next night. Rolling above the Hulahula I saw birds beyond number wheel and glide south in a staggered vee of shaping wings. The flock's form above our starboard wing told me I was leaving the kingdom of natural designs for the realm of hard-angled, manufactured shapes. It struck me then that a short season in the Arctic was a time of

155. Jeff McCarthy – 'a silty river...a big smile'. (*McCarthy coll.*)

absorption in organic patterns carved by the river and by glacial ice, as well as wind and paws and wings. Maybe as climbers we go back to the peaks to make the same motions and feel the same fear because their organic forms hold us, renew us, then send us back into the manufactured world calmed and even determined that industry's patterns are not the only choice.

That experience of self-in-other becomes a wild way of seeing. For Wordsworth nature is restorative. His Romantic nature is the 'benign' place where we retreat when 'from our better selves we have too long been parted'. Fair enough, but I think I've encountered a different dynamic through wild trips through wild places. In a rough corner of the Arctic I could balance just fine, but I was pushed to immerse myself in the land's language of grizzlies, of bogs, and of mosquito hordes. That's the point. Deep attention is the payoff for climbers, and may well be the way of seeing we all take back to this world of cars and bills and bosses. Does it make us ready to be environmentalists like Rowell and Chouinard and Muir and Brower? Maybe not in a direct, slip on a banana peel way, but that attention sure brings me back to this world with a better eye for its subtleties, and a louder voice for its preservation.

Science

156. Simon Pierse, *Beca di Monciair from Rifugio Vittorio Emanuele II*, 2006, watercolour, 42 x 59cm

BRIAN CUMMINS

Measuring Intracranial Pressure in The Himalaya

A 20-year old paper by Brian Cummins introduced by Jim Milledge

In September 1992, when revising our textbook, High Altitude Medicine and Physiology (Ward, Milledge & West) for its second edition, I heard about an extraordinary study carried out by Brian Cummins, a neuro-surgeon working in Bristol. I got in touch with him and briefly discussed the study and the 1985 expedition to Hagshu peak (6330m) in Garhwal (below) on which it was done. He faxed me an article he had written about it but never published. From this I extracted the salient results and mentioned them in the relevant chapter of our textbook as a 'personal communication'. He never published the article or any other about the study except for an abstract presented at a conference of the 8th European Congress of Neurosurgery. Brian retired from the NHS and died in 2003.[1]

I have also briefly discussed the expedition with its leader, Mike Rosser, an AC member, and he believes the article was intended for the AJ. The fax which Brian sent to me is now fading so I made a transcript of it before it was lost forever. I thought that AJ readers should have a chance of learning about this bold piece of high altitude medical research. It has not and never will be repeated, since nowadays ethical committees would not allow such a study. His style, as you can see from the very first paragraph below, is also charmingly free of pomposity and jargon. ***JM***

When you ask a middle-aged neurosurgeon, lazing fatly on a Gower beach watching the more energetic members of the Mountain Rescue team shin up three cliffs or fall off windsurfers, if he wants to come to India next year as medical officer of a HIMALAYAN EXPEDITION, the only answer you deserve is 'yes'. Romance courses through tortuous arteries as briskly as in the elastic days of youth. The trouble is, the silly beggar may want to 'do something', in order to justify his existence. In our case, it was holes in the head.

The purpose of the investigation was serious enough, even if its execution had its light-hearted moments. Acute mountain sickness (AMS) has been the complaint of high altitude travellers since the Spaniards colonized the Andes, and a Jesuit priest thought of casting up his soul in the thin air. Ravenhill noted in 1913 that PUNA (one of the South American terms for AMS) caused headache, unwellness, fatigue and vomiting, which usually settled down but could sometimes cause death, in coma or from acute congestion of the lungs. It was apparent to the early mountaineers that being young and fit did not protect you. Whymper on Chimborazo at 16,664ft

157.
Hagshu Peak (6330m) in the Garhwal Himalaya, the objective of the 1985 expedition led by Mike Rosser.

suffered badly with the two Carrels, while 'strange to relate Mr Perring did not seem to be affected at all'. Mr Perring was 'a rather debilitated man and distinctly less robust than ourselves. He could scarcely walk on the flat road without desiring to sit down.' The despised individual looked after the heroes until they were better.

In 1985, Ross, in the *Lancet* [1985 I p990-1], postulated that the reason that the young and fit were frequently stricken by AMS was the tight fit of their brains into their skulls. The brain is moored in its own cerebrospinal fluid snugly within the skull and has cavities inside (the cerebral ventricles) which act as reservoirs. These ventricles may be of different sizes in individuals, commonly being smaller in the young. The only way out is through a hole at the bottom of the skull, the foramen magnum. If the brain swells, the cerebrospinal fluid is squeezed out until there is no more left and then the pressure in the skull (intracranial pressure, ICP) rises. If it rises close to the arterial pressure, no blood flows through the brain and you die, in coma.

The brain may swell at high altitude because it lacks oxygen. This causes the cells to swell (cerebral oedema) and the cerebral blood vessel to expand in an attempt to increase flow of blood, simply adding to the volume packed into the constricted space of the skull.

In general the younger you are, the tighter the brain fits into the skull; the older you are, the more the brain has lost its cells, the bigger the ventricles and the more CSF there is to bathe it. Individuals vary widely and it is impossible by simple clinical examination to decide the volume of CSF available.

The computerized axial tomographic scan (CT scan) can tell the snugness of fit of the brain to any individual's skull. I felt that this technique might be a way of studying susceptibility to AMS.

Method of investigation

Each of our party had a CT scan before setting off. This was reported by a consultant radiologist and the films put into the safe keeping of Dr Charles Clarke. In ignorance of the results of the CT scans, Margaret Coldsborough, an experienced nurse, conducted a daily interview and symptoms were scored for each member of the expedition. When Margaret left with the trekking party, I conducted the interview, often in retrospect when the climbers came down to advanced base camp at 15,500ft. This interview was structured into the symptoms Fletcher and colleagues suggested in 1985 *Quarterly Journal of Medicine*, 93-100, and accompanied by self-assessment forms scoring the same complaints.

Thus, each day, each climber had to fill in and to confess to whether he was unwell, fatigued, lacked appetite, had headache, was unsteady, and had either irregular or difficulty in breathing. The score was rated 0-3 for each symptom, 0 being 'no problem', 1 'not troubled', 2 'Makes life miserable' and 3 'stops you doing what you want to do'.

This method proved effective, the interview and self-assessments matching well.

Measurement of intracranial pressure (ICP)

Early in 1985 a telemetric button to measure the pressure within the skull became available. This meant that a battery-operated sensor could detect the ICP by a radio signal generated in a coil within the skull. All that was needed was a little hole in the skull, so that the button could rest on the membrane lining it. The pressure could then be measured in any position of the head.

I had already been worried about Duncan, since he had had a head injury that required a shunt to siphon CSF away from the brain. I thought he might have problems at altitude if there was no CSF reserve. Consequently I suggested this technique as a safety device and since I was interested in the physiology, I wanted one too. Mike Rosser, the leader, a completely 'normal' man volunteered himself. In the event, Duncan's monitor proved very useful.

The operation was very simple. I had mine put in the week before the others to make sure it was innocuous. My senior colleague, Huw Griffith, at my behest, drilled the hole, placed the button under local anaesthetic. I was surprised how noisy and how completely painless it was. An hour after

158. Brian Cummins measuring the intracranial pressure measured on a fellow expedition member in the field.

the insertion of the button I was conducting my routine outpatients session. British patients being what they are, none raised an eyebrow at the shaven head and fresh dressing applied to their doctor.

The other two monitors I put in myself. Anxious enquiry by phone the following day revealed that one patient was teaching gymnastics while the other was halfway up a cliff.

At the turn of the century, Alberto [Angelo] Mosso in his *Life in The High Alps* lamented, 'It was my wish to find some one with a hole in his skull who would have been willing to come with me on the Monte Rosa expedition but I was not successful in my search.' We had three.

The general health of the expedition was good once the polluted waters of the lowland had been left behind. The trekkers took home with them one unfortunate climber who had drunk not wisely but too well, and who had contracted very severe fever with diarrhoea which responded just in time to massive doses of metronidazole. Above base camp at 12,000ft we contended with little except altitude and lack of good food. One climber suffered very severely from prolapsed piles brought about by diarrhoea, which played havoc with his otherwise imperturbable self-assessment and interview scores. His stoicism was bent a little by my digital replacement of the fallen parts, reminiscent in fact of the poor King Edward being put to death in Berkeley Castle, whose cries could be heard across the Severn. Within three days he was back on his feet and climbing with the best.

Complaint scoring related to CT scan

Our scoring system began with our walk in from Golhar at 5,900ft. There were few symptoms referable to altitude until we reached base camp at 12,000ft, by which time the trekking party had left. At base camp, the party of 11 consisted of seven climbers, three base camp supporters and the Indian Liaison Officer, who had not had a scan. Baggage to base camp was by mule, and after by backpack, the doctor and his 16-year old son earning their keep by portering while the only woman, Jo, became an expert chapatti maker as well as carrying as heavy loads uphill as the rest. There were days when the party was split, and the three supporters reached no higher than 16,500ft where the highest ICP measurements were made on a glacier. Each individual filled in his complaints scores daily, and the interview scores were completed as soon as possible.

It soon became apparent that one climber was affected by altitude far more than the rest, and at low altitudes. He had had problems on a previous expedition to the Himalaya, and now suffered badly with each gain in height, so that in the end I gave him Diamox, which eased his discomfort considerably. Two others were severely affected by the combination of rapid height gain and load carrying, which did not affect the rest so adversely, although no one was entirely without symptoms.

On return, it was possible to sum the complaints score for four weeks and to compare the results with the radiologist's report of the brain scan [Table 1].

These results support the postulate of Ross, that the tightness of fit of the brain into the skull is an individual phenomenon and determines the susceptibility of the individual to acute mountain sickness.

Table 1.
Results of CT scans, size of cerebral ventricles, and AMS scores.

*Base camp supporters – not above 16,500ft.

**Results weighted by 3 days severe diarrhoea and pile prolapse.

Subject	Age Years	AMS Score Total	Headache Unsteady Score	Cerebral ventricles Size
I.M.	29	99	20	very small
S.C.*	16	49	19	very small
D.M.	28	48	10	small shunt
A.S.	35	**36	0	large normal
M.R.	31	24	5	normal
J.J.	28	25	1	normal
B.C.*	52	16	3	large normal
S.T.	28	15	3	normal
S.R.	21	13	1	normal
J.C.*	28	10	3	normal

Measuring the ICP

After conference with expert colleagues, I decided that the intracranial pressure should be recorded at rest and in the standardized conditions of increasing stress to the system, at each session. Daily, from the beginning of the walk in to the end of the climb, as well as in Delhi and Bristol, ICP was recorded in the three subjects, except when they had climbed higher than I could take the recording instrument.

1. Lying horizontal
   - i) head straight
   - ii) head turned to right
   - iii) head turned to left
2. Body tilted
   - i) up 30 degrees
   - ii) down 30 degrees
3. Lying horizontal
   - i) breath held 40 seconds
   - ii) over breathing 30 seconds
4. Sustained press-up 30 seconds, with breath held terminal 15 seconds.

The pulse rate was recorded at the beginning and end of each session by digital pulse meter. Although this was easy enough at sea level (in Delhi we had done it with handstands) above 12,000ft breath holding for 40 seconds began a test of will, while the press-up was less stressful. Finding 30-degree slopes was no problem, although anchoring the subject to the rock or ice occasionally produced hilarious tangles of man and machine.

We took 776 separate recordings of the ICP, in varying climate and at altitudes up to 16,500 ft. The physiological stresses caused the expected rise and fall in pressures.

At sea level, we were all well within normal limits. Resting level of ICP in mmHg.

Altitude	<15,500 ft	> 15,000ft
M.R.	9.5 +- 3	14.0 +- 2.5
D.M.	9.0 +- 4	9.0 +- 3
B.C.	7.0 +- 3	6.5 +- 3

Table 2 Results of ICP measurements (mmHg) in the three subjects above and below 15,500ft.

At advanced base camp and above 15,500ft Mike's ICP rose to the upper limits of normal (15mmHg) and his stress tests showed more excursion of the values, but were not excessive. My own atrophic brain placidly accepted heights with no change from sea level.

Duncan however, reacted differently. It appeared that his shunt might keep the pressure stable until a certain point when possibly the ventricles were collapsed. Having climbed very hard with a heavy load, he was marooned with two others on a small ledge at 18,800ft for 36 hours. When he came down to camp at 15,500ft, he was exhausted and unsteady on his feet. His resting pressure was 14 mmHg but simply turning his head to either side raised this to 24 mmHg and the press up to 38 mmHg. His resting pulse was 104 and rose to 152 at the press-up. I did not need the ICP monitor to tell me that he was in trouble, but there is little doubt that it confirmed my judgement that he was suffering from altitude sickness compounded by the swelling in the brain. Sorrowfully, and against his protests I took him down to 12,000ft where in base camp within a day he recovered and his ICP returned to normal.

In the end, as it often does, the mountain won, but we learned a lot and I at least had the craven consolation that I had brought all my friends home alive.

159. Brian Cummins having his intracranial pressure measured while doing press-ups.

Comment by Jim Milledge

Although it is 24 years since Brian carried out this study, we still do not know for certain that the symptoms of AMS are due to raised intracranial pressure (ICP) though that seems the most likely explanation. We have no accepted, non-invasive, method of measuring ICP, although a number of indirect methods have been suggested and tried. Not surprisingly, Brian's study was short of numbers of subjects, which is why he felt he could not publish in the medical press. However, his results are in keeping with the hypothesis that oxygen lack at altitude, results in brain oedema, swelling. In people with small cerebral ventricles and therefore small volumes of cerebro-spinal fluid, this causes a rise in pressure within the skull. In those with larger ventricles, smaller brain volumes, the same degree of swelling results in less pressure rise. The rise in pressure causes the well-known symptoms of AMS: headache, nausea and vomiting.

I am grateful to Mike Rosser and Ann Cummins for permission to use their photos and to Mark Wilson for helpful suggestions and gathering the photos. A paper has been published by Mark, based on Brian's work, for the medical scientific press. Wilson, M. H. and Milledge, J.S. (2008). Neurosurgery 63, *970-975*

1. Brian Cummins died on 16 August 2003. *British Medical Journal* obituary at **www.bmj.com/cgi/content/full/327/7422/1053-a**)

Arts

160.Simon Pierse, *Smile of The Buddha*, 1997, watercolour, 53.5 x 58.5cm

SIMON PIERSE

Out of Thin Air

On painting Ladakh
(. . .and three poems by John Gimblett)

The journey to Ladakh is not to be undertaken lightly: by road it is a long and arduous journey across the Himalaya, either from Srinagar, or now more commonly from Manali in Himachal Pradesh. Either way it takes about three days, a trek over some of the highest road passes in the world. By air it is a short hop from Delhi to Leh, but even then there is no certainty of arriving. Pilots have to fly by sight, since radar is rendered useless in the mountain passes; and due to poor visibility, planes are sometimes forced to turn around and return without landing at their destination. My first flight to Leh was cancelled due to bad weather conditions and it was four days later before I finally arrived, and then only after intervention from a local travel agent that facilitated my way onto an overbooked flight from Srinagar. During the short time we were air-borne, K2 was briefly visible through the window, its summit poking above the clouds. As we came in to land, the plane circled, lurched alarmingly, and finally touched down on a steeply sloping runway – a small sliver of land between mountainous valley sides. I knew instantly that I had come to a very special place: a remote land in the rain-shadow of the Himalaya, politically part of India but geographically part of the Tibetan plateau – a place literally beyond the mountains and the clouds. What immediately struck me as I stepped off the plane were the sharp clear light and the intense cobalt blue of the sky, both due to the high altitude and thin air (Leh is 3500m above sea level). No doubt altitude was also behind the heady, breathless feeling I experienced as I made my way to the hotel. In the space of an hour I had escaped monsoon-ridden India and arrived somewhere midway between the clouds and terra firma. Already I could feel my nostrils drying out in the thin air.

I went out later later same afternoon and made a sketchbook study of the deserted and half-ruined royal palace, situated on a promontory above the old town. Already I began to realize that what I wanted to say about Ladakh's landscape was not to be found through slavish topography. The sun was scorching hot and there was precious little shade. Light penetrated the thin atmosphere, exposing the landscape, cutting its edges like a laser. In my head the landscape seemed to be full of colour and yet when I looked, the dry rock, earth and mud-brick architecture were an almost uniform shade of buff-brown. Colour there was, but only in the intensely

161. *Chortens below Tikse Gompa,* 1997, watercolour and gouache, 53 x 73cm

blue sky, the gaily coloured, ubiquitous prayer flags, the emerald snippets of irrigated barley fields along the Indus valley, and the crimson robes of the Buddhist monks in the monasteries or *gompas*.

Two days later I was overwhelmed by the huge gilded Buddhas I saw on visits to *gompas* at Shey and Tikse, where the stark contrast between austere exterior and richly decorated interior reminded me of a geode – a hollow rock split open to reveal a glittering treasure of amethyst or quartz crystals. Slowly, I began to sense a way of painting Ladakh as I saw and felt it. In the presence of the giant *Sakyamuni* at Shey, transfixed by the mesmerising smile that shimmered in the semi-darkness, it slowly dawned on me that the swirls of the Buddha's hair were of a pure and glowing ultramarine blue: a colour, together with ochre and a darkish blood-red, that became a *leitmotiv* in all the Buddha paintings that I made on returning home. I found another kind of *visual essence* in Ladakh's arid and airless landscape with colours such as cobalt violet, cerulean blue and Naples yellow: pigments chosen for their opacity and granulating properties.

Ladakh's landscape has been shaped by more than two thousand years of Buddhism - the whole landscape resounds with praises to the Buddha: countless thousands of acts of devotion make up the mile-long walls of mani-stones, each one engraved with the mantra *Om Mani Padme Hum*. The same endless invocation is spread on the wind by the prayer flags that flutter from every high place. Whitewashed chortens dot the grey-brown desert, dissolving slowly back into the landscape like forgotten sandcastles.

The most awe-inspiring views are from the roofs of the monasteries, where the visitor looks down, as if from an aircraft window, on the Indus valley or across towards the Zanskar Range. I made sketches and took many photographs from these vantage points, often choosing a high horizon line to open up the composition. Tikse Gompa perches like a miniature Potala Palace on a rocky promontory above the coffee-brown, silt-laden Indus where feelings of elation and vertigo intermingle. In *Climbing to Rizong Gompa*, I combined a number of different viewpoints in order to convey the memory of a walk made to one of the most isolated *gompas* in Ladakh, where the only way is on foot, making every journey up and down the steep track a simple daily pilgrimage for the monks who sing and tell their beads along the way. As if the vertiginous landscape itself were not enough, there are also mountainous cloudscapes in the skies above Ladakh. In summer, the clouds roll in around mid afternoon, building into fantastic shapes that appear surreally sharp and sculptural in the thin atmosphere. In *Chortens below Tikse Gompa*, clouds form a dominant part of the composition - applied in white gouache, and while still wet, flooded with stains of grey.

After the second of two journeys to Ladakh lasting around three weeks, travelling on public transport and later by taxi (even to the top of Khardung La at 5350m), the return journey overland to Manali was as spectacular as it was hazardous: the road just cleared of snow and a bridge destroyed by floods only repaired the day before we set out. Back in the studio, a series of small paintings grew out of my attempt to achieve a synthesis of Ladakh's visual and cultural identity. *Alchi fragments* are paintings derived from the ancient mural paintings of the monastery of Alchi: a rare survivor of the invading forces that destroyed so many of Ladakh's monasteries over the centuries. The faded colours and patination of these fragments acknowledge the importance that visual manifestations of Buddhism such as *mani-walls,* prayer flags and mural decorations have in shaping the identity of Ladakh's landscape. Their various rhythms, colours and textures are something that I have drawn on in my work, not in a literal way, but as a means of coming closer to a visual and emotional truth.

I am grateful to the poet John Gimblett, who paid the warmest tribute to my work with three poems written in response to the Ladakh paintings in 2003. He has kindly given permission for these poems to be published here for the first time alongside the paintings where, with enviable economy of style, they eloquently touch on the still and timeless qualities of Ladakh. When I led a cultural tour to Ladakh in the summer of 1996, our small group included the author and art critic Marina Vaizey, who described mountains as 'a state of mind', and later wrote of her experience 'at high altitude, beyond the clouds':

Surrounded by mountains, we drive over the high desert, visiting *gompas*, looking for Buddhas, escorted by Buddhist monks. Some of the temples and monasteries are very old: Alchi is a thousand years old, Tikse is half a millennium ...The views are almost clearer than the eye can cope with; sharp-edged mountains framing, under the achingly blue sky, the valley of

162. Simon Pierse, *Tikse Gompa*, 1997, watercolour, 61 x 91cm

Tikse Gompa

Tikse: a city
of alleys, black
cells steeped
in the whisper
of yak-bells.
Etiolate, racks
of scrolls
rain a holy
snow; where we
go it's winter.

the Indus in Ladakh. The air in this high desert valley of the western Himalaya is thin, its life supported by the narrow strips of cultivation by the great river, curiously heightening the visitor's awareness and apprehension, not only of his own physical self and all around him, but of something beyond. Thin air makes the visitor dizzy; we walk as though through glue, very slowly. Our hosts run, seemingly lighter than air. And our eyes are open, looking on unimaginable vistas.

163. Simon Pierse, *From Lamayuru*, 1998, watercolour with some pastel, 54 x 81cm

From Lamayuru

A trickle of river
to Moonland. Great
yaks, cold clouds of
grey mass, fumble
along pasture. Back
at the gompa, Milarepa
holds the cave in his
fist. A mist hugs the
river to Moonland.

Ladakh's desert landscape continues to have a powerful attraction for me, for reasons I cannot fully explain. Extremely barren but, in a cultural sense, also very rich, the difficulty of getting there, whether overland, or by taking the hair-raising flight over the Himalaya, will always contribute to the visitor's feeling of timelessness and isolation and is surely one of the reasons that Ladakh's fragile culture and customs have survived for so long.

164. Simon Pierce, *Walking to Rizong Gompa*, 1997, watercolour, 61 x 91cm

Walking to Rizong Gompa

Clockwise at the foot
of the hill, bypass the
chorten, a young boy with
a yoke drips Indus onto
the shale snake path,
thudding upwards: a
metronome.

Past the apricot garden
of the nuns, a crack
in the wall hides flat
sunlight, stealing it
from the incisor ridge
of the Zanskar mountains.

At Rizong, we touch the
foul cups to our mouths,
a lone monk watching us
slip butter tea into parched
throats that want to repel it.

I think of a buddha at
Shey: a mischievous smile
like a secret kept to oneself.
We drink thirstily.

A new book by JOHN GIMBLETT: *Monkey: Selected India Poems*, is available from Cinnamon Press, ISBN: 978-1-905614-66-0 (www.cinnamonpress.co.uk).

MARK HAWORTH-BOOTH

The Return of Vittorio Sella

A distant view of a snowy range … has a strange power of moving all poets and persons of imagination – Douglas Freshfield, *Round Kangchenjunga* (1903)

I first heard his name over 30 years ago. I was working with Bill Brandt on an exhibition of 20th century landscape photography at the time. Our show, *The Land*, was presented at the Victoria and Albert Museum in 1975. We included grand mountain photographs, including masterworks by Ansel Adams, Yoshikazu Shirakawa and Bradford Washburn. Vittorio Sella (1859-1943) was reputed to be one of the greatest photographers of mountains. If my recollections are accurate, I looked at Sella photographs at the Alpine Club but failed to find anything I thought would appeal to Brandt. (Maybe the prints weren't in the best condition). If I'd known more about Sella, perhaps I would have travelled to Biella, where he had lived – between Milan and Turin – to seek out his archive. The moment passed, but Sella's name continued to flicker at the edge of my awareness of the history of photography. His kind of photography always appealed to me – I devoured the Sierra Club 'Wilderness' books that came out in the 1970s and curated the first exhibition of Ansel Adams held in Europe (at the V&A in 1976).

It fell to a friend of mine, the late Michael Hoffman – publisher at Aperture in New York – to instigate the long overdue return of Vittorio Sella. Aperture brought out *Summit*, a large-format, splendidly printed, Sella monograph in 2000. On the cover was a breathtaking telephoto image of – appropriately – the summit of Siniolchu as seen from the Zemu glacier in Sikkim. It was taken in 1899 but the peak, as delicately patterned as frost on a window, stood out dramatically against the kind of deep, dark sky that we associate with Ansel Adams. The preface was by Adams himself and reflects the generosity of spirit that made him champion other photographers – from Timothy O'Sullivan in the 19th century to Brandt in his own time. He wrote that 'The purity of Sella's interpretations move the spectator to a religious awe. Sella has brought to us not only the facts and forms of far-off splendours of the world, but the essence of experience which finds a spiritual response in the inner recesses of our mind and heart.'

Adams's words came, of course, from beyond the grave as he had died in 1992. However, his remarks contained his unrivalled experience of photographing in the mountains. He admired Sella, he added, for 'The exquisitely right moment of exposure, the awareness of the orientation of the camera and sun best to reveal the intricacies of form of ice and stone, the

165. Vittorio Sella, 1859-1943, *carte de viste* (*Alpine Club Photo Library*)

unmannered viewpoint…there is no faked grandeur; rather there is understatement…' Adams's preface – so eloquent and exact – was published in the *Sierra Club Bulletin* in December 1946. What was originally published as an appreciation, three years after Sella's death, became – when reprinted in 2000, with minor errors corrected – a major step in the Italian photographer's return to the public domain.

In order to publish a beautifully printed, large-format book like *Summit*, Michael Hoffman brought together not only funding from well-wishers but also a coalition of interests. Ansel Adams was the ideal figurehead, but the supporting cast were also distinguished. The book's foreword was contributed by David Brower, who led the Sierra Club through its most active decades - and had exhibited Sella's photographs and initiated the Adams essay back in 1946. Essays were contributed by mountaineers Greg Child and Paul Kallmes and an art historian, Wendy M Watson (of the Mount Holyoke College Art Museum in South Hadley, Massachusetts). Sella's work belongs to all of these constituencies. Greg Child's essay immediately tells us something that is more obvious to a mountaineer than to a viewer with little experience of the places in these photographs. Take Sella's heroic, six-part panorama from 1909 of the Baltoro glacier, featuring K2 (the world's second highest mountain), Broad Peak (Child: 'a vast empire of a mountain; Manhattan could fit onto its upper snowfields') and Gasherbrum IV. Child remarks that Sella did three extraordinary things in this panorama: he had 'crammed more information into his image than the eye normally sees, and the effect was startling'. Secondly, 'Sella's camera had captured a sense of movement – the relentless ancient ritual of ice, the thirty-five mile long Baltoro glacier, chiselling away the mountain flanks and conveying the rubble at a speed of a few feet a year.' Third, Sella had photographed the mountains as an experienced climber: an expedition nearly 50 years later used this panorama and other Sella photographs of Broad Peak like 'roadmaps to plot their way up its 10,500-foot west face'. (The supposed falsehood of photography has been enthusiastically overstated in recent years).

Paul Kallmes, building on the biography of Sella published by Ronald Clark (*The Splendid Hills*, 1948) and the excellently organised archive at the Fondazione Sella in Biella, provided a most useful guide to Sella's career, including descriptions of his major phases of work and special expeditions from 1879 to the finale in the Western Himalaya in 1909. I have followed Kallmes's outline in the following paragraphs, augmenting his remarks with observations of my own, which derive from visits to the Fondazione Sella in 2005 and 2007. Like others before me, I have had the pleasure and benefit of conversations with two extremely knowledgeable individuals – Lodovico Sella, descendant of Vittorio and head of the foundation, and Luciano Pivotto, conservator of the photographic archive. On the first visit I took part in the lively discussions of a group of international experts included Maria Francesca Bonetti, Régis Durand, Giuseppe Garimoldi – author of the important *Fotografia e Alpinismo* (1995) – Filippo Maggia and Ulrich Pohlmann. On the second visit I spent a week studying Sella's prints, negatives and publications in more detail. I found that his photographs – because of the way tonal subtlety is combined with dynamic compositional organization – constantly reminded me of the early Ansel Adams.

Sella grew up with photography and mountains. His father, Giuseppe Venanzio Sella, not only photographed as a serious amateur but published the first Italian treatise on photography – *Plico del Fotografo* (Turin, 1856). Vittorio Sella's uncle, Quintino Sella, founded the Club Alpino Italiano in 1863. The young photographer grew up in a family that was prominent

166. 'The purity of Sella's interpretations move the spectator to a religious awe,' –Ansel Adams. Siniolchu (68878m) Sikkim, from the Zemu glacier, 1899. (*Vittorio Sella, Alpine Club Collection*)

in industry, through its linen mill in Biella, and politics –Quintino Sella, trained as an engineer and was a statesman in the tumultuous decades of the 1860s and 70s. Vittorio Sella's education included languages – including English and German – as well as drawing. He received lessons from the painter Luigi Ciardi. Sella exhibited a charcoal drawing and a painting, both of mountains, in 1882. As a young man, Sella read Horace-Bénedict de Saussure (*Voyages dans les Alpes*, 1787), John Tyndall (*Glaciers of the Alps*, 1857) and the classic accounts of mountaineering in the 1860s and 70s by Edward Whymper. He took up photography in the age of wet collodion, which – for maximum rapidity of exposure and sensitivity – required glass negatives to be coated and developed on site. His first efforts, preserved at the Fondazione Sella, located in the family's former linen mill, show the usual problems of applying the syrupy collodion mixture evenly to the glass. There are also problems with fogging – light leaking into the camera or the dark tent and onto the negative – and with focusing the lens: the foregrounds are often out of focus and therefore not merely empty of information but aesthetically formless. Sometimes the whole negative was out of focus. However, despite all the technical glitches, from the first box in the archive – *Prime Fotografie, 1879-80* – Sella demonstrated an interest in rhythmical composition. Some of his early alpine compositions are almost abstract. As usual with collodion negatives, the skies in these early photographs came out dead white (because Sella, to avoid the characteristic mottled effect, painted them out). He printed these early efforts on albumen paper.

Very fortunately, Sella persevered with the skills required to photograph with large cameras in the mountains and become a virtuoso of panoramic photography at high altitudes. A new negative came into general commercial production in 1880 – the gelatin dry plate. This not only allowed photographers to leave their mobile dark-tents and chemicals at home but gave them vastly enhanced exposure speeds and improved spectral sensitivity. Sella took a wet collodion apparatus onto the Alps in 1879 – when he made his first ascent of Monte Mars, in the mountain range north of Biella. In 1880 and 1881, he took dry collodion plates (which he had prepared himself in advance). In 1882 he began using the new, factory-coated gelatin dry plates. Soon there was a new printing paper too: Printing Out Paper. P.O.P., as it subsequently became known, was made and marketed from 1884 onwards by J H Obernetter in Munich – a commercial centre important to Piedmont. As its name implied, P.O.P., sometimes called Aristotype, was a paper for printing out in daylight, under a negative in a printing frame. This was the original means of printing, practised by Henry Talbot, the inventor of positive/negative photography. As it happens, several prints by Talbot (apparently once owned by Michael Faraday) belonged to Sella's father and were presumably known to Sella himself. P.O.P. (still in production) gives delicately warm-hued prints with a very long tonal range. These characteristics differed from the other new possibility – gelatin-silver paper (also introduced around 1880) that required print-

167. K2 from Windy Gap, 1909. (*Vittorio Sella, Alpine Club Collection*)

ing by chemical development and produced the comparatively cold-toned black and white image that is characteristic of much of the 20th century. Both these type of prints were usually gold-toned to enhance tonal richness and as a means of preventing the prints from fading – unfortunately, not always successfully. When perfectly preserved, Sella's prints convey the effect of pristine purity he evoked in these words: 'the great cold cleanses the air'. In old age he often toned his prints, in pink and yellow, by hand. Sella also made good use of the newly-perfected photo-mechanical collotype process to print copies of his panoramas in ink rather than silver salts.

The Alps provided Sella's first great challenge as climber and photographer. Although his first attempts with a camera began in 1879, the key year was 1882. In March that year Sella and his guides achieved the first winter ascent of the Matterhorn, a triumph saluted by the Alpine Club in London. Later that same year Sella sent a significant letter to the Dallmeyer Camera Co. in London: 'I beg you to undertake immediately the camera for plates 30x40 cm described in my letter. I beg you to make it in the best mahogany, with every care possible, as I will serve myself of it for taking photographs in the high Alps ... Here we have splendid weather and I burn with impatience to start photographic excursions.'

A camera taking glass negatives approaching 12x16 inches in size makes the 10x8 inch cameras of Edward Weston and Ansel Adams seem modest. Sella's camera, which Kallmes describes as weighing 40lbs (and each negative 2lbs), is in the heroic mould of the great photographers of the American West a generation earlier – William Henry Jackson, Eadweard Muybridge, Timothy O'Sullivan and Carleton Watkins. It would be instructive to see their prints exhibited side by side. As it is, one can compare Sella's work with his European contemporaries quite easily. Many of them appear together in the pages of *The Alpine Portfolio*, edited by Oscar Eckenstein and August Lorria (London, 1889). Even when translated into reproductions printed in collotype, Sella's alpine photographs make those of even distinguished rivals, like the English photographer/mountaineer William Donkin, seem like photocopies. They lack Sella's air and sparkle, as well as his compositional skill.

Sella used his large camera like a magnifying glass. He was aware that such photographs as his could be more than a secondary record of the experience of high places. He once remarked: 'The wish to reproduce faithfully the atmosphere of the panorama even more accurately than it can be seen by the eye or retained by the mind delights the photographer.' Although Sella built a solar enlarger, which still exists, as part of his darkroom and laboratory at San Gafalo in Biella, he preferred to work with large negatives and generally offered contact prints for exhibition and sale. His photographs were distributed commercially for many years by the Spooner agency in London.

Sella extended his range as a climber and photographer very significantly with three visits to the Caucasus in 1889, 1890 and 1896. On the 1889 expedition Sella and his companions made the fifth ascent of Mount Elbrus (5642m), Europe's highest mountain. Kallmes points out that, on returning to his darkroom, Sella inserted figures into his photograph of the summit of Elbrus – 'to add a human dimension to the work and dramatize the scale of the mountains'. This is a practice in which Vittorio indulged on a number of occasions. They are usually easy to identify with the naked eye. Using smaller cameras, Sella was also able to make vivid portraits of the people met with on the three expeditions.

Sella increased his range still further thanks to the patronage of Prince Luigi Amadeo di Savoia, Duke of the Abruzzi (1873-1933). Abruzzi led the first great mountaineering expedition to Alaska in 1897, with Sella as official photographer. It led to the conquest – to use the language of the time – of Mount Saint Elias (5489m) and a substantial volume by Filippo de Filippi, *The Ascent of Mount Saint Elias*, published in London in 1900. The book contains a wealth of scientific data and reproductions of Sella's photographs. Before it was published, however, he had taken part in another major expedition. With the British mountaineer, Douglas Freshfield, Vittorio explored Kangchenjunga in Sikkim and Nepal in 1899. Although heavy snowfalls obstructed the climbing, the fresh snow provided Sella with spectacular photographic opportunities. His image of the summit of

168. Mitre Peak and Muztagh Tower, 1909. (*Vittorio Sella, Alpine Club Collection*)

Siniolchu, one of the cluster of peaks around Kangchenjunga, derives – with many other masterpieces – from this expedition.

The Duke of Abruzzi invited Sella to join him on an expedition to Uganda in 1906. The aim was to explore the Ruwenzori, also known as the Mountains of the Moon, whose snowy peaks rise from tropical forests. No one had climbed the higher peaks before 1906. Abruzzi's expedition not only climbed but mapped and photographed the peaks. Sella also photographed the local people and the flora. A substantial volume – published in Milan in 1908 – recorded all aspects of the expedition. Abruzzi next led a seven-month expedition to the Karakoram mountains in the Western Himalaya. The climbing team failed on K2, but reached approximately 7470m in the ascent of Chogolisa, the highest that any human had yet climbed. According to Paul Kallmes, here 'Sella produced a portfolio of images that stands alone for its time – a striking record of the Karakoram, arguably the finest visual representation of a mountain range that has ever been done'. A volume of nearly 500 pages was published in London to record the expedition's findings, including Sella's photographs, in 1912.

The term 'visual representation' opens up a quite different prospect – the position of Sella's photographs within the history of image-making. Wendy M Watson addressed this in *Summit*, telling us the fascinating fact that Sella read P H Emerson's passionate essay on photographic art – *Naturalistic Photography for Students of the Art* (1887) – shortly before leaving for the Caucasus in 1899. Sella copied a quotation by the painter J F Millet from the book, onto the flyleaf of his expedition diary. Part of it reads: 'We should accustom ourselves to receive from nature all our impressions.' The passage connects with the impulse we find in Wordsworth, in which the poet opens himself to nature as the source of inspiration and goodness. Watson tells us that the bookshelves of the Sella family home contained the works of Wordsworth, Byron and Shelley. The Romantic reverence for mountains was carried deep into the 19th century in the writings of John Ruskin, which were also to be found on the Sella bookshelves. The literary background and many other aspects of Sella's formation as a photographer have been helpfully explored by Marina Miraglia in *Paesaggi Verticali: La fotografia di Vittorio Sella 1879-1943* (Turin, 2006).

I was struck some years ago by the fact that one of the first important early English collectors of fine photography – mainly of landscape – was a poet and a disciple of the 'Lake Poets'. Studying Chauncy Hare Townshend and the photographs he bequeathed to the V&A in 1868 suggested to me that photography was seen by both its artists and their audience as a 'natural poetics' in which nature itself directly impressed not only the artist's receptive spirit but the practitioner's sensitive plate - producing 'sun pictures', as they were then called. Such observations remain speculations, but the whole question of the spiritual meaning of mountains has been refocused with great clarity by Robert Macfarlane in his book *Mountains of the Mind* (2003).

There have been many other changes in recent years in the intellectual and physical landscape in which Sella's photographs are situated. One cannot think with equanimity of the current state of the places he photographed, as great glaciers recede and high peaks are stripped of snow. Sella's achievement now seems not only immense but unrepeatable.

* This essay is based on the foreword to the catalogue written by Mark Haworth-Booth for the exhibition *Frozen in Time: Mountain Photographs by Vittorio Sella (1859-1943)* at the Estorick Collection of Modern Italian Art, London, 25 June to 14 September 2008. Some 50 of Sella's extraordinary vintage photographs and multi-plate panoramas were on display, borrowed from the Fondazione Sella which owns the Sella Museum, established in 1948 at the laboratory in his home town of Biella.

History

169. Simon Pierse, *From the roof, Tikse Gompa*, 1996, watercolour, 61 x 91cm

WILLY BLASER AND GLYN HUGHES

Kabru 1883

A Reassessment

Shortly before 2pm on 8 October 1883, W W Graham, Emil Boss and Ulrich Kauffmann stood some 30 to 40 feet below the summit of a peak to the south of Kangchenjunga. The actual top was an ice pillar. Graham believed they were within an ace of the first ascent of Kabru (7338m) and estimated their height at 'within a few feet of 24,000 feet'. The height then accorded to Kabru by the Great Trigonometrical Survey was 24,015ft. The trio had recorded the highest altitude yet reached by mountaineers. However within a year doubts were expressed and have persisted down the decades such that the first ascent of Kabru is now generally credited to Reginald Cooke in 1935[1]. But is that fair? After reassessing the evidence, Willy Blaser and Glyn Hughes have concluded it is time for a rehabilitation of Graham and his Swiss companions.

William Woodman Graham was a young law student (born about 1859) with an impressive record of ascents of major peaks in the Alps. In July 1882 the Sella brothers, with three guides, had made the first ascent of the lower summit of the Dent du Géant, making use of iron stanchions and fixed ropes prepared by the guides over the previous four days. Three weeks later Graham, with Chamonix guides A Payot and A Cupelin, took advantage of the Sellas' staircase to repeat the ascent. They then lowered themselves into the gap between the two peaks and, using combined tactics, completed the first ascent of the higher north-east peak. This apparently did not endear him to the members of the Alpine Club who blackballed him when he applied for membership later that year.

The following year Graham made his historic journey in the Himalaya. This has been universally accepted as the first instance of travel to the Himalaya with the main object of climbing mountains 'more for sport and adventure than for the achievement of scientific knowledge'. His lack of scientific rigour was to allow some to doubt their achievements. All details of the journey given below, including place names and heights, are taken from Graham's own account [2].

Graham left Darjeeling on 23 March accompanied by Joseph Imboden, a guide from St Niklaus, and marched to Jongri, in the south of the Kangchenjunga massif. From here they crossed the Kang La (17,000ft), and climbed an unnamed peak they estimated to be more than 20,000ft high. They returned to Jongri, from where they trekked north over the Guicho La (over 16,000ft) to the Talung glacier, amidst the main peaks

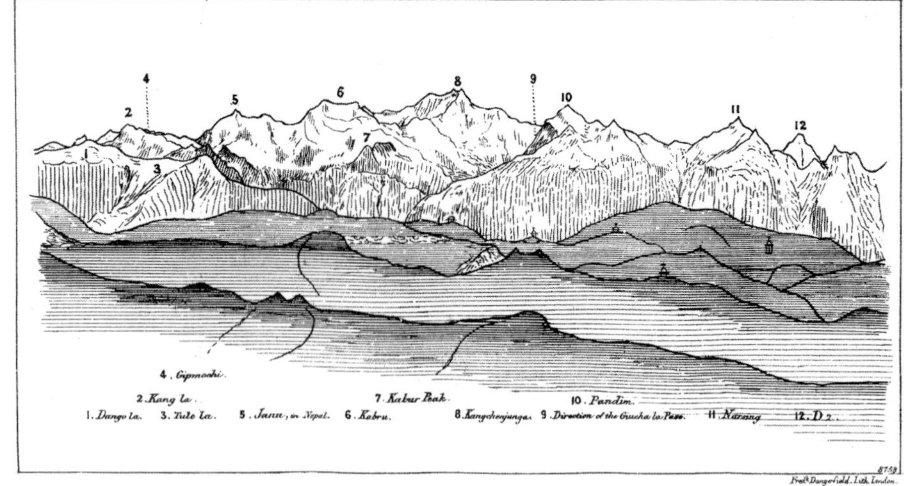

PANORAMA OF THE KANGCHENJUNGA RANGE FROM DARJEELING.
(From a Sketch published at the Surveyor General's Office Calcutta 1882).

170. Panorama sketch from *AJ* XII (1884-86)

of the Kangchenjunga group. They retreated to Jongri in heavy snow. Weather conditions were poor, most of the coolies were unwell, and the last straw was when one of them burned Graham's boots while trying to dry them. They returned to Darjeeling, and Imboden, unwell and homesick, was sent back to Switzerland.

Graham had arranged for Emil Boss, of the Bear Hotel in Grindelwald, to find a replacement for Imboden, but Boss decided to join Graham himself, and brought the guide Ulrich Kauffmann with him. This was particularly fortunate, as Boss was a very experienced alpinist himself, an officer in the Swiss Army, and the previous year had very nearly reached the summit of Mount Cook with W S Green and Kauffman. Kauffman was reputedly 'one of the fastest step-cutters living'. The trio left Darjeeling on 24 June for the Garhwal, where they hoped to attempt Nanda Devi. Their first attempt on the Rishi Ganga failed, and they turned their attention to Dunagiri (7066m / 23,182ft), on which Graham and Boss reached an estimated height of 22,700ft, in sight of the summit only 500ft above before retreating in the face of 'biting hail and wind'. It was the first time any of them had reached such a height, and they reported no 'inconvenience in breathing other than the ordinary panting inseparable from any great muscular exertion'. They also experienced no symptoms of altitude sickness.

The attempt on Nanda Devi was then resumed via a different approach on the north bank of the Rishi Ganga. But once again they were repulsed. Graham was highly critical of the 1 inch to the mile map of the region, finding 'one whole range omitted, glaciers portrayed where trees of 4ft thickness are growing'. This criticism goes far towards explaining some of the subsequent confusion as to which mountains they actually described. Next they successfully ascended a peak indicated on their map as A21 (22,516ft), which they called Mount Monal, because of the number of snow pheasants they saw on it. Finally they attempted a peak in the Dunagiri range shown as A22 (21,001ft), but were turned back by technical difficulties at a height estimated at more than 20,000ft. Thus ended the second phase of Graham's adventure, and the party returned to Calcutta to prepare for their *pièce de résistance*, another trip to Sikkim.

This time they had great difficulty securing good coolies in Darjeeling, and had to make do with 'rather a scratch pack'. Progress was slow and it took nine days to reach Jongri. The weather was very poor with heavy rain, but in spite of this they explored the west side of Kabru, satisfying themselves that there would be little chance of success here. On 6 September they tramped up into the glen immediately south of Kabru in search of some *argali* or mountain sheep (Ovis ammon) reported to be there. They returned the same day empty-handed, but convinced that the south side of the mountain would be even more difficult than the western. After further delays due to porter trouble, they moved camp a few miles north to Ahluthang at the foot of the Guicho La, and the rain continued. On 19 September they left camp to climb Jubonu, but were driven back by heavy snow. On the 23rd they crossed the Guicho La with the intention of climbing Pundim from the north, but found it quite impracticable, so returned to camp again. Eventually the weather cleared on the 29th, and next day they set off to climb Jubonu due east of their base. They camped at about 18,000ft, left at 4.30am, and reached the summit (5936m / 19,475ft) at 11am. Graham described the climb as being 'incomparably the hardest ascent we had in the Himalaya'.

By now the party had climbed one peak (A21) of 22,516ft, one of 21,400ft (not detailed here), reached about 22,700ft on Dunagiri, and more than 20,000ft on another (A22). They had also crossed a number of high passes, and covered a great deal of ground. Graham had also climbed an unnamed peak of more than 20,000ft during his first trip with Joseph Imboden. They were obviously now very fit, well acclimatised, and ready to make a further attempt on Kabru.

Having explored the western and southern flanks of the mountain, without identifying a practical route, the trio now reconnoitred the eastern face, and set off for their attempt on 6 October. Their highest camp was reached on the second day, and was estimated by aneroid and comparison to be 18,500ft. They left at 4.30am the following day, starting up a long couloir, with loose snow threatening avalanche, and continuing up a steep ice slope leading to the foot of the peak itself. From here they enjoyed nearly 1,000ft of 'delightful rock-work' to within 1,500ft of the eastern summit. The last slope was described as pure ice, but because of the recent heavy snowfall there was a coating of frozen snow up which Kauffmann was able to cut steps. Graham felt that the ascent was only possible because of this coating.

He records reaching the lower summit of Kabru at 12.15 and estimated its height to be at least 23,700ft. The speed of their ascent was to be a point of contention later. 'The glories of the view were beyond compare,' he wrote, and they could clearly see Everest to the north-west. They continued along a short arête and after 90 minutes reached a point 30-40ft below the main summit, which Graham described as 'little more than pillar of ice'. Daunted by the 'extreme difficulty and danger of attempting it', and a shortage of time, they left a bottle at their highest point and descended with difficulty to camp.

Even Kabru was not enough for this energetic party and on 13 October they crossed the Kang La, and climbed a peak of nearly 19,000ft from which they examined Jannu. They concluded it was too late in the year for an attempt and returned once again to Darjeeling. So ended Graham's remarkable adventure.

The carping begins...

On 9 June 1884 Graham read a paper describing his Himalayan trip to the Royal Geographical Society. This was published in the Proceedings of the RGS, and also in the *Alpine Journal* [2]. In it Graham was highly critical of the maps of the Nanda Devi region, describing the 1 inch to the mile map as 'highly inaccurate'. He also quotes an earlier traveller (Kennedy) who termed the maps as 'beautifully inaccurate'. Graham said the then new map of Sikkim was 'a work of admirable accuracy up to the snow-line', however because the Survey officers had no training or skills in the arts of mountaineering, their maps 'suffer when they come to the delineation of the ground above snow level'. He suggested that officers should be given alpine training before taking up duties in the Himalaya.

The evening after Graham's presentation at the RGS, Emil Boss, who had been present at that meeting, spoke to the Alpine Club[3] about the ascent of Kabru, amplifying Graham's own account, and confirming that their ascent had only been possible because of the favourable snow conditions. He also expanded on Graham's comments on the maps then available. Boss was very well qualified to comment on this subject; as an officer in the Swiss army he was very familiar with the study and use of maps of mountain regions.

Boss was highly complimentary of the accuracy of the Great Trigonometrical Survey (GTS) of India in general. He also spoke favourably of the then new two mile to the inch map of Sikkim, which he said was 'as good as any map of such a district made by men not, in the Swiss sense, mountaineers could well be'. Of the maps of Kumaon he was severely critical. He expanded on Graham's suggestion that survey officers in training be given training in Switzerland in icemanship and map-making in glaciated areas. Following Boss's address Douglas Freshfield made further comments on the status of maps of the Himalayan regions, which were expanded on in the *Alpine Journal*[3]. He agreed that the criticisms by Graham and Boss were entirely justified. Freshfield also proposed the formation of a Himalayan Club to encourage travellers to publish their own studies of particular areas.

171. From left to right: On the right of black cone is Kabru South (7317m), Kabru North (7338m), below is the round summit of Kabru Dome (6600m), Forked Peak (6108m) and Kangchenjunga (8598m). (*Willy Blaser*)

We have no doubt that Graham's and Boss's criticisms were intended to be constructive, but they were clearly not seen that way in the corridors of the Indian Survey Department. In an article in *The Pioneer Mail*[4], an anonymous correspondent, describing himself as 'for nearly 30 years a wanderer in the Himalayas', and who had read Graham's RGS paper, poured scorn on his claims. There is no record of Graham himself responding to this article but Douglas Freshfield certainly did. In a vigorous and witty response in the *AJ*[5] he takes apart the arguments of the 'wanderer' with great relish, and confirms his total support for the accounts of Graham and Boss.

Martin Conway seems to have missed or ignored Freshfield's article. In the section on Mountaineering that he wrote for *The Encyclopaedia of Sport* in 1898[6] he repeated accusations made by the 'wanderer', dismissed Graham's claims, and claimed that he himself, together with Bruce, Zurbriggen, and two Gurkhas, took the 'record' for the greatest height yet reached (23,000ft) on Pioneer Peak, Karakoram, in 1892. Freshfield again took up the cause, rejecting Conway's arguments in the *AJ*[7] of February 1898. The pair locked horns further on the issue in the May *AJ*[8] of that same year. Freshfield seems to have been the clear winner of the debate, as in a later edition of the *Encyclopaedia* in 1911[9] Conway, co-authoring the Mountaineering section with George Abraham, supports Graham's claims: 'Amongst other great feats, this party climbed almost to the top of Kabru (24,015ft), and, strange to say, until 1909 this remained the record for altitude.' Conway now makes no mention of his own claim to the altitude record.

Next to join the debate was Norman Collie, in *Climbing in the Himalaya and other mountain ranges* published in 1902[10]. Writing of Graham's account Collie said: 'Anyone who will take the trouble to read his account of the ascent of Kabru cannot fail to admit that he must have climbed the peak lying on the south-west of Kanchenjunga, viz Kabru, for there is no

172. Kabru South and Kabru North taken from Dzongri Alm. (*Willy Blaser*)

other high peak there which he could have ascended from his starting point except Kanchenjunga itself.'

However, there were still doubters. In a paper in the *AJ*[11] in 1905 entitled *Some Obstacles to Himalayan Mountaineering and the History of a Record Ascent*, William Hunter Workman described how he had reached 23,394ft on Pyramid Peak in the Karakoram in 1903, which he claimed as the altitude record. In a footnote he dismissed Graham's claim thus: 'The contention that Mr. Graham reached an altitude of 24,000 feet has, on various grounds, whether rightly or wrongly, been so strongly disputed that it must be regarded as far from proved, and therefore the altitude mentioned cannot properly claim a place among those acknowledged to have been made.'

In the absence of Boss (now deceased) and Graham (whereabouts unknown[1*]) Collie again leapt to their defence, as did Edmund Garwood in the absence of Freshfield abroad, in the *AJ*[12] of 1904-5. Garwood quoted Freshfield's belief, forthrightly expressed in *Round Kangchenjunga*, that, 'Much of the criticism bestowed on it [Graham's ascent] has arisen from crass ignorance of mountaineering.' On Freshfield's return, the battle with Hunter Workman continued in the pages of the *Alpine Journal* until the editor finally called time in 1907. It is worth pointing out that Hunter Workman's argument was never that he did not believe Graham's ascent, but simply that without adequate scientific confirmation the ascent was not proven.

If more support from a highly respected Himalayan mountaineer was

[*] According to Walt Unsworth's *Encyclopaedia of Mountaineering* (1992), little is known of Graham's later life. He is said to have lost his money and emigrated to the USA where he became a cowboy.

needed it came from Tom Longstaff, in a paper in 1906[13]. We can do no better than quote him in full. 'A well-known Indian official of my acquaintance, who was in Darjeeling at the time of Graham's visit, says now, and said then, that he fully believed in Graham's bona fides, but thought he had mistaken Kabur (15,830ft) for Kabru (24,005ft), an opinion which has since been quoted by others. Now, for anyone who is a mountaineer, and has seen Kabru, it is impossible to believe that Graham, Emil Boss, and Kauffmann could make any mistake as to which peak they were on. They may have been imposters, but they could not have been mistaken: my point is that we have no tittle of evidence that they were either. Any climber who will carefully study Graham's paper in its entirety, especially if he knows the country at all, cannot but be struck by the strong internal evidences of truth which it bears. That he did not suffer from mountain sickness is no proof of bad faith. That he made little pretension to scientific knowledge is no evidence that he was not a very competent mountaineer. I would add that, particularly in India, it is unwise to believe tales and rumours to the discredit of other people. To quote them is distinctly rash.'

We think it relevant to mention here the Norwegian near-ascent of Kabru in 1907. In the autumn of 1906 two young Norwegians went out to India with vague intentions to climb in the Himalaya. Carl Rubenson's climbing experience was limited to Norway, and his companion Monrad-Aas had never before climbed any mountain. Rubenson gave a full account of their trip in a paper read before the Alpine Club on 2 June 1908, and reproduced in the AJ[14]. They settled on Kabru as their objective, but reaching Jongri too late in the year to make an attempt on the mountain, went off travelling in the East 'lazy beyond measure'. They returned to India in August 1907, and after the usual preparations left Darjeeling on 16 September. Curiously they found the scenery in Sikkim 'not very different from that in Norway'. They established their base at Jongri, and set about climbing the mountain via the Kabru glacier to the south, an approach apparently rejected by Graham's party. Progress was very slow, partly because of problems with supplies and porters, and presumably also lack of fitness and acclimatisation. However from a high camp at about 22,600ft they were eventually able to reach a point 50 or 60ft below the summit before they were turned back by strong winds. Interestingly Rubenson, like Graham before him, reported that they 'did not suffer any real physical inconveniences'.

Regarding Graham's ascent, once again it is worth quoting in full Rubenson's comments: 'As for myself, I must confess that I found it hard to realise that Mr. Graham could have made such progress as he claims to have made in one day; but Mr. Longstaff on his last expedition proved that such rapid progress was not impossible, and I do not venture to dispute Graham's statements any longer.' This refers to Longstaff's account of the ascent of Trisul[15] in which he reports a similar rate of ascent to that reported by Graham on Kabru. According to Eva Selin in her paper in a recent AJ[16] this ascent by the Norwegians provided the inspiration for the founding of Norway's own alpine club, the Norsk Tindeklub.

173. Kabru South and Kabru North taken from Yuksum. (*Willy Blaser*)

Conclusion…

Summarising the above, those who declared themselves firmly on the side of Graham's party in the dispute include Freshfield, Collie, Longstaff, Garwood and Rubenson. Those against include Conway, who apparently later changed his mind, and Hunter Workman, who made it clear that he didn't say they hadn't climbed Kabru, but that it was not proven. Is it a coincidence that both Conway and Hunter Workman subsequently made claims to have made the highest ascents to date, claims which would have been invalid if Graham's Kabru ascent had been accepted?

We are left with the challenge which started off the whole dispute, that by the anonymous 'wanderer' in the *Pioneer Mail*[4]. He raised five specific objections (our rebuttal in *italics*):

1. That an ascent of Kabru from Jongri in the south would be impossible, the south side being 'a succession of precipitous faces of sharp rock where an ibex could not possibly find a footing'. *Graham's party also rejected this approach, which is why they climbed Kabru from Ahluthang in the east.*

2. One of the native guides was reported to say that 'while at Jongri, the tourists (sic) made an excursion northwards towards the snows, and returned the same evening to their camp. If so they could only have gone as far as a peak called Kabur'. *The party was based at Jongri for several weeks, and made numerous excursions from there, including the one on 6 September when they visited the glen on the south side of Kabru, and returned the same day. Possibly this particular informant was only at Jongri for a limited time.*

3. According to 'wanderer', 'There is no evidence that Mr Graham went

anywhere unaccompanied by his native guides'. *It is clear from Graham's account that the climbers were never accompanied by native guides above their higher camps.*

4. Describing the aneroid carried by Graham, 'wanderer' states that 'this instrument is only available for altitudes up to 8,000 feet; its accuracy beyond this limit may be doubted'. *Graham states: 'I carried with me an aneroid barometer by Solomons, graduated to 23,000 feet. The heights it gave corresponded, where comparison was possible, within, generally, 100 feet with the G.T.S. Heights up to 14,000 feet. Above this, measurements taken with it had only a differential value. It was compared and corrected at Calcutta between each of the three tours here described.' It is clear that Graham was well aware of the limitations of his aneroid, but that these were far less serious than 'wanderer' claimed. Also, as Longstaff pointed out*[13], *in respect of Graham's ascent of Mount Monal and near ascent of Dunagiri, 'the altitude of neither of these mountains, nor any others mentioned in Graham's paper, is affected by the fact of the climber having or not having a barometer, or a dozen barometers, with him? They have been triangulated by a succession of most competent surveyors during the space of the last 90 years.'*

5. Finally 'wanderer' notes that Graham named peak A21 Mount Monal on account of the number of snow pheasants seen on it and deduces that as the altitude range of monals is 8,000 to 13,000ft, the mountain climbed could not be higher than this. *Graham, of course, did not claim that the monals were seen on the summit of the mountain, so this argument is irrelevant.*

It is hard to take any of these arguments seriously, so what was the motive behind 'wanderer's' attack? Freshfield[7] puts one argument well: 'The point of view of the average official mind is the same all the world over. It has been tersely summarised in these doggerel lines:-

I am *the* old inhabitant,
And what I cannot do you can't.'

'Wanderer' was clearly in sympathy with the Survey Department, if not actually employed by them, and took Graham and Boss's constructive criticism badly. More difficult to understand, in view of the overwhelming support for Graham's claims by a majority of the serious Himalayan explorers and mountaineers of the day, and the triviality of the arguments of an anonymous critic, is why the doubts persist?

The verdict of Kenneth Mason, a former Superintendent of the Survey of India, and Professor of geography at Oxford University was clearly an influence here. In his important history of Himalayan exploration and mountaineering[17] Mason points out that doubt had been thrown on the validity of Graham's claim, citing staff of the Survey of India (no surprise there), Sir Martin Conway, and 'others in England'. He seems to have been unaware that Conway had completely changed his position to one of support for Graham's claim. He then names a number of people (Freshfield, Collie, Garwood, Waddell, Longstaff and Rubenson) who 'have argued for or against the claim', however fails to point out that of these only Waddell

174. The Kabru peaks, Talung and Kangchenjunga . (*Roger Payne*)

argued against, the rest being strongly for. The specific evidence that Mason cites for believing that Graham had mistaken the mountain that he was climbing was that he made no mention of the Kabru glacier, turned with time-consuming difficulty by Cooke in 1935. Well Graham did mention it, in his account of their sortie on the south side of Kabru on 6 September[2], describing it as 'one mass of broken glacier', and rejecting it as a practical line of ascent. Graham's route was a totally different one.

Once again the doubts of the Survey Department had been allowed to predominate over the convictions of a considerable body of eminent mountaineers. We believe it is time to put the doubts to rest, and give Graham, Boss and Kauffmann their due credit for an extraordinary achievement.

References

1. *Fallen Giants*, Issermann and Weaver, Yale University Press, 2008, 33/4.
2. *Alpine Journal* XII August 1884, 25-52.
3. Ibid XII August 1884, 52-60.
4. *The Pioneer Mail*, Allahabad, 27 July 1884, 82.
5. *Alpine Journal* XII August 1884, 99-108.
6. *The Encyclopaedia of Sport, Volume 2*, Lawrence and Bullen, 1898, 27.
7. *Alpine Journal* XIX February 1898, 48-54.
8. Ibid XIX May 1898, 159-166.
9. *The Encyclopaedia of Sport & Games*, William Heinemann, 1911, 204.
10. *Climbing in the Himalaya and other mountain ranges*, Douglas, 1902
11. *Alpine Journal* XXI August 1905, 506.
12. Ibid XXII November 1905, 626-8.
13. Ibid XXIII August 1906, 204.
14. Ibid XXIV November 1908, 310-321.
15. Ibid XXIV May 1908, 120.
16. Ibid 113 2008, 257-263.
17. *Abode of Snow*, Kenneth Mason, 1955, Rupert Hart-Davis, reprinted 1987, Diadem Books, 94-5 and 274-5 (1987 edition).

ANDREW ROSS

100 Years of The OUMC

A Brief and Personal History

I joined the Oxford University Mountaineering Club in my first week at Oxford in 2001. Back then I had no idea that it would be at the centre of my four years of life in Oxford, and continue to play a role during the years since. I think it was in 2003 that I first realised that the Centenary of the formation of the club was getting close, and it was Steve Broadbent who formed the Centenary Committee in 2005 to ensure that we would have a fitting celebration. I started researching the history of the club, producing an account for the Centenary Ball Programme, and it was this that led to me writing this article. I'll take this opportunity to thank everyone who helped me with the research over the last four years.

175. On the Heather Terrace, Tryfan. OUMC meet, January 1922.

The origins of the club lie back in the 19th century. Following the formation of the Alpine Club, in 1857, members of the AC resident in Oxford decided to form a club to consist of members of Oxford University interested in the objects of the Alpine Club. A meeting was called by Hereford George on 14 February 1876 and the Oxford Alpine Club was officially founded. The club had a limit of 30 members and consisted mainly of

176. OUMC training session at the Horspath Tunnel in the late 1950s. Alan Wedgewood and Colin Taylor on the *Horspath Horror*. (*Richard Gilbert*)

Dons, although there were some undergraduate members. Its main activity was a dinner each year, with occasional lectures. The limit of 30 was lifted in 1883; this helped matters, but when Arnold Lunn started at Balliol in 1907 he could see a need for an undergraduate mountaineering club. There was an unofficial club that met at irregular intervals on the roofs of Oxford and it is likely that this helped form the OUMC.

The exact date of formation is unclear; Lunn originally said it was in 1909 but later changed his mind based on that fact that he had been sent down from Oxford in Trinity Term 2009 for failing exams in the rudiments of Holy Scripture. From other sources I believe the club was formed in Hilary term 1909, and it was on this basis that we celebrated the Centenary in March 2009. H E G Tyndale was elected President at the first meeting, with Lunn taking on the role of Secretary. In those early years the club ran along similar lines to the OAC, with slide shows and dinners being the main activities. Whilst some members were active climbers they did not climb as a club, and only really managed to climb during the vacations. On one occasion in 1912 the club entertained four distinguished Cambridge mountaineers, Geoffrey Winthrop Young, H O Jones, Claude Elliott, and George Mallory. This was the beginning of a partnership that lasted through to the late twenties, and included the production of four joint journals.

OUMC took heavy losses in the First World War and by 1919 it had ceased to exist. In the autumn of 1920 H R C Carr was instrumental in reforming the club. Initially they knew nothing of the pre-war club, although Arnold Lunn attended a meeting a few months later, so they would have known by then. This new OUMC climbed more as a club and their calendar typically consisted of lecture meetings during the term, an annual dinner, and meets during the vacations. The Lake District and North Wales were popular for the Christmas and Easter vacations, while summer drew them to the Alps.

The Oxford University Women's Mountaineering Club was formed for the first time in 1924, and the Irvine Travel Fund founded in 1926 following the death of Sandy Irvine on Everest. In the early thirties it was Cambridge climbers who were leading developments in the UK while OUMC members were more active overseas. Hoyland and Wand made an ascent of the Grépon in 1934, an OUMC team made many first ascents in the Caucasus, and another nearly succeeded on Masherbrum.

The club nearly disintegrated during the Second World War but somehow managed to hold one or two meets each year, at Helyg or Brackenclose. With the return of the servicemen after the war membership increased rapidly. The club began a pattern of activities involving lecture meetings, the annual dinner, meets in the UK during Christmas and Easter vacations and a trip to the Alps in summer. Rationing affected the ability to go climbing at the weekend, and climbing standards were described as very low, and took some time to improve. Scott Russell arranged two joint meets with the Geneva University Club at Zinal in 1946 and Arolla in 1947, and these went some way to improving the Alpine experience of club members. A hard blow was dealt to the club the following year, with the death of three members in an accident on the Matterhorn.

The following years did start to see an increase in standards, particularly when Tom Bourdillon came up to Oxford in 1948, tackling climbs like *Hiatus* and *Gimmer Crack* in poor conditions given the equipment of the time. His approach to hard climbing made a tremendous impact in the Alps and rubbed off on other members. With Mike Ball he made the first British ascent for many years of the Mer de Glace face of the Grépon, and the following year with Dick Viney and John Saxby he did the Ryan-Lochmatter route on the Plan, and with Nicol the Roc-Grépon traverse and the north face of the Petit Dru.

It was in the early fifties that the President's invitation meet was formed. Held in the CIC Hut below Ben Nevis, it was the scene of many incidents. In 1951 Nicol and Rawlinson fell about 600ft down *Zero Gully* after, 'The pitons came out like studs from a dress shirt.' The following year whilst soloing *Gardyloo Gully* David Collis fell, knocking off Alan Blackshaw, but retaining his honour by turning and exclaiming 'Good Lord, I'm sorry!' after the fall.

The bridges at Horspath were a popular venue with the club at this time. They lie about 5 miles south-east of Oxford along a railway line. The steep walls were excellent stamina training and the tunnel faces provided technical climbing on small holds. The faces are still occasionally visited by

OUMC climbers, although many of the finishing holds have fallen and routes become overgrown.

Members of OUMC were active in the Himalaya during the fifties, with a number of University expeditions including to Gangotri, Haramosh and the Chitral. The story of Haramosh is one of the great epics of mountaineering, and is told in *The Last Blue Mountain* by Ralph Barker. The club also had two members on the Everest expedition in 1953 – Tom Bourdillon and Michael Westmacott. The fifties also saw Nicol taking part in the first British ascent of a route graded TD, and of an ED in the western Alps. With Bourdillon, Nicol made ascents of the Ratti-Vitalli on the Aiguille Noire de Peuterey, the north face of the Petit Dru and the first British ascent of the east face of the Grand Capuçin.

In 1957 when Michael Binnie arrived at Oxford, it was Cambridge climbers who were filling the guidebooks and journals of the time. But not for long, as Michael explains:

'Enter the new President, Colin Mortlock, a man for whom non-conformity was almost an art form and who personally raised university climbing to stellar heights. Together with Peter Hutchinson he put up a series of hard routes on Millstone Edge as well as climbing many of the harder classics in the Pass and on Cloggy. A notable first ascent was *Jubilee Climb* on Dinas Mot. In the company, variously of Hutchinson, Wilf Noyce and Rhodes Scholar, Jack Sadler, he climbed the east face of the Capuçin, the *Brown/Whillans Route* on the Blaitière and made first British ascents of the *Welzenbach Route* on the Dent d'Hérens, a direct on the Furggen ridge and on the Signalkuppe. It was not so much what Colin climbed. His intense personality and presence, coupled with the fact that in the vacations he climbed with the Rock and Ice, gave Oxford mountaineering a certain frisson in the late fifties. Colin went down in 1959. The hard men that followed him were of a different order but continued to keep standards high. These were the triumvirate of Alan Wedgwood, Colin Taylor and Richard Gilbert who, as a job lot, were as eccentric as they come!'

The Oxford University Women's Mountaineering Club had been reformed for a third time in 1953 and regular meets were held in Wales and the Lake District. Some of these were held in the same area as an OUMC meet so that the groups might benefit from the presence of each other. By 1955 the ladies were invited to attend OUMC meetings and bus meets, with the ladies extending the same offer to the men. By 1959 women were permitted limited membership of the OUMC, invited to all but the annual dinner, with the events on the term-cards being the same for the two clubs. In the AGM of 1961 a motion was passed to give ladies full membership rights, and Janet Wedgewood remembers the OUWMC was certainly disbanded by Michaelmas term that year. A new position on the Committee was created, the Ladies' Representative, and for the first 15 years or so this was held by a female member of the club. Eventually the post was filled by a male member and it was only a few more years before the position was dropped entirely. The club first had a female president, Elizabeth Jolley, in

1983 and has had four since.

John Wilkinson has probably the best view of the club in the latter half of the 20th century, and provided me with most of the information for this section. He studied for a D.Phil in the late sixties, and was Senior Member from 1977 to 1997. In 1966 the OUMC, like the CUMC, was still one of the premier clubs. The President was invited to the Alpine Club dinners, the journal was widely distributed, and the club even received books for review.

An important element in building club spirit was that back in the 1960s there was very little private transport and the main meets went by coach. Later in the 1970s this was replaced by mini-buses, of which one belonged to the Clubs' Committee. Climbing was never recognised as a sport by the University, and so did not receive the kind of funds that the 'real' sports could get. John did manage to get some money for equipment and Brian Smith along with some dons from St Catherine's College managed to get a small climbing wall built at the Iffley Road sports centre at the start of the '80s. The holds were made by DR walls and the wall built by the University bricklayer, at a total cost of £3000. It was popular with club members up until the wall at Brookes was built, and then underwent a revival in 2000, when the holds were numbered and a bouldering competition held. The wall now boasts hundreds of problems, and has its own guidebook.

177. OUMC at Stanage, 1975. Andy Brazier tries an unconventional approach to *Goliath's Groove*. (*Geoffrey Grimmett*)

The year typically started with a Freshers' meet to gritstone and another to Wales. Those that survived (by choice rather than physical elimination) were more or less left to fend for themselves. Coach meet venues included Wales, Derbyshire and Swanage, with destinations further afield being saved for the vacation. The Avon Gorge was immensely popular with the club, and it was there in November 1973 that Stephen Venables almost killed a novice French member called Pierre. Stephen was belayed to a single knife-blade piton at the top of *Suspension Bridge Arête* when Pierre got into difficulties, climbed above a runner and then fell off. This created a

178. OUMC in Snell's Field, Chamonix, on a summer vacation meet; left to right Mike Harrop, Nick Barrett, Nevil Hewitt and Chris Harris. (*Simon Richardson*)

huge jerk and pulled Stephen off too. They both fell about 80ft and ended up see-sawing from the one runner the rope was clipped into – an old peg halfway up the chimney. Stephen suffered a dislocated shoulder, smashed knee and rope burns almost through to the bone. He appeared on the national news that night, telling a cameraman where to put his camera, and, unfortunately, generated all the usual nonsense about putting the public rescue services at risk. Pierre, thank God, was merely shaken, but was never seen again at an OUMC meet.

The best mountaineers of the club tended to do their own thing in the summer, but most years a group would head to Chamonix, with Snell's Field popular in the eighties. An increase in the number of graduates and people spending up to seven years in Oxford meant there were some very experienced mountaineers in the club. Rock-climbing standards were also high. In the seventies, Phil Bartlett and Andy Brazier climbed *Quiver* on Clogwyn Du'r Arddu, which was Britain's first E6. Don Ballance wrote in the 1987 journal that Sean Myles and Mike Dawes were regularly climbing E5, with half a dozen members climbing E3. Many members were climbing HVS or E1 by the time they left Oxford.

In the mid nineties novice climbers weren't much of a priority for OUMC. The club remained relatively obscure within the University, but there were a number of very competent climbers around at that time. Simon Milward's outing on the Central Pillar of Frêney and Anthony Spate's ascent of the Walker Spur set the bar for OUMC climbers. In 1998 this began to change, with the new President, Mark Naylor, making changes in priorities and embracing the changes to University sport in general. Sessions took place at Brookes wall every Tuesday, and the first few meets each year were very much geared to novice climbers.

A significant event occurred around 2001 when the University introduced rules requiring all 'coaches' to be registered with the Sports Federation. This included any leaders climbing with less-experienced climbers on club meets, and would require a formal assessment of their ability. This kind of regulation clearly did not fit with a sport like climbing, and Steve and Katja Broadbent, being the more senior club members, got deeply involved. The club made plans for disaffiliation if that became necessary, and the debates ended with an EGM in the spring. The back room of the Gardener's Arms was full to bursting, with almost the entire club, along with representatives from the University and Sports Federation. Fortunately the outcome was in the club's favour and the club has enjoyed a good relationship with the University since then.

That was my first year at Oxford. The pattern of the club had not changed much. There were four meets a term, a Christmas dinner and an annual dinner. Each vacation, members would go on various unofficial trips. For some reason Skye became a popular New Year destination, and we put up around 40 new rock climbs, both in the Cuillin and on the sea-cliffs of Flodigarry. Most summers people would head to the Alps, with Saas Fee being quite a popular destination along with Chamonix.

I served as OUMC President in 2003-2004. By the time I left Oxford in 2005 the club was beginning a particularly successful period. Lydia Press was President in 2006 and she managed to broaden the horizons of club members, and bring together a wide variety of climbers. It came as a huge blow to the club when she was tragically killed in the Alps in 2008.

Rock-climbing standards reached new heights thanks to Eddie Barbour who was in a league of his own, making ascents of *End of the Affair* (E8), *Simba's Pride* (E8) and *Tolerance* (E8) as well as his Fairhead project, *The Rockafella* (E7). Around six other members have made ascents above E5 in recent years. In the mountains things have been quieter, with few notable ascents. Alpine ascents have been limited to mid-grade routes, but a number of us have been further afield, including my trips to South America. More recently India has received some attention with two trips in the last two years to the Miyar Nala.

We have recently held our Centenary Ball, attended by 150 past and present members, including members from the early fifties. Steve Broadbent produced a video of the club history based on my research, and Elie Dekoninck put together an excellent gallery. For me, the number of people who chose to attend goes to show how important the club has been in their lives. It's fair to say that for many, OUMC was more important to their University lives than their college, or friends from their course.

I'll end with a quote by Felix Ng from the club logbook.

'It's 12:16am and I can just write. Keep this club going. It's not just a good laugh. I love it.'

C A RUSSELL

One Hundred Years Ago

(with extracts from *The Alpine Journal*)

> As we reached the summit of the pass the cliffs and glaciers of the Lauterbrunnen Jungfrau, backed by the sharp pyramid of the Eiger rose beyond a misty abyss of shadows. Every curve in the swelling snows, every crag and buttress of the Blümlisalp cliffs was lit up by the mellow rays of the mountain moon.

This description of a winter scene above the Tschingel Pass in the Bernese Alps was recorded by Arnold Lunn who left Kandersteg on 2 January 1909 accompanied by Professor F F Roget and three guides engaged as porters to commence his ski traverse of 'the Oberland from end to end'. Staying in huts and other accommodation, Lunn and his companions reached the Lötschental by way of the Petersgrat and continued over the Lötschenlücke in perfect weather. After climbing the Finsteraarhorn on 6 January the party completed the final stage of the traverse, reaching the Grimsel road and arriving at Guttannen late on the following day.

In the same region, also on 2 January, Rudolf Schloss, G Licht and O D Tauern made the first ski ascent[1] of the Ebnefluh. Other expeditions of note completed with the aid of ski included a traverse from Zinal to the Val d'Hérens and Zermatt by W A M Moore and J R Dixon with the guides Louis and Benoît Theytaz and, at Easter, an ascent of the Grossglockner by Max Winkler and Fritz Strobel.

Although conditions in the Alps were cold and unsettled for much of the summer the climbing season was memorable for a number of successful expeditions undertaken during brief spells of fine weather by leading climbers of the day. In the Mont Blanc range on 12 August Hans Pfann and Franz Gassner completed a difficult route on the Italian side of the Grandes Jorasses, reaching Pointe Walker by way of the Pra Sec glacier and the upper section of the south-east, Tronchey ridge. A few days later, on 16 August, H O Jones with Laurent Croux and a porter traversed the Aiguille Blanche de Peuterey, forcing a route from the Frêney glacier up the steep west spur of the north-west summit and descending to the Brenva glacier.

In the Zermatt district on 31 August Geoffrey Winthrop Young and Josef Knubel joined forces with Oliver Perry-Smith to establish a new route on the north-east face of the Weisshorn. Earlier in the month, on 4 August, in the Bernese Alps Young, George Mallory and Donald Robertson made the first complete ascent of the long south-east ridge[2] of the Nesthorn. In the Bernina Alps on 30 July another long expedition was undertaken by G

179. West face of K2 from the Savoia glacier, June 1909. (*Vittorio Sella*)

L and C G G Stewart who with Ferdinand Summermatter and Alphonse Simond made the first ascent of the south-west, Sella ridge of Piz Roseg.

In the Eastern Alps two notable climbs were completed: in the Dolomites the first ascent of the north-east, Dibona edge of the Cima Grande di Lavaredo – the Grosse Zinne – by Emil Stübler with Angelo Dibona in August; and, on 22 September, a new route to the summit of the Dachstein by the guides Georg and Franz Steiner who opened a direct line up the south face.

180. K2 from the north-east, June 1909. (*HRH the Duke of the Abruzzi*)

Early in the year work was resumed on the construction of the Lötschberg Tunnel under the Bernese Alps between Kandersteg and Goppenstein. Following the collapse of the northern, Kandersteg heading[3] and the completion of a fresh survey it was decided to realign part of the route away from the unstable ground below the Gastern valley and to introduce a series of curves – the first major Alpine tunnel to incorporate a curved alignment.[4]

On 25 July celebrations were held to mark the official opening of the first section, from Le Fayet to the Col de Voza, of the *Tramway du Mont Blanc*.

> The train takes one hour to accomplish the distance between these two places, and a splendid but limited view can be enjoyed from the summit of the Col.

In September Mont Blanc itself was the scene of considerable activity.

> The Janssen Observatory on the summit of Mont Blanc is about to be demolished by workmen, probably during the next few days. It has several times been in danger from snow-drifts, but the storms of last winter were so severe that the building was nearly buried in the snow.
>
> All the valuable scientific instruments in the observatory, which was completed in 1893[5] under great difficulties, have been removed to the Vallot Observatory, which is at a lower altitude.

During the year many expeditions were undertaken in other mountain ranges. In July Helene Kuntze, another active climber, travelled to the Caucasus where she explored the Laboda and Sugan districts in the central region. Accompanied by the guides Josef Schaller and Rafael Lochmatter and by an interpreter named Julian Abuloff she completed a number of successful climbs including, on 5 August, the first ascent of the south, higher peak (4490m) of Sugan Tau.[6]

On 15 April the Duke of the Abruzzi arrived at Srinagar to commence his expedition to the Karakoram. The Duke, who hoped to attempt the ascent of K2 (8611m) and 'to contribute to the solution of the problem as to the greatest height to which man may attain in mountain climbing', was accompanied on this occasion by Marchese Federico Negrotto, his aide-de-camp, as topographer, Vittorio Sella as photographer and Filippo De Filippi as physician and naturalist. Three guides – Joseph Petigax and the brothers Alexis and Henri Brocherel – and four porters,[7] all from Courmayeur travelled with the party which was completed by Erminio Botta, Sella's assistant. At Srinagar the Duke was assisted by Sir Francis Younghusband, then British Resident in Kashmir, who arranged for A C Baines, an experienced traveller in the region, to join the expedition as transport and supply officer.

On 25 May an advanced base was established at 5030m below the south face of K2. After heights of more than 6000m had been reached during unsuccessful attempts on the south-east, Abruzzi spur and the north-west ridge the party moved round the peak to examine the north-east ridge. Although this ridge was ruled out as impracticable the Duke with Petigax and a porter was able, on 25 June, to reach a height of some 6600m on the south ridge of Skyang Kangri (7544m) from the head of the Godwin-Austen glacier.

Having completed the reconnaissance of K2 the party established a base below the north face of the north-east summit of Chogolisa (7654m)[8] and placed a light camp on the Kaberi saddle at 6335m. On 18 July in dense mist and dangerous snow conditions the Duke with Petigax, Henri Brocherel and a porter ascended the south-east ridge to a height of 7500m – the greatest climbing altitude attained at that time.

Another visitor to this region was Tom Longstaff who spent four months exploring a large area of the eastern and southern Karakoram. Accompanied initially by Morris Slingsby and Dr Arthur Neve, Longstaff located and crossed the Saltoro Pass (5547m) in June to find a great unknown glacier – the upper reach of the Siachen glacier – flowing to the south-east; he also discovered and named the Teram Kangri group of peaks across the glacier to the north. Later in the year with the assistance of D G Oliver, British Joint Commissioner in Ladakh, Longstaff approached the Siachen glacier from the south. On 18 September, after ascending the ice for 16km he was able to estimate the total length of the glacier – some 72km – and to ascertain its true location.

This outstanding piece of exploration enabled Longstaff to confirm the correct position of the main, northern axis of the Karakoram and to add the Teram Kangri peaks and the approximate area of the Siachen glacier to the existent map.

Further east Dr Alexander Kellas returned to Sikkim where on 14 September, accompanied by two local men, he made the first ascent of Langpo Peak (6950m). Kellas also made unsuccessful attempts to climb other peaks including Pauhunri (7125m) and to reach the Nepal Gap (6300m) on the north ridge of Kangchenjunga (8586m).

In the Southern Alps of New Zealand on 4 March L M Earle with Alex[9] and Peter Graham and Jack Clarke followed a new line, now known as *Earle's Route*, to the High Peak of Mount Cook (3764m)[10] by way of the north-west ridge above the Sheila glacier. Later in the year, on 1 December, Earle and Bernard Head with Clarke and Alex Graham made the first ascent of Mount Hamilton (2997m) in the Malte Brun range.

In the Canadian Rockies notable expeditions included the ascent of the unclimbed North Tower (3525m) of Mount Goodsir[11] on 16 August by J P Forde and P D McTavish with Eduard Feuz senior and, in September, the first complete traverse of the long summit ridge of Mount Victoria (3464m) by G W Culver with Eduard Feuz junior and Rudolf Aemmer. To the west in the Selkirk range the guideless party of F K Butters, E W D Holway and Howard Palmer completed a number of new routes including, on 23 July, the first ascent of Augustine Peak (3283m), the highest point in the Bishop's group.

In Britain increasing numbers of climbers were active in all the principal regions. In Wales two new routes of note were completed: *Central Arête* on Glyder Fawr at Whitsun by Guy Barlow and H B Buckle; and, on 23 September, *Paradise Climb* on the East Buttress of Lliwedd by H O Jones and R F Backwell. In the Lake District on 7 April Fred Botterill and John Hazard made the first ascent of *Abbey Buttress* on the Napes, Great Gable. Several months later, on 26 September, an attempt to climb the neighbour-

181. Siachen glacier and Teram Kangri peaks, 15 June 1909. (*Tom Longstaff*)

ing Eagle's Nest Ridge ended in tragedy when T J Rennison, leading Botterill, Oliver Thorneycroft and Fred Aldous, slipped and fell to his death. In Scotland on 12 April Harold Raeburn, climbing with W A Brigg and H S Tucker, completed the ascent[12] of a famous route – *Crowberry Gully* on Buachaille Etive Mor.

An event which aroused considerable interest was the publication of *The Climbs on Lliwedd* by J M Archer Thomson and A W Andrews, the first of a series of guides issued by the Climbers' Club. The guide was soon in demand and received a favourable review in the *Alpine Journal.*

> On the whole the authors have succeeded in avoiding the merely sensational, while laying due emphasis on the extreme difficulty of many climbs which they describe.

A welcome development at the end of the year was the formation on 8 December of the Association of British Members of the Swiss Alpine Club.

> This Association has been formed, with the full approval and recognition of the authorities of the S.A.C., to bring together those members of the S.A.C. who live in Great Britain.

The first President of the Association was Clinton Dent, an honorary member of the Swiss Alpine Club and a former President of the Alpine Club.

On 9 January the death occurred of Count Henri Russell-Killough, a pioneer of Pyrenean exploration and an early member of the Alpine Club. An ardent traveller in his youth, the Count is remembered for his association with the Vignemale (3298m) where he constructed a series of grottoes and spent long periods alone, on many occasions watching the sunset fade 'or in grave meditation stalking slowly to and fro across the moonlit snows'.

In conclusion it seems appropriate to recall in Longstaff's own words[13] his great achievement in the Karakoram.

> We had stolen some 500 square miles, from the Yarkand river system of Chinese Turkestan, and joined it to the waters of the Indus and the Kingdom of Kashmir.

References

1. A ski ascent is defined by Sir Arnold Lunn as 'an expedition on which ski were used until the foot of the final rock or ice ridges'.
2. The ridge had been descended by John, Charles and Edward Hopkinson, Cecil Slingsby, G T Lowe and a porter on 4 September 1895.
3. See *AJ113,* 270,2008.
4. As a result of the realignment away from the original straight line the total length of the tunnel increased by 800m to 14.605km.
5. See *AJ97*, 238, 1992-93 and *AJ98*, 225-226,1993.
6. The first ascent of the north peak (4467m) had been made by Vittorio Sella and Emilio Gallo on 22 August 1896.
7. The porters were Ernest Bareux, Emile Brocherel, Laurent Petigax and Albert Savoie.
8. The Bride Peak. Named by Sir Martin Conway during his expedition to the Karakoram in 1892.
9. Alex Graham was known to everyone as Alec.
10. For details of a recent alteration to this height see *AJ99*, 221, 1994.
11. The first ascent of the South Tower (3562m) had been made by C E Fay and H C Parker with Christian Häsler and Christian Kaufmann on 16 July 1903.
12. Considered by some authorities to be the first ascent under winter conditions. Raeburn had completed the route with E B Green on 10 April 1898 when 'the quantity of snow was exceptionally small for the time of year'.
13. Tom Longstaff, *This My Voyage.* London, John Murray, 1950.

Area Notes

181. Simon Pierse, *Ciarforon from Rifugio Vittorio Emanuele II,* 2006, watercolour, 42 x 59cm

Area Notes

COMPILED AND EDITED BY PAUL KNOTT

LINDSAY GRIFFIN

The Alps 2008

This selection of ascents in 2008 could not have been written without the help of Jonathan Griffith, Andrej Grmovsek, Tomaz Jakofcic, Rolando Larcher, Tony Penning, Claude Rémy, Hilary Sharp, Luca Signorelli and Ueli Steck.

Starting in late June, Diego Giovannini and Franco 'Franz' Nicolini took 60 days to complete the first non-mechanised link-up of all 82 Alpine 4000m summits that appear on the UIAA's official list. The pair opted to track from west to east, ending with Piz Bernina. Until the early 1990s there was no definitive list; some opting for as low as 52 (the number of completely separate mountains), others adding more, with alpine specialist Richard Goedecke listing a staggering 150 individual tops and bumps. At the end of 1993, in an attempt to put an end to the debate, a joint UIAA and Italian Alpine Club committee came up with an 'official' list of 82, which they hoped would be used as the benchmark for future attempts. This list came too late for Simon Jenkins and Martin Moran, who in the same year made the first non-mechanised traverse of 74 summits from the Piz Bernina to the Barre des Ecrins. Perhaps the most notable attempt to complete the 82-peak traverse began in the winter of 2004, and ended after 65 summits when Patrick Berhault fell to his death.

Ecrins Enchaînement

An impressive event in the **Ecrins Massif** took place over 11 days, ending in October, when Aymeric Clouet and Christophe Dumerest made a more-or-less continuous north to south traverse of the range, linking eight respectable north faces. Two or three of these alone would keep most people happy for a season. The pair started with the *Z Couloir* on the **Meije** and finished with the *North Ridge* of **Le Sirac.** In between they climbed the *North Couloir* of the **Col du Diable**, *North Couloir* of the **Brèche de la Somme**, *Grand Central Couloir* on the north-west face of the **Dôme de Neige des Ecrins**, *North-West Face* of **Ailefroide Occidentale**, *North-East Couloir* of **Les Bans** and *North Couloir* of the **Brèche des Bruyères**. They saw no other climber in the massif during the entire trip.

Mont Blanc Massif

At the end of September Enrico Bonino and Paolo Stroppiana squeezed a new line into the now well-explored east face of **Mont Maudit**, when they climbed an icy ramp through the rock buttress immediately above the diagonal traverse of *Blaireaux* (just left of the 1978 *Gabarrou-Maquennehan Central Couloir*, later renamed the *Direttissima Roger Baxter-Jones*). The 500m

183. Marko Lukic making a free ascent of the Dru Couloir Direct (First complete ascent Accomazzo/Sorenson, 1977 with two short sections of A3) (*Andrej Grmovsek*)

route, named *Rêve Caché*, was climbed in 17 pitches up to WI 5+ and F4c. Not long after starting the difficult section, Stroppiana was hit on the leg by a large rock and finished the route with some difficulty.

On the **Grand Capuçin**, Alex Huber evoked old ethics of the legendary Paul Preuss by free soloing up and down the *Swiss Route* (300m: 6b). Huber climbed the route from the top of the approach couloir in one hour on 5 August. Preuss, who soloed many climbs in the first years of the 20th century and was noted for his purity of style, felt that one should ascend only those routes that can be down-climbed safely.

On the east flank of the **Dent de Jetoula** above the Rochefort Glacier,

Elio Bonfanti, Enrico Bonino, Luca Maspes, Rinaldo Roetti and Paolo Stroppiana climbed *Diretta allo Scudo, le Demon du Midi* (250m: 6c/A0, 6b+ obl) on the east-southeast face of **Punta 3095m**. The right edge of this formation was climbed in 1990 by Giancarlo Grassi, the last of many routes in the Mont Blanc Massif that he opened before his untimely death in the spring of 1991. A second route was added in 2005 by Dave Hope, Nick Mullin and Tony Penning, who climbed a corner system left of a prominent shield of slabs: *Voie Pellin* (500m of climbing, British E4 6a). The new Italian route climbs directly up the shield, but in complete contrast to *Voie Pellin*, uses a large quantity of bolts, a situation that saddens Penning, who had one day hoped to return and attempt the line in good style. Bonfanti has approached the Courmayeur municipality, proposing that Punta 3095m (actually 3093m) be renamed Punta Grassi.

From 19-24 February, Benoit Drouillat and Pascal Ducroz, both French guides, and the Belgian Vanessa Francois made most likely the second winter and, indeed, a very rare ascent of *Manitua* on the north face of the **Grandes Jorasses**. The team was unable to climb the final and crux pitch onto the crest of the Croz Spur, and instead made a series of very tenuous skyhook moves left to reach the top section of Bubu Bole's route, *Le Nez*. Here, they aided up Bole's protection bolts to complete the ascent. Sadly, within the next 12 months both Drouillat and Ducroz would lose their lives in separate climbing accidents.

On 17 February Tina di Batista and Tomaz Jakofcic made a rare ascent of Yvan Ghirardini's *Rêve Ephemere d'Alpiniste* on the north face of Pointe Young. They climbed the route free in 11 hours at a surprisingly reasonable M5+.

On the left extremity of the Jorasses north face, 57-year old Patrick Gabarrou plugged the obvious gap between Couloir Douce and the Petit MacIntyre. This snow/ice face with a mixed exit was climbed with Michel Caranotte, and is Gabarrou's ninth new route on the wall. Graded TD, the line was named *Hugues d'en Haut* after Hugues d'Aubarede, a 61-year old French grandfather who was one of the victims of the 2008 K2 tragedy.

In January, on the north face of the **Grand Dru**, two Slovenian teams made completely free ascents of the *Dru Couloir Direct*. First up was the tried and tested partnership of Andrej Grmovsek and Marko Lukic, who completed the route in 13 hours at VI/6+ and M8, with each pitch climbed on-sight. Grmovsek said it was the best mixed climb he'd ever done. It was repeated later at the same grade by Tina di Batista and Tomaz Jakofcic.

On the Grandes Montets Ridge of the **Aiguille Verte**, Jonathan Griffith and Will Sim climbed some new ground with their 450m *Choco and Vanilla Go Climbing*. However, most of this route appears to coincide with *Hot and Cold*, put up by Thierry Renault with Abigail Crofts in April 2007. The route loosely lies on the north-east (Argentière) face of **Pointe Farrar** but well to the right of the summit fall-line. In the upper section, Crofts and Renault avoided a rocky nose via mixed ground on the left, while Griffith and Sim passed it on the right. The meat of both routes appears to be the same; three sustained mixed pitches in a corner system that were II 4+ and M5 for Renault, and III M6 (easy Scottish 7) and A1 for the British pair.

On the right side of the north face of the **Petit Clocher du Portalet**, Claude and Yves Remy have added *Plaisir Immédiat*. This eight-pitch route (6c) is now the best equipped (65 bolts) and least demanding on the steep monolithic wall. The Remys also replaced many of the original bolts on their 1983 jamming classic *Etat de Choc* (7a). On the east pillar of **Le Satellite**, a modest summit just north of the Petit Clocher, the Remys put up *La Raison du Temps*, a five-pitch bolt-protected line up cracks and corners at 6b.

184. *Left:* Duncan Tunstall climbing the steep chimney beyond the shattered tower, pitch 33, day 3, on the first ascent of the south-west spur of Punta Baretti. *Right:* approximate line of Richardson/Tunstall route. (*Simon Richardson*)

South-west Spur, Punta Baretti (1200m ED1)

Punta Baretti (4013m) is considered to be the most remote of all the 4000m peaks and lies on the south side of Mont Blanc on the lower Brouillard Ridge. Its forgotten south-west side plunges 1600m to the Miage glacier and is defined by two spurs separated by a couloir. The lower-angled right-hand spur was climbed by Baretti himself in 1880, and has only been repeated once. The upper section was followed by Blodig in 1908 who traversed onto Baretti's route from the upper Mont Blanc glacier during his quest to complete the 4000ers.

The south-west aspect of Baretti was ignored for nearly a century until May 2006 when Pierre Tardivel climbed, and then skied, the couloir left of Baretti's spur. The couloir was repeated by an Italian team in July 2009,

185. Yves Remy repeating his recently re-equipped 1983 classic, *Etat de Choc* (Remy/ Remy: 300m: 7a), on the North Face of the Petit Clocher du Portalet. Here he is on pitch six (6c). (*Claude Remy*)

which prompted Simon Richardson and Duncan Tunstall to attempt the steeper unclimbed spur leading directly to the summit.

The pair left the Miage glacier at 4am on 7 September and ascended 400m of brittle ice up the steep snout of the Mont Blanc glacier to gain the spur which they climbed in more than 40 pitches over a series of knife-edge towers to the final snow slopes. They reached the summit at 2pm on the third day and descended to the Eccles Hut.

The ascent of a new 1200m route leading to the summit of a 4000m peak is an unusual event; according to the Italian mountain historian Luca Signorelli, the south-west spur of Punta Baretti was 'one of the last remaining virgin features on Mont Blanc'.

[*A full account of this ascent is planned for the next AJ.*]

Bernese Oberland

Records were set and then broken on the **Eiger** during the winter. On 28 January, Simon Anthamatten and Roger Schäli climbed the *Classic 1938 Route* in just six hours and 50 minutes, a time that until quite recently would have been a good three hours faster than the record for a roped party. In 1969 Peter Habeler and Reinhold Messner turned the world of alpinism upside down by racing up the climb in an astonishing 10 hours. This was an achievement light years ahead of its time and remained more or less unbeaten by a roped pair until very recently, Schäli himself, with Hanspeter Hug, knocking two hours off the record in October 2007. Prior to his 2008 ascent, Schali had climbed the route nine times. Incidentally, film buffs will recognize Anthamatten and Schäli as the actors playing Andreas Hinterstoisser and Toni Kurz in Joe Simpson's film, *The Beckoning Silence*.

For Schäli it was part of a remarkable achievement of climbing all six 'Great North Faces' of the Alps, one after the other, between 8 January and 22 February. Apart from the Eiger and Badile (see next page), his routes were as follows: Cima Grande, *Via Camillotto Pellissier*; Matterhorn, *Classic Schmidt Route*; Dru, *Dru Couloir*; Grandes Jorasses, *Shroud*.

The Anthamatten-Schäli record did not last for long: less than a month later Daniel Arnold and Stephen Ruoss climbed the *1938 Route* in six hours and 10 minutes.

Of course this sort of time is quite leisurely for Ueli Steck. The noted Swiss alpinist, who already held the speed record for the ascent, returned to the face on 13 February and, without a rope, stormed up the 1938 Route in two hours and 47 minutes (and 33 seconds!). As the weaving nature of the line makes the distance climbed more than twice the 1800m vertical interval of the face, Steck was moving at over 20m a minute.

An innovative feat took place on the very steep rock wall that forms the right edge of the north face, when on 6 August American Dean Potter soloed *Deep Blue Sea* (300m. 7b+), wearing a parachute to protect a possible fall. Fortunately, it was never put to the test. Potter traversed into the route above the lower, less steep and looser terrain, where a fall would not have allowed him enough time to deploy the parachute. He concentrated

186. Monte Disgrazia from the north-northeast. (E) East Summit (3648m). (C) Central Summit (3650m). (M) Main Summit (3678m). (N) North face. (1) North East Spur (Anderegg/Prat/Barlow/Still/Taugwald, 1874: AD+). (2) The approximate line of *Moonlight* (Baletti/Cavalli, 2008: 450m of climbing: VI and 75°). (3) Hypergoulotte (Baletti/Ranaglia, 1989: 330m: ED1: 95° and V). (4) Couloir dell'Insubordinato (Casarotto/Federico/Gogna/Mario/Mauri/Molin, 1979: 300m: D/D+: 65° max). (4) The classic Corda Molla Ridge (First integral ascent Bonola/Corti/Corti, 1928: 500m: AD+). (*Lindsay Griffin*)

his efforts on the slightly impending headwall, five pitches of which he'd climbed the year before, roped to Beat Kammerlander.

Late in August, Steck returned to the north face, and with Stefan Siegrist free climbed *Paciencia*, creating what the Swiss pair feel to be the most difficult alpine sport route on the Eiger. The route, which climbs through the Rote Fluh and continues up the front face of the Czechoslovak Pillar, was equipped, climbed but not redpointed in 2003. Paciencia has 27 pitches, one of which is 8a, two are 7c+ and nearly all the remainder vary between 7a and 7b+.

Bregaglia-Disgrazia

Arriving at the summit of the **Piz Badile** on the 20 February, after a bivouac at the foot of the east-northeast face, and three more on the wall, Fabio Valseschini completed the first solo winter ascent of the *British Route* (Isherwood/Kosterlitz, 1968: 600m: ED1: climbed free by Rossano Libera at 7a). This was only the second time the route had been climbed in winter: the first, in 1982 by two young alpinists from Czechoslovakia, Zusanna Hofmannova and Alena Stehlikova, remains one of the most impressive performances ever by an all female team on a major route in the Alps. AC member Martin Moran made the first solo ascent in 1979, and as access to this route has become increasingly difficult over the years, it is not clear if

187. The west face of the Sass dia Crusc (2825m) rises above the Badia Valley. (A) The left-hand or Livanos Pillar. (B) The Central Pillar. (1) Livanos Pillar (VII- [5.10b], 500m, Gabriel-Livanos, 1953). (2) Meyerl Diedre (VII [5.10d], 550m, Mayerl-Rahracher, 1962). (3) La Perla Preziosa (IX+ [5.13a/b], 375m/eight pitches of new climbing, Sartori-Tondini-Zandegiacomo, 2008). (*Claudio Cima*)

there have been any more before Valseschini.

One day later, Rossano Libera started up the *Cassin Route* alone, and after two bivouacs made the first confirmed winter solo. Unusually, there appears to have been a lot of compact névé and he climbed much of the route using ice tools, finding difficult mixed ground and dry tooling in the upper chimneys. However, just a few days earlier the *Cassin* had received a remarkably fast ascent by Simon Gietl and Roger Schäli, who completed it in a day and rappelled the *North Ridge* the following night. This may have been only the third winter ascent of the historic route, one of the traditional 'Six Great North Faces of the Alps'.

Benigno Baletti added his 19th (!) new route to **Monte Disgrazia,** when with his wife Giovanna Cavalli (completing her ninth new route on the peak) he climbed *Moonlight* (450m: 75° and UIAA VI). The pair began on the ice slope left of the Hypergoulotte on the north-northeast flank of the south-east ridge, but at half height crossed the couloir and finished up a pronounced rock rib of excellent serpentine.

Dolomites

Continuing his philosophy of trying to create hard traditionally-protected routes on the great Dolomite walls, Nicola Tondini, has made a free ascent of *La Perla Preziosa* (Precious Pearl) on the magnificent west face of the **Sass dia Crusc** (aka Sasso della Croce or Heiligkreuzkofel) in the Fanis. Tondini began working on the route, which lies to the right of the now classic Meyerl Diedre, in 2005. Stumped by a section of very rotten rock, he was forced to climb out right on a superb compact wall and agonized for more than a year about the problem of protection, before finally placing two bolts and climbing the crux at UIAA IX+.

Florian and Martin Riegler made the first free ascent of *Vint ani do*, a 350m line on the south face of the **Meisules de la Biesces** in the Sella Group first climbed in 2004 by Stefan Comploi and Ivo Rabanser at VII and A2. The brothers climbed the 12-pitch route at 8a+ to produce what is now considered the most difficult line in the Sella-Sassolungo region. Surprisingly, they made this free ascent during the winter season – on 2 March.

Rolando Larcher climbed a superb and exposed line left of the classic *Solda Route* on the south-west face of the **Marmolada di Penia**. Larcher employed his usual style, climbing from the ground up, using natural protection where possible and only resorting to bolts - as always, drilled by hand – when faced with totally compact rock. In the end he placed only 11 protection bolts. Although he managed to free each individual move of the 17-pitch *AlexAnna*, Larcher was unable to make a redpoint ascent due to unseasonably inclement weather but estimates the eventual grade at 8a+/8b.

On 15 August Thomas Huber completed a previously attempted project of linking hard routes on each of the summits of the **Tre Cime di Lavarado** in less than 24 hours, descending from the summits by parachute. With Peter Anzenbeger he started up *Alpenliebe* (UIAA IX) on the north face of the **Cima Ovest** at 10.30pm on the 14th, reached the summit at 4am but had to wait until dawn to make the BASE jump from near the top of the Squirrels' Ridge. At 7am he was beginning *Das Phantom der Zinne* (IX+) on the north face of the **Cima Grande** with his brother Alex. They reached the top at 2pm and then descended to the Ring Band, from where Thomas made his second BASE jump. At 3.30 he was tackling *Ötzi Trifft Yeti* (VIII+) on the south face of **Cima Piccalo** with Martin Kopfsguter, who apparently had to wake Huber numerous times on the belays. However, the pair reached the summit at 7.30pm after Thomas had climbed a total of 48 pitches. From there, he chose to descend the *Normal Route* at a more leisurely pace.

DEREK FORDHAM

Greenland 2008

Greenland was as popular as ever in 2008 and 69 land based 'sporting' expeditions, as the Danes like to refer to them, applied for permission to be in the National Park or on the Inland Ice. As usual the majority of these, 51, were to cross the Inland Ice following, with a few notable exceptions, the trade route between the Ammassalik area on the east coast and Kangerlussuak on the west. Of these 69 expeditions, 14 responded to your correspondent's request for information.

Weather in 2008 seemed to be rather better than the previous year when a number of Inland Ice expeditions were thwarted by poor conditions of weather and ice, although with the low percentage response to information requests it is difficult to draw overall conclusions. Last year's expansion of objectives to embrace more of the lesser-known mountain groups did not seem to continue. Perhaps this was due to the problems experienced last year of aircraft sinking into soft snow and eliciting threats from pilots and air charter companies that they would be limiting activity to such areas in future, but no hard evidence of this limitation has yet been reported.

One of the most interesting expeditions across the Inland Ice was that undertaken by Björn Leander and Andreas Classe (Sweden) who skied from **Qaanaaq** to **Kap Morris Jessup**, the most northerly point of mainland Greenland. They started with pulks weighing 150kg on 20 May after a 16-day delay due to bad weather, and encountered much soft snow followed by surface water on the ice necessitating a southerly detour, which also helped them gain height and cold snow. 500km into the journey, they encountered bear tracks close to their tent and 400km from the nearest coast. After 1200km and 50 days, they sighted Peary Land and much appreciated the relative warmth of entering a huge dry land. A large lake that they had intended to cross on the ice had also enjoyed the warmth and the lake ice was totally melted. Having in earlier lives had contacts with the military, they were able with a satellite telephone to summon a helicopter, which arrived after seven days' wait. A few minutes in the air and they were a lot lighter in wallets and only 350km from their destination in an area never visited before. The terrain was mainly dry valleys with glaciers and plenty of wildlife. Near the coast a lot of river wading was necessary resulting in wet equipment, but after 74 days, running out of food and 15kg each lighter they reached the small hut at Kap Morris Jessup to be picked up by helicopter. In their words, 'we had reached the objective but also emptiness was it not more'.

Much further south **Christian Eide (Norway)** made his sixth crossing of the Inland Ice leading a group of eight from Umivik, south of Ammassalik,

188. The Tasermiut valley with the Hermelnbjerg on the left and the Tininnertu-up group on the right, British Tasermiut Fjord Expedition. (*Ruben Gutzat*)

to Austmannadalen following the line of Nansen's first crossing in 1888. They started on 20 August and experienced generally good weather with just two days lost to the *piteraq*, the coastal katabatic wind common in this area. The surface of the ice lake at the head of Austmannadalen, which they reached on 13 September, was found to have dropped by about 80m and the lake split into three, probably due to glacial retreat allowing much water to drain away.

Following the trade route, **Harald Fuchs** and **Andre Felbrich (Germany)** left Isortoq, after being delayed a few days by problems with the helicopter that took them to the edge of the Inland Ice, on 21 April. They experienced a couple of days delay due to the *piteraq* after which they were able to make use of their kites to aid progress. Perhaps it was the stress of kite skiing that caused a broken ski in early May but repairs were effected and the pair reached Kangerlussuak on 22 May having remained in touch by satellite telephone with a contact in Germany who maintained an up to date website for the expedition throughout the traverse. On virtually the same route, Grzegorz and Szymon Gontarz, and Piotr Zasko of **Wazari Team Poland** set off from sea level at Nagtivit on 9 August and reached Point 660m at Kangerlussuak on 12 September. Out of their total traverse distance of 665km, they used kites for 80km although high winds up to 150km/hour gave problems as well as assistance. A storm towards the end of the journey caused concern when heavy snow reduced their progress to 10km/day and the party, already on rather slender rations, thought they would run out of food. Also on the same route, but leaving Nagtivit four days behind, were **Camilla Ianke** and **Bjørge Selvåg (Norway)** who reached Point 660m via

Camp Raven, as the old early warning station DYE 2, which all parties following the standard route pass, is now known, on the 4 September and thus without mentioning it must have passed Wazari Team Poland en route! They had no serious problems other than 1.5 days tent-bound and some extensive melt water on the west coast.

Starting earlier in the year on 9 May, **Timo Palo (Estonia)** and **Audun Tholfsen (Norway)** who might have expected reasonably settled weather encountered storms, wet snow, overcast, and rain! However, moving at 'night' after reaching 1700m altitude the skiing conditions improved and just after passing the highest point the temperature dropped to -30°C. Problems were encountered with the breakage of the metal bar which locates the toe of a nordic ski boot (in this case Alfa Skarvet GTX SNS) in the binding. They were able to repair it at Camp Raven and from there carry forward a few spare bits which were all needed. After Camp Raven, in one 17-hour day they managed 59km. Leaving the Russell glacier area of the Inland Ice and gaining Point 660m proved difficult with many crevasses and much melt water on the ice cap and a 36-hour day was necessary to break free after 26 days en route.

The **Polar Explorers Greenland Crossing** was a west-east dog sledge supported ski traverse led by two guides Annie Aggens and Keith Heger who started from Kangerlussuak with an international team of six and met up with their dogs, sledges and East Greenland drivers at a camp on the Inland Ice 72km from Kangerlussuak. (Dogs from East Greenland are not allowed to be taken into West Greenland.) They left Dog Camp on 17 May and reached the east coast near Isortoq on 6 June. They experienced changeable weather with more low-pressure windy days than good ones and they found not much difference between night and day travelling conditions and had one big storm with high winds gusting to 120km/hour.

The **Great British/Tiso Trans Greenland Expedition (Scotland)** consisting of Alex Hibbert and George Bullard covered 2300km between 25 March and mid July, taking 113 days fully unsupported. The route was from near Ammassalik on the east coast to near latitude 74°N on the West Coast and then back again. They laid depots at intervals on the outward leg. They experienced heavy sastrugi for the first 250 km and heavy crevassing on both coasts. On the return journey, the last two depots had been destroyed and so the final 10 days were completed on dangerously low rations. This expedition is now claimed to be the longest ever unsupported polar journey although it would not appear to match the unsupported 2771km south to north traverse of the Inland Ice made by Rune Gjeldnes and Torry Larsen from the Kap Farvel area to Kap Morris Jessup in 1996.

The **Wings over Greenland Expedition (France)** consisting of Thierry Puyfoulhoux, Cornelius Strohm and Michael Charavin left Qaleragdlit Fjord near Narsaq in the far south of Greenland on 1 May and reached Qaanaaq in the far north after a journey of 2215km on 31 May. The team all made extensive use of various types of kites and averaged 76.4 km/day. They started with 375kg of equipment and during the journey lost

189. Tony Stone high on the 1971 route on the Hermelnbjerg. Summits of the Tininnertuup group behind. (*Ruben Gutzat*)

three days waiting for wind and carrying out repairs. They reached speeds of 55km/hour in good conditions although they encountered 800km of sastrugi! Later in the year on 19 June the **'Girls in a Gale' Expedition (Norway)** formed of Ingrid Langdal, Saskia Boldingh and Silje Haalandset also set off from Narsaq using kites and after a journey of 2300km on 22 July reached MacCormick Fjord in the far north, where they claim to have had a celebratory swim. Their best day's travel was an amazing 312km helped by their later start, which meant that much of the sastrugi had reduced by melting. The trio are claiming a world record as the first girl expedition to cross Greenland south to north.

High standard big wall climbing was the objective of the **British Tasermiut Fjord Expedition (UK)** consisting of Ged Desforges, Dan McManus, Tom Spreyer, Tony Stone, Es Tresidder, James Vybiral and Ruben Gutzat. They found their chosen objectives, the Minster and Cathedral groups, inland from Kap Farvel to be too broken and moved to the Tasermiut (Ketilsfjord) area where they employed a lightweight approach to tackling the big and hard walls they encountered. The first, Tininnertuup ll, 1725m, proved that the combination of climbers and this approach technique could give good results, and high standard routes on that group were followed by ascents on the towering wall of Hermelnbjerg, 1912m, which overlooked their base camp and provided hard climbing and a difficult unseen escape abseil.

Further north and centred on the Watkins Mountains, **The Arctic Summits Expedition (Germany)**, formed of George Csak and Dominik Rind, having flown on to the ice cap east of the Knud Rasmussens Bjerg by helicopter, became the first Germans to ascend the four highest peaks in the Arctic (the highest being Gunnbjornsfjeld at 3699.96m) and also descend them on ski. A further six ascents were made in the Gronau Nunattaker and Knud Rasmussens Bjerg groups. Ascents, and ski descents, in the Watkins group were notable for unusually extensive areas of hard blue ice, perhaps resulting from the warm summer of the previous year. During the descent of the peak known as Paul Emile Victor in the Watkins Mountains the weather deteriorated very rapidly and the pair were left in total white-out conditions. They had not left marker wands on their ascent route or recorded any GPS waypoints, other than that of their tent, which they were very lucky to find after a 28-hour day. After further travels the pair were picked up by Twin Otter from Paul Stern Land after a week's delay due to bad weather.

In the interior of Scoresbysund, **The Greenland Renland Expedition (UK)** Nat Spring, Crispin Chatterton and Rob Grant was flown into its base camp in central Renland by a helicopter, which then took out an expedition from **Queen's University Belfast MC (UK)** that had been following up explorations made the previous year by the West Lancashire Scouts Expedition. The Renland expedition's stated objective was to climb unclimbed peaks in a remote area by routes of PD/V Diff standard although the actual standard of some routes completed was rather higher. They climbed four new peaks, all just under 2000m, as well as making the second ascent of Bodger, a peak first climbed by the West Lancashire Scouts in 2007. They travelled the full length of the Edward Bailey glacier and carried out a survey of plant life in the area.

The 'Arctic Riviera' section of the north-east coast seemed to attract a different type of group this year, perhaps more in tune with the legacy of the old trappers who used to live and travel in the area.

At Mestersvig Hans Laptun and his **Nor–Fra 2008 (Norway)** group spent two months ski touring and travelling in the area. Jørn Breinholt and Inge Mortensen with their **Sommerferie 2008 (Denmark)** expedition undertook an interesting kayak trip in the fjord region of the north-east coast. Starting on 19 July and using folding kayaks they travelled from Daneborg through Young Sund past Zackenberg to Moskusheimen. Then down Loch Fyne and overland to Moskusoksfjord and on to Strindberg Land, down Kejser Frants Josef Fjord, passing Teufelsloss, to Blomsterbugten, on to Polarheimen and through Antarctic Sund ending the trip at Ella Ø on 19 August. They saw many musk ox and met polar bears on three separate occasions. The **Wappen von Bremen (Germany)** expedition set out by sailing boat from Reykjavik on 18 July intending to enter Scoresbysund. At that time of year the pack ice off the entrance to Scoresbysund had not loosened and since they were unable to pass into the fjord they sailed south to Nansen Fjord before sailing on down the east coast to Isortoq before heading back to Iceland, reached on 10 August.

Recent editions of these Greenland notes have all finished with the ongoing story of Dennis Schmidt's quest for the most northerly land on earth which must lie somewhere off Kap Morris Jessup (referred to also

190. Midnight sun behind the silhouette of Gunnbjornsfjeld, observed from the top of Paul Emile Victor peak, 3609m, The Arctic Summits Expedition. (*George Csak*)

in the first expedition mentioned in these notes). In 2008, a helicopter was used in an attempt to rationalise a lot of recent claims and eliminate those that refer to patches of ice-borne moraine or other non-island phenomena. It seems that many of the 'islands' reported as seen and then not seen fall into the non-permanent glacial deposits group. The most long-lived at 84 deg. 42min. is now called Eclipse Ø but Dennis's view is that these most northerly 'islands' are lacking in substance and deserve his earlier name of *kimmiapahluit* or 'stray dogs'. He suggests they are more important as an idea than as a physical reality.

Correction

In the item about the **SMC East Greenland** expedition in the Greenland Notes, *AJ* 2008, p291, the reference to problems with some types of MSR stoves and Jet A1 fuel should be substituted with the following: The old MSR XGK ll stoves worked well with Jet A1. It was the newer Dragonfly and 2 MSR Whisperlite stoves (600 and Internationale) that did not work with Jet A1 fuel.

SIMON RICHARDSON

Scottish Winter 2008-2009

It was a sensational season on **Ben Nevis**. One of the most glittering prizes in Scottish climbing fell to Andy Turner and Tony Stone in early March, when they made the first winter ascent of *Sassenach*. This provocatively named climb was first climbed by Joe Brown and Don Whillans in April 1954. It was the first route to breach the impressive front face of Carn Dearg Buttress, which bristles with overlaps and hanging grooves. *Sassenach* takes the prominent chimney in the steep central section, and is defended at its base by a severely overhanging corner. Brown and Whillans aided through this and then continued up the chimneys and grooves above. The route was graded Very Severe (the highest grade at the time) and was climbed free 15 years later by Steve Wilson at E3 6a, although the chimneys themselves are thought to be worth E1 5b in their own right.

A winter ascent of this great line had been considered for nearly 30 years and Al Rouse talked about it in the early 1980s. The route is rarely in condition, so ever the innovator, Rouse had a plan to divert a stream at the top of the cliff so it ran down the line and would ice up the following winter. Rouse never did attempt the route, but during the cold snowy winters of the 1980s the lower section did indeed ice up. Snow melt from the ledge above formed an icefall that led past the aid section, but the upper chimneys remained typically bare and nobody took up the challenge.

The explosion of mixed climbing standards over the last few years has transformed *Sassenach* from an unlikely ice climb to a demanding technical mixed challenge. Carn Dearg Buttress is not often in mixed condition, but it does hold hoar frost and powder snow most winters. Turner attempted the line with Steve Ashworth in February 2008, and succeeded in climbing the lower part of the route through the aid section using two rest points, but the pair ran out of steam and abseiled off. They left a few pieces of gear in place in the overhanging corner that they were unable to retrieve because the route was too steep.

Early in March 2009, Turner returned with Tony Stone to attempt *Sassenach* once again. The pair were full of confidence having made the third winter ascent of *Centurion* (VIII,8) with Iain Small three days before in a very swift eight hours. More importantly Carn Dearg Buttress was white with powder snow. 'This is a route that needs specific conditions,' Turner explained on his blog. 'The whole of the Ben can be plastered white after a storm but that part of Carn Dearg always stays black. What it needs is the 'Perfect Storm' – north-west gale force winds and loads of snow.'

Stone led the first pitch and soon Turner was facing the crux. 'When Don Whillans first led this pitch he used several pieces of aid,' Turner contin-

191. Iain Small on the first winter ascent of *Castro* (VII,8), Sgurr an Fhidhleir, 8 February 2009. (*Simon Richardson*)

ued. 'There are no useful footholds anywhere. On the left wall everything slopes the wrong way. Clipping the frozen Friend and Bulldog I placed the previous winter, it never crossed my mind that the Friend wouldn't hold a fall. Trying to remember any useful holds was useless, as ice had changed the whole appearance of the pitch. At one point my feet ripped and I was left hanging with my feet dangling in space. I've never understood the use of 'power screaming' but I found myself screaming my lungs out just to force myself on. Several sketchy balancy moves later saw me standing relieved at the base of the chimney.'

Stone immediately went to work on the next pitch. 'He set off slowly, getting higher and higher, and further and further into the mountain. The chimney was drawing him in. At one point he had to take his helmet off just to turn his head to see where he was going. I think a good old gritstone apprenticeship was the order of the day. Eventually the thrutching ended and a belay was found.' The rest of the chimney passed relatively uneventfully and the pair finished up some beautiful icy grooves. They reached the summit of the buttress, just as darkness fell, with the historic first winter ascent of *Sassenach* (IX,9) in the bag.

Other highlights on Ben Nevis included first winter ascents of *Heidbanger* (VIII,8 – Rich Cross and Andy Benson), *Metamorphosis* (VIII,9 – Iain Small and Gareth Hughes), *Devastation* (VII,8 – Ian Parnell and Andy Benson), *The Brass Monkey* (VII,8 – Pete Davies and Tim Marsh) and *The Minge* (VII,8 – Pete MacPherson and Mark 'Ed' Edwards). In contrast, Iain Small and Simon Richardson bucked the trend of climbing summer routes with *The Cone Collectors* (VIII,8), a winter-only line on the North Wall of Carn Dearg. In a similar vein, across in the Mamores, Dave MacLeod and Malcolm Kent added the fierce sounding *Yo Bro* (VIII,9) on the granite crag on Mullach nan Coirean.

A series of cold snaps in the early and middle part of the winter brought the North-West into good condition. One of the highlights was the first winter ascent of the very technical *Hung, Drawn and Quartered* (VIII,8) on **Sgurr nan Gillean** on Skye by Martin Moran and Nick Dixon. Graded E4 in summer and overhanging for much of its height, this is said to be the most difficult summer gully climb on the island. Back on the mainland, Ian Small and Simon Richardson made the first winter ascent of *Castro* (VII,8), the prominent line of weakness on the 300m-high Magic Bow wall on **Sgurr an Fhidhleir**, and nearby on the West Face of **Quinag**, Andy Nisbet, John Lyall and Mark 'Ed' Edwards made the first ascent of the spectacular overhanging chimney of *Assynt of Man* (VI,6).

Beinn Eighe was another scene of intense activity and the Fuselage Wall area saw a number of new additions including *Spitfire* (VII,8 – Viv Scott and Steve Ashworth), *Mosquito* (V,7 – Andy Nisbet, John Lyall and Jonathan Preston), *War Games* (VI,7 – Nisbet and Lyall), *Grand Slam* (V,7 – Nisbet, Lyall and Pete MacPherson) and *Ace* (VI,7 – Malcolm Bass and Simon Yearsley). On West Central Wall, the showpiece crag on the mountain, Guy Robertson and Tony Stone pulled off a notable coup with the first winter ascent of *Chop Suey* (VIII,8). This summer E1, which was described as 'dangerously loose' by the first ascentionists, resulted in a superb winter route.

The big event on Beinn Eighe was the first ascent of *Bruised Violet* (VIII,9), to the right of Chop Suey, by Ian Parnell and Andy Turner. After a couple of failures and a nasty avalanche incident earlier in the season, Parnell was in a determined mood when he returned in early March. His first attempt to climb the initial overhang on the second pitch was thwarted when the ice clipper krab on his harness became wedged into a crack. Higher up he went the wrong way, down-climbed, and then had his arms lock up due to cramp and dropped a tool. The pair eventually finished the five-pitch

192. Iain Small on the first ascent of *The Cone Collectors* (VIII,8), Ben Nevis, 14 December 2008. (*Simon Richardson*)

route in darkness. For Parnell, a new route on West Central Wall was the realisation of a long held dream, and he explained afterwards that the route 'doesn't really follow the slabbier summer lines of the two E2s here, but searches out steeper ground with deeper better hooking cracks… The hardest thing on this wall is finding the line and convincing yourself that the route will go through such hostile looking territory.'

Without doubt the most significant ascent in the Northern Highlands however, and one of the most important Scottish winter routes for several years, was the first ascent of *The God Delusion* (IX,9) on the Giant's Wall on **Beinn Bhan** in the Northern Highlands. This 200m-high vertical cliff in Coire nan Fhamhair between Gully of the Gods and Great Overhanging Gully has an aura of impregnability that is truly jaw-dropping. The sandstone face is close to vertical, bristles with overhangs and has no continuous lines of weakness. Its defining gullies are sought after winter prizes in their own right, and when Martin Moran and Paul Tattersall climbed the line of *The Godfather* (VIII,8) up the left side of the wall in 2002 it was seen as a significant step forward in North-West climbing. *The Godfather* finishes up a vertical corner, the only significant feature on the upper wall, so when news of a new route to its right appeared on the Internet, it created real excitement.

The God Delusion (IX,9) was the work of Pete Benson and Guy Robertson, one of the most successful Scottish winter partnerships of recent years. They are no strangers to the cliff and made a spirited second ascent attempt on *The Godfather* with Es Tresidder a couple of seasons ago. Unfortunately Benson took a fall within a few metres of easy ground at the top of the route and broke his ankle. The ensuing retreat down seven pitches of vertical to overhanging terrain in the dark, followed by a long walk out was a sobering experience, but both Benson and Robertson were struck by the possibility of adding another line to the wall.

They first attempted *The God Delusion* in December, but Robertson took a big fall when he pulled off a TV-sized block on the sixth pitch. They returned a few days later, climbed the first two pitches in the dark and by early afternoon they had reached pitch 6. It was very steep and there was no obvious way to go. 'You look up and all you see are roofs,' Robertson recounted. 'But incredibly each roof was fringed by a turf moustache! I tried to probe a way through the steepest section to the left, but on the second try I looked across and saw a more promising line. For about 15 metres the climbing was pretty futuristic, but when manteling onto an undercut ledge I realised that I was absolutely spent. I said to Pete that I'd lost it and just let go. One of my tools pulled, but the second tool stayed in and I was left hanging from my spring leash. Fortunately I was able to prusik back up the leash and continue the pitch.'

December days are short, and they completed the last couple of pitches in the dark to emerge on the summit plateau under a brilliant starlit sky. The pair thought the crux pitch was technical 9, but every other pitch was 7 or 8 making it the most difficult winter climb yet achieved in the Northern Highlands. But it was not just the sustained difficulty of the route that caught everyone's imagination, but the style the route was climbed. 'If you stick to traditional ethics,' Robertson explained, 'there's no avoiding the total commitment required to climb hard mixed routes in Scotland, especially new ones. No summer knowledge, no pre-inspection, no fixed gear. Just rock up and go for it, bottom to top. That's the gauntlet; anything else is heresy.'

MIKE MORTIMER

Morocco 2005-2009

This report covers developments on the **north side of Jebel El Kest.** The Cicerone Guide *Climbing in the Moroccan Anti-Atlas* by Claude Davies describes climbs around the market town of Tafraout (or Tafroute – most names inevitably have multiple spellings) and above the Ameln valley i.e. to the south of the Jebel el Kest massif. Since the publication of the guide (2004), increasing numbers of climbers have visited the area and many additional climbs have been discovered as the new route books in the Hotel Les Amandiers testify.

The true north side of the massif received no attention until March 2005 when Geoff Hornby and Susie Sammut climbed several routes on the impressive but easily accessible slabs at Dwawj and these have seen considerable activity since that time. However, the major development of the north side did not start until 2007, when Steve and Katja Broadbent started developing the crags close to the idyllic village of Annamer and Lower Eagle Crag was subject to assaults by teams made up of Ben and Marion Wintringham, Paul Donithorne, Emma Alsford and Steve Findlay, Chris Bonington and Dave Absalom, Derek Walker, Mike and Marjorie Mortimer and Jim Fotheringham. This was the start of extensive exploration that has continued apace to the present day, aided by the new road between Idagnidif in the east and Tanalt in the west.

The rock of the massif is composed entirely of an excellent quartzite, highly suitable for climbing as it is generally firm, well supplied with holds and readily takes natural protection. Drilled protection is unnecessary as is the carrying of pitons and hammer. Although most crags are vegetated to a greater or lesser extent, it is usually possible to climb clean rock with little or no gardening. Many of the crags are not particularly steep so those expecting routes in the modern idiom may be disappointed, although a few routes of around E5/E6 have been found recently. The emphasis is on adventure with routes of up to 800m of climbing on the largest crags and the discerning eye will spot many possibilities for further exploration. Inevitably, the crags that have received most attention have been those close to the road, very few being more than 10 minutes' easy walk. However, there are many attractive and presumably virgin crags for climbers not afraid of one or two hours of toil in the Moroccan sun.

The north side is situated about an hour and half's drive south-east of the popular holiday resort of Agadir (regular flights from the UK and readily available car-hire) where very comfortable accommodation is available at the spectacular Kasbah Tizourgane close to Idagnidif. The Kasbah has the advantage of close proximity to the crags but it lacks the amenities of the

193. Jim Fotheringham on *Dream of White Butterflies*, Waterfall Walls, Jebel El Kest, Morocco. *(Mike Mortimer)*

traditional centre of Tafraout, 50 minutes drive further south, where the favoured hotel is Les Amandiers. The climate of Jebel El Kest is that of a semi-desert region and as such good weather for climbing is generally to be relied on, the best months for the north side being March, April and October. Summer is far too hot and the winter months are likely to be rather cold for the north-facing crags.

As only a handful of routes have had second ascents the following account is inevitably a personal account of the longer climbs that have been made. Details of climbs can be found in the Amandiers route books and an on-line guide by Steve Broadbent is available at **https://sites.google.com/site/quartziteclimbing/Home** Ben Wintringham is also planning an on-line guide.

Lower Eagle Crag is the finest of the crags readily accessible from the new road with a fair spread of grades and easy descents at either end (the goat herders' path at the west end is well worth seeking out and the start is clearly marked with cairns). As one approaches from Idagnidif the 200m north-east facing wall of the Sanctuary is very obvious with two vertical black stripes giving spectacular climbing (*Saladin*, 200m HVS and *Otello*, 200m E1) whilst further right is the challenging Bon Courage Wall (*Bon Courage*, 200m, E1). The most attractive looking line on the main part of

Lower Eagle takes another black streak (*Black Beauty*, 250m E1) but there are many excellent climbs hereabouts.

Just over the ridge to the north of the Eagle Crag group is the incredibly beautiful valley in which is situated the communities of Tamza and Tmdkrt (or Tamdakert). Abundant water supplies (by Moroccan standards and especially after the exceptional rains of the last winter) mean that the hillsides together with the valley bottom are lush and green: terraces with fig trees and vines as well as cereal crops and well-stocked vegetable gardens are not unusual here. The contrast with the multicoloured cliffs that tower above the valley has created a magnificent and unusual climbing environment. The valley, which does not appear to have a name but is often referred to (by us) as Shangri La, can be reached from the east by turning off the new road down a dirt track by a small mosque on the right about five miles from Idagnidif (I believe this is called Ighir). The surface of this track varies from year to year but is negotiable by two-wheel drive cars if care is taken.

On entering the valley, various attractive-looking rocks appear but the first of any size suddenly appears as the road bends left and starts to drop. The Tamza wall stretches for several kilometres and attains a height of 300m but boasts only a handful of routes. The wall is breached by a broad gully, Ice Box Canyon, which is taken by the Tamza-Annamer path. The north-facing wall, which gives the gully its name, is the home of some fine routes on excellent steep rock; the natural approach is from Tamza but the routes are most easily reached from the Annamer side. Right (i.e. west) of the Tamza wall is the Flatiron, a huge slabby monolith that has seen considerable activity with three great outings up the left side with the Wintringhams' *The Edge* (200m E2) looking particularly fine.

Beyond the Flatiron the track drops quite steeply to the heart of Shangri La, the community of Tmdkrt, dominated by the mighty Waterfall Walls and the great ridges of Aylim giving as romantic a location for climbing as one could wish for. In October 2007 Donithorne and Findlay made the first breach of the former when they fought their way up the forbidding looking *Continuation Corner* (600m E2) whilst Fotheringham and Mortimer, having been repulsed by smooth and protectionless black slabs right of the waterslide, consoled themselves with the mainly easy but potentially classic *Great Ridge of Samazar* (650m HVS) up the massive Aylim. Even longer and equally fine looking is the Broadbents' *Labyrinth Ridge* (800m AD) added the following year. Worth noting also are two routes up the east face of Aylim, *East Face Direct* (450m HVS) by the Broadbents and *Pipeline at the Gates of Dawn* (250m HVS) by Richard Hazsko, Bonington and Graham Little. Meanwhile Fotheringham and Mortimer renewed their acquaintance with Waterfall Right Hand to produce *Terminator Wall* (600m E2), a mountaineering route with some vegetated bits and a big atmosphere.

Right of Terminator Wall is The Pimple, apparently part of Waterfall Right Hand but with a true summit and an abseil descent (most unusual in Shangri La) and crammed with character-full lines most of which give superb climbing; *Lady in Black* (200m E1) with five varied pitches is well

194. Fig Tree Wall. *(Mike Mortimer)*

worth seeking out. The exceptional rainfall of the last winter meant that the waterfall was particularly spectacular and really added to the atmosphere of *Dream of White Butterflies* (550m E2) which takes the line of slim slabs and ribs right of Continuation Corner to give what may be the most beautiful climb in the valley.

Beyond the Pimple the road rises steeply in a series of hairpins to a col before continuing downhill to Tanalt. On the right of the col is the south face of Agouti sporting three pleasant looking climbs; the Broadbents' *Stairway to Heaven* (195m MVS) gives an entertaining route to a summit which is an exceptionally good view point. Opposite Agouti the attractive West Buttress of a Cloggy-like crag called Fig Tree Wall (actually part of Aylim) offers several fine routes and the Wintringhams' *Braveheart* (210m HVS) is another potential classic.

In summary, this is a great place to climb, adventurous but not overly serious, lonely but quite easy to reach with a wide variety of climbs and a unique ambience.

HARISH KAPADIA

India 2008

New ascents, high peaks, exploration of new areas and most importantly, challenging climbs by Indian mountaineers – all were part of the 2008 season in the Indian Himalaya. This year will be remembered for some energetic climbs and rather settled weather. In total 65 foreign expeditions climbed in India. Since the Indian Mountaineering Federation opened a liaison office at Leh to collect fees locally, **Stok Kangri** has become their most profitable peak, with 21 official ascents. Counting this with Indian teams and unofficial climbing, this peak will be in the record books for the most climbed peak above 6000m.

Kishtwar area, once a paradise for challenging mountains, was closed due to terrorism in Kashmir. The routes from the valley were too dangerous to approach. A British-Canadian-American team tried to approach Kishtwar-Shivling from the north, crossing Umasi la. But a small incident en route scared porters and they refused to descend into the valley. According to their observation, terrorists were watching them and they do not like any nationalities – the three above or Indians. So Kishtwar will have to wait till things improve. Another show of energy was on **Chong Kumdan II**. This virgin 7000m peak had beaten two expeditions previously, both from the east. The Indian-French team approached from the south over a high pass and finally reached the long summit ridge. After a camp on the high ridge, they traversed to the summit and back in a long day. This was perhaps both the longest approach and longest climb in recent years. There were worthy climbs in **Garhwal** too. Conrad Anker and friends climbed Meru Shark's Fin despite bad weather, Mick Fowler challenged **Vasuki Parbat** by a daring route (see page 3) and the Japanese climbed **Kalanka** by the north face (p64). But the iconic climb was on **Kamet** by a two-member Japanese team (p62). They acclimatized on the 'normal' route and established supplies for their return. Then in one push they climbed the steep south-east face to the summit and returned by the normal route. With most of the climbing above 7000m, this expedition too can enter the fitness race with those above.

195. South-east face of Nya Kangri, an unclimbed peak in Arganglas valley, East Karakoram. *(Divyesh Muni)*

With 57 expeditions during the year, Indian teams were not too far behind in terms of excellence in climbs. **Thalay Sagar**, up to now the preserve of strong foreign teams, received Indian climbers for the first time. A small team from Bengal reached the summit. Similarly, **Tirsuli West** was climbed for the second time by an Indian expedition. This high peak in earlier years had defeated several strong teams. Maiktoli south face, Srikanta and Manirang were other high peaks climbed by the Indian teams. This is a very welcome sign and it is hoped that a new breed of young mountaineers in future will explore climbing without fixed ropes and support by Sherpas, as was done this year.

Others either climbed in new areas or opened new valleys for the future. Irish teams explored Gramang Bar in Kinnaur and climbed in the Debsa valley of Spiti. Two Indian teams took on challenges of Nya Kangri and Plateau Peak. Both are challenging peaks in the Eastern Karakoram that will take strong teams to tackle them in future. On the historic trail was a British team exploring to reach the Zemu Gap and planning for its first crossing. Their route from high Guicha la to the Talung valley was not without difficulties. Ahead lay the icefall, and approaching bad weather stopped their movements. Hopefully some team will return here to reach the Zemu Gap, a first after H W Tilman.

This list below covers important expeditions to the Indian Himalaya in 2008.

UTTARAKHAND: KUMAUN HIMALAYA

Changabang (6866m)

Team: Czech Republic. Leader: Michal Bernard
From 7-17 September, six members of the Czech team attempted the W face. They reached 6100m but had to give up because heavy snowfall made further climbing hazardous.

Kalanka (6931m)

Team: Japanese. Leader: Fumitaka Ichimura
Ichimura with Yusuke Sato and Kazuki Amano completed a new route on Kalanka's N face. After enduring a short spell of bad weather, they started from base camp on 14 September. They had to stay three nights at 6600m on the face due to more bad weather and finally reached the summit on 22 September, returning to base camp on the 24th. They had permission to climb Changabang (6866m) also, but abandoned it, as Kalanka had left them exhausted. (Account page 64)

Tirsuli West (7035m)

Team: Indian Mountaineering Foundation. Leader: Gautam Dutta
The team of 12 climbers with some high altitude supporters followed the route of the first ascent (by a team from Nehru Institute of Mountaineering in 2001). They fixed the entire route from base camp till near the summit, establishing four camps, the highest (Camp 4) at 6630m. On 12 June, Amresh Kumar Jha, Debraj Dutta, Goutam Saha, K Wallambok

Lyngdoh, Mohan Lal, Subrata Chakraborty and three high altitude supporters Phurba, Tashi and Dorjee Sherpa reached the summit. It was the second ascent of the mountain, which had been attempted several times earlier.

Maiktoli (6803m)
Organisers: Indian Mountaineering Foundation. Leader: Col Vijay Singh, VSM
As Maiktoli lies on the southern rim of the Nanda Devi sanctuary, it can be attempted only from outside the sanctuary walls, i.e. the S face. A Japanese team first climbed this route in 1977. On the same route in 1992 four climbers from an Indian expedition from Almora, Uttarakhand, died in a fall from the ridge. The Almora team again attempted the route in 1995 without success. The IMF team of nine climbers followed the same route finding it very steep and fixing 880m of rope. In bad weather, they reached 6200m on 10 September. Knowing the history of the deaths on the S face, the leader wisely called off the expedition.

GARHWAL HIMALAYA: GANGOTRI AREA

Thalay Sagar (6904m)
Team: Indian. Leader: Basanta Singha Roy.
Comprising nine members with four Sherpas from Darjeeling, this team proceeded from Gangotri, and established base camp at Kedar tal. From here, they followed the W ridge and established Camp 3 (summit camp) at 6400m, fixing ropes en route. The summit camp was the junction of the snowy W ridge, which connects the Jogin group of peaks and the vertical rock wall of Thalay Sagar. On 29 August they fixed ropes for 550m to almost within 100m of the summit. After sitting out snowfall on the 31st they set out at 4am on 1 September, finishing up 100m of steep snow to reach the summit at about 8am. This was the first ascent of Thalay Sagar by an Indian team. Summiteers were Basanta Singha Roy and Sherpas Pasang, Pemba and Phurba Gyalgen.

Meru (6660m)
Team: Korean. Leader: Se Joon Kim
The Korean team of three climbers climbed a new direct route on the N face of Meru. The leader with Wang Jun Ho and Kim Tae Mam reached the summit late on 13 July.

Meru Central (6550m)
Team: American. Leader: Conrad Anker.
Attempting the peak in September 2008 via the 400m prow of the Shark's Fin, Anker, Jimmy Chin and Renan Ozturk reached the summit ridge after 19 days only to be thwarted 100m from the summit by an overhanging gendarme and exhaustion.

Shivling (6184m)
(1) Team: Swiss. Leader: Nellen Michael
All three climbers of this Swiss team successfully reached the summit by the traditional W ridge. On 28 May the leader with Simon Schydrig and Wellig Diego climbed to the top at 5pm.
(2) Team: Korean. Leader: Boun Hyun Park
The five-strong team climbed the W ridge. The leader with Young Jik Yoo and Seon Tae Jang reached the summit on 31 May, three days after the Swiss expedition. The Koreans also attempted Meru but could not climb beyond 5900m due to heavy snow.
(3) Team: Iceland. Leader: Arnar Emilsson
The team of five climbers attempted the W ridge but was unlucky with the weather. They reached Camp 3 (6000m) after fixing ropes all the way from Camp 2. There was heavy snowfall and they could not climb the overhanging route ahead. There were avalanches on both sides of the route so they backed out. Despite returning in bad weather, they cleared all their fixed ropes.

Sudarshan Parbat (6507m)
Team: Japanese. Leader: Toshio Yamagiwa
The Japanese team followed the east ridge route, pioneered by an Indian-French expedition in 1981. They established two camps en route and a top camp at 5800m. S Kazama, N Suzuki and K Hirano with guides Laxman and Wallambok reached the summit on 19 August.

Vasuki Parbat (6792m)
Team: British. Leader: Mick Fowler
Mick Fowler and Paul Ramsden attempted the W face of the 'King of Serpents' (Vasuki). It would have been a new route but they could reach only 6400m. Mick describes his experience as follows: 'We tried the buttress line catching the sun and reached a point about two-thirds of the way up. I think we might have completed the technically hardest climbing but an earlier spell of bad weather meant that we did not acclimatise as well as I would have liked and we just ground to a knackered halt going slower and slower (and feeling we were getting more and more wobbly). It was also surprisingly cold to the extent that we could not use bare hands on rock.' (Account page 3)

Srikanta (6133m)
Team: Indian. Leader: Anand Mali
The expedition approached the mountain from Jangla village near Uttarkashi on the Gangotri road and established two camps at 5200m and 5600m. On 12 September, five climbers reached the summit of this rarely visited mountain. The last successful attempt was in 1997. Anand Mali with Tekraj Adhikari and Krishna Dhokle and two high altitude supporters Gyalbu and Pasang reached the top after 16 days of efforts. Kalyan

Kadam, the fourth member, reached the summit camp. They fixed about 1100m of rope between their top camp and the summit.

CENTRAL GARHWAL

Kamet (7756m)

(1) Team: Japanese. Leader: Hazuya Hiraide

The two-member team of Hazuya Hiraide and Kei Taniguchi climbed the formidable SE face of Kamet. They set up base camp on 1 September and acclimatised by climbing to Mead's Col on the normal route. There was heavy snowfall from 18-24 September. Starting on 29 September, they climbed a direct line up the face and reached the summit at 10am on 5 October. This was the first ascent of the SE face (commonly called east face) and the pair are the first Japanese summiteers of Kamet. Just before this expedition, Hiraide had summited Gasherbrum II and Broad Peak. (Account page 62)

(2) Team: Japanese. Leader: Isao Hidehiko

Before the above-mentioned spectacular ascent, another Japanese team of seven climbers attempted Kamet in the pre-monsoon season. Taking the normal route, on 12 June they reached Camp 4 at 6050m which proved their high point. They had a curious situation when the soles of seven new boots they were using came off. They were trying the new model for a possible attempt on Everest. We do not know the brand of the manufacturer.

Nilkanth (6596m) - Correction regarding 2007 'ascent' (*AJ* 113, p304)

The Himalayan Club had sponsored an expedition to Nilkanth in Garhwal in 2007, organised by its Kolkata Section. The expedition leader AVM (Retd) A K Bhattacharyya reported that the team had reached the summit of Nilkanth after a difficult climb. As doubts were expressed regarding the authentication of this climb the Himalayan Club appointed Jagdish Nanavati, (President Emeritus) as Ombudsman. On examination of details and photographs the Himalayan Club Managing Committee accepted the report of the Ombudsman and concluded that the summit of Nilkanth was not climbed by this expedition. Hence, the record of ascent of this peak should be corrected. The Ombudsman's Report is available on the website of the Himalayan Club at **www.himalayanclub.org**

HIMACHAL PRADESH: KINNAUR

Rangrik Rang (6553m)

Team: French. Leader: Ferron Odilon

Three young mountain guides (all 22 years) completed the second ascent of this beautiful mountain in Kinnaur. The original route, followed by the 1994 Indian British expedition led by Chris Bonington and Harish Kapadia, climbed directly from the glacier to the col. This was the intended route of the French alpinists, but because of heavy snowfall, they found this route dangerous and hence followed an alternative longer route to the summit. They traversed over Mangla peak to the col with the main peaks and followed it to the summit. The leader with Rumebe Jeremy and Audibert Slvoin reached the summit. The climb was completed in only two days reaching the top on 1 October at 7.30pm. They bivouacked on the summit for 10 hours and returned to their top camp on 2 October late in the evening.

Gramang Bar (6248m)
Team: Irish. Leader: Seamus O'Hanlon
Gramang Bar is located NW of peak Sesar Rang and east of Morang village in the Kinnaur Himalaya. This expedition of five members approached the peak from Morang and followed Paltha – Khokpa nala to the Timchhe glacier. They experienced good weather and explored the valley thoroughly, reaching a high point of 4800m, but did not climb the peak because water supplies at their base camp dried up. They had received information about the area from veteran Irish mountaineer Paddy O'Leary who had been to this area in 1993. Unfortunately, this information was no longer valid due to terrain changes and the approach to the mountain had become dangerous. They surveyed NW aspects of the mountain and thought that the W ridge would be possible for a future attempt.

Manirang (6593m)
Team: Indian. Leader: Dr. Anjan Choudhury
This high peak is situated on the border of Kinnaur and Spiti areas of Himachal Pradesh. A 10-member team climbed it after establishing three high camps. They climbed via Manirang pass and placed the summit camp at 5734m. Shushanto Mondal, Tapan Mukherjee with two high altitude supporters reached the summit on 12 September.

SPITI
Kanamo (5975m)
Team: British Royal Navy. Leader: Andrew Wagstaff
The name of this small but attractive peak implies 'White Hostess' and this easy peak welcomed a 12-strong RN team. Situated near Shilla and Chau Chau Kang Nilda peaks, Kanamo is now easily approached by road from Kaja. On 6 September, all members except one reached the summit. They climbed the SW ridge and had warm, sunny weather except on summit day.

Lhakhang (6250m)
Team: British. Leader: Michael Borroff
Six senior citizens (60+) from the Yorkshire Ramblers Club accompanied the leader to attempt this mountain in Spiti during the post-monsoon season. They established their advanced base camp on the lateral moraines

on the west of the Dhhun glacier, which allowed detailed reconnaissance of the NW face. Unseasonal and widespread snowfall on peaks in the northern Spiti caused them to abandon the climb. They reached 5660m while exploring the glacier.

Khhang Shiling (6360m)
Team: Indian. leader: Anath Bandhu Ghosh
In 2004, a team led by Mumbai climber Divyesh Muni first climbed Khhang Shiling in the Khamengar valley of Spiti. The present team of six members followed the route of the first ascent. They established their summit camp at 5950m. On 1 August, Raj Kumar Dhara with two high altitude supporters reached the summit.

P. 6135m (Debsa nala)
Team: Irish. Leader: Gerard Galligan
This three-member team entered the Debsa nala in western Spiti and established base camp at Thwak Debsa. After exploring the surroundings, they climbed an unnamed and previously unclimbed peak of 6135m, on Upper East Debsa glacier. They suggested the name Ramabang (peak of Rama). On 22 June the leader with Darach O'Murchu and Paul Mitchell climbed the SW ridge to reach the summit. Later, the expedition crossed a high pass at the head of Bauli Khad (Debsa valley) to the Parvati valley.

KULLU – LAHAUL-ZANSKAR

Menthosa (6443m)
Team: Italian. Leader: Bruno Moretti
This team of 10 was not successful on Menthosa, but climbed four other peaks in the area, p.6046m, p.5770m, p.5760m and p.5577m, all in September.

Dharamsura (White Sail) (6446m)
Team: Indian. Leader: Barun Mazumdar
Located near Manikaran in the Kullu valley of Himachal Pradesh, Dharamsura (Peak of good) is also known as White Sail due to its shape. The four-member team followed the normal route and established four camps. Summit camp was placed at 6400m, from where on 26 July Arindam Jana and Sujit Bag with high altitude supporters Pasang Phutar and Phurba Sherpa reached the summit.

Papsura (6451m)
Team: Indian. Leader: Prosenjit Mukherjee
This expedition of seven members reached 200m short of the summit on Papsura (peak of evil), a higher neighbour of Dharamsura. On 11 June, they stopped their climb due to verglas on rock and a shortage of rock anchors and fixed ropes.

Sanakdank Jot (6044m) (as per Survey of India 6360m)
Team: Indian. Leader: Dr. Ujjal Ray
The seven-member team reached Tandi at the confluence of Chandra and Bhaga rivers and entered Shipting nala. They approached this peak in Lahaul area from the Shipting glacier. On 30 August, Rajib Bhattacharjee, Surajit Bhowmik and Bibhas Ganguly with high altitude supporters Madanlal Thakur and Neelu Negi started at 3.30am from camp 2 at 5050m and reached the summit.

Shinkun East (6081m)
Team: Himalayan Club. Leader: Subrata Chakraborty
A team of seven members climbed in the Zanskar area, near the popular trekking route across Shinkun la (formerly Shingo la). Base camp was at Chuminakpo at 4650m and a second camp was set up at 5190m. They reached the top of an unnamed point 5912m on 9 September and established their summit camp here. On 10 September, starting from the summit camp, they negotiated a cornice and two rock bands of about 70m each, traversed another rock band and reached an ice slope leading to easier ground to the summit. The summiteers were the leader with Debraj Dutta, Jayanta Chattopadhay, Goutam Saha, Rudra Prasad Halder and HAP Harsh Thakur.

P. 6184m (Jankar nala)
Team: British. Leader: Stuart MacDonald
The peak is located north of Gangstang. The nine-member team approached the mountain from Jankar nala turning SW from Kuddu for the base camp. Massive snowfall on 19-20 September made progress difficult. One of the members, Jamie Emberson, suffered multiple fractures in the upper arm and shoulders and was evacuated by helicopter on 26 September. The team reached a high point at 5900m on 29 September before calling off the attempt.

CB – 13A (6240m)
Team: Polish. Leader: Pawel Krawczyk
The peak is situated in the Chandra Bhaga range of Lahaul and is often visited by climbers. The Polish team consisting of three members attempted the NE ridge. On 13 August, one climber, Mariusz Baskurzynski reached the junction of the N and E ridges at 6000m, which was the high point of the expedition. The continuation ridge was complicated due to loose rocks and they decided to turn back.

Shib Shankar (6011m)
Team: Japanese. Leader: Shoji Sakamoto
A team of five members successfully climbed this mountain in the Pangi valley. The peak is located at the head of the Dharwas in the Lujai nala, near the Sersank pass on the Pangi-Zanskar divide. Attempted by a British

expedition in 2006, Shib Shankar is surrounded by many hidden crevasses. On 19 July, Kazuo Kozu, Hidetaka Lizuka and Miss Reiko Maruyama with three high altitude supporters reached the summit.

LADAKH AND EASTERN KARAKORAM

Rimo I (7385m) Correction regarding 2007 ascent (*AJ* 113, p309)
The IMF organised an expedition to high peak of Rimo I in the eastern Karakoram in 2007. The team leader Major K. S. Dhami reported that the team, including himself, reached the summit in poor weather. They had followed the same route as the first ascent by the Indo-Japanese expedition in 1988. However, on examination of details and photographs the IMF Authentication Committee concluded that the summit of Rimo I was not climbed. Hence the record of ascent of this peak should be corrected.

Kishtwar Shivling (6000m)
Team: American-British-Canadian. Leader: Kevin Thaw
This international expedition of three climbers could not even reach the base of the mountain as their porters refused to carry loads over the Umasi la and they had to turn back. Despite the desire by climbers to visit this area it remains a difficult and sometimes dangerous place to access.

Pologongka (6632m)
Team: Indian. Leader: Karuna Prasad Mitra
The team reached the Pologongka pass and followed the south ridge. It was the same route as followed by the 1998 British expedition. On 27 August, Dipankar Ghosh and Bhagwan singh Thakur reached the top – the first ascent of the mountain.

Chalung (6546m)
Team: Indian. Leader: J S Gulia
The team approached via the Rupshu valley from Sumdo Ribil. After establishing base camp at 5200m and a high camp at 5900m, they decided to tackle the W ridge. On 29 June, the leader with Gaurav and Amardeep along with two high altitude supporters Fateh Chand and Pyare Lal reached the summit at 1pm. This was the second ascent of the peak and first by the W ridge. A Japanese team made the first ascent in 1997.

Nya Kangri (6480m)
Team: The Himalayan Club. Leader: Divyesh Muni
Nya Kangri is a beautiful pyramid-shaped peak of the Arganglas valley in the Eastern Karakoram. It dominates the entrance to the valley. A four-member team attempted the peak in June–July, establishing base camp at Phonglas on the right of the Argan nala at 4600m. The attempt was made from the SW side. A higher camp was established on the south slope at 5400m. The south ridge was approached from a 700m gully flanked by a

rocky ridge on one side and a huge hanging glacier on the other. On 26 June, the team opened a route through the gully and fixed four ropes to 5800m. It snowed heavily over the next two days and with a series of slab avalanches the attempt was called off.

Saser Kangri IV (7410m)
Team: Indian. Leader: Samir Sengupta
Starting from Panamik, the 26-member team approached via the Phukpoche glacier to their base camp, then placed two camps on the W ridge of the peak. They reached c7000m on Saser IV on 5 August, however terrain difficulties defeated further progress. A large amount of equipment was left at Camp 2.

Chong Kumdan II (7004m)
Team: Indian-French. Leader: Chewang Motup Goba and Paul Grobel
This team accomplished the first ascent of one of the last unclimbed 7000m peaks in the Eastern Karakoram. The 12 members approached via the Mamostong valley and crossed the NW ridge of the Mamostong Kangri by a high col to reach the South Terong glacier. From the glacier, they climbed to the Nup Col overlooking the Chong Kumdan glacier, then gained the S ridge of Chong Kumdan II. On 20 August, the main peak was climbed by Konchok Thinless, Samgyal Sherpa, Maurine Bernard, Raiot Dominique, Paul Grobel and Sebastiano Audisio.

Plateau Peak (7287m)
Team: Indian Mountaineering Foundation. Leader: Wing Commander N. K. Dahiya
The IMF organised an expedition of 11 members to this virgin seven thousander in the Eastern Karakoram. The team approached from Panamik in the Nubra valley in northern Ladakh. Base camp was set up on the Phukpoche glacier at 3950m, reached on 26 July. The members had to ferry loads between the road-head and advanced base camp (4875m), as very few porters were available. From ABC they climbed the SW slopes to reach the west ridge and established Camp 1 at 5650m. They continued on the west ridge, fixing ropes. Camp 2 was to be established at 6400m from where they had planned to attempt the summit. Their 1100m of fixed rope was not sufficient, so seven climbing ropes were also fixed. Bad weather and unconsolidated snow defeated the attempt at 6900m on 3 August.

Zemu Gap (5891m)
The expedition was organised by Colin Knowles, with Adrian O'Connor and Jerzy Wieczorek. Its objective was to link together two treks – the 'Goecha La' trek, which leaves from Yuksom and terminates at the Goecha La, and the 'Green Lake' trek, which follows the Zemu Chu from Lachen to the eponymous lake, and back. To make the connection it would be necessary to cross the Talung glacier, gain the Tongshiong glacier and cross

the Zemu Gap (Zemu La) – a *brèche* on the SE ridge of Kangchenjunga, before descending to the Zemu glacier and thus to the Green Lake. The Zemu Gap (5891m) has a remarkable place in mountaineering history. The northern approach, via the Zemu glacier, is relatively straightforward, and documented visits include Alexander Kellas (12 May 1910), John Hunt (18 November 1937) and H W Tilman (9 July 1938). Tilman then crossed the gap, experiencing some interesting adventures on his descent from the Talung glacier.

The Gap only really sprung to prominence when Tilman became suspicious about a claimed ascent from the southern (Talung) side by Captain Boustead on 8 May 1926. Tilman went to investigate and failed to climb it from the southern side on 13 May 1936. His suspicions seemed justified as Captain Boustead's account did not fit with his experience. However, unbeknown to both there was a prior claim to the first ascent from the south by N A Tombazi in 1925. He had mounted a photographic expedition to the area. Regrettably, he had not taken any photographs as the weather had been unfavourable. However none of these protagonists had gone on down to the Zemu Gap, so the first true south to north crossing of the La was still awaiting. Since that time the only other documented visit to the La from the south was by a group from A J S Grewal's Talung Expedition in 1975. They were prevented from crossing the Gap 'by two big open crevasses approx. 40ft in width' just 200ft short of the col. '...it is clear that the Gap can be reached if one goes prepared to bridge the two crevasses.'

The Burma Hump

During World war II, flights that took off from Assam for Kunming in China had to cross the high ridge in the eastern Arunachal Pradesh, nicknamed the 'Burma Hump'. These non-pressurised old planes had to fly at night and in a circuitous route to avoid attention by the Japanese. More than 1000 planes crashed on these high mountain areas. Not many crash sites are located as yet. An American team, with the support of the Indian Air Force, was permitted in this border area of the Siang valley. After many difficulties, they located one of the crash sites at high altitude. These eastern areas are likely to see more such expeditions in the future.

DICK ISHERWOOD

Nepal 2008

I would like to thank Elizabeth Hawley and Lindsay Griffin, in addition to many of the climbers named below, for information in these notes.

Stability seems to have returned to Nepal, at least for the moment, as the former Maoist rebels came out in front in the national elections in April 2008, and have had the doubtlessly interesting experience of forming a government and actually running the country. Trekkers are back in large numbers and the government has reduced peak fees in an effort to keep the climbers coming. All peak fees have been discounted in autumn, winter and 'summer', though not in the main spring season, and peaks west of the Dhaulagiri range (e.g Kanjiroba, Saipal, Api and Nampa) are exempt from peak fees altogether.

The **Everest** scene in spring 2008 was dominated by the Chinese project to carry the Olympic Torch to the summit by the north ridge route. This was achieved on 8 May by no less than 26 people, following an ascent by seven others the day before. Unfortunately, perhaps, the arrangements for this great deed, and the unrest in Lhasa and elsewhere in the Tibetan regions of China, severely disrupted the economic growth engine of commercial expeditioning. At least 65 parties were booked to climb Everest and Cho Oyu from Tibet in the pre-monsoon season, and all were forced to cancel. The Chinese authorities also leaned heavily on the Nepalese government, basically preventing movement high up the mountain on the south side until the torch show was over. Permits were delayed and Nepalese security forces limited rope fixing in the Khumbu icefall until mid-April. Nevertheless 391 people reached the summit from the Nepal side, including 76-year-old Min Bahadur Sherchan, a Nepali from the western part of the country, who beat the previous age record, held by a Japanese climber, by a good five years. An American carrying a Tibetan flag on his pack above the base camp was arrested, deported and banned from Nepal for two years, which seems a bit hard given the number of Dalai Lama images and Free Tibet slogans one sees in Kathmandu.

In the post-monsoon season permit delays and problems continued in Tibet, in part because decision-making had been pulled back from the provincial authorities in Lhasa to the central government in Beijing. Around 30 groups switched from Cho Oyu to Manaslu due to permit difficulties. In the end 35 expeditions attempted Manaslu and 11 were successful, all by the standard north-east face route. 17 parties eventually got permits for Cho Oyu and 11, including three Chinese groups, reached the summit by the north-west face. Six parties went to Everest from Nepal in the post-monsoon season but none were successful.

In the 2007/8 winter **Annapurna II** (7937m) had its first winter ascent, by the German climber Philipp Kunz with three Sherpas, following the original British route from the north side over the shoulder of Annapurna IV. Two winter attempts on Makalu, the only 8000m peak in Nepal not to have had a winter ascent, were unsuccessful in 2007/8, though the 'indestructible Himalayan strong man' (according to Planetmountain.com) Kazak Denis Urubko returned a year later with the Italian Simone Moro, and succeeded on the standard route in January 2009.

Also in winter the Russians Vladimir Belousov and Alexander Novikov made a difficult 1200m mixed route on the north face of **Kwangde Lho** (6187m) with two bivouacs on the ascent. Their line seems to have been to the right of previous routes established here in the eighties, and reached the ridge between Kwangde Lho and Kwangde Nup very close to the summit of the former. The standard was M4, WI4, and they reached the summit on 10 January after a very cold bivouac on the summit ridge. They descended the original route on the mountain, into the Lumding valley on the south side, and had a long walk home over the Lumding La.

In the spring season a large international expedition was on the south face of **Annapurna**, attempting a line far to the east of the main summit, and close to the route climbed solo by Tomas Humar in 2007. A good deal of fixed rope was used and the Russian climber Alexei Bolotov reached the middle summit (8061m) alone, where he reportedly dedicated his ascent to the new Russian President Dmitry Medvedev. Sadly the Spaniard Iñaki Ochoa de Olza died of cerebral and pulmonary oedema at 7400m on the east ridge despite heroic efforts by his teammates and also by the Swiss climbers Ueli Steck and Simon Anthamatten, who had been attempting a different line on the face, and Denis Urubko, who came out by helicopter from Kathmandu, to get him down. Annapurna would have been Inaki's 13th 8000m peak, all climbed without oxygen, which seems to show that however extensive your past experience you are not necessarily safe from serious altitude illness (article *The Spirit of Mountaineering* p83).

Kangchenjunga had one ascent in the spring, by an Indian expedition on the south-west face route. **Makalu** had at least 19 ascents by its standard north-west face route.

Earlier in the spring, as acclimatization for their planned Annapurna climb, Ueli Steck and Simon Anthamatten climbed a very impressive and direct line on the 2000m north face of **Teng Kangpoche** (6487m) in Khumbu. Their route required three bivouacs and they graded it VI, M7+. It was climbed in Alpine style with the second jumaring with both packs on some steep pitches, and finished with a bivouac on the knife edged summit ridge. They reached the summit on 24 April. (article *Checkmate* p56) Their route is well to the left of the 2004 British Bullock-Carter route. A Spanish party also made an ascent on this face that seems to share much ground with the British route. Like them they reached a point well west of the

196. High on Teng Kangpoche – Ueli Steck and Simon Anthamatten's successful ascent of the coveted north face of this Khumbu peak. (Steck coll)

summit and were unable to continue along the ridge to the summit of Teng Kangpoche.

A Japanese pair (Kenro Nakajima and Hiroki Yamamoto) made what may have been the first ascent of **Dingjung Ri** (6196m) in the Rolwaling valley by its east ridge. They reached the summit on 15 March, after fixing rope on a loose rock section. Also in the upper Rolwaling, Pete Athans and Theodore Hessler made an apparent first ascent of **Kang Kuru** (6320m) on 16 April by its west ridge.

On **Ama Dablam** the Italian Francesco Fazzi and Spaniard Santiago Padros climbed a line on the west face that started up, or very close to, the Japanese 1985 route but then went left and up unclimbed ground to the summit at grade V+, M5+ with 80 degree ice. They bivouacked on the summit and descended by the standard south-west ridge route. They named their route, perhaps provocatively, *Free Tibet*. The standard south-west ridge route had numerous ascents in the autumn, despite continuing icefall danger in the area of the 'dablam', the high hanging glacier which now seems to be falling down altogether.

In the post-monsoon season two notable new routes were climbed on high mountains. The American climber Vince Anderson and the Slovenian Marko Preselj climbed the west face of **Kangchungtse** (Makalu II, 7678m), mainly on ice with some mixed climbing high up, at a standard of M4-5, in a 16-hour round trip from a camp at 6700m. Their subsequent attempt on the west face of Makalu itself was defeated by bad weather.

On **Nuptse** two French climbers, Patrice Glairon-Rappaz and Stéphane Benoist climbed a direct route on the south face, starting left of the original British route, and climbing very steep ground (M4-5, and some vertical ice) before joining the original route in the snow couloir below the summit ridge. They reached the ridge at around 7700m at 7pm on 28 October and were forced by extreme cold to descend without going to the 7864m main summit. (article *Are you Experienced?* p51) The whole climb took four days and Benoist needed helicopter evacuation from their base camp with frost-bitten feet. Glairon-Rappaz had attempted this route solo in 2006 but re-treated in bad weather. They commented that it was a bit harder than the north face of Les Droites.

Another route was climbed on **Teng Kangpoche** in the autumn, on the north-east face, by Japanese climbers Yasushi Okada and Hiroyoshi Manome. Their 1900m route was climbed in Alpine style on rock and steep ice, and required three bivouacs. They reached the summit on 15 November and descended in 12 hours using an 80m abseil rope. They graded it ED in the traditional system. En route they found an old piton at 5750m, probably left during a French attempt in 2002. Around the same time another Japanese pair attempted a line further left on the same face, reaching 6250m on very steep mixed ground before being forced to retreat. Both these routes are to the left of the impressive central pillar of Teng Kangpoche's north face, whereas the Steck/Anthamatten and Bullock/Carter routes are to its right.

American climbers David Gottlieb and Joe Puryear made an ascent of **Kang Nachugo** (6735 m) in the Rolwaling Himal, which they believe was the first ascent of the mountain. They first attempted a direct line on the south face but were forced to retreat around 150m below the summit in bad weather. They then climbed the long and very narrow west ridge over five days in alpine style, summiting on 17 October. The *Himalayan Index* records two previous ascents of Kang Nachugo in 1980 and 1995, but they appear to refer to a peak considerably further west.

Also in the autumn Nick Bullock attempted the west face of **Peak 41** (6623m) north of the Mera La, with Andy Houseman. They were required by the Tourist Ministry to pay for a liaison officer, who never even left Kathmandu. All their gear was stolen from their unguarded base camp above the village of Thangnag, and by the time they could replace it Andy had to go home. Nick found a new companion, who had little experience, and finally made a solo attempt, reaching 6200m on steep mixed ground (Scottish V-VI) and some very loose rock.

LINDSAY GRIFFIN & DICK ISHERWOOD

Pakistan 2007

This summary was compiled from extensive notes collected by LG. We thank Mr Saad Tariq Siddique of the Alpine Club of Pakistan, and the climbers named below, for their assistance.

The Pakistan authorities approved 83 expeditions for 2007. As in Nepal, peak fees have been steeply discounted to keep the climbers coming, and a permit for K2 now costs only $6000. Peaks below 6500m have no fee at all, and (perhaps the best news of all) liaison officers are no longer required outside the Baltoro region.

On **K2**, 29 climbers from eight expeditions reached the summit, out of 130 starters. A Russian expedition climbed the west face by a new route, much of it on the very steep central rock buttress, using plenty of aid but apparently little oxygen, and put 11 people on the summit on 21/22 August after over two months' effort. They considered the route to be more difficult than the 2004 Russian ascent of the north face of Jannu, and it is almost certainly the hardest route to date on K2. A good deal of gear was left behind.

Denis Urubko and Serguey Samoilov from Kazakhstan attempted a new line up a shallow spur on the north face of K2 late in the season, but abandoned their attempt low down in bad weather and traversed onto the Japanese route on the north ridge, reaching the summit on 2 October. This was the latest summit date ever for K2 and another impressive achievement for this pair, climbing fast and unsupported and without oxygen.

Among other parties on K2, Bruce Normand with American Chris Warner and Canadian Don Bowie made an ascent of the Abruzzi Spur after attempting two new lines on the east spur and south-east buttress. They climbed without oxygen but with a good deal of fixed rope, and were variously helped and hindered by a number of other parties, several using plenty of oxygen and some willing to both steal gear and abandon their weaker members high on the mountain. Bruce has written vividly about the selfishness and incompetence of many participants. A Czech climber, Libor Uher, was the sole member of a party on the *Cesen route* to reach the summit, and needed extensive assistance on the descent of the Abruzzi. A number of climbers were evacuated by the Pakistan Air Force at the end of the season.

On **Broad Peak**, 19 expeditions were successful, putting a total of 77 climbers on the summit. One was an Austrian party celebrating the 50th anniversary of the Buhl/Diemberger first ascent. Hidden Peak (**Gasherbrum I**) was climbed by 27 people, but the normally very popular **Gasherbrum II** had only one successful ascent as avalanche danger on the

197. The Russian line on the west face of K2. Six camps were used on the rock buttress over two months. (*Anna Piunova/Russian K2 Expedition*)

standard route killed one climber and deterred many others. **Nanga Parbat** was climbed by 17 people from five expeditions.

In the 2007/8 winter attempts on Nanga Parbat and Broad Peak were both unsuccessful. Simone Moro's party reached 7800m on the latter. No one has yet succeeded on an 8000m peak in winter in Pakistan, though some have come very close.

In July, the Spanish climber Luis Carlos Garcia Ayala made the first ascent of the south-west face of the **Red Queen**, a granite peak close to the Nameless Tower in the Trango group. His companion, Ali Mohammed, had been his cook on his only previous trip to the Karakoram seven years earlier, and had no technical climbing experience. Ayala quickly taught him the essentials and they made the ascent and descent of the 900m face in four days at a free climbing standard of 5.10b, with very little aid. This may be a landmark in the history of climbing instruction.

A large team of young climbers from the Siberian city of Krasnoyarsk, Russia, completed two first ascents on the 2000m north-west face of **Great Trango (6286m)**. A four-man party climbed new ground close to the original 1999 *Russian Direct* route. On the upper section, they found traces of previous passage and their route seems to have shared some ground with both a 1990 attempt and the *Azeem Ridge*, climbed by Kelly Cordes and Josh Wharton in 2004. Although no grade has so far been quoted, the climb is reported to be 75% free. At the same time six of their comrades were on the left side of the face, attempting to finish the line climbed to within a handshake of the summit ridge in 2003 by an Odessa team, which is rather less amenable to free climbing. They completed the climb in 11 days at a standard of 5.11/A4, after enduring some bad weather. The combined team, all on their first visit to the Karakoram, then moved on to attempt Broad Peak.

Two new lines were established on the 5885m **Shipton Spire**. The

198. The American-Slovenian first ascent route on K7 West. The main summit of K7 is on the right; the rock spire in the centre remains unclimbed. (*Marek Holocek*)

Spanish climber Silvia Vidal, known for a number of hard solo ascents in Pakistan and India, spent 21 straight days on the north-east face in capsule style, making 20 solitary bivouacs before reaching the notch on the north-east pillar at c5300m. Her route didn't follow any strong features and therefore required continuous hard aid: several pitches of A4 and a crux of A4+, finishing with mixed climbing. She declined to continue to the summit over difficult mixed ground. Perhaps notably for today, during her stay at and above advanced base she was entirely alone and carried neither radio nor phone, commenting that it was 'a great experience'.

A four-man Russian team also spent 20 days on their route during very much the same period as Vidal was climbing hers. The Russians originally planned to attempt the unclimbed south face of the Spire but found the approach up the chaotic glacier too difficult and dangerous. Instead they switched to an independent line up the available rock between two previous routes on the south-east face, *Baltese Falcon* and *Women and Chalk*. The four Russians climbed capsule style, following a prominent right-facing corner/depression in the upper section. They reached the top of the wall after enduring a full week of bad weather and having climbed pitches of 5.10d and A4. They then continued up the taxing mixed summit ridge to the highest point, which they reached on July 30. In all 32 pitches were required for this 1300m route.

Two Americans, Cedar Wright and Renan Ozturk, made the first ascent of the higher south-west summit of the striking **Cat's Ears** (5564m) near the Shipton Spire. They encountered much dubious rock on a line that corkscrewed around the pinnacle via two long traverses and climbed the wobbly summit block at up to 5.11, A2.

In the Charakusa valley Steve House, Vince Anderson and Marko

Prezelj made the first ascent of **K7 West** (6858m) by its south-east face in four days with 5.11 rock-climbing, steep ice and some very steep and unstable snow near the top. This summit had seen several previous attempts going back to the seventies. Their subsequent attempt on **K6 West** from the Charakusa glacier was defeated by dangerous icefall conditions. A number of other difficult rock climbs were done by several parties on the lower peaks of the Charakusa valley.

On the west side of the Hushe valley a Polish party climbed the west summit of **Honboro Peak** (6430m, and about 20m lower than the main summit which may still be unclimbed.) Their route up the south-west ridge took 53 hours of almost continuous climbing, much of it on poor rock.

In the central Karakoram, an American party (Doug Chabot, Mark Richey and Steve Swenson) climbed the peak known as **Choktoi I** (6166m) from the south-east, making an alpine style first ascent of this beautiful triple-summited mountain over two and a half days. The climbing was mostly on snow and ice, and the name Suma Brakk has been proposed: Suma means three summits in Balti. They subsequently attempted the north ridge of **Latok I** (7145m) but were forced to retreat from 5900m. This ridge, the 'Walker Spur of the Karakoram' has now had more than 20 attempts by a variety of highly talented parties, though none has come close to the first, Jim Donini, Michael Kennedy, George and Jeff Lowe, who reached c7000m in 1978.

Two young Chamonix climbers, Julien Herry and Roch Malnuit, climbed the south-west ridge of **Latok III** in mid-September to make the probable 4th ascent (third in alpine style) of this 6949m peak in a six-day push base camp to base camp. The original Japanese ascent in 1979 used 2000m of fixed rope, much of which remains in place.

In the western Karakoram Yannick Graziani and Christian Trommsdorff made the first ascent of **Pumari Chhish South** (7350m) by its 2700m south face in six days of difficult mixed climbing. This was their third attempt on this peak.

Pat Deavoll and Lydia Bradey from New Zealand attempted the first ascent of **Beka Brakkai Chhok** (BBC) (6882m) in the Batura Mustagh from the Baltar valley, but retreated from around 6000m in poor snow conditions. A Japanese party attempted **Pamri Sar** (7016m), also in the Batura, but had to retreat from 5500m in bad weather.

An eight-man Polish expedition attempted the west ridge of **Kampire Dior** (7168m), the westernmost major peak in the Karakoram, but retreated from 6500m in bad weather. This would have been the second ascent of the mountain, first climbed by a Japanese party in 1975.

A large Greek party attempted **Buni Zom** (6551m) in the Hindu Raj, but had to settle for its 6200m south summit. One party member died in a fall on a subsidiary peak. A French party made a new route on a 6058m summit in the northern Hindu Raj just south of **Koyo Zom**, the highest peak in this range, at a standard of Alpine Difficile. This peak had probably been climbed before, from the north side.

JOHN TOWN

China and Tibet 2008

The past year was not a good one for the people of Tibet or Sichuan, nor for climbers with ambitions to climb there. In March riots broke out in Lhasa and a range of other centres within the Tibetan areas of the Tibetan Autonomous Region (TAR), Sichuan, Qinghai and Gansu. The Chinese closed the borders of TAR and other affected areas and most expeditions abandoned their plans. Initial assurances to groups heading for the north side of Everest proved worthless, as the area was sealed off to avoid the chance of any further protests concerning the Olympic torch. Most diverted to the south side, where the paranoid behaviour of the Nepalese authorities in response to Chinese pressure to eliminate protest did them little credit. The torch's 8 May 'Journey of Harmony' apart, no other expeditions reached the summit from the north in either the pre- or post-monsoon seasons.

On 12 May a massive earthquake hit the mountain regions of Sichuan, killing over 69,000 people and making nearly 5 million people homeless. Disruption of the infrastructure made travel difficult or impossible. Taken together these events ensured that most mountaineering activity was limited to the latter part of the year:

Qonglai Shan

In September Americans Chad Kellogg and Dylan Johnson completed the first ascent of the impressive south-west ridge of **Siguniang (6250m)**, taking an epic nine days to complete the 72-pitch route.

Daxue Shan

French guides Sébastien Bohin, Pascal Trividic, and Sébastien Moatti visited the Minya Konka group in late September and October. Bohin and Trividic made the third ascent of the beautiful **Riuchi Gongga (5928m)**, via the south-east ridge. The team also attempted the 1600m West Face of **Jiazi (6540m)** but were turned back at 5400m by poor weather.

In late November, Tom Nakamura and three companions explored one of the last unclimbed 6000m peaks in western Sichuan – a 6079m peak south of Minya Konka, provisionally named **Ren Zhong Feng**, before moving on to investigate **Xiaqiangla (5470m)**, a spectacular unclimbed pyramid north-west of Danba town in the Dadu River basin.

Hengduan Mountains

The Hengduan mountains stretch down from Tibet into the northern part of Yunnan, but the Yunnan section is rarely visited. In January Booth

Haley (USA) and Juan-Antonio Puyol explored the **Tza-Leh (Cali)** group that lies north of the Baima Shan Pass, south-east of Deqen, on the Yunnan-Tibet border. They climbed **Peak 5600m**, south of the highest peak, which is shown as 5621m on some maps.

The Nu Shan, situated in the Deep Gorge Country of south-east Tibet, forms the watershed between the Mekong and Salween rivers and consists of three massifs – from north to south these are Dungri Garpo, Damyon and the Meili Xue Shan. In October and early November Tom Nakamura and two Japanese companions explored the first of these massifs from its western side, braving both landslides and deep snow. They were eventually rewarded with stunning views of **Dungri Garpo (6090m)** and a range of other peaks (article Travels Beneath Blue Skies p91).

Nyenchen Tanglha East

A party from the Tohoku University Alpine Club, consisting of Junichi Imai, Kenji Tajiri and Hiroshi Okada visited the Yigrong Tsangpo gorge in March. A road built in 2007 reaches as far as the village of Ba, from where they explored the Jianpu valley. They were unable to reach the Jianpu glacier in the two days available but did obtain photos of the unclimbed **Peak 6694m** at its head. The party then trekked for three days from Ba, via Bake, to Rika (Rigonka, Ragoonka) village. From Rika they crossed the main river and followed an unexplored subsidiary valley south-west for two day to reach the village of Long Pu. This lies at the junction of the Nenqeng, Shindoboma, Tamboo and Yumo valleys and they were able to see a variety of fine peaks, including **Tsepurong (6648m)**, as well as to visit the Shindoboma glacier. Returning to Rika, they then attempted to repeat Kingdon Ward's 1935 traverse of the main gorge but had to retreat three days short of their objective when Imai suffered a broken leg.

An elderly party from the Osaka Eiho Club, lead by Takatsugo Shiro, continued their 2007 exploration of five new glacial lakes in the Botoi Tsangpo valley, this time equipped with a kayak as well as climbing gear. After a variety of aquatic trials they succeeded in reaching the icebergs of the fifth lake, which lies directly below the glacier.

Tien Shan

Paul Knott, Guy McKinnon and Bruce Normand visited the Chinese Tien Shan in August 2008 (article p19). All three made the first ascent of **Hanjaylak I (5424m)**, and McKinnon and Normand also made the first ascents of **Hanjaylak II (5424m)** and **Yanamax (6332m)**.

Himalaya

Three members of a seven-man Japanese expedition were avalanched and killed on 1 October during an attempt on the unclimbed North Ridge of **Kula Kangri (7538m)**. Yoshinobu Kato, Satoshi Arimura and Susumu Nakamura had been fixing ropes above camp 1 on a snow spur leading to the ridge.

KESTER BROWN

New Zealand 2008 - 2009

This report covers developments in the New Zealand mountains from May 2008 to June 2009.

The **Darran Mountains** in Fiordland National Park continue to be New Zealand's pre-eminent destination for alpine rock development. Richard Thompson, Dave Vass and Richard Turner furthered their contribution to a wealth of new routes in the Central Darrans with a second line on Patuki's north face. The route is six pitches, grade 20 and unnamed. Two very high quality new routes were added to the north face of Mt Moir. Nick Craddock, Murray Ball and Milo Gilmore completed a six-pitch climb, named *Vindication*, grade 25, on the right hand side of the face. Sarah Adcock and Kester Brown finished off an old aid route in the middle of the face, adding three pitches to what is now an all-free route: *El Braveth* goes at grade 25. Ian Brown and Tom Williams made the probable first ascent of the north-east ridge of Mt Madeleine in February over two days. The pair encountered fresh snow and rock gendarmes that made for difficult travel on the upper ridge. They bivvied at 1400m and thought the route would be about grade 3 on the Mt Cook scale.

The **Mt Aspiring Region** whilst eternally popular, new alpine route development in the past year has been limited to just one line on the west face of Mt Aspiring. *Pride of the Hotaka* was climbed in January '09 by a Japanese team comprising Takeshi Tani and Masayoshi Kohara. It is a direct line that tackles the upper headwall of the face directly and is graded AI5, M5.

Motivated **Queenstown Region** locals have continued to pluck new gems from the south side of the Remarkables Range. During winter '08, Aaron Ford and Rupert Gardiner climbed a new line on the west face of **Double Cone**. They called it *Sumo*. It's an eight-pitch mixed line graded at M6. Dave Bolger and Reese Doyle established one rock route during the summer months. *After Glow* is on **The Telecom Tower** and is grade 18. The early stage of the '09 winter season has already seen one new mixed line put up in the same vicinity, unnamed as yet. The first ascensionists were Sally Ford, Aaron Ford and Tony Burnell. Over in the **Lake Alta Cirque**, controversy over bolting raged briefly, but was swiftly quashed with beer and sensible conversation. Subsequently, the rock route *Judas Goat* had two direct pitches added and was rerouted in its upper reaches to create a high quality addition to the DB Eh Buttress.

Aoraki Mt Cook and Westland: new route activity has steadily slowed in the high Alps in the last few years, grinding almost to a complete halt in the last year; just two notable additions to the peaks surrounding the upper

199. Simon Young on pitch two of *Super Styling* (WI3, Mt Cook 4+), south-west face of Mt Haast, upper Fox Glacier Neve. (*Garry Phillips*)

200. West face of Double Cone, Remarkables Range, showing the line of *Sumo* (8 pitches, M6) climbed by Aaron Ford and Rupert Gardiner. (*Aaron Ford*)

Fox Glacier Neve. The first was by Australians Garry Phillips and Simon Young, who added *Super Styling* to the south-west face of the west peak of **Mt Haast**, mostly ice, and grade WI3, Mt Cook 4+. The second is a possible new ice route on the south-west face of the **Bismarck Peaks**, entailing eight pitches of moderate ice climbing, put up by Tom Wilson and Steve Dowall. Further south and on the other side of the divide, in the Huxley Range, Tony Clarke and Andrew Somervell climbed the south face of the rarely visited **Gilkison Peak** from the Ahuriri/Hunter col. The route is grade 2 on the Mt Cook scale and was almost definitely unclimbed before this ascent.

On **North Island**, Daniel Joll and friends climbed some new mixed routes on the **Cathedral Rocks** and around the **Tukino** ski field, **Mt Ruapehu**, in September '08. The routes consist of mostly vertical rock and ice terrain and are all one to two pitches in length.

ANTONI GÓMEZ BOHÓRQUEZ

Cordillera Blanca

The following historical note aims to resolve the confusion that has arisen in relation to the summits of **Taulliraju Sur** and **Tuctubamba**.

Part of the problem lies with inaccurate sketch maps. The map from the guide *Yuraq Janka* by John F. Ricker (1977) shows a definite SSW ridge of Taulliraju (5830m) descending to the Punta Union pass (4750m) without any marked peak. The south-east ridge, by contrast, shows a prominent peak with no height or name. On the east ridge of this unnamed peak are two minor peaks of 5420m and 5030m, which Ricker named in his book 'Nevado Tuqtubamba' and 'Tuqtubamba Este'. These summits were climbed on 12 July 1960 by Andrea Farina and Nino Poloni as part of the Italian expedition led by Bruno Berlendis, which gave the names Nevado Antonio Locatelli to 5240m and Nevado Leone Pelliccioli to 5030m.

The SSW ridge was presented differently on sketch map 93 in Mario Fantin's book, *Pioneri ed epìgoni italiani sulle vette di ogni continente* (1975), this time showing a 5000m summit named Nevado Unión. This name was given by the 1960 expedition led by G Dionisi, who believed they were the first to reach this peak, from the col that allows passage from the Santa Cruz gorge to the Huaripampa. The Italian team was unaware that the previous year H Adams Carter, his son of 15 years and a friend of the same age had reached the same top. Another notable difference in Fantin's sketch is that it shows the south-east ridge of Taulliraju as uncertain until it reaches peaks 5420m and 5030m, and does not mark the prominent unnamed peak.

The real terrain differs from that represented in these sketch maps. Looking north-east from the head of the Santa Cruz gorge highlights that on the SSE ridge of Taulliraju, the unnamed south-west peak is the one that really goes down to Punta Union. Such differences between sketches and reality, as well as the imagination of new authors, led to confusion between the prominent unnamed peak and its neighbour nevado Tuctubamba, and in some cases with Nevado Unión.

Taulliraju Sur, Taulliraju Sureste or Taulliraju Chico (c5400m)

When Slovenians Tomaz Štrupi and Tone Stern tried to climb this prominent unnamed peak on 8 July 1995, they found pitons and coils of rope on the north-west face. They reached the south-west ridge, but not the summit. Afterwards, they sought details of who had left the material and whether they had attained the summit. They could identify nothing of relevance in the *Revista Peruana de Andinismo y Glaciología (RPAG)* or the *American Alpine Journal (AAJ)*. The problem seems to be that the relevant reports in these publications are subject to many interpretations, since they

201. South side of Taulliraju Sur (c5400m) from the upper end of the Quebrada Huaripampa. *(Ignacio Ferrando)*

lack a line in a photo showing the exact route.

RPAG, No 12, 1976-1977, p. 15: Giulio Fiocchi organised the Spedizione CAI Lecco with the aim of climbing the west wall of Taulliraju. They approached by the Santa Cruz gorge and made their base camp near the Taullicocha lake. In subsequent days, they climbed the ridge towards Taulliraju Chico, ESE of Taulliraju summit, but failed 100m from the top due to technical difficulties and avalanche danger.

AAJ, 1977, p.216: Taulliraju attempt. Our expedition consisted of Mario Conti, Pino Negri, Giuseppe Lanfranconi, Angelo Zoia, Roberto Chiappa, Dr. Galluzi, Denis Bertholet and me [Giulio Fiocchi] as leader. We reached Base Camp at the head of the Santa Cruz gorge on the Taullicocha lake on July 10 [1976]. We worked out a route north of the peak over a pass, across under the north face and up an icefall to the northeast face. Conti, Zoia, Negri, Lafranconi and Chiappa set out on an eight-day attempt. They climbed gullies and compact granite slabs. Bad weather drove them back to Base. In four more days they got to 17,725 feet, some 1400 feet below the summit, but dangerous ice conditions forced them to give up.

AAJ, 1978, p 567: Taulliraju attempt. Clark Gerhardt, Christian (Del) Langbauer, Todd Thompson and I [Craighead McKibben], accompanied by Juan Henostroza and Aquilino Moreno, established the base camp on 26 June [1977] below the impressive west face of Taulliraju. Ignorant of the 1976 Italian attempt, we repeated some of their mistakes and had some exciting but ultimately futile climbing to a high point on the south ridge.

Thus, the material found by the Slovenian team could be from the Fiocchi expedition, although the McKibben team might also have made a drop. It is also possible that it was discarded by the French guides Jean Luc Fabre, Jean Paul Balmat, Daniel Hervé Thivierge and Monaci, who climbed to the left of the Italian attempt when they reached the summit of Taulliraju in alpine style in 1978.

This report ends with a further correction note. Some guides after Ricker suggested, in confusion, that the unnamed south-west peak of Taulliraju was the Tuctubamba (5420m) climbed by the Italians in 1976. So, six years after Štrupi and Stern's attempt, four American climbers approached the same peak in the belief that it was Tuctubamba. Clay Wadman and

202. West side of Taulliraju from the vicinity of Taullicocha lake. *(Antonio Gómez Bohórquez)*

Christian Beckwith tried to climb a couloir on the south face. Absent, among other things, were the granite slabs covered with ice and snow. Their companions Topher and Patience Donahue had more luck climbing the north-west side; see *AAJ* 2002, p.296 and 2003, p.305. The two brothers reached that peak of about 5400m, unnamed on the maps, arbitrarily named Taulliraju Chico and Taulliraju South, although it might be called Taulliraju South-east.

MARCELO SCANU

Argentine Andes 2008

The reports are ordered from North to South. **Chañi Chico** (5571m) in Salta, North Argentine Andes, is a minor summit in the **Chañi** (5896m) massif. The highest summit was sacred and 100 years ago, an Inca mummy was found and extracted from there. Its incredible south wall has been a dream for many generations of Argentine climbers, so this ascent is very remarkable. Argentines Humberto Vázquez, Fernando Gutiérrez and Facundo Juárez opened the line called *Siete Dolores* (*Seven Pains*), 960m 6c (min. 5+), on 9 September. They completed the ascent in 12 hours. The rock was rotten and had much rockfall, and many cracks had hard ice. They bivouacked on the shoulder next to the summit and rappelled the route the next day.

Cachi is another important sacred 6380m mountain in Salta. Nicolás Pantaleón and Nicolás Yannito, both from Salta, ascended the virgin north face in November. They began on the 8th, camping at 3300m and camped twice more at 4000m. On the fourth day, at 4935m, they reached snow that they could melt for water. Otherwise, the mountain is dry. Switching onto the ridge, they erected two more camps on the long route, one at 5578m and the last one at 5830m, where they had heavy snowfall during the night. Finally, on the sixth day, 13 November, they reached the summit at 10.45am. They descended quickly, reaching Salta the next day.

During the year, climbers made the first descent of the crater of **Bertrand's Volcano** (5207m). No-one had previously descended to the crater's bottom as it was sacred from Inca times. This volcano lies amongst the highest volcanoes on earth and in one of its driest zones. The crater is an incredible 4.5km in diameter and more then 300m deep. The Incas made the first ascent of the volcano. In 1965 the European couple of Verena and Anders Bolinder with the local hillman Víctor Bustamante made the first modern climbing ascent. Thirty years after their ascent, Marcelo Scanu solo climbed the summit and found the papers left by the 1965 party. From then on, he had in his thoughts the descent to the deepest point in the crater.

In January-February 2008, José Luis Querlico and Marcelo Scanu travelled to the high barren zone in Catamarca province. They camped west of the crater in an area with little volcanic cones 10-20m high and a lagoon that was red from volcanic minerals. From there they ascended to the crater rim at around 5000m and descended through a dry creek full of enormous rocks, walking virgin territory to the crater's bottom at c4850m. The crater was like a lost world: rock, stones and volcanic ash with virtually nothing

203. The line taken by Siete Dolores (960m 6c) on Chani Chico (5571m). *(Nono Vázquez)*

living. The crater's walls fall steeply from the main summit and from the north summit (5188m). Scanu solo climbed the north summit (his companion had to descend because of work), finding a modern cairn at the top but nothing else. Before going to Bertrand, Querlico and Scanu had explored the region, especially the conic and beautiful **Peinado** (the combed one) volcano. Scanu also ascended here solo a virgin volcanic cone of c4900m called by the locals **Hijo del Peinado** (the Peinado's son). In its summit is a 15m diameter crater. They had lots of snowfall and minus 15°C.

On 11 July (southern winter) Argentines Guillermo Almaraz, Nicolás Pantaleón and Javier Echenique made the first absolute ascent of elegant **Cerro Pabellón** (5331m in Argentine maps) by the south face. They began

204. Crater view from the north summit of Bertrand's Volcano (5188m). *(Marcelo Scanu)*

their ascent from Las Grutas, the border police post near the border with Chile. Almaraz states that the mountains in this region are higher than the maps report. They measured 5405m with STRM (Shuttle Radar Topography Mission) and 5424m by GPS. In 1913, the German geologist Walther Penck claimed to be the first to ascend in the region a mountain called Pabellón of more or less the same height. As the modern group didn't find any trace of Penck (nor of the Incas), surely he ascended another nearby mountain. Pabellón is a common name for mountains in the region.

Incahuasi (6638m) lies on the border between Chile and Argentina, being one of the highest volcanoes on Earth. It was one of the highest points ascended by the Incas for religious purposes. On 19 April, Guillermo Almaraz, Eduardo Namur and Nicolás Pantaleón opened a new route, the south-east. They approached by the Valle (valley) de Las Peladas up to the mountain's base at 4600m. Previously two expeditions had visited the south face, but this one took instead a canal in the south-east. The climbers camped at 5200m and 5750m and ascended the south-east nevé with 50° ice and short passages of climbing to reach the summit plateau at 6250m. They continued to the 6638m summit that emerges from the snow and is part of the huge crater rim. The last metres consisted of loose rock where a simple Inca temple was erected 500 years ago. Prior to the climb, they ascended virgin **Cerro de las Peladas** (4650m), near the place of the same name.

In the Central Argentine Andes, Argentine Herman Binder and Spaniard Alex Gárate made the first traverse of some of the highest volcanoes on Earth. This traverse included the highest volcano on Earth **Ojos del Salado** (6879m), **ATA** (6527m), **Walther Penck** (6682m) and **Nacimientos** (6463m). The unsupported traverse was 21km long (from the base of Ojos del Salado to Real del Rasguido) and never went below 5800m. Binder and Gárate completed it in six days during February 2008, finishing in a lunar eclipse.

On **Aconcagua,** there were fewer climbers on the mountain during the 2008-9 season (4041 against 4548 in 2007-8). A high proportion of the climbers came from outside Argentina. The two first weeks of January were the most popular with 590 and 533 climbers respectively. Unfortunately, there were nearly 300 rescues compared to 278 last season, and a higher death toll at six people. An Argentine guide and his Italian clients had a big accident that led to a major rescue and an unpleasant media circus. The guide and an Italian woman died. There were several interesting climbs by some Aconcagua porters who are also leading climbers in Argentina. Ariel di Carlantonio, Fernando Arnaudi and Mariano Galván made the second ascent (30 years after the first by Argentines Vieiro, Porcellana and Jasson in 1978) of the 2800m *East Glacier and South-east* route, also known as *English Glacier*. The last camp was at 6600m near the Polish Glacier's exit. Mariano Galván also made a new route to the right of the Polish Glacier. He went from Plaza Argentina to the summit alone in 14 hours for 2800m. He had ice and mixed terrain with 6th grade rock. He named the route *Los Porters* because of his and his friends' activity in Aconcagua. Ariel and Fernando meanwhile ascended the south face of nearby **Ameghino** (5883m), on which they had up to 80° ice and rotten rock. They finished via the normal route to the striking little summit. It is likely that this was a new route, although apparently Pizarro and one of the Benegas brothers earlier ascended part of the route.

205. Reaching the lowest part in Bertrand's Volcano's crater. *(Marcelo Scanu)*

Mount Everest Foundation Expedition Reports

SUMMARISED BY BILL RUTHVEN

The Mount Everest Foundation (www.mef.org.uk) was set up as a registered charity following the first successful ascent of Everest in 1953 and was initially financed from the surplus funds and subsequent royalties of that expedition. It is a continuing initiative between the Alpine Club and the Royal Geographical Society (with the Institute of British Geographers).

Its purpose is to encourage 'exploration of the mountain regions of the Earth'. This is exploration in its widest sense, not just climbing expeditions but also the application of other exploratory disciplines, such as geology, botany and zoology. It has now distributed well over £900,000 to almost 1,600 British and New Zealand expeditions, mostly to ambitious young climbers.

In return for supporting an expedition, all that the MEF asks is a comprehensive report. Once received, copies are lodged in the Alpine Club Library, the Royal Geographical Society, the British Mountaineering Council and the Alan Rouse Memorial Collection in Sheffield Central Library.

Donations to assist the work of the MEF are more welcome than ever, so if you have previously benefited from MEF grants, why not include a bequest to the Foundation in your will?

The following notes summarise reports from the expeditions supported during 2008, and are divided into geographical areas.

AMERICA – NORTH AND CENTRAL

Buckskin Glacier Take Two, Alaska 2008 Jon Bracey with Matt Helliker (April-May 2008)

With only three big wall 'aid' routes on the east face of Bear Tooth (3207m), this pair of climbers hoped to establish another one up the central fault line or the continuous corner system on the left- hand side of the face. Unfortunately, they arrived in the area just after a massive storm had deposited almost a metre of fresh snow over the entire range. Their intended objective was therefore out of condition, so they turned their attention to the Moose's Tooth (3150m) on the eastern side of Ruth Gorge. On this peak they climbed a big fault line on the right-hand side of the east face, achieving a 1400m new route *There's a moose loose aboot the hoose* (ED4, M8, A2, AIG), stopping on the north ridge 100m short of the summit because of a dangerous sérac. They also climbed a probable new route on the north-west face of the Mini Moonflower Buttress of Mount Hunter, (4442m) to the left of the Prezelj/Koch route *Luna*. MEF 08/10

AMERICA – SOUTH AND ANTARCTICA

Welsh Central Tower of Paine 2007 Mike (Twid) Turner with Bob Brewer, Geoff Hibbert and Peter Jones. (March 2008)
Few expeditions can have undergone as many changes between conception and completion as this one. Following changes to leadership and three team members, the trip was postponed from late 2007 into 2008, which was most unfortunate, as during that time, their prime objective was climbed by an Italian team. But that didn't deter these stalwarts, who turned their attention to the deep Bader Valley to the south of the Central Towers massif. Here they succeeded in making the first ascent of a 700m granite pillar on the east face of Cuerno Norte (2400m). They called their 20 pitch (ED 5.10 A4) route *The Devil Rides Out*.
MEF 07/24

British Darwin Range 2008 Simon Yates with Andy Parkin (September 2008)
After failing to set foot on Monte Frances (2200m) during an attempt in 2007 (MEF 07/10) due to adverse winds and weather, this team returned to have another go. After sailing from Ushuaia to Caleta Ola with Capt Wolf Kloss on the yacht Santa Maris Australis, they found that this year the south face was devoid of ice, so they turned their attention to the unclimbed west ridge. On this they reached 2100m before being forced to retreat due to a storm. Back at the yacht, they discovered that Kloss and Luis Tura had just made the sixth ascent of Monte Francis by the 'standard' south-east ridge. They then sailed back to Puerto Williams, from where they made their way to Yendegaia for an attempt on Roncagli III. Although they made some progress on this, reaching a bergschrund snow cave on the east ridge, they were once again forced to retreat due to storm and bad snow conditions. Nevertheless, they felt that the weather and conditions for climbing in the Cordillera Darwin at this time of year seemed more favourable than in the summer.
MEF 08/15

Cordillera Blanca 2008 Tony Barton with Olly Metherell, also (part time) Tom Chamberlain from UK and Jim Sykes from USA (June-August 2008)
This was a multi-part expedition to Peru, which started with a short acclimatisation trip to view objectives in the Quebrada Rajururi. They then embarked on a trip to the Nevado Pongos/Raria massif, but retreated when the leader became ill. While recovering back in Huaraz, they were joined by Sykes, with whom they undertook the third phase, making the first ascent of Huaytapallana II (5025m) (apart from the summit block) by two separate routes, *Cop Out* (11 pitches, E1,5A) on the west face and *Last Exit* (7 pitches, also E1 5A) on the north ridge. Finally, they explored the little visited Quebrada Puchua, which offers excellent potential for new routing. MEF Ref: 08/18

Pompey - Eastern Blanca - Peru 08 Ken Findlay with Kieran O'Sullivan, Brian Swales and Keith Waddell (July-August 2008)
In 2006, Paul Hudson made a solo reconnaissance trip (MEF 06/14) into the Eastern Cordillera Blanca of Peru which proved that there was still much left to explore: as a direct result, this team hoped to make the first ascent of the south ridge of Nevado Copa (6188m) from a base camp at Lago Allicocha, but only reached 5000m.
Late one night while Findlay and Swales were on the mountain, two masked bandits entered BC and attacked the cook: they slashed his hand and hit him on the head with the butt of a rifle before being disturbed by the other climbers but escaped with a load of money. MEF 08/24

Chimanta 2008 Anne and John Arran (September 2008)
For this year's exploration of the tepuis of Venezuela, this pair chose the more remote steep rock walls of Chimanta (2700m), formed from a very hard type of sandstone, some of the oldest in the world. Previous exploration of the peak by cavers and ecologists has been limited, due to it having the most overhanging wall in the world (100m+). Although the main wall remains unclimbed, they made the first ascent of a hard (E7 6b) route on Amurita, where the overhang sheltered them from the heavy rain that fell on several days: however the resultant rise in river levels added to the hazards of the jungle, delaying their return journey. MEF 08/26

GREENLAND

Queen's University Belfast MC Greenland 2008 Anthony Garvey with David Leonard, Fred Maddelena and Les Ross from UK plus Jonathon McCloy and James McKevitt from Ireland. (June 2008)
To some extent this expedition to Renland in East Greenland was a follow-up to the West Lancashire Scouts Expedition in 2007 (MEF 07/19). With Tangent Expeditions providing the transport etc, this team planned to explore around the Edward Bailey glacier system and make as many first ascents as possible. In this they were successful, achieving two new peaks summited on ski and three subsidiary peaks and two impressive summits climbed in alpine style over rock and snow. Grades varied from PD to TDinf. MEF 08/03

British Tasermiut Fjord 2008 Ged Desforges with Dan McManus, Tom Spreyer, Tony Stone, Es Tresidder and James Vybiral plus Ruben Gutzat from Bavaria (July-August 2008)
This team hoped to establish high standard alpine big wall routes in the Cape Farewell area, in particular on the 500m-600m west faces of the Minster (1940m) and Cathedral (2030m). However, on accessing the area they discovered that the rock was very shattered, so abandoned their primary objectives and concentrated on climbing from an underdeveloped valley by the Hermelnbjerg (1912m) and Tininnertuup (1725m) groups of mountains. On these they were successful in putting up seven new routes with grades up to

E5 6b and also repeated two other routes. In addition, Gutzat carried out a survey of wildlife in the area while Vybiral, a visual anthropologist, filmed the expedition, planning to use the footage to produce both an anthropological piece as well as a conventional climbing film.

MEF 08/13

Greenland Renland 2008 Nat Spring with Crispin Chatterton and Rob Grant (June-July 2008)
As with the expedition from Queens University Belfast (MEF 08/03) this was a follow-up to the West Lancashire Scouts Greenland Expedition 2007 (07/19) with the intention of extending the exploration of a little visited area of East Greenland and making first ascents of peaks by routes up to Alpine PD/V Diff standard, although this turned out to be a conservative estimate. They were actually flown in on the helicopter that was evacuating 08/03. From their base camp, they explored two glaciers (travelling the full length of the Edward Bailey glacier) and made first ascents of three major peaks up to 1997m via snow and ice lines, together with one subsidiary peak and a minor point via a rock route. They also carried out a survey of plant life at various altitudes.

MEF 08/25

HIMALAYA – INDIA

British Zemu Gap 2008 Colin Knowles with Adrian O'Connor and Jerzy Wieczorek (March-April 2008)
This exploratory trip to Sikkim, in the style of Shipman and Tilman, hoped to make the first south to north crossing of the Zemu Gap (c5850m) from Yoksum via Gochi La and then on to Green Lake and Lachan, thus linking two major trekking routes. Although going very close to Zemu Peak (7780m) – a contender for the 'world's highest unclimbed mountain' – they did not plan to tread any summits but nevertheless the 'trek' was likely to involve very steep ice-climbing. Unfortunately unseasonal heavy snow prevented them from reaching the Gap in time to complete the circuit and return safely. They did however reach a height of 5100m below the Tongshiong glacier.
MEF 08/01

Obra Valley 5000m Peaks 2008 Derek Buckle with Toto Gronlund, Martin Scott and Bill Thurston (September-October 2008)
When their plans for a return trip to Nyenchen Tanglha had to be abandoned due to the Chinese ban on trips to Tibet, this team was fortunately able to select this alternative destination in the Western Garhwal that did not require a permit. They planned to explore the upper reaches of the Obra Valley and Devkir glaciers, and make first ascents of as many peaks as possible over 5000m. They visited three major cols overlooking the Maninda Supin and Zupika valleys. Heavy snow and zero visibility thwarted their attempt on Peak 5760m, however they did achieve the first ascent of Peak 5165m by its north-west ridge at PD.

MEF 08/05A

Edinburgh Altitude Research 2008 David Hall with Richard Benson, Richie Dargie, Nikki van Gemeren, Stewart Jackson, Nicky Salmon, Kirsty Steggles, David Veitch, Maddy Whitehouse and Rob Young (June-July 2008)
This group of medical students originally intended to carry out its research in Pakistan but transferred to India when the political situation in Pakistan became threatening. Their aim was to investigate the cognitive effects of altitude – particularly reaction times – while undertaking a high level traverse in an under-explored region of the Zanskar Himalaya, a task that was achieved with great success, although it will take some time to analyse all the results. The traverse entailed the team, complete with pack horses, crossing the Shingo La (5049m) and Phitse La (5560m) passes and culminated in a classical Himalayan climb (without the horses!) of Friendship Peak (5289m). MEF 08/14A

British Sikkim 2008 Roger Payne with Owen Samuel, also Claire and Simon Humphris and Norwegian Tom Midttun during acclimatisation phase. (October-November 2008)
For some years, Roger has been hoping to obtain permission to make the first ascent of the south ridge of Gurudongmar (6715m) in North Sikkim, and although under a barrage of requests the Sikkim authorities seem to be gradually relaxing their attitude towards foreign expeditions, Gurudongmar still remains off limits. However, after acclimatising in North Sikkim with first ascents of Marpo Peak (c5400m), Ta Peak (c5300m) and Changma Peak (5000m), Payne and Samuel moved to West Sikkim, to attempt the south-east ridge of Rathong (6679m). Mixed climbing up to UIAA grade IV/V rock and grade II snow/ice took them to a very exposed bivouac at c6300m. Very strong winds made it dangerous to continue on the exposed ridge above this point, so they aborted, descending with 18 abseils. MEF 08/28

HIMALAYA – NEPAL

British Phari Lapcha (Machermo) 2008 James Thacker with Andrew Turner (November 2008)
Phari Lapcha (aka Machermo, 6017m) stands adjacent to the well-trodden route to Gokyo, and this pair hoped to climb a new route on the left-hand side of its north face. However, at approximately half-height, they encountered unconsolidated snow and very difficult mixed ground. They retreated and turned their attention to the north side of Dawa Peak (aka Phari Lapcha West, 5977m) on which they made probably the third ascent of *Snotty's Gully* (ED1) first climbed by Bracey and Bullock on MEF 06/23.
MEF 08/06

Khumbu Alpine Style 2008 Nick Bullock with Andy Houseman then Dave Noddings (September-November 2008)
Bullock and Houseman planned to make the first ascent of the south summit

(6575m) of Peak 41 by climbing the steep west face, then traversing to the main summit before descending via the Slovenian 2002 route. However, after a brief acclimatisation trip, they descended to their base camp to find that everything – boots, tents, clothing and food with a total value of £10,000 - had been stolen. They returned to Kathmandu, from where Houseman flew home. Fortunately, after a series of urgent emails, Bullock persuaded Noddings – although with limited experience – to take immediate leave from his job and fly out to join him, bringing 60kg of replacement clothing and gear. They then returned to the Hinku Valley where Bullock made a solo attempt on the intended route, but abandoning at 6200m due to steep mixed loose rock.
MEF 08/08

Ethnobotany Nepal Himalaya 2008 Paul Egan with Carol-Ann Cunningham, Marloes Eeftens and Cearúil Swords (July-September 2008)
Working in conjunction with Tribhuvan University (Kathmandu), this multi-national group of scientists from the University of Aberdeen (one UK, two Irish and one Dutch) carried out a multi-disciplinary study of medicinal plants, growing at an altitude of up to 5000m in Langtang and Manang. Unfortunately, the flowering season for the main species – Himalayan Poppy or Meconopsis – is between July and September, so the team was forced to contend with monsoon weather plus leeches and other associated hazards. Nevertheless they were successful in their aims, though full analysis of the data will take some time. The team collected soil samples in addition to plant samples.
MEF 08/11

PAKISTAN

Beka Brakkai Chhok 2008 Pat Deavoll with Malcolm Bass (June-July 2008)
Beka Brakkai Chhok (6940m) is a peak in the Batura range of North Pakistan. Having failed on it with a two-woman team in 2007 (MEF 07/16) New Zealander Deavoll returned for another attempt with Bass from UK. After acclimatising on Baktoshi Peak (6050m) they turned their attention to the icefall to the west of the south face of Beka Brakkai Chhok, establishing a camp at 6000m just below the col on the south-west ridge. At 3am next day they started for the summit, but after two hours thick clouds moved in and it started to snow so they abseiled back to the tent. Bad weather continued for 10 days by which time their eight-day rations were virtually spent, but nevertheless, they had one more attempt at the summit. Climbing a slanting line up the south-west ridge, they reached 6300m where they were stopped by a long sharp corniced section composed of suspect snow with no sign of possible protection. Considering this to be unjustifiably dangerous, the attempt was abandoned.
Note: The south peak of Beka Brakkai Chhok was climbed in early August by two Italians using the same route Deavoll and Bass had attempted, but there is apparently some doubt as to which spot on the ridge is the highest point.

UK-Canadian Distaghil Sar 2008 Bruce Normand with Ben Cheek and Peter Thompson from UK and Don Bowie from Canada (June-July 2008). Distaghil Sar (7883m) in the Hispar Range of Pakistan has had four previous ascents; this team hoped to make the first ascent of its north ridge. The one previous attempt on the ridge had been stopped by the Upper Malangutti glacier, so this team planned to bypass the glacier by adopting an innovatory approach from the east. The peak is high, remote and very committing and they knew that the trip would involve a considerable level of exploration. However, on arrival at P6247m, they discovered that in the past 10 years the whole area had changed beyond all recognition – presumably the effect of climate change – and the terrain had become extremely dangerous. They abandoned the expedition with no further climbing attempts.
This expedition received the Nick Estcourt Award for 2008 MEF 08/19A
Note: On completion of the above expedition, Ben Cheek set out on his own to make a second attempt on the unclimbed north face of Shimshal Whitehorn (6303m) – described as 'one of the most beautiful mountains in the Karakoram'. Despite helicopter searches by the local military and land searches by his colleagues, he was never seen again. We would like to express our deepest sympathy to Ben's family and friends.

British Hispar Sar 2008 Rufus Duits (solo) (September-October 2008) Although subject to several earlier attempts, Hispar Sar (c6400m) remains unclimbed, but this man hoped to make its first ascent climbing solo via the south-west face couloir line attempted by Parkin and Yates in 2004 (MEF 04/14). To acclimatise, he made the first ascent of a nearby 5684m peak which he named Emily Peak; he climbed the south-west face at AD-. Duits then turned his attention to Hispar Sar, his first attempt soon being abandoned due to a surprise snow storm. With the return of more stable weather conditions and climbing up to A1 IV/V, he then reached a high point of 6000m in the couloir before encountering precarious slabs covered in unconsolidated snow, which forced a retreat. MEF 08/29

CENTRAL ASIA AND THE FAR EAST

New Zealand Harturtay Paul Hersey and Graham Zimmerman, both from New Zealand, plus Yewjin Tan from Singapore (June-August 2008)
These strong technical climbers planned to make the first attempt on the steep west face of Harturtay (5127m) in the Schurovkovo Valley in SW Kyrgyzstan. However, when they saw the face for themselves, they realised it had large sections of rotten rock bands, from which they witnessed a number of rock-falls, so they shifted their objective to the impressive north face. On this they made the first ascent of the 1400m Central Rib over three days, recording grade 5.10, AI4, & M4. The valley contains many opportunities for first ascents, but their own efforts on these were thwarted by the onset of bad weather with heavy snowfall.
Note: Local name for Harturtay is 'Kyzyl Muz' and for Schurovkovo is

'Jiptik', and it is recommended that these names be used in future references to the area. MEF 08/04

Eagle Ski Club Ak-Shirak Dave Wynne-Jones with Derek Buckle, Jerry Seager, Mike Sharp and Robert West (April-May 2008) After planning an expedition to the Kangri Garpo range of Tibet, this team was able to switch to an alternative venue in Kyrgyzstan when much of Tibet was closed early in 2008. The new plan was to make a west-east traverse of the Ak-Shirak range on ski, then strike north to make a circuit of the largely unexplored glacier systems of the North Eastern Ak-Shirak range. Unfortunately high winds and clear days had stripped snow from south-facing slopes, making the intended route impossible. However, they did achieve the first ski crossing of the Kyondy Pass (4327m) and first ascents of five peaks between 4767m and 5004m plus first British ascents of two others of 4837m and 4966m, the routes ranging from PD to AD. MEF 08/09A

Oxford University Tien Shan 2008 Ben Sutton with David Jorden, Chris Lloyd, George Margerison and Tom Sutherland (August-September 2008) This team planned to explore and make alpine-style ascents from the Cholok-kanchigai valley in the south-east corner of the Borkoldoy range, but when they arrived in Kyrgyzstan, they discovered that the access road had been washed away. They therefore based their expedition in a valley in the Dy-andjiger range instead: from here they climbed nine (non-technical) peaks up to 4818m, all believed to be first ascents. MEF 08/20

MISCELLANEOUS

Elbrus Dragon 2008 (scientific) Nick Cochand with Sabina Aziz, Prof Damian Bailey, Jon Bailey, Sarah Buszard, Peter Davies, Kevin Evans, Rhodri Evans, Sam Harrison, Ian Lane, Sile Murphy, Jamie Naughton, Jo Organ, Alex Patau, Caroline Taylor, Cicely Warren, Ross Whitehead, Mike Wild and Dr Richard Wise. (July-August 2008)
This was a group of healthy volunteers from Swansea and Cardiff universities (including doctors and medical students) who planned to undergo simple non-invasive tests before, during and after an ascent of Mt Elbrus (5642m) in order to assess the morphological, biochemical and metabolic factors predisposing to AMS. Prior to departure, all team members underwent Magnetic Resonance Imaging (MRI) and Trans Cranial Doppler (TCD) to determine their normal states: these were repeated following the expedition. The experiment was greatly assisted by the presence of a cable car that enabled the subjects to gain access to a hut at 3800m without undertaking any 'normal' acclimatisation. Initially the weather was excellent, but it began to deteriorate as summit day approached, and the ascent had to be aborted at 4900m. Nevertheless, very useful data was acquired, including from a number of inevitable, but fortunately minor, medical problems experienced, including AMS. MEF 08/12

Reviews

MOUNTAIN LITERATURE FESTIVAL

Personal Recollections

Jim Curran

It seems quite extraordinary that for almost a third of my life I spent a day a year at the International Festival of Mountain Literature. Nineteen of these were held at Bretton Hall and two at Kendal. Now, the instigator, Terry Gifford, has relinquished the reins of the IFML and its like may never be seen again.

'Extraordinary', because it seems only last year that a small audience gathered in a strange, acoustically-challenged crescent-shaped room to hear Dave Cook set the bar so high with his lecture 'Running on Empty' that it was hard to imagine anyone challenging him. 'Extraordinary', because however hard I tried, Terry managed to hook me every year bar one, to attend (and I only escaped that by going to Patagonia). And most extraordinary because of the cast list that Terry invited, cajoled, bribed and, for all I know, blackmailed into performing to an increasingly knowledgeable audience. Suffice to say when your list of speakers has included Catherine Destivelle, Kurt Diemberger, Al Alvarez, Charlie Houston, Bob Bates, Paul Piana, Doug Scott, Chris Bonington, Paul Nunn and Walter Bonatti, you can call your festival 'International' without a qualm of conscience. Also, like both the Alpine and Climbers' Clubs, it was the first of its kind, so there was no need for 'British' or 'English' to qualify the title.

I have to confess that although the Festival had always had a strong Sheffield input, the so-called 'Sheffield Mafia' initially viewed it with deep suspicion and took a few years to admit both its importance and how enjoyable the day had become. Their misgivings were not entirely without foundation and I think it is only fair to say that over the years the event has featured a few pretentious and worse, boring events. There is often a thin line between intellectually challenging and self-indulgent posturing. The audience at Bretton were always amazingly tolerant and polite, sometimes too much so, and even in debate tended to be cowed into submission by the same old voices (Ken Wilson).

So what were the Festival's highlights? It would, I think, be cheating to look up the cast list year by year, so I will try to rely on my increasingly unreliable memory, on the basis that if I've forgotten a presentation it wasn't much good and vice versa. Likewise, there is no attempt at chronology.

Heading the list is, as already mentioned, the late Dave Cook, asking awkward questions of our elitist attitudes to sexism and racism. Gill Lawrence, the following year, gave a spirited reply (embarrassing me in the process). Ed Drummond recited his poems from the top of a 40ft tripod. Johnny Dawes wrote an article set for him during the festival. He had three hours to write it. 'Climbers – their Writing and History' was delivered by economic historian, bon viveur and doyen of British mountaineering, Paul Nunn, whose death in 1995 left an un-fillable void.

As well as the lectures, there were other diversions. The winners of the *High* writing competition had their work read out by Ian Smith, who performed the duty throughout the Festival. The judges' verdict on the Boardman Tasker Award was repeated, normally a week later than the award itself, held in the London bastion of Charlotte Road. This was an event enjoyed more by the winner and the audience than the runners-up, who, if present, had to hear their work dismissed for the second time in a week (ok, I'll admit it, it was normally me).

Talking of the Boardman Tasker Award reminds me of another great highlight of the Festival, Harold Drasdo's hilarious reading 'On Falling Off' from his book *The Ordinary Route*. This, in all the years of Boardman Tasker judges' idiosyncratic choices, still takes the biscuit for the 'Best Book Not to be Shortlisted'. Indeed, re-reading it recently, I am amazed it didn't win. But there you go.

Terry normally managed to mount an exhibition of paintings at the Festival as well as musical interludes. This combined with decent breaks at lunch and teatimes and with a bookstall from Jarvis Books provided time for informal discussions and socialising. Terry always tried to make the day as full as possible, and for many of us the breaks were as good as the presentations.

As the Festival's reputation spread the speakers also grew in stature. Charlie Houston and Bob Bates, both in their eighties, gave a memorable joint performance, re-living their K2 adventures, as did Kurt Diemberger. Al Alvarez was persuaded to come up from Hampstead and maintained that Apsley Cherry-Garrard's *The Worst Journey in the World* was the only example of the Festival genre he could think of that counted as real literature, a view hotly contested by the audience (and Ken Wilson).

Chris Bonington gave a surprisingly personal and emotional account of how his huge output of writing has evolved, even if it didn't rate too highly on the Alvarez scale of literary worth. And then there was Walter Bonatti, Terry's greatest coup. Unfortunately the Festival that year was held in Leeds University in a huge freezing cold auditorium, but Bonatti gave a superb and riveting performance, even though he needed an interpreter.

As well as the 'heavy duty' performers, Terry has always given us fun and humour from a diverse set of personalities. Maggie Body's life of editing climbing giants stands out, as does Steve Ashton's theatrical performances, Rosie Smith's irreverent songs and Sid Marty, from the Canadian Rockies, whose dry wit entertained us on several occasions. And when scraping the barrel, Terry occasionally had to resort to this writer for some low humour.

So, life goes on; nothing stays the same etc etc, and Terry's Festival is no exception. On behalf of everyone who made up the audience at Bretton Hall, a big thank you to Terry for all your efforts in bringing us such a rich orgy of stars (many of whom came to my house later, but that's another story).

BOARDMAN TASKER AWARD 2008

The Boardman Tasker Award for Mountain Literature for 2008 was won by Andy Kirkpatrick for *Psychovertical*, reviewed in this *AJ* by Jim Curran. It was Kirkpatrick's first book and he enthusiastically pocketed the winner's cheque of £3,000.

Three of the other four shortlisted books are also reviewed here: Jonathan Trigell's novel *Cham* (Serpent's Tail), Frank Westerman's *Ararat* (Harvill Secker) and Maurice Isserman and Stewart Weaver's history of Himalayan mountaineering, *Fallen Giants* (Yale University Press). The fourth book, John Harlin III's *The Eiger Obsession* was reviewed in the 2007 *AJ*, 372-3, following the book's first publication in the USA. This latest UK edition is from Random House.

The judges for 2008 were Tim Noble, former editor of the *Climbers' Club Journal*, Alison Fell, poet and novelist, and Phil Bartlett, teacher and author of *The Undiscovered Country* (1993).

Delivering the judgment at a ceremony that has become one of the highlights of the Kendal Mountain Festival, Noble said that 'despite its title and front-cover hype' *Psychovertical* was a compulsive read. Kirkpatrick had managed 'a minor miracle'.

Noble continues: 'In measured and balanced writing, larded generously throughout with wit, self-deprecation and mordant humour that he keeps in fine check, he finds the perfect measure of himself on some of the planet's most dangerous climbs. It is perhaps because he knows himself so well that we accept both his expressed incompetence in climbing and writing (he is dyslexic) and efforts to overcome it without demur. Here is no case of classic British irony.

'We warmed to this author – to his urge to live life to the full; to understand his limitations as son, husband and father. The loss of a father figure in particular points to an underlying theme over 30 years of mountaineering biography; but none of us could recall a more sensitive and less self-indulgent treatment of the theme than here presented.

'The book is very cleverly structured (we all wonder if the Hutchinson editor gets credit here). The cuts from scene to scene and climb to climb work wonderfully well – a sort of mountaineering *Day of The Jackal* – as Kirkpatrick comes closer and closer to his nemesis on Reticent Wall. And it is this climb, the running narrative of the book, that grips the most. Fourteen pitches of aid climbing, unrelieved by conversation with a partner should by rights be boring. But it grips the heart further and further. These chapters are without exception exceptional – the best writing about aid climbing we've read, and make for sweaty-palmed page turning. On this basis alone the book is a winner. Taken as whole it stands as a beacon for the next generation of young Turks: a challenge to pick up the pen and overcome their own reticence. Kirkpatrick has taken up the baton on behalf of Generation X and, at just the right moment, has said "Yes I can".'

Psychovertical
Andy Kirkpatrick
Hutchinson, 2008, pp 278, £18.99

What a rollercoaster of a book. Rarely has a climbing memoir been so 'in your face'. To attempt a calm, detached review seems unlikely and almost undesirable. But here goes, and I'll start with a diversion.

A few years ago I had the misfortune to appear on the same bill as Andy at the Fort William Mountain Film Festival. I was comprehensively upstaged and outgunned by an extraordinary barrage of surreal humour, outrageous tales of derring-do and the sheer exuberance of Andy's performances in front of an audience who loved every moment. I drove home reflecting that here was a new star in the ascendant – as well as resolving to add Andy to small children and animals, never to perform with.

So the appearance of *Psychovertical* was one that I looked forward to but wondered whether Andy could carry his 'stream of consciousness' lecturing style into sustaining the written word for a whole book, particularly as Andy's dyslexia is well known. He had, of course, written gear reviews in the magazines that were often quite hilarious, but a book ... ?

Well, he has done it – and how! This is a comprehensive page-turner as Andy exorcises his demons in an epic solo ascent of Reticent Wall on El Capitan. The story pans from a broken home in Hull via many Alpine and Patagonian epics to the overhanging environment of El Capitan and two long and lonely weeks of self-imposed effort before topping out.

My only criticism of the book is that it follows the current trend of dividing the main Reticent Wall story into bite-sized chunks juxtaposed with the account of his life leading up to the climb. Both are absorbing and both can stand on their own. The endless switch-backing from chapter to chapter implies an admission that neither can stand on its own. It seems to be a disease caught from television, which assumes that nobody can concentrate on anything for more than five minutes. What's wrong with a beginning, middle and an end?

But despite this structural quibble, I read the book in one long, sweaty-palmed sitting. I can think of only three or four climbing books that sustain tension from beginning to end; *The Last Blue Mountain*, *Touching the Void* and *The Shining Mountain* come readily to mind; and *Psychovertical* is up there with them. Indeed, I can't think of any previous book that has put the fear of God into me while describing aid climbing. But this is no 'dangle and whack' tedium. It is the excruciating tension of long run-outs edging on skyhooks barely gripping on finger-nail sized flakes, of placing tiny copperheads into expanding cracks, the shock of a huge fall with protection unzipping to be stopped by an ancient rusting nut before the long plunge into oblivion. I could go on – the storms, the hypothermia, the constant fight to stay in control – but I will refrain – read it for yourself.

A postscript: Andy has a real artistic talent and managed to get accepted on an Art Foundation Course in Hull, only to be rejected by a degree course at Sheffield. Having spent nearly 30 years teaching on foundation courses, Andy's rejection brought back painful memories of other talented students similarly treated. But reading Andy's story, it is gratifying to realise he has had the last laugh. For once the Boardman Tasker judges have got it right and Andy has won the biggest prize in mountain literature. Congratulations Andy – and I can't wait to see what comes next.

Jim Curran

Fallen Giants
A History of Himalayan Mountaineering from the Age of Empire to the Age of Extremes
Maurice Isserman and Stewart Weaver
Yale University Press, 2008, pp600, £25

Halfway through *Fallen Giants*, a determined assault on the imposing summit of a one-volume history of Himalayan mountaineering, two climbers face a similar conundrum. Charles Evans, high on Everest, decides against his partner Tom Bourdillon's suggestion of pushing on to the top, preferring to retreat from the South Summit. Hermann Buhl, meanwhile, at the other end of the Himalaya, watches his partner turn back down Nanga Parbat before pressing on alone towards the summit.

Despite being born in the same year, Evans and Buhl, authors Maurice Isserman and Stewart Weaver conclude, choose contrasting options because they are climbing in different eras. Buhl is heralding the determined individualism of the modern age, while Evans comes from a more patrician and courtly age, albeit one tainted with colonialism, where discretion and teamwork are placed ahead of a desperate gamble.

There's certainly some truth in this view. The British Everest expedition of 1953 was in many ways a continuation of the pre-war efforts. How much truth is another question. The answer depends on your outlook on the causes of history. The subtitle of *Fallen Giants* 'A History of Himalayan Mountaineering from the Age of Empire to the Age of Extremes' is a nod to the Marxist historian and cosmopolitan communist Eric Hobsbawm.

Isserman himself is a historian of radical movements in the United States; Stuart Weaver is a historian specialising in British colonial history at Rochester University. Both are enthusiastic hikers and climbers. Their stated aim in *Fallen Giants* is to locate the story of Himalayan climbing within a broader socio-political framework as a way of understanding what motivated the men and, very occasionally, women who were at the forefront of Himalayan exploration. Were these extraordinary individuals simply that –extraordinary and individual – or agents of the cultures they emerged from.

'Though [George Mallory] famously disavowed any motive in climbing Mount Everest beyond the fact it was there,' the authors say in their Preface, 'the expeditions he joined in the 1920s followed the high colonial imperative of exploring, surveying, and ultimately subduing the Himalayan frontier. Throughout this book, these are the sorts of associations we have drawn in order to situate the arcane activity of Himalayan mountaineering fully in the context of its times.'

All historians, certainly since Marx and his ideas of historical materialism, have to wrestle with finding a balance between competing strands: the impact our cultures have on our actions and ideas, our material needs and the demands of our own personalities. Mountain climbing, inevitably, contains all these imperatives to a lesser or greater extent. Which of these you emphasise usually coincides with your own political standpoint. As the authors themselves explain:

'The expeditionary culture of the age of empire, perhaps best exemplified by the Everest expeditions of Mallory's day and some years thereafter, was a paradoxical thing. It was bound up with visions of imperial destiny that assumed the rule of white Europeans over darker-skinned Asians and drew many of its conventions from the hierarchical order of the English public school and the British Army. At the same time, it harboured individual climbers who were often misfits in their own societies, romantic rebels who found a spiritual purpose and freedom in the mountains…'

The other big idea the authors want to advance, and implicit in the title, is that Himalayan climbing follows the classic parabola of rise and fall. Expeditions, particularly a certain kind of American expedition, used to be full of fellowship and mutual support, whereas these days, in the age of extremes, Camelot has been overrun by barbarians more interested in making a few quid and getting their picture in the papers while destroying the mountain environment. 'Hypertrophied commercial individualism' is their phrase for this. (The book is far more readable than this phrase might suggest.)

Fair play. When trying to corral a subject as vast and sprawling as the history of Himalayan mountaineering, it's useful to have a big lasso and historical materialism provides one. And until the end of the book, when the authors' thesis and storytelling begins to go awry, it proves highly effective. The book is very much a romp across rugged terrain, the first of its scale since Kenneth Mason's *Abode of Snow* from the 1950s and in most ways far superior. Packed full of incident, flashes of humour and the succulent fruits of a great deal of reading, it really is indispensable to anyone with an interest in the history of mountaineering.

It opens with a tour de force, a magisterial geographical overview of this prodigious region. From there we spin through the first faltering steps of Himalayan exploration and the curious interface between Empire and sport. Familiar stories and faces loom out from the haze of memory refreshed and successfully reinterpreted. There are, for example, pithy and good-humoured takes on figures like Martin Conway and Douglas Freshfield, although they're too hard on A F Mummery, whose instincts were correct, just hopelessly anachronistic.

I found the sustained assault on institutions, particularly English ones, a little flat-footed. Like Hollywood movies, where an English actor is cast as the villain, the authors don't much care for the English establishment. Fair enough. Kick the Alpine Club, by all means; I'm a big fan of that myself. But Isserman and Weaver are sometimes not astute enough in their cultural judgements. The Alpine Club has never been a subversive organisation, but study the intellectual positions of its most famous Victorian members and it starts to look much less like just another extension of the establishment.

A more powerful line of enquiry would be to examine in closer detail the background of the Everest men of the 1920s. Mallory, of course, is there in spades, and is admired for his links to left-wing intellectuals. Likewise Charles Bruce, presented as the quintessential imperial cartoon. But there is nothing about the missionary work of Howard Somervell, who offers fresh ground for their kind of approach. The Quaker and educationalist Robin Hodgkin is mentioned only as someone lucky enough to run into Charles Houston, but the Masherbrum expedition of 1938 would have offered a useful frame for a fresher, deeper and more informed discussion of British mountaineering before the war.

Ditto, writing about Chris Bonington, the authors note approvingly that his mother was a member of the Communist Party and that growing up in a single-parent family somehow put him in the same social bracket as the proletarian heroes Don Whillans or Joe Brown. Yikes! Don't tell Sandhurst. It's true that Bonington is a far more complex figure in British climbing history than many of his own contemporaries allowed, but not because he was a working-class hero. Anyway, joining the communists in the 1930s was almost *de rigueur* for a portion of the English elite. Just ask Anthony Blunt.

Where the authors' take on English colonialism really tripped them up, however, was in their treatment of the aftermath of the 1953 Everest expedition. It's well known that relations between Tenzing and Sir John Hunt were strained in Kathmandu, as political concerns hijacked the celebrations for the conquest of Everest. The Foreign Office was borderline racist in its treatment of the Tibetan-born Sherpa, but that charge cannot possibly extend to the British climbers.

It is true that Hunt could have been more emollient towards a proud but essentially decent man. But the authors go much further, suggesting that while the British contingent toured the world making money for the Himalayan Committee, Tenzing was hard at work setting up institutions to benefit his people.

In fact, the Himalayan Mountaineering Institute in Darjeeling was a way for Nehru to make political capital from Everest, cementing relations with independent-spirited hill people who were ethnically Nepali on the mountainous fringes of India while leaving real control of in the hands of the Indian Army and Delhi. All of which sounds rather colonial, don't you think?

Ultimately, however, my main concern is that *Fallen Giants* doesn't always get to grips with the most important context of all – the climbing. True, all the people who make an appearance in this book were the product of a particular time and place, but they were also riveted by the idea of climbing mountains. How you do that, what constitutes a challenge, what is perceived as an advance, all build into a culture of their own and have to be understood properly or the project abandoned. Hermann Buhl had a vision; he imagined new possibilities. Some of his inspiration came from his nature, some from his background, but much of it came from within mountaineering itself.

Isserman and Weaver largely get to grips with the driving forces in the Himalaya up until the 1950s, which they regard as a golden age, but their interpretation begins to wobble soon after. They're not totally fixated by 8000m peaks, but they do tend to see everything through that prism. Reinhold Messner provides a useful continuing strand in the Hobsbawm theory of mountaineering history, the arch-individualist making good. Likewise the commercialism that followed Messner is covered. There's an entertaining glance at feminism in mountaineering, with the male huffing that followed the 1978 Annapurna women's expedition.

But it's all a little simplistic. The last four decades are skipped over in just 50 pages and quite a lot of that is spent on disasters afflicting commercial expeditions. Guys, trust me, a lot more went on. True, after first national ascents, most countries lost interest in mountaineering as national aggrandisement, to be replaced on Everest by self-interested consumerism. That's an important trope. But there are other strands to examine. Eastern European mountaineering, particularly by the Poles and Slovenians, offers rich material, both in pure mountaineering terms and in the social context the authors enjoy.

They mention Jerzy Kukuczka, but fail to record his incredible achievement of climbing all the 8000m peaks bar one either by a new route or a first winter ascent. Ascents that more or less define modern mountaineering, like the west face of Gasherbrum IV, Great Trango or the Golden Pillar of Spantik simply don't appear. The names Voytek Kurtyka, Mick Fowler, and Jenez Jeglic aren't there. There's a lot more about Bill House than Steve House. They could have had a field day with the impact Reagan and Thatcher had on climbing, but the project seems to have run out of steam.

I think that for all their materialist historical credentials, there's a dreamy streak in both the authors. The history of Himalayan climbing no longer holds much appeal for Isserman and Weaver after the golden age. The romance has gone out of it for them. Their expedition ideal is very much the American ventures led by Charles Houston before and after the war, a man with direct links to the Kennedy administration, whose world-view perhaps matches their own. For a couple hell-bent on exposing historical materialism and the imperial narrative in mountaineering, that's rather touching. But it does leave them more in the camp of James Ramsay Ullman than Eric Hobsbawm.

An example. The book finishes with a reflection from Houston after he returned with Bill Tilman from the first Western exploration of Khumbu, a world he regarded as 'a beautiful oasis in a troubled world'. It was hard, Houston says, to leave 'this happy primitive land'. That's a sentiment straight out of Rousseau. But Khumbu was no oasis. It had its own history, one that included suffering, hardship, and exile as well as beauty, a world capable of all the prejudice and intolerance of our own, masked by those friendly faces.

Ed Douglas

Cham

Jonathan Trigell

Serpent's Tail, 2007, paperback edition 2008, pp224, £7.99

I read this book from two points of view, the objective and the subjective. If literature has rights, the most basic arise from the words that appear over the doors of the Victoria and Albert Museum, 'The excellence of every art must consist in the complete accomplishment of its purpose'[1]. Determine the purpose, and read accordingly. This is the objective view.

This little book is intended to be a light read, the sort you pick up on the way to Chamonix if your flight is delayed. It is an amusement, a diversion. And if it irritates you it is to be tossed aside lightly, not thrown with great force[2].

The dust jacket tells us, 'the writing soars when describing the sublime mountain scenery...' Well, maybe, but given the purpose of this book it would be unfair to search for and fail to find those passages of soaring literature here. Yes, there are descriptions, one or two, which trigger the imagination, the magic road to Chamonix 'raised on great soaring stone pillars...looted from the temple of the Titans', and a clever reference to the dog shit that emerges in spring from the winter ice. But these are few and far between.

More often the descriptions are slightly inaccurate; he refers to the 'Glacier de Pendant' when descending what, to all English speakers (his main readers), is the 'Front Face' and if he is going to be French about it, he might as well get it right; Glacier de la Pendant. In English we say Mountain Guides, not High Mountain Guides. Sometimes he is just plain wrong; pisteurs do not help out on rescues in Col du Plan. There are several other examples in this vein which all have the effect of halting the storytell-

1 Joshua Reynolds, 1870
2 With apologies to Dorothy Parker, 1957.

ing while the book is (unfairly I admit) hurled across the room.

If airport reading is meant to be plot driven, and I think it is, this book is weak in that area too. There are two plots here; the main plot, a psychological one, centres on Itchy's deplorable sex life and is described with near-pornographic repetition. (pages 9, 24, 27, 33, 60, 82, 70, 76, 81, 87, 133, 149, 178, 243, and 251). All this stuff is apparently driven by low self-esteem and even lower esteem for the women he uses, until he is rescued from himself by 'The Nightingale', a pretty young French women, with almost no character description to call her own. A psychological novel needs strong character descriptions to drive it, and so does this book.

The subplot, promising at first to be a thriller, appears to be based on the true story of the rapist caught in Chamonix in 2001. The book opens with the rape scene, informing the reader that the rapist and his detection will be the main plot line. But that information is wrong. Other than providing prurient word sketches of the rapes there is no point to this sub plot which terminates with the culprit being accidentally caught by Wendy (a transvestite who clearly owes her literary existence to Roberta, John Irving's magnificent creation in *World According to Garp*.)

In summary, does Cham work as a light read? Is it a page-turner? Yes, but only just. I freely admit, it is a better novel than I could produce, but even so, the scenery is scarce, the characters are thin and the plot weak. This is my objective assessment of the work. Now for the subjective: Do I like it? No, not really.

Victor Saunders

First Ascent

Stephen Venables

Cassell Illustrated, 2008, pp192, £25

In *First Ascent*, Stephen Venables has produced a grand chronology of the most famous moments in mountaineering history and the climbers who created them. It is a broad canvas which he describes as 'the whole game of mountaineering from the smallest boulder to the summit of Everest', introducing those iconic climbers who opened the door for others to follow. Not always immediately. The first recorded alpine ascent in 1492, when a French army captain attacked Mont Aiguille in the Vercors on the orders of the King, using ladders and prototype pitons, was not repeated for 342 years.

The 150-year-old story of popular mountaineering that unfolded via the great Alpine summits and their dramatic history to the Himalaya and beyond, led to the renaissance created by a new school of climbers seeking the steeper, harder, faster challenges that set new physical, intellectual and emotional limits. Venables presents this history in crisp and engaging style paying homage to past generations of mountaineers and respect to a new generation achieving first ascents that are inevitably harder to find and more challenging to achieve.

The book is large format and is handsomely illustrated; some well-known historical images, portraits and engravings with some spectacular double-page colour spreads.

First Ascent is the story of men and mountains told by a mountaineer with a formidable personal record as the first Briton to climb Everest without oxygen, pioneering a new route on the Kangshung Face. This has modest mention but Venables' knowledge of the sport and understanding of his fellow mountaineers make his account a significant addition to the mountaineering record.

Ronald Faux

Paths of Glory
Jeffrey Archer
Macmillan, 2009, pp 404, £18.99

It is symptomatic that after all the years of research that Archer claims to have done, that he believes Everest to be a granite mountain, and that the Royal Geographical Society is the ultimate arbiter on the question of whether or not it is possible to climb a mountain. This is a singular achievement. But as Archer explained to me himself, he is a storyteller and does not feel himself bound or unduly hampered by the constraints of the facts – the detail of history. Archer is a believer in the old adage, 'don't let the facts spoil a good story'. As such he could have warded off serious criticism and censure, had he included an honest admission to that effect, informing the reader that he has freely rewritten history to suit his own ends. But Archer has chosen to present this 'historical novel', as being essentially 'true' if not correct. It is a fascinating and revealing distinction, true but not correct – i.e. not corresponding to the historical facts – that then begs the question, *true to what*? To the spirit of George Mallory as Archer subjectively divines it, irrespective of all those tiresome facts to the contrary? We are in an entirely subjective world here where Archer, ideally, would have no objective criteria to validate any truth claims or consequently, to enable us even to distinguish truth from falsehood, fact from fiction. But outside the pinchbeck fantasy world of Jeffrey Archer's make-believe, the historical facts, like the testimony of the rocks, remain.

Reading the novel it quickly becomes clear that Archer is a man who manifestly has no love of the hills and therefore, has no interest in or understanding of climbing. This inevitably disables and vitiates his book at the outset from being a credible account. But Archer is seemingly sublimely unaware that this might even be a problem. He has simply proceeded to superimpose a template that he can understand and relate to onto the subject, which is one of competition, keen rivalry, and the overwhelming (overweening?) desire and drive to be the first. It is a territory where he feels completely at home. And to be the first man on top of the highest mountain in the world, that really does capture Archer's imagination. Thus the *Archerized* version of events boils down to it being the story, or rather the melodrama, of Archer's fictional Mallory, 'who loved two women and one of them killed him'; the pair, of course, being Ruth Turner, his Guinevere, and Everest, his Jezebel. To this 'heady tug-of-love' Archer adds a sub-plot about the fierce rivalry between George Mallory and George Ingle Finch. Condemned as the two climbers are to having to provide some drama in the hope of sustaining the reader's interest, they must compete against each other to be the first to reach the ultimate summit and achieve undying fame.

Faced with a novel that is such a travesty of the historical facts and which presents such a 'collideoscape' of anachronisms, inconsistencies, absurdities and schoolboy howlers, it is hard to know where to begin. But it is singularly apparent that Archer has decided not to consult maps and even more bizarrely, not to work from photographs. Hence, when it comes to describing Everest and Archer's prose soars – as soar it must – to meet the challenge, he describes the summit as follows: 'Her noble head rested on a slim neck, nestling in shoulders of massive granite.' A few lines further on, he has Mallory doubt if he is, 'capable of climbing onto even the shoulders of this giant, let alone scaling her granite ice face'. Later we are assured that, 'Those members of the RGS who had predicted that Chomolungma would be like Mont Blanc, but a little higher, were already looking foolish.'

Curiously, Archer makes an incomprehensibly confused and confusing muddle of Mallory's politics. On first meeting Rupert Brooke at the Fabian stand, during Freshers Fair, Archer has Mallory say, 'I have long believed in the doctrines of Quintus Fabius Maximus.' Later on, when he is a teacher at Charterhouse, he will have Mallory complain of a friend and colleague that, 'he showed no interest in climbing, and even less in the beliefs of Quintus Fabius Maximus.' But Quintus Fabius Maximus Verrucosus (he had a wart on his lip) was an elected Roman dictator not an intellectual socialist with a passionate belief in social democracy. It was for his successful military tactics of attrition against a superior enemy, Hannibal, that the Fabian Society named themselves after him, not for his political beliefs.

In an unguarded and strikingly revealing moment, that discloses an extraordinary lack of self-awareness, Archer has Mallory, whilst still a history teacher, complain aloud to a colleague: 'Marking the lower fifth's essays on the Armada', said George, 'I do believe that lot find a sadistic pleasure in rewriting history.' Which inevitably leaves one wondering about the nature of the pleasure that Archer himself gets out of the rewriting of history. It is the question that hangs over almost every page of this novel.

Later on, in a letter home to Ruth from the Front, Archer has Mallory write, 'Do you remember Siegfried Herford? What a difficult decision he had to make, having a German father and an English mother.' But of course Herford's father, as anyone with an ear for that patronymic would know, was English; it was his mother who was German. And it was Siegfried's mother also, who made that difficult decision for him. As Herford's biographer Keith Treacher movingly relates: 'It is your country,' she told him laconically, 'and you must fight for it.' Archer's muddled version is typical of his general sloppy inattentiveness and his lack of historical knowledge. The result is always the thoughtless, clumsy mistake – Herford a German patronym – and the subsequent, inevitable trivialisation of the real, historical facts.

This is Archer's first attempt at an historical novel, so how does he fare in describing the historic, 1924 summit assault – one of mountaineering's most legendary and fiercely debated climbs?

After adjusting their mouthpieces (the oxygen supply Archer describes owes more to the 'Undersea World of Jacques Cousteau' than to the Irvine MK. V prototype) the ill-fated pair set out on the climb. Soon they face, 'a vertical rock, covered with ice that never melted from one year to the next'. They climb this we are told, for forty minutes. But, 'Once Irvine had climbed up to join him, George checked the altimeter: 112 ft left to climb.' The altimeter here is seemingly an oracular device, as the exact height of Everest was at that time unknown and also, Archer's Mallory does not seem to have done any mental arithmetic either to make even a remotely credible stab at such an observation. Archer subsequently goes on, 'He looked up, this time to be faced with a sheet of ice that had been built up over the years into a cornice overhanging the East face, which would have prevented a four-legged animal with spiked hooves from progressing any further.'

You would have thought that faced with this obstacle, the years of research that Archer claims to have done could have paid off handsomely. We surely should have had here a memorable description of Mallory's legendary, superb step cutting skills. Not a bit of it. Jeffrey doesn't really 'get ice-axes' – anyone for a spot of glacial moraine croquet? – so Mallory simply raises his boot to meet the challenge. But no sooner does he venture forth his intrepid boot than the mountain is struck by lightning down below. Cue the thunder. The thunder duly claps. This is the very stuff of high drama, and Archer relentlessly carries on the cliffhanger suspense in consummate, office memo prose. Mallory 'assumed he would be engulfed by a storm, but as he looked down, he realized that they were far above the tempest venting its fury on his colleagues some 2,000ft below.'

Throughout Archer's Mallory is almost invariably addressed, by other members of the expedition, deferentially as 'skipper'. So, rather like the quondam chairman of the Tory Party himself, he doesn't have companions, he has colleagues.

But what about the obstacle of that sheet of ice, the ice-axe surely might be useful but, 'Once again, George lifted his boot and tried to gain some purchase on the ice. The surface immediately cracked and his heel skidded back down the slope. He almost laughed. Could things get any worse?'

Sure enough they do. 'After a dozen such steps the narrow ridge became thinner until he had to fall on all fours and begin crawling. He didn't look to his left or right, because he knew that on both sides of him was a sheer drop of several hundred feet.' Several hundred feet! I hear you cry in disbelief. So you will understand why it is just as well that Archer's Mallory doesn't look down to his left or right, otherwise he too would be alarmed – aghast to discover that approximately 10,700 feet had somehow mysteriously disappeared from the Kangshung Face; a disquieting anomaly for even the most seasoned mountaineer. Those of you who have been high or higher, will no doubt be starting to recognize some of the hitherto completely baffling topographical features of the mountain that Archer's Mallory has been climbing, and will now have the sneaking suspicion that we are not in the Death Zone at all, but in a confused and confusing fantasy zone – the dreadful old tosh zone in fact – and that this can be none other than the treacherous, false summit of the legendary Rum Tarradiddle. That benighted peak in the heart of Rajwearistans Morcrassian Range, that lies forever in the mighty shadow of the sublime Rum Doodle.

But what of Archer's Mallory, the 'skipper' on his hands and knees in that terrifying situation still, with those frightful, vertiginous drops of 'several hundred feet' on either side. Have no fear! The 'skipper' has to boost his flagging morale in this desperate situation, the most wise and heartening counsel. It is a maxim no climber would wish to be without, 'Look up, ignore everything around you and battle on.'

Archer's Mallory usually thinks in these painfully risible, jolly hockey sticks clichés. For a man whom Archer has translating Homer's Illiad and reading Joyce's Ulysses, Archer's 'skipper' sadly, seems to owe his all to Angela Brazil with just a pinch of Bulldog Drummond.

But I like to think that, in the terrible bathos of this situation, Mallory, so ignominiously reduced to shuffling along on all fours, and in such 'extreme peril', would have thought of happier days, and recalled to mind a snatch of that droll verse, written in a 'shanty' bath at Pen y Pass, after a memorable day on Lliwedd, by his friend and climbing mentor Geoffrey Winthrop Young:

Ye Mallorys of England that still guard
our native screes! . . . My Kingdom for a horse
or, better still, a mule . . .

Sadly though, Archer's 'skipper' must 'battle on'; this is a serious business. 'Another yard forward, another half yard back.' No laughing matter. Somehow the 'skipper' seems to have puzzlingly slid back on to that 'sheet of ice', to be sliding back and forth so, but Archer does not trouble to make it clear as to why the 'skipper' should be sliding back down the ridge, even though he has taken to proceeding in this most resolute and determined manner, shuffling along 'on all fours'. But any thought of using his ice-axe here has deserted him. (You could be forgiven for thinking that this might be due to the debilitating effects of altitude, but as this is Rum Tarradiddle remember, any thought of the tiresome problems of altitude has been expediently forgotten). The 'skipper' resolutely sticks to his hands and knees throughout and progresses painfully slowly along the 'narrow ridge', 'a yard forward, another half yard back', doing what one can only suppose is the Chomolungma Shuffle. At the height of this torment Archer's 'skipper' not unreasonably asks, 'Just how much can the body endure?' One might also wonder just how much can the reader endure.

Mercifully though, this being Rum Tarradiddle, the 'skipper' does not encounter or have to contend with the high altitude wind – 'the biting wind' as Archer, always ready with the tired cliché calls it – until he has climbed up on to the summit itself – just a tantalizing sixty odd feet away. Down here, at a mere 28,970ft approximately, the wind, doubtless having a touchingly soft spot for the high endeavours of Oxbridge alumni, does not even make its inclement, never mind rude appearance. But such, of course, are the absurdly comic anomalies on Rum Tarradiddle. Likewise, the cold is seemingly not a serious problem on halcyon Rum Tarradiddle, hence the redundancy of gloves, irrespective of other features that might suggest the need – i.e. the presence of snow and ice. It perhaps says something that not even Archer can dispense with snow and ice. Old Jeffrey knows a thing or two about mountains.

It is another twenty minutes, we are told, before 'George Leigh Mallory' (a truly momentous occasion such as this requires all the gravitas that a full moniker can give a chap) 'puts his hand, his right hand, on the summit of Everest. He pulled himself slowly up on top and lay flat on his stomach. ' "Hardly a moment of triumph", was his first thought.'

'Hardly a moment of triumph' doesn't really begin to fathom the full bathos of this hilariously absurd account of the 'achievement' of the summit. But there can be no doubts left now about this being the first account of an ascent of Rum Tarradiddle.

Before starting the descent from the top of the highest mountain in the world, in a final bathetic travesty, Archer's 'skipper' – more yellow stockings and cross garters than Kashmir puttees – an Aldermanic or Rotarian Malvolio making his obsequious obeisance – pays this absurdly pompous, British Empire fustian salutation to the mountain: '"The King of England sends his compliments, ma'am," he said, giving a bow, "and hopes that you will grant his humble subjects safe passage back to their homeland."'

After that, I feel that the only adequate response to the above would be the blowing, by Chomolungma, of a seismically felt tectonic raspberry! Lawksamercy, ma'am: what a *true* load of old cobblers.

Charles Lind

Maurice Wilson: A Yorkshireman on Everest
Ruth Hanson (foreword by Doug Scott)
Hayloft, 2008, pp200, £12.50 (profits to Community Action Nepal)

It was not the mark on history Maurice Wilson had hoped to make. The war hero from Bradford set out in May 1933 determined to become the first man to climb Everest by landing a light aircraft on its lower slopes and striding to the summit powered by sheer physical toughness and a spiritual will to succeed. That he had never flown in an aircraft or had the least idea of how to climb serious mountains were secondary to an obsessional determination to succeed. The result was inevitable. He died and his bones occasionally reappear as the East Rongbuk glacier, in which he was buried, grinds its way down the flank of Everest.

The most extraordinary fact about Wilson's one-man expedition is that he managed, against what should have been insuperable odds, to get within striking distance of the North Col, which allows Ruth Hanson an admiring view of what he achieved. Her biography of Wilson, who was dubbed 'the mad Yorkshireman', is a thorough sifting of the evidence from the diaries he left and from the man's difficult history.

It was the disappearance of Mallory and Irvine on Everest in 1924 that first fired Wilson's imagination but other powerful influences helped shape his stubborn, bull-headed nature. He fought in the trenches during the First World War and was awarded the Military Cross for conspicuous gallantry under heavy shell and machinegun fire. He was wounded and never fully recovered from his injuries or his experience of the carnage of the Great War. After two failed marriages he devoted himself to a regime of fasting, faith in God and a determination to demonstrate to the world the power of his belief by conquering Everest, a quixotic tilt at the world's most formidable windmill.

The story has been well recorded. Wilson bought a Gypsy Moth biplane, which he named Ever Wrest, and then learned how to fly it. He was not a naturally gifted pilot but against the best efforts of the government to stop him, less than a month and 5,000 miles later his aircraft spluttered on the last of its fuel into India. Hanson recounts the frustrations and refusals placed in Wilson's way by the authorities that drove him to subterfuge. Wilson described in his diary how disguised as a Tibetan Buddhist monk he 'crept out of Darjeeling on bended knees to camouflage height'. With him were three Sherpas who had worked for the Ruttledge expedition the previous year. Although Wilson's training for Everest had been to walk from Bradford to London they covered the 300 undulating miles through Sikkim and Tibet to the Rongbuk monastery in 25 days. He then confronted the thin air and technical challenge of the climb to the North Col, fully expecting that the steps and fixed ropes of the previous year's expedition would be there for him to use. They were not. Wilson had no crampons and was taught by a Sherpa how to use an ice-axe as he twice attempted to reach the North Col.

Hanson rejects the idea that this was an elaborate suicide. She puts Wilson's lack of preparation down to naïve optimism rather than reckless stupidity or a wish to die making a name for himself. His story became almost stranger than fiction, reappearing as Wilson the Wonder Athlete in the *Wizard* comic, as the tormented character in Barry Collins' one-man play *The Ice Chimney* and as the central figure in Mike Harding's book *Yorkshire Transvestite Found Dead on Everest*. This followed rumours of a high-heeled shoe and items of women's underwear found at one of the old English camps but there was no positive evidence to suggest they belonged to

Maurice Wilson or that he was a cross-dresser. He even made 'guest appearances' in Salman Rushdie's *The Satanic Verses* when Rushdie's character Alleluia Cone comes across Wilson during her own Everest bid. From the non-fictional world came the unlikely suggestion that Wilson may have climbed considerably higher than the North Col, based on evidence of a pre-second world war tent found high on the mountain. This has been rejected as improbable. A Union Jack Wilson intended for the summit was still in his rucksack where his body was found.

Hanson acknowledges it will never be known exactly how far up Everest Maurice Wilson reached before exhaustion, cold and exposure finally took their toll. That is not the key part of the story. He was naïve, inadequately prepared and did not sensibly retreat when he could have done but he deserves respect for his conviction in what he was doing, admiration for his strength and commitment and applause for getting as far as he did. Hanson concludes: 'The sensible way is not always, for everyone, the true way. Having given all he could to make his crazy dream reality; to me at least he becomes a hero.' It would be another 19 years before Everest was climbed and a further 46 years before Reinhold Messner reached the summit alone in the style of Maurice Wilson.

Ronald Faux

The Struggle for Everest

George Ingle Finch, edited by George W Rodway

Carreg, 2008, pp 232, £20

How odd that this significant record of early British attempts to scale Everest should be first published in Germany as *Der Kampf um den Everest*, and that it has taken 84 years for a full translation into English. *The Struggle for Everest* by George Ingle Finch gives a fascinating view of the problems and politics of those early expeditions and the important role Finch played both in developing ways to deliver supplementary oxygen to climbers at high altitudes and persuading the establishment of the benefits. Politics, prejudice and personal dislikes seem largely to blame for the delay.

Finch's original text has been edited by George W Rodway, an assistant professor at the University of Utah and an honorary research fellow in the Centre for Altitude, Space and Extreme Environment at University College, London; a specialist who clearly recognises Finch's contribution to these first attempts on Everest, despite persistent rejection by the Everest Committee.

Finch was born in New South Wales, Australia, and aged 14 moved with his family to Europe. Educated in Switzerland, his interest in mountaineering began almost immediately. He studied chemistry at the *Eidgenossische Technische Hochschule* in Zurich before a distinguished professional scientific career that led to a long association with Imperial College of Science and Technology in London. By 1921 when the reconnaissance expedition was chosen, Finch was already established as a highly able mountaineer and an ideal candidate for the team. His record of alpine routes climbed without a guide was impressive and his performance in the pressure chamber, where high altitude could be simulated, demonstrated extraordinary fitness. Even so, Finch was rejected as physically unfit.

Despite his climbing record, Finch found himself at odds with some members of the selection committee on a number of counts. He was not of the Oxbridge elite who commanded the sport at the time; his enthusiasm for combating altitude with supplementary oxygen was regarded by some as unsportsmanlike and thoroughly un-British. A similar rationale denied parachutes to pilots in the Royal Flying Corps.

Even so Finch was selected for the 1922 expedition when a late order of 10 oxygen sets was obtained from the Ministry of Aviation, the type being used by pilots in the final stages of the Great War. Finch reflected that science had handed mountaineers a weapon for combating high altitude, one that became known among the porters as English air. The doubters still persisted, one 'expert' insisting it was equally important to determine just how high a human could climb without oxygen as to create artificial conditions 'which have nothing whatsoever to do with honest mountain climbing'.

The men actually on the mountain were more impressed by Finch's experiments comparing the performance of climbers with and without an oxygen supplement. He also demonstrated the benefits of breathing oxygen during rest periods, which he found sharpened the appetite, and of using down as protection in jackets as well as sleeping bags. Some of his other views however do not survive modern scrutiny. He advocated the invigorating and well-known stimulating effects of nicotine as it affected the respiratory process in a pleasant way. There was an exhausting need to concentrate on breathing at all times, but after the first few inhalations of cigarette smoke, mountaineers discovered that their breathing changed to the involuntary, automatic kind, the effect of a single cigarette lasting for up to three hours.

Finch also held some curious ideas about how human skin might be hosed with oxygen to encourage absorption, and his view that climbers with long legs and short trunks had an advantage over climbers with short legs and long trunks would surely be disputed by men in the Whillans mould.

When Finch made his assault on Everest with Captain Geoffrey Bruce, a cousin of the expedition leader General C G Bruce, and Corporal Tejbir of the Gurkhas, he expressed absolute determination to make it to the top. 'Nothing, absolutely nothing could cast a doubt upon this conviction. It could even mean defeat if a single man were to be doubtful, experience internal surrender, or falter in any way.' he writes. In the event, Finch and Bruce reached 8326m on the final ridge, a record at the time and only 208m short of the point reached the following year by Norton and Somervell. Bruce, a far less experienced mountaineer, was close to collapse when the pair turned back.

It was never clear as to why Finch chose to have *The Struggle for Everest* published in German but his book *The Making of a Mountaineer*, published in 1924, proved an inspiration to a generation of climbers. His writing style is frank and unadorned and this edition has many diary extracts and photographs of the pioneers with their baggy tweeds, clinkered boots and stoic ambition.

Finch was not invited on the 1924 expedition. Perhaps old reservations surfaced, and there was a spat with the Everest Committee over earnings from lectures following the 1922 attempt. Reflecting on the failure in 1924 and the loss of Mallory and Irvine, Finch points out that the climbers were two to three hours late in reaching the spot where they were last seen, which could only mean an earlier failure in the oxygen equipment. Irvine was known to be carrying a flag that would have been easily visible flying from the summit.

In a postscript to the book, Stephen Venables raises an intriguing question. How might history have been re-written if on that final attempt Mallory, the impractical romantic but determined mountaineer, had been partnered on that final summit attempt by Finch, one of the best mountaineers of his day and able to contribute his methodical, scientific professionalism to the Everest problem?

Ronald Faux

Dark Summit

Nick Heil

Virgin Books, 2008, pp 271, £18.99

Everest, another catastrophe, another book. Nick Heil, an American journalist and specialist in climbing at dangerous heights, describes the extraordinary coincidence of events on the north side of the mountain in 2006 when 40 mountaineers, on their way to the summit, climbed past one man who lay dying, when another left for dead revived and managed to clamber back to safety as 10 others perished in relatively fair weather in the so-called death zone.

The incidents caused an international sensation and presented the mountaineering community with some solemn questions. Sir Edmund Hillary issued his own scathing indictment that a man was left by fellow mountaineers to die. Though *Dark Summit* opens with the parable of the Good Samaritan, Heil remains non-judgmental, leaving readers to form their own opinion on the wealth of evidence he has gathered.

There is much in mitigation for the mountaineers. The world below Everest is radically changed from the time Hillary and Tensing strode its summit. The highest point on earth, poking its beckoning finger into the fringes of outer space, has become an iconic goal for increasing hundreds of individuals prepared to pay US$20,000 for a place on a guided expedition to the summit. As Heil points out, Everest is now big business, its base camp a crowded multilingual community firmly connected to the outside world by satellite phone, laptop, i-pod, dvd, meteo and medical service with constant scrutiny by internet channels ready with instant analysis of every action and decision made on the mountain. It is an age apart from time of the pioneers.

Hillary had proved Everest was possible, Messner and Habler demonstrated it could be climbed without supplementary oxygen, the north side was reopened and the highest point on earth came within ordinary ambitious reach. Heil reflects that, far from reducing numbers, the 1996 Everest disaster, in which nine climbers perished, inspired even greater demand after it was described in Jon Krakauer's book *Into Thin Air*.

More commercial outfits offered to guide climbers to the summit and the numbers mushroomed. Among those inspired was David Sharp, a 34-year-old engineer from Guisborough, who had already twice attempted Everest. Climbing independently with no Sherpas, guide or radio, carrying minimal oxygen equipment and unsupported by any of the commercial outfits, Sharp was a loner who 'wanted to get Everest out of his system'. On his third attempt he was last seen climbing slowly, alone and late in the day towards the summit. Whether he succeeded will never be known. The next day he was found below the first step on the summit ridge in a cave that already held the corpse of an Indian climber, known as Green Boots, who had perished some 10 years earlier.

Heil describes how the first climbers to reach the cave as they headed up the mountain were dumbfounded to discover a second, unknown, figure inside. They yelled at him 'Hey! Let's go! Get moving!' – but without response. He lay, eyes closed, hugging his knees to his chest. He wore no oxygen mask but tufts of breath escaped from blue lips. He was comatose, unable to move. Other climbers passed the cave without realising there were two bodies in there and it was later in the morning that two more Sherpas found Sharp, pulled him from the cave and gave him oxygen to no effect.

They could do no more. A later attempt to revive Sharp by another Sherpa who fed him oxygen succeeded with the climber mumbling a few barely audible words. 'Just want to sleep,' he said. Three other climbers, one an amputee whose stump sockets were blistered and bleeding from the friction of his prosthetic limbs, could do nothing to help, faced with the impossibility of evacuating an unconscious, immobile body from a point so high on the mountain. As one climber recalled: 'It is one thing to pass by someone long dead, the corpse welded to the landscape; it is a different experience to pass by a man still dying.'

Heil vividly describes the chaotic scramble of exhausted climbers along the summit ridge blundering their way through the narrow weather window that allowed access to the summit. Lincoln Hall, a seasoned Australian climber and client with one of the five commercial operations, set out on the final ridge with determined focus accompanied by three Sherpas. In darkness they climbed strongly, passing the cave oblivious to the bodies inside and reaching the top at 7am, that day's first arrivals. But the descent became a debacle, one climber collapsing and dying and Hall becoming delirious and eventually collapsing 28,200ft high on the mountain with darkness approaching. The Sherpas fought for nine hours lowering him down the ridge. They shouted at him, shook him, fed him oxygen, prised open his eyelids and poked his eyeballs with their fingers but Hall remained completely unresponsive. They believed him dead.

How he was found at daybreak, by four climbers bound for the summit, is brilliantly described. They discovered him sitting cross-legged about two feet from the 10,000ft drop of the Kangshung Face apparently changing his shirt. Hall wore no hat, gloves or sunglasses and had no oxygen mask, sleeping bag, mattress or food. 'I imagine you're surprised to see me here,' he said. Incredibly, he had survived to be led safely down the mountain. One dead man had lived as one live man had been left to die, opening a wider moral debate.

Dark Summit is an excellent analysis of the present state of Everest as an industry, as a right of passage challenge where Russell Brice, dynamic head of Himex, the major commercial outfit, uses his telescope, radio and detailed knowledge of the mountain to operate traffic control on the summit ridge, monitoring his clients and organising his Sherpas as they struggle at an altitude where the human body begins to self-destruct.

After a year spent talking to those who had climbed or tried to climb Everest, Heil felt no closer to understanding why people were so willing to risk their lives doing it. He concluded that rather than being a transformational power, the summit of Everest appeared to give only a weathered fatigue, a yearning to return to families, a warm bath and a soft bed. Maybe that was it, he reflects, reaching a point so close to our own extinction that made every mundane detail of our lives numinous again.

Ronald Faux

Forget Me Not: a Memoir

Jennifer Lowe-Anker

The Mountaineers Books, 2008, pp256, US$24.95

It is impossible to avoid being drawn in by the mesmerizing jacket cover of *Forget Me Not*, Jennifer Lowe-Anker's biography of her late husband, Alex Lowe. An almost mystical panorama of the Tetons is silhouetted against a stormy Wyoming sky, with forget-me-not flowers superimposed on the deepening shades of blue. Jennifer's own painting, it was her response to Alex's written request from Trango Tower in 1999: 'Everywhere I look, the little Alpine forget-me-nots are blooming... I know how much you love those delicate little flowers and I have pressed some and keep them with me... Do you think you could come up with an idea for a painting that ties together these flowers and our love for each other?'

His request – and her painting – set the tone for this long-awaited story of one of the most talented and respected American alpinists, Alex Lowe.

While still in the prime of his life, Alex was killed in an avalanche on Shishapangma in 1999. Jennifer was determined that she should be the one to tell Alex's life story and for years the climbing community waited patiently. While talking with Jennifer about her efforts to write this book, she confided that she just couldn't seem to get at it. Not too surprising, considering the emotional upheaval she had endured, as well as the increased responsibility of raising three active sons whilst continuing her painting career and starting a charitable foundation in Alex's name. She expressed the need to escape her daily responsibilities, if only for a few weeks, to concentrate on the book. She finally did, enrolling in the Banff Mountain Writing Program in 2006 for a month of uninterrupted focus.

She later described the feeling of arriving – alone – with her computer, her letters from Alex, her notes and a few personal things. She moved in to her simple apartment/writing studio, spread everything out to her liking, and prepared herself for that most difficult task: facing her memories of a life with Alex.

The result, published 10 years after his death, is not a traditional biography of an exceptional climber. It is rather a love story that encompasses two extended families, a man and a woman, deep friendships and even deeper loss. Rather than one main character there are two: Alex and Jennifer. The story begins, not with their meeting but much earlier, with their respective childhoods, growing up in the state that they both loved so much, Montana. The core values instilled in them by each set of parents defined them as adults and permeate the entire book: fierce independence, loyalty, responsibility and a sense of adventure.

As a young couple, Alex and Jennifer shared many adventures together: climbing, travelling, paddling and just trying to earn a living. They appeared a perfect match, and Jennifer's rendition of their experiences suggests a charmed existence. It wasn't until child-rearing responsibilities emerged that their life of adventure shifted, with Alex heading off alone more and more frequently. By this time, Alex had assumed an almost legendary reputation as an athlete. His appetite for training, his enviable climbing skills and his caffeine-enhanced energy levels were intimidating to most. As his reputation grew, so did the opportunities, including one that shaped the latter part of his climbing career. Invited to become a member of the elite North Face climbing team, Alex soon found himself on a never-ending series of expeditions to exotic locales, inevitably followed by an equally prolonged series of lectures and sales meetings arranged by his generous sponsor.

But from every precipitous portaledge perch, claustrophobic ice cave excavation, or frenetic outdoor equipment convention, Alex stayed in touch with Jennifer, and it is his letters that provide this book with a very personal, intimate glimpse into an unusual family. The letters, together with his journal entries, help to illuminate the struggles and compromises that were a necessary part of a relationship where one partner attempts to understand, and accommodate, the other's need for adrenalin, adventure and

– ultimately – risk.

Still, throughout all of his climbing expeditions, Alex had an unwavering confidence in his ability to survive, as well as his steadfast commitment to family. In a letter to Jennifer written just prior to a three-month guiding job on Everest, he said; 'Although I will always want to climb, I will continue to weigh my decisions according to the desire to grow old with you... I will base my mountaineering judgment upon the promise and commitment to return to you.'

The supporting cast in this warm and touching memoir includes their three sons, Sam, Max and Isaac, a number of close climbing friends, a few family members and, most importantly, Alex's good friend and most frequent climbing companion, Conrad Anker. The shared joy in their friendship fairly jumps off the page of the jacket back cover photograph of Alex and Conrad, taken by photographer Chris Noble while they were together on a climbing expedition in Kyrgyzstan. Conrad was also Alex's partner on the tragic Shishapangma expedition, and it was an instantaneous instinctive reaction to run one way rather than the other that saved Conrad's life and snuffed out Alex's. The depth of Conrad's despair at Alex's death was considerable. In a letter to Jennifer he admitted, 'A terrific guilt is upon my soul...' But along with that guilt, emerged another feeling – one of enormous responsibility and, finally, love. He grew increasingly close to Jennifer and the three boys and eventually, they became a family. Ironically, it was Conrad who was eventually able to realize Alex's dream, which Alex articulated in a letter years earlier: 'Makes me realize that what I really want to do is climb more with my sons and show them what I love in mountaineering.'

This volume explores many important themes of Alex's life, particularly his deep feelings for his family and his love of wild landscapes and mountaineering. But although we learn of Alex's expeditions to the most remote corners of the globe, including one of his favourites, to Queen Maud Land in Antarctica, we see them primarily from Jennifer's perspective. Other than his letters, which are mainly of a personal nature, there is insignificant input about these important, difficult, sometimes groundbreaking ascents from his climbing partners. We glean little information about the historical context of his climbs and have a limited grasp of their difficulty or technical details based on his reports. That history of Alex Lowe, alpinist, remains to be written and, based on the significance of his climbing career, it deserves to be documented.

Candid and remarkably well told, *Forget Me Not* is a story of adventure, passion, struggle, and hope. Most importantly, it is a story of love. It was the winner of the American National Outdoor Book Award for mountain literature in 2008 and was a finalist at the Banff Mountain Book Festival.

Bernadette McDonald

Himalayan Tribal Tales
Oral Tradition and Culture in the Apatani Valley
Stuart Blackburn
Brill, 2008, pp300, €69

Stuart Blackburn's first task in setting about the study of the oral tradition of the Apatanis in Arunachal Pradesh was to learn the language, not easy when there is no written text and the Apatani villagers are not particularly interested in talking to you. He solved it by loitering at a roadside shop that sold soap, candles and other dry goods, and by riding the local bus, trying out phrases on people going to market, getting his language lessons 'on the sly'.

It was four frustrating weeks before Blackburn was able to record his first tale – of two sisters (one good, one stupid) and a snake-husband – and this followed his attendance at a ritual in which a priest had slit open the belly of a small pig and examined the three sections of its liver for omens. Often the circumstances of Blackburn's research are as engaging as the stories themselves. The result is both a serious piece of academic work that adds to our understanding of oral traditions around the world and a highly readable account of the role of myths, legends, trickster tales and ritual chants in the life and identity of the Apatanis.

The Apatanis are a tribe of sedentary agriculturalists living in a narrow valley at 5,000ft in the eastern Himalaya. There are about 30,000 of them, speaking an unwritten Tibeto-Burman language and following a form of animism – though as Blackburn points out, contrary to the general idea of animism rendering spirits visible in some form, what distinguishes the 150 plus Apatani spirits from humans is their invisibility. Maintaining what sounds like an uneasy truce or alliance with this spirit world through the chanting of ritual texts and sacrifice requires constant observance.

The meat of book are the stories collected by Blackburn, a folklorist at the University of California, Berkeley, on extended visits between 2000 and 2006. He divides them into three categories: Tales, with man-eating monsters, magic trees and mistreated heroines in a Grimm-like panoply; Myths and Histories, dealing with the beginnings of the world and the Apatani ancestors, migration over the mountains from Tibet (an origin Blackburn regards as unlikely despite its hold in the tribal story); and the all-important Ritual Texts, delivered in a special speech, mostly by male priests, to communicate with the spirit world to, for example, ensure prosperity or protect someone from danger. Interestingly, for all the exotic cast of their stories, Apatanis do not make the usual distinction between myth and legend (as believed to have a kernel of truth) and 'once upon a time' folktales. All are believed to have happened.

Irrepressible throughout is the figure of Abo Tani, the first human and the father of all the Tani people of central Arunachal Pradesh. He is a variant of that international folk hero, the trickster – 'clever, amoral and sexually ambitious... a Rabelaisian character who mocks authority and stricture,' as Blackburn puts it. But Abo Tani is more than that; the son of a spirit, he is also the negotiator in that delicate alliance between spirits and humans and today, as 'ancestor', he has become an identity figure for the Apatanis in a changing world. Half a century ago, Abo Tani, like the spirits, was never seen; now his image is everywhere – 'hair wound into the distinctive knot and skewered with a brass pin, a large machete slung over his shoulder' – on posters, calendars and even the signs of the Abo Tani Wine Shop.

Himalayan Tribal Tales forms part of publisher Brill's Tibetan Studies Library. The reviewer came across the book by chance at the British Museum, on sale in conjunction with an exhibition 'Between Tibet and Assam – cultural diversity in the eastern Himalayas'. Blackburn acknowledges that not all of the Apatani's stories are 'a good read' – particularly the ritual texts, but that's not their purpose – however the challenge he set himself was to take readers at least some way inside a tribal and animistic culture. In that he has succeeded. Those for whom travel in the mountains has led to a keen interest in the myriad individuals tilling plots of buckwheat by the wayside, bearing burdens of firewood and fodder, or serving trays of *dal bhat*, will be enlightened by this book.

Stephen Goodwin

Explorers of the Infinite

Maria Coffey

Tarcher/Penguin, 2008, pp288, $26.95

This is a book that will either fascinate or frustrate, or possibly both. It won the American Alpine Club Literary Award in 2009 and carries an endorsement from the American Boardman-Tasker winning novelist Jeff Long for 'daring to tackle the taboos and sacred cows'. It is a follow-up to Coffey's series of interviews about grief reported in her book *Where the Mountain Casts Its Shadow* (2003) and its sub-title tells you how: *The secret spiritual lives of extreme athletes – and what they reveal about near-death experiences, psychic communication, and touching the beyond.*

Explorers of the Infinite begins with the issue of high altitude mountaineers seeing ghosts and goes, in its final chapter, 'Beyond Extremes' to the author's own return from death by drowning. Surfers, cyclists, kayakers, BASE jumpers, deep water freedivers, high-wire walkers, ultra-marathoners, polar explorers, skiers and skydivers join climbers and mountaineers in revealing some weird experiences that represent what Coffey calls their 'secret spiritual lives'. In the opening chapter addiction to the mental state achieved by climbers pushing themselves very hard becomes, in the words of the Mexican mountaineer Carlos Carsolio, 'spiritual addiction'. Chapters on 'Fear' and 'Suffering' lead to cases of intense connection with the environment, including interspecies communication. A chapter on anticipating death is titled 'Remembering the Future'. 'Spirit Friends' leads to

'Wandering Spirits' and then to 'Spiritual Tools'. The latter, it turns out, are closely related to forms of controlled breathing and link levitation, out-of-body experiences and apparent returns from death. These are, indeed, fascinating dimensions of human experience that few of us will not have either encountered ourselves, or read about more than once in mountaineering literature.

In my limited experience it is misleading, even sensationalising, to associate this realm of perception with the most extreme achievements of mountaineering. One person's easy route is another person's extreme experience. Soloing, for example, at any level, will sooner or later bring about an unexpectedly intense encounter with the materials in hand. I remember finding myself inexplicably in tears at the end of a long pitch of friction climbing in Tuolumne Meadows. It didn't feel like fear or relief from fear, but a kind of joy at oneness with the grains of that herringbone rock. I didn't need to call it a spiritual experience – more like an animal one – but some people do. On the other hand, it is surely useful to review the possibilities of one's death before an Alpine climb, hoping that such dreams do not provide Maria Coffey with another case of 'remembering the future'. Ultimately my frustration with this book is not concerned with the language given to these dimensions available to human life in risk-taking relationships with the elements. It is with the disconnection between different kinds of language, the anecdote and the scientific research.

This book is really a kind of anthology of stories and some possible explanations, except that the scientific material is not discussed and evaluated as an adequate or inadequate explanation, but rather dropped in between the anecdotes. In one page the text can jump from a lively spoken narrative to the specialised discourse of one researcher and back again. I'm all in favour of giving each mode of discourse equal status, of science speaking to experience, and of anecdote in dialogue with research findings. The problem is that the style of this book is simply to juxtapose these two voices without any linking evaluative discussion that might help readers begin to sift the blazing insights from the bullshit. All voices from all adventurers and all scientists are regarded as being equally true. In fact, we know that in this field of enquiry in particular, it is just possible to find a joker or a charlatan. The sense of a neutral anthology of material being offered to the reader is endorsed by the fact that the selected references for each chapter simply list books by adventurers and researchers.

But I've not given a sense of the insights such juxtapositions can sometimes produce. BASE jumpers have to process information fast in freefall. What the Swiss neuroscientist Peter Brugger calls a 'Type 1 error' is in perceiving a pattern where none exists. A 'Type 2 error' is failing to recognise a pattern when it does exist. From an evolutionary perspective, he points out, 'if you miss the tiger hiding in the grass, you're dead. If you're always seeing tigers, you're running away a lot, but you're not dead.' Coffey goes on to tell a story about the BASE jumper from New Zealand, Duane Thomas, who, with his friend Shaun Ellison, was assisting Leo

Holding and Tim Emmet in their first jumps from a cliff in the Lauterbrunnen valley. Then Thomas made his own jump. He was seen to reach back to deploy his parachute and, without apparent struggle, he simply left his hand there on the pilot chute and hit the ground. Shaun Ellison is convinced that when, unusually, he had shaken the hand of Thomas before his jump, Thomas had seen a premonition of his own death in Ellison's eyes. 'Don't ever look at me like that again', said Thomas, totally out of character. Ellison's conclusion is: 'I think we were both tapping into other levels of consciousness.' Coffey's conclusion is: 'An early warning. Ignored. A Type 2 error – fatal.'

In the same way that some mountaineers take Jim Curran's history of K2 to read at K2 base camp, this might be a book to take on a trip, not just to fuel hours of storm-bound discussion, but to learn to avoid 'remembering the future'.

Terry Gifford

A Man's Life: Dispatches from Dangerous Places
Mark Jenkins
Rodale Press USA, 2007, pp368, US$25.95

Mark Jenkins readily admits to what he describes as 'the incurable disease of mountain guides, foreign correspondents, and all kinds of adventurers: We yearn to go, but we don't want to leave.'

It wasn't always that way for Jenkins. Travelling hard since the age of 16, he is a veteran of hard beds, bad water and pain. Former monthly adventure columnist for *Outside* magazine, Jenkins wandered the globe, from the mountains of Afghanistan to the Turkish coast of Gallipoli. His partners were often legends in their own right: Greg Mortenson, Yvon Chouinard, Aron Ralston. His destinations were such that arrival was often uncertain and intact return, even more so. His passion for travel was intense: 'I cannot get enough of the world. To smell it, walk through it, sink the teeth of my mind into it.' Fortunately for his readers, his insights and literary talents produced equally passionate tales of his physical, intellectual and spiritual journeys. *A Man's Life* is the second volume of his almost 10 years of work at *Outside* magazine, following *The Hard Way,* published in 2002.

But *A Man's Life* is not simply a chronological sequel. Jenkins' approach to travel and adventure, to danger and risk, has shifted in this volume, and its title belies what is really going on. Of course he is older and presumably more mature, but the fundamental difference is that his personal life has changed. Now a family man with a wife and two daughters, Jenkins' departures become increasingly painful and his own spectacular experiences on the road are constantly weighed against the more poignant home life he is inevitably missing: birthdays, first steps, dinner parties and childhood bruises. He describes his departure for an unclimbed peak in Burma when his daughter Addi was 20 months old. She happily helps him pack, playing with his climbing equipment and climbing into his cozy, alpine sleeping bag clad only in her diaper. Everything is going along swimmingly until the airport, when Addi finally figures it out. 'Daddy…' she says, lip quivering. As Jenkins recalled, 'The look of shock and hurt and betrayal in her huge brown eyes crushed me more than any avalanche ever could.'

Yet he manages the knife-edged balancing act and gets out there, month after month. Long days, rock-fall, unconsolidated snow slopes, punishing temperatures, surly armed customs officers and campfires are his companions. Many of his stories are about climbing. He is an accomplished climber, yet writes deprecatingly and with humour about his exploits. Despite his refreshingly light approach, his position on climbing ethics is firm. 'Why we climb is personal, but *how* we climb… is communal. How we climb defines the spirit of our sport… directly impacts not just the practice and future of mountaineering, but the health of the mountain environment.' Although a strong supporter of the Tyrol Declaration, Jenkins ultimately throws the decision on style back to the individual. 'We are what we do. And style *is* substance.'

The 37 stories in *A Man's Life* are vivid, amusing, gritty and infused with raw emotion. Winner of the 2008 Banff Mountain Book Award for adventure travel, it was described by jury member John Harlin as 'the definition of excellence in serious writing about serious adventure'. Harlin concludes, 'The only thing that rivals Jenkins's enthusiasm for putting himself into harm's way in exotic places is his love for crafting stories after coming home to his family in Laramie, Wyoming.'

A Man's Life is the result of that love and talent for crafting stories and I would highly recommend it.

Bernadette McDonald

Revelations

Jerry Moffatt (with Niall Grimes)

Vertebrate Publishing, 2009, pp 256, £20

I'm pretty well convinced that the high point of technical 'trad' climbing, and sport climbing for that matter, was the 1980s. It was the decade when training techniques approaching athletic rigour were applied to the more open-ended mindset of the aid-eliminating pioneers of the Seventies, with spectacular results. The classic super-desperate and serious test pieces of today, *Parthian Shot*, *New Statesman*, *Master's Wall*, *Indian Face*, *The Quarryman*, *Mandela*, *Revelations*, *Gaia* and *Totally Free* were all products of the Eighties. Since then, progress has been one of degree, with the application of a bouldering mentality to sport routes (just how small can the holds be?), a highball bouldering mentality to the ever-dwindling supply of unclimbed lines on grit (just how injured are you prepared to be if you fall off?) and a near-soloing mentality to the super-bold routes from the likes of MacLeod and Birkett on mountain crags (just how dead are you prepared to be?).

Back in the Eighties, one of the leading lights of the climbing scene, and certainly one of its most colourful characters, was Jerry Moffatt. His autobiography, *Revelations*, co-written with Niall Grimes (and edited by Ed Douglas), is the story of a remarkable climbing career.

Moffatt started climbing whilst at school near Llandudno and the early part of the book chronicles the all too familiar pattern of death-defying early days on rock. It's said that God protects drunks and small children, and the latter is particularly relevant to Moffatt's early escapades.

As with most climbing autobiographies, it's the early, non-climbing detail that proves the most interesting. We discover, for example, that Jerry had learning difficulties (in the literal sense, not the PC euphemism) and dyslexia as a child – but excelled at sport, particularly rugby. Once Moffatt discovers climbing, his life changes and there are familiar tales of living rough and obsessive climbing behaviour, the latter resulting in prodigious bouldering skills and a long line of spectacular climbs, including an orgy of soloing on Dinas Cromlech, which culminates in a death-cheating first ascent of *Master's Wall* on Cloggy.

The book goes on to describe Moffatt's involvement with gear development, motorbikes, competition climbing, and a fight with career-threatening injury caused by over-training. *Revelations* provides insight into a crucial decade in world climbing by one of its most influential players.

Bernard Newman

A Passion for Nature: The Life of John Muir

Donald Worster

Oxford University Press, 2008, pp535, £18.99

To come straight to the point, this book lacks an essential reference to the *Alpine Journal* and as a consequence fails to fully engage with Muir as either a mountaineer or as a mountaineering writer. Sir Edward Peck, in *AJ* No 99, 1994 (reprinted in *John Muir: His Life and Letters and Other Writings*, Bâton Wicks, 1996), evaluates Muir as a mountaineer and suggests that Muir's account of his solo first ascent of Mount Ritter 'belongs to the finest tradition of mountaineering literature'. The American historian of mountaineering literature, David Mazel, says that 'Muir was the most skilled American climber of his day' (*Pioneeering Ascents: The Origins of Climbing in America, 1642-1873*, 1991, p. 233). Rather than using Mazel, in his new biography of Muir, the environmental historian Donald Worster uses James Ramsey Ullman's 1956 *The Age of Mountaineering* to contextualise Muir's attitude towards mountains as a mountaineer. This leads him to Ruskin and the old misunderstanding that Ruskin believed that 'mountain gloom' was a quality inherent in the mountains themselves. In fact, Ruskin was referring in *Modern Painters* to the crucifixes and the morbid gloom he found in the indigenous human culture in the Alps. So for Worster to say that 'Muir saw only glory, and never any gloom, in his mountains' (188) is to repeat Muir's own misreading of Ruskin to claim the 'glory' of mountains for himself in contrast with Ruskin. With these reservations out of the way, one can welcome this new biography of Scotland's major contribution to American environmental and mountaineering history.

This is only the second life of John Muir that has gone back to original sources and it is a great advance upon Frederick Turner's *Rediscovering America: John Muir in his Time and Ours* (1985). Here is a more complicated and a more contextualised Muir whose contradictions are not avoided: Scottish, educated in America, professional engineer and part-time botanist, a sustainer of friendships with women who could not broach marriage, a serious horticulturalist who could resist the pull of the wild for a decade, a wealth-accumulating businessman who valued simplicity, friend of those railroading America who nevertheless spoke for wilderness, and ultimately man of compromise whose writings demanded entrenched conservationist positions. Worster has produced a fresh and more nuanced version of Muir that is a riveting read.

Although Worster is shaky on general Scottish historical background (Surely even Americans should know that Mary Queen of Scots was beheaded, not 'hanged'?) his detailed research in the National Archives of Scotland reveals that Muir's father was a wealthy and powerful man in Dunbar, popular with voters and with a reputation for probity. But it was the rejection of every form of church available that took Daniel Muir to Edinburgh to hear Alexander Campbell speak of the clergy-free gatherings he had established in America. Within a few months Daniel Muir determined that the family would 'take the boat', along with Highland families at the height of the Clearances in 1849.

It is in the richness of its detail and its historical contexts that this biography makes its mark. Worster's knowledge of the environmental history of the West leads to some telling observations: 'Muir had arrived in the West at precisely the moment when new careers in scientific exploration were being made'. But actually government sponsored geologists and botanists were funded to promote industrial and agricultural exploitation of the landscapes they explored. Muir's devotion to both empiricism and spiritual renewal sometimes resulted in his missing the political motivations of others. This gives an interesting and topical twist to the old and continuing debate of the preservationists versus the conservationists which resolves itself into the issue of 'How much use?', or indeed, 'How much management?' – the very issue which provoked the foundation of The John Muir Trust here in the UK in the face of encroaching signage, trails, and visitors' centres, or military usage of wilderness.

Like the original motivation for the JMT, Muir wanted to provide and publicise a good example that others might be encouraged to follow. But the motivations of some of the others established a context in which to be a non-interventionist was to win the moral battle, but lose the landscape war. The later Muir's lobbying with a politically astute publicist – Robert Underwood Johnson – won many local and short-term battles, but actually probably lost the long-term war, we might observe as we review the

Bush legacy. Saving some forests and parks did not ultimately challenge the American dream's notion of growth, or its values grounded in wealth, which have regularly won the big political debates about landscape values. (Has saving some Scottish estates by the JMT offered strong enough alternative values to challenge the capitalist power driving the necessary alternative energy business in Scotland? Victory in the battle against bolts in the Alps [by no means assured] would be pyrrhic if in waging it we ignore the greater war against climate change, or even consort with the enemy by flying so much. I speak as one more sinning than sinned against.)

Worster does not duck such issues. Muir was prepared to sacrifice 'ordinary' landscapes (Lake Eleanor, within Yosemite National Park) to save 'extraordinary' ones (Hetch-Hetchy Valley, also within the park). 'Politically, the distinction would be difficult to make and susceptible to economic influence,' comments Worster. During the long years of San Francisco's campaign to turn the Hetch-Hetchy Valley into a reservoir for the city's water supply, Muir and the Sierra Club were 'not paying attention' when a bill was passed permitting water conduits through the National Park.

And ultimately Muir was not supported in this fight by his rich friends: 'The sad lesson staring Muir in the face was that those who already had plenty of wealth could be weak, undependable allies in the struggle.' Muir had dictated his memoirs of Scotland and Wisconsin, *My Boyhood and Youth*, at the Lake Klamath country retreat of the West's railway magnate, Edward Harriman. (Worster points to a current debate that Muir ignored about draining the Klamath Basin, a nationally important wildlife refuge, for agricultural land.) But Harriman failed to support Muir in the Hetch-Hetchy campaign. The openness to nature that Muir found in some of his rich friends did not ultimately moderate their belief in 'economic growth, national expansion, and material values above everything else'.

This is very far from being a biography that is sceptical about Muir's sustained influence. With the strong regional and national presence of the Sierra Club in America, a worldwide network of national parks, a thriving and increasingly urgent international conservation movement and the establishment of a John Muir Trust in the UK, how could it not be? But it is a biography that thoughtfully raises issues for readers in the present. Muir's dilemmas and compromises still face us in new forms, not least in the issues of wind farms, dams, and other environmental balancing acts being debated in the land of Muir's birth. This wonderfully readable book ends with the words: 'Muir was a man who tried to find the essential goodness in the world, an optimist about people and nature, an eloquent prophet of a new world that looked to nature for its standards and inspiration. Looking back at the trail he blazed, we must wonder how far we have yet to go.'

Terry Gifford

Meetings on The Edge
Mags MacKean
The In Pinn, 2008, pp198, £14.99

In 2005 Mags MacKean did what so many of us only dream of; she abandoned her 10-year career as a BBC journalist and took to the mountains. She wanted to 'originate her own stories' instead of interpreting those of others second-hand and to continue a love affair, begun during her ascent of Kilimanjaro, with 'the process of moving uphill'.

These restless urges took her around the globe on a series of extreme physical challenges. It was a long road of emotional and spiritual awareness, peopled by unusual and often influential characters whose random acts of kindness led her to question and redefine her understanding of security. Their outstretched hands marked the landscape she moved through in a way that maps never could: 'It is the human face of the environment that makes its geography so memorable.' A lady of remarkable independence of spirit led her to the mayor of Baillestavy in the eastern Pyrenees who provided her with food and shelter, saving her from an uncomfortable night in a primitive woodstore. Phillipe, a Belgian encountered in a mountain hut, taught her to find the way through unpredictable terrain and to adapt to its demands on her energies and resourcefulness.

MacKean's 70-day solo walk across the Pyrenees forms the backbone of the book whilst other journeys and expeditions weave in and out, illuminating a train of thought begun earlier or establishing a pattern in friendships made along the way. Climbing in the Cascades, ascending Denali, mountaineering in New Zealand, attempting Pisang Peak: all these natural classrooms afford her the opportunity to consolidate skills and bind herself to her companions with an understanding forged out of endurance and mutual support.

The writing is immensely readable, compact and cinematic in its descriptions and peppered with a lively sense of humour, largely generated by unlikely juxtapositions - the naked flasher she encounters on her first day in the remoteness of the Pyrenees, the exotically handsome Nepali film star on holiday with her in Mull, the giant spiders which cause her to scream repeatedly during a strictly silent retreat in the Garhwal.

MacKean evokes a strong sense of place, not merely as a backdrop but as a commentary on her emotional development. At first she finds the landscape hostile, the uncertainty of the way ahead disturbing, but as her journey continues she finds a harmony in her surroundings and an understanding of 'resourceful outdoor living' which shapes and strengthens her reactions to future events. Most telling of all, she begins to understand her focus should not be on continual activity – seeking a new goal as soon as she has realised the last – but on knowing herself well enough to understand what would be best to do next. As she states so succinctly: 'Life is never a destination to reach but a state of becoming.'

Val Randall

Himalayan Playground: Adventures on The Roof of the World, 1942-72
Trevor Braham (foreword by Doug Scott)
The In Pinn, 2008, pp120, £9.99

Trevor Braham's climbing career spanned the 'golden age' of Himalayan mountaineering, when the principal peaks were climbed one by one, and climbing parties penetrated into hitherto unmapped and unvisited areas. The first trip recorded in this book is a trek in 1942 along the well-known Singalila Ridge. Approached from Darjeeling (where he went to school), the Ridge goes due north towards Kangchenjunga, along the border between Nepal and Sikkim. Clearly it was for him a case of love at first sight.

Four further visits to Sikkim are recorded here, with increasingly ambitious objectives. The series was interrupted, if that is the right word, by an invitation to go as a 'guest member' (no doubt also a very useful, if unofficial, liaison officer) with a Swiss party in Garhwal in 1947. With them Trevor climbed Kedarnath Dome, finding himself surprisingly fit at 6830m. On return, he left the party, they going west to Gangotri while he struck east, then south and finally north-east, to the Bhyundar Pass, and so east and south-west over the Kuari Pass to 'civilisation'. Travel through the mountains, rather than peak bagging, was always his first love. But he thought he ought to learn to climb 'properly' and took himself off to the Valais, where he had three seasons with his friend Arthur Lochmatter, the last in 1956.

Apart from Sikkim and Garhwal, visits to other areas are recorded – Kulu and Spiti, visited with Peter Holmes at a time when the environment could be described as 'mediaeval' and streams had not been bridged, even by a log – Karakoram, Swat/Kohistan, Kaghan. Even this list is not exhaustive. Based initially in Calcutta, where he was apprenticed to his father's import/export business, Trevor was able to get away to the hills almost every year. He was also incidentally a very active member of the Himalayan Club, editing the *Himalayan Journal* and serving as Vice-President and a committee member for many years.

He just mentions a trip in 1968, when he joined Sally and me, and Hugh Thomlinson, in a visit to the Kotgaz glacier of the Hindu Kush, close to the border of Afghanistan. By this time he was living and working in Pakistan. We took advantage of his familiarity with the local political setup (rather feudal at that time) and ability to organise our journey into the mountains. Unfortunately he and Hugh had to leave us before they could repeat our ascent of a 5680m peak on the frontier, or try any others.

I confess that I approached the book with some misgivings, wondering if it would consist largely of reprints from his *HJ* articles. Some of those, probably written more or less directly from diaries, have paragraphs more than a page long, full of detail about the routes followed – useful for people following in his footsteps but somewhat tedious to read. I need not have worried. In just a few cases the book covers much the same ground, but more briefly and very readably. There is a lot about his travels through the mountains, often accompanied only by porters, which is new to me and very interesting. Good diagrammatic sketch maps, and very good photos, almost all Trevor's own, enable one to visualise his journeys. This is a most enjoyable book.

Mike Westmacott

Ararat: In Search of the Mythical Mountain
Frank Westerman (translated by Sam Garrett)
Harvill Secker, 2008, pp236, £16.99

While Mount Ararat is found in modern Turkey and is the nation's highest peak at over 4200m, it is nevertheless displayed at the centre of the Armenian coat of arms. The mountain is a national icon to the Armenians, who depict it topped by a massive boat to recall the statement in Genesis that Noah's Ark ran aground on Ararat as the waters receded from the great flood. AC members who have stood there will vouch that in reality no vessel sits stranded on the summit, yet the search for archaeological remains goes on. Frank Westerman is no 'Arkaeologist' himself (the pun is irresistible) but in a wider sense he too is searching.

Christians have scoured Ararat for fragments of wood as physical testimony to a faith they appear already to possess in abundance. Westerman's interest in the mountain is more nebulous. His book explores the relation between religious belief and modern scientific knowledge by charting the way in which education displaced Christianity from his life. The facts of evolution and the earth's great age could not be reconciled with his parents' Protestantism. Although *Ararat* made the shortlist of the Boardman Tasker Prize for mountain literature this is not a book about mountaineering or even about mountains. Instead it uses Ararat as a metaphor for human and personal struggles with religion, science and nature.

At the heart of the flood story is man's relationship with the unpredictable, dangerous natural world, evoked in some of the book's most vivid passages. Westerman describes trekking across Holland's treacherous tidal mudflats in training for his climb and also childhood memories of a drilling rig swallowed following a gas eruption and of nearly drowning in a river surging with water released from an upstream reservoir. These passages contribute to *Ararat*'s intimate and often tentative tone. Some of the book's ideas are presented repeatedly but others are only hinted at. For example, Westerman notes that the retreat of Ararat's ice may be attributable to climate change, but he evades the terrible connections between the story of carnage brought about by human civilisation told in Genesis and the future that glacier retreat shows drawing closer.

Towards the end of the book, describing the days before his attempt at climbing Ararat, Westerman narrates an encounter with a pair of 'real authentic Ark-seekers' from Russia. When a companion asks whether they have found the Ark, Westerman recoils from his sceptical friend's mockery of the inevitable response, that they have seen a boat-like object but could not quite reach it:

The fragile world of the Ark-seeker, I realised existed by virtue of not finding; his goal always had to remain beyond reach – this was what kept him going and lent purpose to his life. The Ark-seeker owed his singularity not to the Ark, but to the fact that he was seeking. And what I was doing, I reckoned, came down to exactly that.

It follows that the climb itself forms a coda to this thought, a journey made with the desire to have an experience, but not to be overcome.

Kathleen Palti

Contact
Mountain Climbing and Environmental Thinking
Edited by Jeffrey Mathes McCarthy
University of Nevada Press, 2008, pp242, £22.50

This collection of essays could stand alone as a worthwhile anthology of mainly American writers waxing about their engagement – sometimes intense – with nature through climbing. But Jeffrey McCarthy has a more ambitious purpose, namely to demonstrate his thesis that climbing matters. Really? While climbing matters to me personally, I rather thought Lionel Terray had caught its overall significance in that wonderful title *Conquistadors of the Useless*. But McCarthy begs to differ, seeing in climbing narratives, or at least in the best of them, the leading edge of society's attitude towards nature and the possibility of a cultural shift, reconnecting humans as part of nature and vice versa.

Perhaps the sharpest example of this connection comes in Yvon Chouinard's account, reproduced here, of his and T M Herbert's eight days on El Cap's Muir Wall in 1965. Physically exhausted yet so attuned to their vertical world, by day seven their senses are vivid. 'Each individual crystal in the granite stood out in bold relief,' Chouinard recalls. They're transfixed by cloud shapes and by tiny, brilliantly coloured bugs on the rock. 'This unity with our joyous surroundings, this ultra-penetrating perception gave us a feeling of contentment that we had not had for years.'

How could it be otherwise on the Muir Wall? The prophet of Yosemite permeates this book. Chouinard's heightened perception after a week on the wall sounds very similar to John Muir's own state on his ascent of Mount Ritter. Momentarily he becomes crag-fast, convinced he is going to fall while climbing a 50ft cliff, then 'life blazed forth again with preternatural clearness... muscles became firm again, every rift and flaw in the rock was seen as through a microscope'. And up he goes.

Muir, Chouinard, and probably some of you, it's a fairly simple sum: exhaustion + fasting (whether involuntary or Muir's dry crust frugality) + plus a nerve edge situation = intense perception and a powerful feeling of unity with surrounding nature. But where does it get us? McCarthy isn't claiming that climbers are about to save the Planet; rather that we might be an indicator species, and that our writings, in moving from narratives of conquest to those of connection, presage a shift in society's attitude to nature.

Contact is a book where the Introduction is essential first reading. In it McCarthy explains the three categories into which he divides the collection: conquest, which is flags on summits of course, but interestingly the opponent might also be internal, 'the hungry, quivering, unruly self'; caretaking, which is probably where most folk are at the moment, it's national parks and conservation, but that's still treating nature as a resource for human use; and finally connection, where the climber and physical world cease to be separate but attain a harmony.

Inevitably the categories overlap and not all the stories stay in their appointed boxes. Besides Muir and Chouinard, the 23 authors featured include Steve House, Arlene Blum, Gary Snyder, Doug Robinson, Cam Burns, Henry David Thoreau and Terry Gifford. It's quite a cast and McCarthy marshals their stories well. While philosophers and ecologists cast about for a changed consciousness to solve environmental problems, McCarthy contends that narratives such as these offer a lived expression of the very shift they seek.

Stephen Goodwin

Auldjo
A Life of John Auldjo
Peter Jamieson
Michael Russell (Publishing) Ltd 2009, pp253, £24

Students of Alpine history will be familiar with the fact that John Auldjo made the 19th ascent of Mont Blanc in 1827 and published his highly readable account the following year. Some may also know of his time in Naples and his important studies of Vesuvius, which led to his being admitted to Fellowship of the Royal Society. Few, however, will know much more of the intriguing life of this Victorian gentleman traveller and Peter Jamieson's book amply fills this void.

In painting out the vivid scenery of Auldjo's life, Mr Jamieson demonstrates that he is a master of digression. However, his digressions are invariably well informed, often fascinating in their own right and always relevant to his main theme. So, one is transported in turn to Montreal at the beginning of the 19th Century and the Scots run fur trade, Regency London, Naples and its vibrant social life in the 1830s, Constantinople, London again in the 1840s and 1850s and finally to Geneva in 1865 where Auldjo became Honorary British Consul in 1871. He finally died in Geneva in 1886. Along the way, Auldjo encounters many of the leading players of the era: Sir Walter Scott, Bulwer-Lytton, Dickens, Thackeray, Sir William

Gell, the Duke of Sussex, the Duke of Brunswick and even that other famous ascensionist of Mont Blanc, Albert Smith. The 'Index of Persons' runs to some 500 entries; indeed, there are so many characters in the book that it is sometimes a little difficult to keep track and at least an Auldjo family tree might have made life a little easier.

The latter part of Auldjo's life was marred by a major financial disaster, which caused him to sell up in London and flee to France and ultimately Geneva, effectively bankrupt. The causes of this have never been clear, but Mr Jamieson has appended an intriguing hypothesis to his book, which the reviewer will certainly not spoil for you.

This book certainly left one more than interested in pursuing further accounts of several of the events and many of the people described. The bibliography provided by Mr Jamieson not only facilitates this, but also demonstrates what a well-researched book this is.

Jerry Lovatt

The Apprenticeship of a Mountaineer:
Edward Whymper's London Diary 1855-1859
Edited by Ian Smith
London Record Society Volume XLIII, pp267, 2008, £25

This work comprises a transcription of all six notebooks, kept as daily diaries by Whymper in the five years leading up to the year of his first visit to the Alps, which was to determine the course of the rest of his life. However, it is not only that. In addition the editor has provided an extremely helpful introduction, which ably sets the context for Whymper's early life, covering his family background, the relevant social milieu of South London in the 1850s and an interesting section on wood engraving, the heart of the family business in which the young Edward was serving his apprenticeship. There is also a useful synopsis of his later life and several helpful appendices, in particular the Whymper family tree and key biographical details of more than 400 of the principal characters featuring in the Diary. Mr Smith's footnotes are also apposite and generally illuminating.

In the last major biography of Whymper, written by Frank Smythe and published as long ago as 1940, the author in transcribing a proportion of the Diary comes to the conclusion that it is a 'sad document' and that the young Whymper led a life of 'appalling monotony'. While there may be some truth in the latter, the former comment in no way does it justice. Smythe contended that its sadness lies in the fact that it shows how Whymper's spirit, intelligence and potential were somehow stultified by the monotony of his daily grind. Be that as it may, there is another side to the coin and that is that the effort to overcome these obstacles in his early life almost certainly made Whymper into the determined, strong, if difficult man he became in later years.

Whatever one's view on that, the Diary itself is far from sad for, whenever the monotony begins to take hold, some fascinating cameo appears, whether it be the saga of the launch of the Great Eastern, the first investitures of the Victoria Cross, an update on the latest from the Crimea or the Indian Mutiny. The young Whymper certainly lived in interesting times. Not only that, but he was also a strikingly mature and self-confident commentator on these events, for one who was a mere 14 years at the commencement of the Diary.

While there are virtually no hints of any interest in mountaineering, even as close as a year from his first Alpine tour, the Diary gives ample evidence of the strength of body and purpose that were to serve him so well in later years.

All in all, Mr Smith and the London Record Society have done us a considerable service in making more available this remarkable document and in presenting it in such a usable and interesting form.

Jerry Lovatt

Who's Who in British Climbing
Colin Wells
The Climbing Company, 2008, pp575, £20

The last book Colin Wells wrote was the splendid *A Brief History of British Mountaineering* which was completed in just six weeks to coincide with the opening of The National Mountaineering Exhibition at Rheged in July 2001. In contrast his most recent epic, *Who's Who in British Climbing* is a Very Big Book and has taken over six years to come into fruition. Nearly 600 pages long and containing some 700 mini-biographies of climbers, many dead, some still alive, it has involved a monumental amount of research on Colin's part. The result is not your traditional kind of *Who's Who*, which could have been dry and boring, but a funny, highly entertaining and often wholly irreverent and outrageous account of those who in Colin's totally non-scientific selection have done something interesting or significant to help make British climbing what it is today.

The idea for *Who's Who* was first mooted after Colin produced 'The 100 Most Memorable British Climbers of the Millennium' for *On the Edge* magazine in December '99. Apart from the extra time needed for research for this book, rumour has it that publication has been delayed for years while some entries were thoroughly scoured in case they were deemed possibly libellous for him and the *Climb* team. The idea has definitely been to entertain and in the preamble Colin quotes General Bruce, *Himalayan Wanderer*, 1934, 'This book has been written purely for amusement. Carping critics are asked to be indulgent to the author, who makes no claim to literary merit.' Carping critics there are as Colin forecast in his introduction when he identifies four groups of people who will hate this book, the main two being 'Everyone who is in it and... Everyone who isn't in it!'

One well-known Lakeland cragrat of the '50 and '60s complained to me that there were 13 errors in his entry, but when I checked and found that most of the info had come from my old mate Trevor Jones's *Cumbrian Rock* I remembered that Trevor would never allow a bit of historical accuracy to ruin a good story. And Rossy does get two and a half pages. Despite some errors that have emerged and which Colin acknowledges, the majority of readers will find this book great for dipping into, but beware – it's addictive, very difficult to put down, and not to be taken too seriously.

An alphabetical layout has been adopted starting with two heavyweights, The Abraham Brothers (*Make it snappy*) and ending with another, Geoffrey Winthrop Young (*Romantically-inclined monoped who dreamt up the BMC – he's to blame*). These witty (and sometimes corny) by-lines follow each name. Other examples are two of the several Joneses featured in the book: Crag – *Taff at the top* and Eric – *Two mugs of adrenaline and a flapjack please!!*

In between the Abrahams and GWY the 300 substantive entries are interspersed with briefer descriptions of climbers who have been grouped together under titles such as Lakeland climbers '50-60s; Welsh Wizards 1930-80s; Cider Drinkers: SW significant others; '80s Glam Rockers; Mountain Men and New Wave Alpinists. Although those featured are not in their normal alphabetical position, they can be easily found by reference to the index.

Alpine Club members past and present naturally figure prominently in this book and some may be offended or infuriated by Colin's wacky style. But for those with an interest in mountaineering history and who are prepared to accept that this is not intended as a definitive reference book, but rather a light-hearted charge through the activities and achievements of the key players in our strange sport, then they should have a copy.

Derek Walker

Östlich des Himalaya: Die Alpen Tibets

Tamotsu Nakamura

Detjen-Verlag, Hamburg 2008, pp288

Nyainqentanglha East, Kangri Garpo, Deep Gorge Country, Daxue Shan, Qonglai Shan... the names of the ranges capture the imagination and go on and on.

Tamotsu (Tom) Nakamura is single-handedly responsible for opening the eyes of the world to the fantastic mountain ranges between Lhasa and Chengdu – his 'Alps of Tibet'. As at April 2008 he lists only five of the 251 peaks exceeding 6000m here as having been climbed. Sometimes statistics say a lot.

The fact that this book is in German should not put off any non-German readers with an interest in the area. Here we have 288 pages packed full of stunning photographs and maps that capture the topography and culture of the area better than anything I have ever seen before. Tom has devoted his retirement to exploring this part of the world and this is his most comprehensive and revealing publication yet. A truly mouth-watering array of photographs and maps come together to form an absolute must for anyone with even a passing interest in the mountains and people 'east of the Himalaya'.

Tom has made some 30 visits to the area, making him by far the most knowledgeable person as to its secrets. He is masterful at recording what he sees and meticulous in his efforts to gather information from diverse sources in order to publish photographs and definitive maps for the benefit of adventurous-minded souls. A combination of satellite detail and skilful use of the latest mapping technology results in the maps standing out as inspirational pieces in their own right. The detail is such that I forever find myself revisiting them.

And it is not just the maps and mountain photographs that are inspiring. Even with only a rudimentary knowledge of German, text and photographs combine to give a vivid insight into both history and cultural heritage. This is a book for anyone with an interest in the area, not just mountaineers.

Die Alpen Tibets has been on my bedside table ever since I received a copy. Tom's photographs have already motivated me to visit the area four times. Now I find myself overwhelmed with more inspiring objectives and future plans. Suffice to say that few other books have had a look in since.

Thank you Tom.

This is an absolutely essential purchase for all with even the slightest interest in the 'Alps of Tibet'.

Mick Fowler

Shadows of a Changing Land
Peter Freeman
Polecat Press, 2008, pp184, £25

This is a spectacular book of photographs by Peter Freeman with the extra bonus of a fascinating polemical essay about the fate of upland landscapes by John Capstick.

Peter Freeman's photographs cover the Yorkshire Dales and the Lake District, effectively celebrating its beauty in all types of weather and season, while John Capstick's essay presents a history of the two national parks, very well informed from a farming, institutional, and local industry point of view, that presents the case for understanding the landscape as something forever changing, its present form being largely the result of centuries of action and industry by its inhabitants. He argues for preserving the dynamism and diversity of these landscapes in the face of popular and institutional assumptions that everything must stay the same.

The photographic images are memorable, (I liked particularly the one of Gable), with inventive cropping and often with an emphasis on the sky. He certainly has been repeatedly in the right place at the right time, making an effort to find new viewpoints to take pictures from. There are informative notes on his planning technique using maps, fieldwork and Azimuth tables to make sure of the angle of light for a good picture (though the printing sometimes seems to me over-saturated with colour, sacrificing subtlety for impact).

The images of the Dales are quieter, and on the whole they show more interestingly the man-made contribution to the landscape of walls, barns, viaducts, and so on. There are some particularly fine photographs of Swaledale and Wensleydale showing the pattern of walls and barns covering the valley bottom and sides, illustrating one example of significant landscape change driven by economic demands – the enclosures of the 17th and 18th centuries – damned at the time, but which are now celebrated as beautiful and essential to the character of the landscape. Perhaps wind turbines will be similarly appreciated one day.

Capstick's essay shows that aesthetics on its own is a bad guide to what is right for the health of a landscape, and fundamentals like economic diversity, local pride and ecological wisdom are more likely to lead to a landscape that happens to have beauty as its by-product. What I find rich and fascinating about upland landscapes is what can be directly seen and read off the surface of the fellside about the long history of give and take between man and nature, geology and weather, long and short time-scales. The more one knows the more one can see of this, and Capstick's essay has certainly educated me. He makes the point that by taking advice from farmers as well as the host of government, academic, and NGOs that form the 'countryside management industry' we might get a better answer to the question 'what kind of upland landscape do we want?'

Julian Cooper

Climbing: Training for Peak Performance (Second Edition)
Clyde Soles
The Mountaineers Books, 2008, pp224, £14.99

It's a sad and unavoidable fact that wisdom is born of twenty-twenty hindsight. So the longer you live the wiser you get. Obvious you might cry, but application of wisdom once acquired is not a foregone conclusion, especially amongst climbers. Now, I'm not going on about that seemingly endless string of toe-curling indiscretions and *faux-pas* (usually alcohol induced) that stretch back to our collective youth, but a different kind of abuse, namely what we have put our bodies through in the pursuit of climbing. I shudder now at the retrospect of non-existent or ill-informed physical preparation and dangerous ego-driven party-tricks (arm-wrestling, dear God!) that were the norm back when 'Ah were a lad…' Admittedly bouldering and climbing wall training were going through a super-steep learning curve during the early Seventies, but most of us never stood back from it all to assess how to get the best out of our bodies and at the same time protect them from damage, immediate and latent. Ignorance was bliss.

Nowadays, of course, the average novice climber is infinitely better informed, or should be. There have been many informative articles on training and physical conditioning for climbers in the magazines over the years and most 'how-to' books include these topics.

One such book is *Climbing: Training for Peak Performance* by Clyde Soles. This is the Second Edition and something of a gem. The first thing you notice is that the author is no downy-chinned juvenile; that face beaming out of the photo has a few miles on the clock, which is reassuring. The whole tone of the book and writing style is liberally endowed with wit and pragmatism and in places a refreshing scepticism.

The author sets out not to stroke the honed, ripple-shouldered youth of the bouldering mats with unlimited time on their hands, but to provide training regimes relevant and accessible to the majority of climbers from all age groups, with mortal bodies and who inhabit a real world of conflicting priorities.

Soles provides that rare experience, text book attention to detail in a hugely readable form. Basically there's just about everything you need to know here about how training affects the body, what exercises do what and what regimes to follow to improve your climbing and reach your particular goals, whether it's bouldering, trad climbing, sport climbing, ice climbing, trekking and mountaineering. Soles also stresses the importance of 'cross-play' – those activities we do to complement climbing: running, road biking, mountain biking etc.

Gym-work is described simply and clearly, such as which resistance exercises work which muscles, important tips on how to do them safely and which exercises to avoid if you suffer from various injuries/chronic conditions.

The section on nutrition is detailed and enlightening, (oh, those days on Cloggy with no food or drink) and here Soles unleashes his irony on the hype surrounding patent diets and food supplements – a joy to read. Basically, there is, and always has been, only one weight controlling diet: take on fewer calories than you expend and you'll lose weight – and *vice versa*. Indeed, myth-busting seems to be a thread running through the whole book.

All the tailored eating and training regimes are presented in clear tabular form, with explanatory notes on why some things are of benefit and others a waste of time.

Throw in a straight-talking section on injury and rehab, and a hope-springs-eternal page for the ageing climber and you are presented with a must have, must read book.

So as I step back into the time-portal behind the climbing wall, having given the half-naked, half-baked youth with chalky hands an hour-long lecture on why he should pull his finger out and make something of his life, I hand him Clyde's book: 'Here, read this.'

Bernard Newman

The Complete Guide to Rope Techniques
for climbers, mountaineers and instructors
Nigel Shepherd
Frances Lincoln, 2007, pp 358, £12.99

Previous editions of Nigel Shepherd's book have been essential reading for trainee instructors for many years. Published first in 1990 as *A Manual of Modern Rope Techniques*, it soon superseded Bill March's *Modern Rope Techniques*, which was my reference when an aspirant mountain leader and instructor in the 1970s and 80s. It was complemented by *Further Modern Rope Techniques* in 1998, and the two volumes were combined into the *Complete Guide* in 2001. The latest edition brings the text up to date with recent developments in equipment, such as belay plate design and mini ascending devices, and has a much-improved range of over 200 clear colour photographs illustrating the techniques. Occasional anecdotes are used to illustrate and enliven a text that otherwise might be very dry. The revised layout and improved photography in this edition mean that it is straightforward to navigate and easy to understand.

As would be expected of a well-respected book that has undergone such an evolution, written by a past Training Officer of the British Association of Mountain Guides, there is little to fault in the techniques and how they are explained. The very few instances that I noticed were:

- The section about the placing of a Deadman anchor in snow is a minor exception to the clarity of the rest of the book. There are no photographs illustrating it, and no explanation of why the angles of placement quoted are so critical.
- There are occasional very small discrepancies between the instructions given in the main text and those in the captions to the photographs, such as in the explanation of passing a knot while lowering.
- There is no discussion of the potential dangers of backing up an abseil by clipping a French prusik into a harness leg loop, or of the alternative of extending the abseil device using a sling threaded through the harness and clipping the prusik into the harness belay loop.
- The discussion of the Croll ascender does not mention that it allows the much more efficient method of having the footloop ascender attached above the Croll, as is done by cavers.

While there are still a number of sections specifically aimed at those preparing for assessment for the Single Pitch Award and Mountain Instructor Award, much of the material that was presented separately in previous editions has been integrated into the main text. Many recreational climbers could learn much from studying this book during the occasional hut- or tent-bound wet day.

Steve Lenartowicz

Everyday Masculinities and Extreme Sport
Male Identity and Rock Climbing
Victoria Robinson
Berg Oxford, 2008, pp256, £19.99

For the majority of rock climbers this book is unlikely to offer an easy read. Without a familiarity with concepts of gender and arcane sociological language, the main tenets of the thesis are elusive. Throughout, there is a puzzling mixture of laypersons' language such as 'everyday', contrasting with such sociological terms as 'problematize', 'illusio' and 'hegemonic masculinities'.

Those who do enjoy a literary challenge in the genre of social science could be tempted to reflect on aspects of their identity and where they might place themselves along a continuum of masculinity. Their musings might lead them to consider whether they experience discord or harmony in moving between their sport and domestic or social situations. It may even cause them to reflect on how friends and colleagues who do not climb find their behaviour bizarre. In chapter 6 there are some interesting references to male climbers who describe emotional aspects of their experiences on rock and the intimacy they share with other climbing partners.

This must have been a challenging and complex topic to explore. The author is a climber and has relatives and close friends who are active in the sport. However, as an active mountaineer for more than 50 years I believe that only a minority of male or female climbers would be so introspective as to scrutinise their behaviour either on or off the crags. Most of them would be preoccupied with getting on with the activity by responding to the physical challenge and very personal enjoyment of the sport.

The author describes the nature of the background investigation as 'empirical'. As a scientist, I find the method more characteristic of a pilot study and the book is essentially discursive. The outcome of statements from a sample of 47 people who were given a semi-structured interview is used throughout to draw inferences on everyday masculinities. (Fourteen of the 47 were female but six of these did not climb.) Apparently this is a small, heterogeneous sample and it seems to me to be quite unrepresentative of the current population of climbers.

Furthermore, there is an unfortunate time gap of more than five years between the interviews and the publication of the book. During this time, attitudes to gender differences in sport, and particularly in climbing, have changed. There is now far less of a distinction between the performance and climbing technique of males and females. The process of standardising masculine behaviour using comments from the interviews allows little room for the variation and individuality which are the essence of human behaviour. Unfortunately, many of the statements quoted from the interviewees are so banal. In contrast, the complex language used by the author to extract from them any significance to illustrate her thesis lacks conviction. For example, in the context of masculinity, 'you need to go out and scare yourself, you need to go out and remember...'

To those AC members and other climbers who are social scientists this book could provide some interesting perspectives on masculinity and extreme sport. To those in other disciplines it offers some insight into how theories of gender and feminism add other dimensions to this sport and the sub-culture to which we belong.

Marjorie Mortimer

Staying Alive in Avalanche Terrain
Bruce Tremper
The Mountaineers Books, 2008, 304pp, US$18.95

Staying Alive in Avalanche Terrain provides a comprehensive overview of the issues connected to safe travel in snow-covered mountains; and the author, Bruce Tremper, is an acknowledged avalanche expert in the USA. The first edition (2001) set the current standard for avalanche textbooks, and this second edition (2008) brings the original work up to date, for example by including new techniques for stability tests. The challenge for any avalanche education is to be able to explain the causes and avoidance of avalanches in a way that distinguishes the key principles from interesting detail. Such discrimination is not an easy task in a textbook. In this case, to help make his message as user-friendly as possible, Tremper draws from his considerable personal experience and uses a modest approach, informal style, and thought-provoking quotations.

The book draws on an extensive body of data gathered in North America and Europe, and gives some global perspectives. However, as would be expected given the author's work and location, there is a bias towards the circumstances and hazards that are typical in North America. Hence, it is important to be aware that in other mountain regions the balance of considerations will be different to answer the key question anyone travelling in avalanche terrain should consider, that is: how to avoid being an avalanche victim.

The usual persuasive key facts are highlighted (perhaps the most important being that in a very high percentage of fatal avalanche incidents the trigger was the victim or another person). The text is supported with many diagrams, graphs and photographs, which would be improved if they were in colour. The use of analogies will work for some readers, and not for others.

As the author makes clear, the book is not a substitute for training and practice in the field. If you are considering a career as a snow sports professional in North America then this book is an essential text; for others it is a useful reference point for a deeper understanding of what is both a simple and complex subject, which when pursued as a mountain traveller can be most unforgiving of errors and omissions.

Roger Payne

Scottish Winter Climbs
Andy Nisbet, Rab Anderson and Simon Richardson
Scottish Mountaineering Trust, 2008, pp386

I was surprised and somewhat flattered when the *AJ* editor asked me if I wanted to review the SMC guidebook to Scottish Winter Climbs. I am pleased to say that Scottish winter climbing has always had a strong pull on the Tunstall body; my early years of climbing in the eighties often saw me leaving work in London with a full rucksack to meet up with Fowler and the other equally mad individuals prepared to drive the 10 hours plus to some remote outpost of the Highlands, typically arriving just in time to park the car and start the walk-in to the crag of choice. It was no surprise that some 20 years later when the opportunity arose, I switched base and moved from being a London-to-Scotland commuter to being a 'local', living in Aboyne, Aberdeenshire.

After the move I found I was no longer climbing exclusively with my own friends but had started to spend time with other 'locals', several of whom are the main drivers behind the SMC guides. Tom Prentice, Simon Richardson and Andy Nisbet have all been recent climbing partners, though I'm not sure 'partner' is the correct word. I meet them where they choose, try and keep up on the walk-in and then belay them, usually in bad weather on some obscure cliff while they tick off yet another unclimbed line.

My other confession, prior to starting a review, is to confess that I've spouted on for many hours to anyone who would listen as to how I have found the SMC guidebooks to be works of climbing art. Never does the Cairngorm guide get carried to a crag. That role is given to previous editions, amended if a recent route is to be attempted, while the latest guide holds prime position on the lounge table, waiting to be read as and when TV gets boring, which is often. I don't understand how it came to be overlooked by the Boardman Tasker judges.

Given the above, you would expect that my order for *Scottish Winter Climbs* would have been lodged well before publication date. But why buy a general guide when you have the regional ones? (I acquired that Scottish tendency, never spend money unless essential.) Then winter turns up, dousing the Cairngorms in metres of snow and somehow missing the Ben, while freezing Skye and the Southern Highlands down to temperatures not seen for years. Expert advice was needed so I called Tom Prentice who was quick to say, 'Aha, in these conditions go to Beinn an Dothaidh, it will be in perfect nick.' The clever man, it was a cliff not in any guide I owned. So out came the credit card and an order placed.

The route we climbed was excellent and in condition, so no complaints there, and to my surprise this new selected climbs guide has more or less replaced the regional guides for my own winter use. It wastes no words so is lighter yet seems to increase the options as regards which mountain best fits the latest conditions. The guide is clearly working, as I'm finding that cliffs I would have expected to be making fresh tracks to often have several parties there, even midweek.

Following the latest BMC international meet I have been climbing with an Italian who is working in the oil industry in Aberdeen. He raves about the book; initially surprised by the 20 pages of introduction, he'd none the less found them all useful, and was inspired by the photos, showing both mixed and pure ice action. Even I, after 25 years of climbing in the Highlands, am inspired by the photos. Just seeing the image of *The Lamp* on Aladdin's Buttress, a route I had never heard of, made me want to kit up and start walking. Others like *Cut-throat* on Beinn Udlaidh make me pray for a rapid coming of the next ice age. The crag pictures with clear route lines make approaching and finding climbs as easy as it has ever been. The route descriptions are excellent, as one would now take for granted from these authors, although the pedant in me wondered why some routes get individual pitch descriptions while others do not.

As to their use of the star system, it was certainly hard to explain to my Italian friend how a climb with a two and a half hour approach that we climbed in less than 30 minutes could get three stars, or how another route in the same area qualified for four stars when, in his words, it has 'less than 50m of climbing'. We couldn't but notice that the sustained three-pitch mixed route of the same grade that we enjoyed the following weekend only received only one star. Maybe the time has come to remove the stars from selected climbs guides as surely if a climb is crap it won't be included.

In summary, yet another brilliant book from Messrs Nisbet, Anderson and Richardson. It is a book that should be bought by all members of the Alpine Club, read, enjoyed, studied in detail and then acted upon. Hopefully the activists among you will be further inspired to root out some of the many unclimbed lines that remain in the Highlands. These lines have revitalised my climbing life. I hope they do the same for you.

Duncan Tunstall

Ben Nevis: Britain's Highest Mountain

Ken Crocket & Simon Richardson

Scottish Mountaineering Trust, 2009, pp416, £27.50

A silver lining to this *AJ* running way behind its production schedule, is that it enables me to flag up one of the most desirable books to cross the editor's desk this year. Crocket and Richardson's update of SMT's 1986 history of 'The Ben' – also by Crocket – is simply superb. Besides the authors, much of the credit should go to Tom Prentice who designed and produced the book. For anyone who has climbed on the mountain, and for those that aspire to, there are simply hours of pleasure stored here, from Timothy Pont's 1585 sketch of 'Bin Nevesh' as part of the first topographical survey of Scotland to Andy Cave's first ascent of *Techno Wall* (V,6), wrapping up the 2008 winter, and Dave MacLeod's extraordinary first ascent, the following July, of Echo Wall, extreme technical difficulty and minimal protection combining to form 'one of the most difficult rock climbs in the world', according to the authors.

What strikes you from this edition is just how much climbing has advanced on the Ben over the last two decades. Seven chapters have been added covering new developments, all authored by Richardson who was a key player in the 'mixed revolution' he chronicles. Not only are the climbs themselves impressive, but the stories are told in such compelling style that a quick dip to check a point of history turns into an hour of rapt reading. A full review of this great book will appear in the next *AJ*, by which time this deserves to be among mountaineering publishing's best sellers. ***SG***

Climbers' Club Guidebook Centenary Journal
Edited by R F Allen
The Climbers' Club, 2009, pp304, £16.99

'...many who thought they knew Lliwedd fairly well will find a feast of...pleasures revealed to them by this little volume.'

Such was the verdict of the *Alpine Journal* in 1909 on Archer Thomson and Andrews's *The Climbs on Lliwedd*, the first-ever climbers' pocket guidebook. And much the same could be said of this latest offering from the Climbers' Club, celebrating a century of CC guidebooks, except that it is not a 'little' volume. The authors ably marshalled by Bob Allen cover a lot of ground, from the big cliff itself, through a veritable degree course in guidebook history, to musings on the idiosyncrasies of authors and how they have occasionally led us astray.

The book begins with a complete reprint of the 1909 guide, a work of 99 pages that set the concise style of route description, plus photographs and topos and lists that has been standard to climbing guidebooks ever since. Mike Bailey, in an informative essay on J M A Thomson and the advent of guidebooks, notes the early resistance of the Pen y Gwryd establishment to publishing route details, or even divulging them to passing visitors. Men like Oscar Eckenstein were, says Bailey, 'fiercely protective of the Corinthian spirit of the early days and anxious that the romantic side of exploration and discovery should not be compromised.'

Then along came rude commerce. The door to the *Lliwedd* guide and 100 years of definitive followers seems to have been pushed open by O G Jones and the Abraham brothers with *Rock Climbing in the English Lake District* and then, *sans* Jones, with the same for North Wales. These were hardly pocket guides and were laced with lively narrative, but they had let the climbing secret out of the bag. The CC responded.

The *Guidebook Centenary Journal* fits precisely that 'bedside...dip-into' mould and is confirmation once again that the essay is the perfect form for writing about climbing. Don't skip the reprint of the 1909 guide. It did not mark a complete swing away from the Romantics; take Andrews's part of the Introduction (the pair wrote a section each) as he sets the scene, approaching by Llyn Llydaw: 'A short walk along its banks, and an ascent of the screes which lie at the foot of the grim walls of Lliwedd, carry us to a world which has caught no note of modern storm or stress.' So they felt the need of such resort even then?

There are plenty of familiar names here from CC circles – Harold Drasdo, Derek Walker, Tim Noble, Dave Gregory, Terry Gifford and more, all of them on form. And there are gems tucked away like Jill Sumner's 'glimpse or two' into the background of the mid-Wales guides written by her late husband John. There's the Sumners' first audience with Joe Brown while researching *Central Wales* – 'a bit like meeting the Godfather' – and a meeting with farmers, 'on neutral territory' by a lane in the Cywarch valley. Jill describes the farmers as having faces set 'with bottled umbrage'. Not only did they object to some of the crags having English names, they objected to English route names, with that of *Crucifix* causing particular offence to Methodist sensibilities. When, in a moment of mischief, Jill said they were thinking of naming a route *The Holy Grail* one man nearly lost his dentures. *Mid Wales* came out with *Crucifix* changed to *The Technician* and no *Holy Grail*. As was said at the beginning, this collection, rather like that first *Lliwedd* guide, contains a feast of pleasures. *Stephen Goodwin*

Mountain Words
British hill and crag literature: into the 21st century
Chris Harle and Graham Wilson
Millrace, 2009, pp184, £14.95

Another quirky, thought-provoking, beautifully produced little book from the Millrace stable is always full of surprises, but this one turns out to be a combination of a Neate-style list for the last 25 years and five essays on mountain literature by Graham Wilson. The complete list takes the same period as the duration of the Boardman Tasker Award, so there's a list of BT short-lists and winners too. To provocatively fill the gap backwards there is a list of 50 recommended books published before 1983. Finally a book search by category is born of Chris Harle's bookselling experience of vague enquiries in 'Outside' at Hathersage.

You have to pay attention to the parameters of the main list: 'British walking/climbing interest' omits *Touching the Void* (it's in the BT list) and includes Wainwright, fell-running and *The Book of the Bivvy* (a gem if you've not discovered it). For all bibliophiles this is going to be an indispensible and contentious book. Neate's best mountaineering book of all time, Whymper's *Scrambles*, does not make this 'best fifty' list. But nor does Leslie Stephen, both being of 'Alpine' rather 'British' interest. Members of this club might feel that there is something unsatisfactory about this. Of course, the same restrictions applied to Graham Wilson's previous Millrace book of essays on this subject, *A Rope of Writers: A look at mountaineering literature in Britain* (2006). Millrace prides itself on producing 'idiosyncratic' publications.

So what of the essays? The opening sentence cites *Scrambles* and *Touching the Void* as pinnacles of British mountaineering literature. No deviation from the press's characteristic quality there then. And in their delightfully rambling way, these essays do address some tricky questions concerning 'Why so much writing about climbing?', 'What do words have over pictures?', 'How reliable are biographers?' 'Can walking literature make the grade?' and 'When is climbing fiction successful?' Along the way there are many instructive insights and incisive critiques of, among others, Andy Cave's *Learning to Breathe*, Dennis Gray's novel *Todhra*, Elizabeth Coxhead's *One Green Bottle* and M John Harrison's *Climbers*. Wilson is strong on telling comparisons: Sutton and Noyce's *Samson* with Jim Perrin's *Menlove*, Whillans and Ormerod's *Portrait of a Mountaineer* with Perrin's *The Villain* and Douglas Milner's photograph of 'Crack of Doom' with W H Murray's account of the climb in *Mountaineering in Scotland*.

What Wilson's admirable work indicates is the need for an inclusive and critical overview of mountaineering writing in English. It is amazing that we don't have one. Meanwhile *Mountain Words*, in its two halves, provides plenty to argue about and take back into re-reading this ongoing rich heritage in which the Boardman Tasker Award can now be seen to play a central role.

Terry Gifford

Eighty Years on Top
The History of the Himalayan Club
A DVD written and produced for the Himalayan Club
by Karamjeet Singh, Ascent Films

'In a hundred ages of the Gods, I could not tell thee of the glories of the Himalaya.' So, with the words of the *Puranas* begins this film, which, nonetheless, does a pretty good job of covering those glories in 25 minutes.

Eighty Years on Top traces Himalayan history from the early wanderers of the high passes to the era of exploration and mountaineering. It includes rare footage from the HC's archives and records the Club's activities from the days of founders such as Younghusband and the Duke of Abruzzi. Early members such as Pandit Nain Singh, Shipton and Tilman are featured and there is footage of the exuberant Gurdial Singh doing his headstand on the summit of Trisul in 1951, plus some words by him today recalling the experience.

From recent times, and always against the background of the mountains, we see Chris Bonington, Harish Kapadia, Dr M S Gill and others, and the film concludes with the Nanda Devi Sanctuary and some excellent words on the future by current HC president, Suman Dubey.

Eighty Years on Top was premiered recently in the presence of Mrs Sonia Gandhi, leader of the Congress Party. It is a fascinating history, but more than that is the abiding impression of 'the glories of the Himalaya' that the film conveys with wonderful visual richness.

The DVD is available in the UK for £4 (£5 including postage) - from me at 18 Howitt Road, London NW3 4LL or from India, details on **www.himalayanclub.org**

Martin Scott

In Memoriam

The Alpine Club Obituary	**Year of Election**
John Blacker	1964
Riccardo Cassin	Hon 2009
John D Evans	1986
Terry Hartley	1970
Charles Houston	1935
Robert (Bob) Lawford	1967
Arne Naess	Hon 1991
John Noble	1972
Peter Owen	1965
Bill Packard	1951
Reginald Parker	1952
Sir Edward Peck	1944
DG (David) Smith	1960
FD (David) Smith	1961
Johannes Somerwil	1965
Elizabeth (Jen) Solt	1987
Trevor Southall	1983
John Stanton	1974
Arthur Wadsworth	1944
George Watkins	1990
Eileen Wilks	LAC 1949
John Wilks	1950
Edward Wrangham	1955

As usual, the Editor will be pleased to receive tributes for any of those not included in the following pages.

Dr John George Carlos Blacker 1929-2008

John Blacker, who died on 28 September 2008 aged 78, was a distinguished demographer whose many interests included mountaineering, sailing, music, scholarship and gastronomy. Above all, he had a genius for friendship combined with an innate modesty that contrasted somewhat with the exuberance that characterised the more exotic members of his highly gifted family. His great-grandfather had married a Spanish Peruvian grandee, though not before siring a strain of Peruvian Blackers whose unexpected continuation of the family line gave John particular satisfaction. His grandfather Carlos, a dashing gentleman of independent means and brilliant gifts had, for many years, been Oscar Wilde's closest friend until Wilde irresponsibly breached Blacker's strictest confidences about the notorious Dreyfus case. John's father, Dr CP Blacker who won both an MC and a GM, was an eminent psychiatrist, a pioneer of family planning and a friend of the Bloomsbury literati. His elder sister, Carmen, was a Professor of Japanese at Cambridge, and his second sister, Thetis, the outstanding British batik artist of her generation.

John followed in his father's footsteps to Eton and Balliol, where he switched from physics to modern history. He had boxed at school but at Oxford his main sporting pre-occupation was rowing as a member of the Leander crew that won the Grand at Henley in 1949 and in the winning Oxford boat in 1950. He continued to scull well into his 70s. After Oxford, he took a PhD in demographic history at the LSE which well suited his multi-disciplined, independent mind. A thirst for adventure and a commitment to public service led him to take up his first professional demographic appointment in 1958 with the East African High Commission in Nairobi, which became his spiritual home and professional base for the next 18 years. During this time, John's demographic work for 16 different countries produced population censuses and surveys that changed the face of African demography. After various assignments for the United Nations and other international agencies, he joined the permanent staff of the Centre for Population Studies at the London School of Hygiene and Tropical Medicine in 1976 where he worked for the next 15 years, making further important contributions to demographic research in Pakistan, Bangladesh, Indonesia, Bahrain and Central Asia. He retired in 1992, but remained very active professionally, producing many internationally acclaimed studies including those on child mortality after the First Gulf War; a re-appraisal of Kikuyu mortality after Mau Mau; and a seminal contribution to the demography of AIDS, which was cited by Nelson Mandela. A gratifying conclusion of John's 1990s demographic survey of AC members was that our life expectancies were six years above the average. Apart from a massive corpus of demographic literature, John meticulously edited *Have You Forgotten Yet?*, his father's First World War memoirs, and made an important contribution to Mark Hichens' *Oscar Wilde's Last Chance* describing his grandfather's pivotal role in the Dreyfus Affair.

John Blacker 1929-2008

John's serious mountaineering career began at Oxford and, between 1951 and 1955, his four guideless Alpine seasons accounted for well over 20 classic routes in the Tarentaise, Oberland, Pennine Alps and Mont Blanc massif. His main companions at this time were Sandy Cavenagh, David Pasteur, Peter Cox and, particularly, Nicholas Woolaston and JGD Warburton with whom, during their 1953 season, he climbed the Allalinhorn, Fletschhorn, Lagginhorn, Weissmies (north ridge), Rimpfischhorn (north ridge), Zinalrothorn, Ober Gabelhorn and Dent Blanche. In 1958, John joined the Mountain Club of Kenya (MCK), a time of renaissance following the recently resolved Mau Mau emergency, when old huts were refurbished, new ones built and new routes put up. As the MCK's Hut Bookings Secretary, he became heavily involved in the club's climbing and social life, and in 1962/3 served as Vice-President.

A mandatory ascent of Kilimanjaro was followed by numerous trips to Mount Elgon and Meru, the Aberdares, and the MCK's rock climbing playground at Lukenia. But Mount Kenya itself was ever the lure. On his first expedition in 1958, he climbed its satellite peaks Lenana, Thomson, John and Pigott, and also made the first crossing of the challenging Firmin Col. A second venture in 1960 was abandoned on the mountain due to what John described as his companions' 'indisposition'. Two years later, he climbed Nelion and Batian via the Gate of the Mists in a party of four, with John and Geoff Newham on one rope, and Robert Chambers and Ulrich Middleboe on the other. Disaster struck on descent when a large chunk of rock broke off. Newham was badly injured after falling 20ft. In the dramatic rescue that followed over several days, John made a breakneck descent of Nelion with Chambers, before racing down the Naro Moru track to raise the alarm with the owner of the first farm he came to – Beryl Markham the famous aviator.

In 1964 John and Charles Richards organised an expedition to the Ruwenzori which I was lucky enough to join. In uncharacteristically good weather, we climbed Speke; did the traverse of Moebius, Alexandra and Margherita on Stanley from the Elena hut to the Irene Lakes in less than 10 hours; climbed Semper via Edward on Baker; and put up a new route on Philip via the Savoia Glacier. Later that year, John was elected to the Alpine Club, and served on the committee in 1981.

John climbed regularly on homeland hills, and particularly relished New Year reunions at the PYG. However, his penchant was for the less frequented ranges, particularly if mountaineering could be combined with his other passion, sailing. While in Africa, he had traversed the length of Lake Victoria in a tiny boat. On return to England, he embarked on a succession of adventurous cruises in his beloved 25' Vertue class yacht, *Foresight*, usually accompanied by adoring ladies. *Foresight* became his base from which to climb along the west coasts of Scotland and Ireland, the Norwegian fiords and Lofoten. In 1979 he sailed her to Iceland and back, via Shetland and the Faroes, with Basia Zaba and Guy Howard. The wind was against them most of the way; navigation was by dead reckoning and they climbed Iceland's highest mountain Snaefell (1833m) in thick fog. Thereafter, he sailed *Foresight* south to the warmer waters of the Mediterranean, stopping off at Corsica, Malta, Crete, Turkey, Greece, and finally Croatia, where he shared a new boat with Rob Hale.

John's mountaineering ranged from the Americas, the Alps, both polar regions, the Pyrenees, the Ala Dağ and Lycian Alps of Turkey, Mt Olympus and the Pindus in Greece, the Julian Alps, and the Himalaya. We trekked together *en famille* in Bhutan and Sikkim, and he particularly cherished his ascent of the previously unclimbed Wohney Gang (5589m), as a member of the Alpine Club's 1991 Bhutan expedition. John particularly delighted in a mountain's historical associations and literature, quoting effortlessly passages from Whymper, Tilman or whoever else took his fancy. In 1994 he returned to the Vignemale, whose Arête de Gaube he had climbed 20 years earlier, with Peter Lowes, Bob Maguire, Baroness Simone De Lassus and others, to commemorate a memorable ascent by Baron Bertrand De Lassus (a forebear of the Baroness's late husband) with the famous Pyrenean pioneer Count Henri Russell.

John was an accomplished viola player and had legendary culinary skills. His friends Elizabeth David and Claudia Roden might have demurred at some of the imaginative 'Catering on Mountains' recipes he wrote for the MCK Bulletin and Mount Kenya guidebook, but never his gourmet dinner party creations. During the last decade of his life, John fought a tenacious and unflinching battle against cancer. When he attended the Alpine Club's 150th anniversary celebrations at Zermatt, his pace might have been slower, but his spirit and good humour were undimmed. He faced adversity with never a murmur of self-pity, and his willingness to be used as a guinea pig for experimental cures in the cause of medical science was typical of a man whose courage, generosity and integrity were an inspiration to his innumerable friends and colleagues. John's reliability, sound judgement and unflappability made him an incomparable climbing companion. He never married, but his girl friends were legion.

John Harding

Riccardo Cassin 1909 - 2009

Riccardo Cassin died at his home at Piani Resinelli, near Lecco on 6 August 2009. In January he had celebrated his 100th birthday and in May he had been made an honorary member of the Alpine Club. It was an accolade bestowed decades too late. Cassin had long since attained an almost god-like status in the climbing world. His greatest routes, the Walker Spur on the Grandes Jorasses, done in 1938, and the Cassin Ridge on Mt McKinley, remain among alpinisms most coveted prizes.

Cassin's stock was not always so high, at least not in the eyes of the British mountaineering establishment. The old guard of the Alpine Club regarded the methods used in the 1930s by Cassin and a new wave of continental climbers to scale the vertical walls of the Dolomites and the great north faces of Alps as cheating. This disdain may also have had a cultural undertone. Cassin, like many of his contemporaries, was a working class lad at time when alpinism, from a British perspective, was still the preserve of gentlemen. The social revolution that saw northern tradesmen such as Whillans and Brown lead a surge in domestic climbing standards did not occur for another 20 years. Though this quickly extended to the Alps, by then the ambitious Italian was leaving his mark in the Himalaya.

Riccardo Cassin was born in San Vito al Tagliamento, lower Fruili. His parents were peasants and Riccardo started work at age 12 as a bellows-boy in a blacksmith's shop. He had no memory of his father. Cassin senior went to America when Riccardo was age two and was killed in an accident at work. Looking to better himself, the young Cassin moved to Lecco in northern Italy and took a job as a mechanic. On his first Sunday there, he went with friends up Punta Cermenati, the main peak of the Resegone, and two weeks later he discovered the Grigna. This popular climbing area north of city was to become Cassin's training ground and the scene of string of first ascents in the early 1930s. First was the east face of the Guglia Angelina, climbed with Mary Varale who later introduced Cassin to Emilio Comici. The master from Trieste tutored the Lecco boys in the use of pitons, double roping, and *etriers* – the methods of 'steeple-jacks' on factory chimneys according to Col Strutt, editor of the *Alpine Journal*.

Cassin acknowledged the purity of the free-climbing ethic and claimed to keep his home-made pitons to a minimum. 'On routes where I had

Riccardo Cassin 1909-2009
(Ken Wilson)

used 50 pitons, other people used 70. So I climbed with less aid than other climbers,' he said. He admired the audacious Austrian Paul Preuss, a great advocate of free climbing, but when Pruess fell to his death, aged only 27, while attempting a solo first ascent in the Gosaukamm, Cassin observed dryly that he had become 'a victim of his own theories'.

After their Grigna apprenticeship, Cassin and his Lecco friends in the Nuova Italia Club moved on to the Dolomites. In 1935, he and Vittorio Ratti authored a masterpiece on the gigantic Torre Trieste, a 50-hour climb up the tower's exposed south-east ridge. The beauty of the Cassin/Ratti line was reflected in the comment of one observer who told them: 'On those 700m of rock you wrote a poem.'

Lecco was a nursery of talented rock climbers, whose skills combined with Cassin's power and determination (he was a boxer as a youth) spelt success where others quailed. This was strikingly evident in what he called his 'Alpine Triad' – first ascents of three major north faces, battered by storms on each occasion. First, in 1935, came the north face of the Cima Ovest di Lavaredo, a 60-hour epic, enduring lightning, hail and snow. Always highly competitive, Cassin had raced to the Dolomites on hearing that two Germans were encamped below the face waiting for the weather to clear. On returning victorious to Lecco, he and Ratti were welcomed by the town band.

Next in the Triad, in 1937, was the north-east face of Piz Badile. Cassin and Ratti were joined by Gino Esposito. Success, however, was marred by the death of two Como climbers who asked to join forces with the Lecco trio at the first bivouac. Cassin could hardly refuse, but the pair proved unprepared for a 52-hour ordeal on such a face and died on the descent from cold and exhaustion. These were the only deaths associated with a Cassin climb, a remarkable record given the seriousness of his routes over such a long career.

All eyes were now on the north face of the Eiger. Climbers were literally dying in the race to be first up the *Nordwand*. Hitler was offering medals for valour – presuming it would be climbed first by Germans – while the gentleman of the AC regarded it all as 'an obsession for the deranged'. Cassin, Esposito and Ugo Tizzoni arrived at Kliene Scheidegg just in time to watch Germans Heckmair and Vörg and Austrians Kasparek and Harrer take the prize.

Cassin thought hard for alternative and week later, with Esposito and Tizzoni set out for the Mont Blanc range, intent on a *dirrettissima* on the north face of the Grandes Jorasses, the Walker Spur. This was wonderfully audacious. None of the trio had ever visited the Mont Blanc group and they had to get directions to the face from a hut warden, dumbfounded at their naivety. The Walker was to be Cassin's greatest climb, completed over 82 hours with, as ever, a lashing from the elements. He led throughout, penduluming beneath the most awkward overhang and hammering in a total of 50 pitons – 'not that many' over such a distance in the opinion of Chris Bonington.

War put climbing on hold. Cassin joined the partisans, but kept his job in a factory producing military equipment – a reserved occupation – to avoid suspicion. He became the leader of a rock climbers' section, liaising with partisans in the mountains and hiding arms and ammunition in his house. Lecco was strategically important and the scene of fierce street fighting in April 1945. Cassin's close friend Vittorio Ratti was shot dead at his side in one exchange while Cassin himself was injured in the arm and face.

After the war, Cassin's life as an alpinist matured. He turned more to the greater ranges for adventure and adopted a father role to the next generation of Italian climbers. In 1946 he was asked to be the leader of the newly-formed *Ragni della Grignetta* (Lecco Spiders). More first ascents and some notable repeats followed. Today, when so many top climbers turn professional, it is interesting to note that Cassin crammed his routes into holidays and weekends, and was always back at his bench on Monday morning. Later it was a desk, as he rose from shop floor to manager and then founded his own company manufacturing ice-axes and so forth.

In 1953, came his first trip to the great peaks of Asia, and with it the seeds of bitterness. Ardito Desio was organising a major expedition to K2, then unclimbed, intent on planting the Italian flag on the world's second highest summit. Cassin escorted Desio on a reconnaissance up the Baltoro glacier, spending 32 days on the march. But to his intense disappointment and anger, he was excluded from the main expedition the following year.

Purportedly, Cassin was dropped on health grounds, but he believed Prof Desio was afraid being overshadowed by a 'simple' climber who was a sporting hero to Italians. Both men regarded themselves as leaders, and the autocratic scientist was unlikely to have taken kindly to advice from a former bellows-boy. Cassin's retort came in the autumn of 1957 when he returned to the Baltoro as leader of an expedition to Gasherbrum IV. Walter Bonatti and Carlo Mauri reached the 7925m-summit after some of the hardest technical climbing then accomplished at altitude.

Cassin's reputation as an indomitable alpinist was sealed in 1961 with success on Mt McKinley (6194m) in Alaska, the highest mountain in North America. With five of his "boys" from the Lecco Spiders, he made a first ascent of McKinley's south face by an elegant spur that bears his name – the Cassin Ridge. It was a post-war equivalent of the Walker Spur, a line of steep ice and rock that remains an absolute classic. The climbers endured violent storms and extreme cold, several suffering frostbite on the descent as snow fell continuously for 75 hours. Cassin called it 'a superb victory for Lecco' and the expedition received congratulatory telegrams from the presidents of the USA (Kennedy) and Italy (Gronchi).

Expeditions followed to the Caucasus (1966) and the Andes, where in 1969 he led the first ascent of the west face of Jirishanca (6126m). All six team members reached the summit, with its cornice of fragile ice. Cassin was indescribably happy. 'With 60 years behind me, and those good lads beside me, I looked at the world from that peak: my mind seemed drugged by infinite silence.'

Most mountaineers would be powering down by this stage in life, but Cassin was still hungry. In 1975 he returned to the Himalaya as leader of a CAI attempt on the south face of Lhotse (8501m). The precipitous 3000m wall had 'last great problem' status stamped all over it, but though the team made good progress and reached 7500m, the elements proved too severe. After a second avalanche smashed through base camp, Cassin reluctantly conceded defeat.

Lhotse was Cassin's last big trip, though he continued to climb rock at a high standard. With three sons and a clutch of grandchildren, he devoted himself to family life, the Cassin factory and his role as an elder statesman of alpinism. In 1987, on the 50th anniversary of his first ascent of the north-east face of the Badile, the Lecco legend turned in a bravura performance, climbing the route twice in one week – the second time for the benefit for the late arriving Press. He was 78 years old, on a route still beyond most recreational climbers despite all the advances in risk-reducing equipment.

The certificate according Cassin honorary AC membership was accepted by one of his sons, Guido, at a dinner in Chamonix during the Piolets d'Or festivities last May. By then Riccardo was too frail to travel, but he wrote a gracious letter to the Club wishing 'good climbing to everybody'.

Stephen Goodwin

Ernest Terence Hartley 1924 – 2009

Terry Hartley, who died in March 2009 after a long illness, was one of the outstanding British ski mountaineers of his generation as the organiser and leader of numerous tours and expeditions, and as an administrator who served as President of the Alpine Ski Club, the Eagle Ski Club and the Ski Club of Great Britain.

Born on 18 April 1924 at Upper Milton, Oxfordshire, of an old farming family, he was educated at Dauncey's School. After the war, having married Rachel Wilson at the tender age of 22, he took over the family's farming operation in Oxfordshire which was to occupy his working life. Both

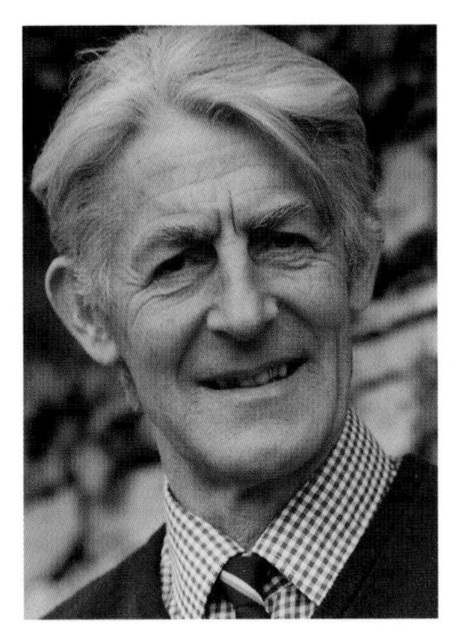

Terry Hartley 1924-2009

Terry and Rachel became skiing addicts, and Grindelwald, with its close Alpine fraternity, was adopted as their second family home. The Bernese Oberland was Terry's first mountain love, and it was from this base, during the 1960s, that he was particularly active as an innovative ski mountaineer at a time when British ski mountaineering, under the overall leadership of Neil Hogg, was at last beginning to emerge from near obsolescence.

During that decade, Terry organised and led a series of guided Eagle Ski Club parties repeating classic, but what were then relatively rarely attempted, ski mountaineering traverses including the High Level Route in both directions, and both the Bernina and Bernese Oberland. En route, his parties climbed many peaks including the Dufourspitze, Morteratsch, Piz Palü, Piz Bernina, Wildhorn, Wildstrubel, Balmhorn, Mönch, Grosse Wannenhorn, and Finsteraarhorn. Other ski ascents over this time included the Grosses Fiescherhorn, Äbeni Fluh, Mont Blanc, Mt Vélan, Grand Combin, Aletschhorn, and Schinhorn. In 1967, to celebrate Arnold Lunn's 80th birthday and the Golden Anniversary of his first ever ski ascent of the Dom (4545m), Terry led a small party to emulate Lunn's historic feat.

Outside the Alps, Terry led one of the earlier British ski expeditions into the High Atlas in 1965, when his party climbed four 4000m peaks, Toubkal, Buguinnousiene, Ras N'ouanoukrim and W'ouanoukrim. In 1966 he was active in the Pyrenees, and in 1969 led an Eagle Ski Club expedition to Iran's Elburz mountains, climbing Demavend and Touchal on ski. In 1970, he was elected to the Alpine Club.

Thereafter, bowing to the demands of family and farming, the tempo of Terry's ski mountaineering activities abated somewhat. He continued to climb and ski regularly, and was such a familiar and popular figure in Grindelwald that he was made a Freeman of that town. He also undertook ski tours in Norway and trekked in the Himalaya, but as Rachel's health deteriorated, the family's holiday focus switched more to long distance walking, sailing, and travel in further flung places including Canada, the Indian Ocean, and later, Antarctica. Terry's other activities and interests were many and varied. He played hockey for both Oxfordshire and Gloucestershire; was a member of the MCC and helped establish the Shipton Cricket Club, subsequently becoming both its Captain and President. He worked tirelessly for the local community and was a popular after-dinner speaker, blessed with a prodigious memory for people and places.

Two years after Rachel's death in 1993, Terry embarked on his second very happy marriage, at the ripe age of 71, to Catherine Tudor-Evans, a family friend of many years. Catherine's selfless love and care gave Terry boundless support during the difficult closing years of his life, when his health sadly deteriorated. He was ever a most devoted husband and father who will be remembered with the greatest affection by all who knew him as a charming, courteous and generous gentleman, and one of the most inspiring ski mountaineer leaders of his time.

J G R Harding

Dr Charles Snead Houston 1913 - 2009

Charlie Houston's territory was the "thinne aire" of big mountains. He almost gasped his last of it in 1953 during an epic retreat on K2 and later immersed himself in the study of why we get sick at high altitude, and sometimes die there.

The archaic quote was a favourite of Houston's, from Father Jose Acosta, a Jesuit missionary who vividly described his symptoms on crossing the Andes in the late 16th century. Acosta attributed his retching and vomiting to air so "delicate as it is not proportionable with the breathing of man".

The priest was on the right track, but it was not until the publication of Houston's *Going Higher: Oxygen, Man, and Mountains* in 1980 that climbers and medics were offered a clear understanding of the cause and effect of the main types of altitude sickness, together with sound advice on staying healthy.

Charles Snead Houston was born in New York in 1913 and brought up

Charlie Houston at the Kendal Mountain Film Festival 2004.
(Bernard Newman)

in East Coast privilege. At the age of 12 he walked with his parents from Geneva to Chamonix, reading Geoffrey Winthrop Young's classic *On High Hills* along the way. The die was cast. While a medical student, he joined the Harvard Mountaineering Club, teaming up with four other putative big names in US climbing – Bob Bates, Bradford Washburn, H Adams Carter and Terris Moore – to form the so-called 'Harvard Five'.

In 1933 he was invited by the more experienced Washburn to climb on Mount Crillon (a near miss) and a year later returned to Alaska on an expedition led by his father, Oscar Houston, to make the first ascent of Mount Foraker. Also on Foraker was T Graham Brown, with whom Houston climbed in the Alps and, in 1936, co-led an expedition to Nanda Devi. The party was an intriguing mix - four cocky Americans, all members of the fledgling Harvard MC - and four veteran Brits, including Bill Tilman and Noel Odell who together reached the 7816m summit on 29 July. Houston seemed set for the first ascent, but at the last camp fell ill with food poisoning - a treacherous tin of meat - and descended to enable Tilman to take his place alongside Odell. Tilman recalled: 'Bad as he (Houston) was, his generous determination to go down was of a piece with the rest of his actions.'

Houston and Tilman teamed up again when in 1950 Oscar Houston unexpectedly obtained permission to explore the Khumbu valley towards the Nepal flank of Everest. Enthralled, the party hiked into Namche Bazar and on up the Imja Khola river valley to Thyangboche monastery. Houston and Tilman prospected further, camping on the Khumbu glacier and wondering at the great icefall obstructing the Western Cwm. Both thought it too hazardous for laden porters and doubted that Everest could be climbed by this route. History proved them wrong.

Charlie Houston, however, is most famously associated with K2 to which he led two expeditions; the first, in 1938, an acclaimed 'reconnaissance' when he and Paul Petzoldt became the first to reach the Shoulder at almost 8000m on the Abruzzi Spur. It had required a supreme effort, wading in deep powder snow. 'I felt that all my previous life had reached a climax in these last hours of intense struggle,' wrote Houston. This paved the way for another American attempt on K2 a year later, a messy affair that gained another 400 metres but ended with the death of its sponsor, Dudley Wolfe, and three Sherpas.

War service over, Houston returned to K2 in 1953 with a strong team, including his close friend and companion from the 1938 trip, Bob Bates. Storm and struggle accompanied the team up the Abruzzi Spur; even so by the beginning of August they were encamped just below the Shoulder and optimistic the summit was within grasping distance. Just three good days were needed. But foul weather again confined them to battered tents - the flimsy nylon shelter occupied by Houston and George Bell was torn away completely. In retrospect, Houston was philosophical about their 10-day battering at Camp VIII. 'Perhaps it is this conquest, conquest of one's self through survival of such an ordeal, that brings a man back to frontiers again and again,' he said.

On 7 August as the cloud lifted and the climbers crawled out of their tents, the young geologist Art Gilkey collapsed unconscious in the snow. He had developed phlebitis, with blood clots in his left leg. As both a doctor, Houston knew there was little chance of getting Gilkey back to Base Camp alive, but there was no question the team would not try to save him. Avalanche risk and pitiless weather delayed them for another three days, until, as Gilkey's condition worsened with clots carried to his lungs, descent became imperative.

With Gilkey wrapped in a sleeping bag and the smashed tent, the team began inching him down the mountain in a blizzard. All were near exhausted and encrusted in ice. The sick man had just been lowered over a cliff when George Bell, who had frostbitten feet, slipped, dragging his rope mate, Tony Streather, with him and dislodging others. Amazingly the five hurtling climbers were halted on the lip of the abyss by the strength and superb belaying technique of Pete Schoening, who also held the weight of the suspended Gilkey.

How they had survived was doubly a mystery to Houston who lay unconscious on a narrow shelf until urged back to life by Bates, who recalled it thus: '"Charlie," I said with the greatest of intensity, looking directly into his eyes, "if you ever want to see Dorcas and Penny again (his wife and daughter) climb up there *right now*". Somehow this demand penetrated to his brain, for with a frightened look and without a word, he turned...and fairly swarmed up the snowy rocks of the cliff."'

Battered and bleeding the party struggled to the nearby Camp VII, then three of them went to fetch Gilkey who had been left anchored by two ice-axes. He had vanished, together with the anchors. It was presumed Gilkey had swept been away by another avalanche, though in recent years Houston became convinced that Gilkey had 'wiggled himself loose' in order to save the lives of his friends. The close team was shocked by the loss of Gilkey, but as Kenneth Mason observed in *Abode of Snow*, perhaps the mountain had been merciful. Gilkey's seven companions would never have abandoned him, nor in their exhausted state could they have brought him down alive.

It was another four days of nightmare descent before the team stumbled gaunt and hollow-eyed into the embrace of their tearfully relieved Hunza porters. Houston was at times delirious. At a reunion 25 years later he revealed how close he had come to ending it all above the tricky House's Chimney, descended in darkness. He feared he would knock his friends off the mountain if he fell. 'Better jump off to one side and get it over with,' he'd thought. 'I knelt in the snow and said the Lord's Prayer. Next thing I can remember is being grasped by strong arms and helped into Camp IV.'

It had, as Mason said, been an 'Homeric struggle'. Houston was deeply affected by the loss of Gilkey and also, quite unreasonably, by a sense of failure. Though he gave up climbing almost completely, the conversion was not quite so Pauline as often presented. His first thought was to have another shot at K2 a year later and he was stunned to find it already booked by the Italian explorer-geographer Ardito Desio. The news, when Compagnoni and Lacedelli reached the summit, came as a heavy blow to his spirit. However on the dictum that 'style is everything' Houston's men win hands down in the story of K2. Theirs had been a bold, lightish-weight push to within an ace of the summit - in a manner still regarded as the finest of mountaineering styles. Desio, on the other hand, laid siege to K2, employing military tactics, 500 porters, and bottled oxygen for his top climbers.

Houston had permission for an attempt on K2 in 1955 but did not take it up. A growing family and rural medical practice increasingly filled his time. Five years - 1957-62 - were spent in Aspen, Colorado, working at the Aspen Institute and walking and fishing in the surrounding mountain country. Then came a big change as director of the US Peace Corps for India, an ideal post for someone so devoted to the wellbeing of his fellow human beings. Houston loved it, visiting almost every corner of India, plus Nepal and Afghanistan. He was called to Washington to develop the worldwide doctor Peace Corps but his internationalist dreams were snuffed out by the Vietnam War and the doctor draft.

In his last decade, Houston's liberalism reasserted itself and he would stand on a soapbox in Burlington city park railing against the warmongering of George W Bush and the shameful absence of universal medicare in the US. He was a man of complex emotions, as revealed in a fine biography by Bernadette McDonald, *Brotherhood of the Rope* (Bâton Wicks, 2007), with an abrasive, critical streak that caused difficulty in his professional life. He suffered periods of depression and, in his self-criticism, unjustifiably underrated his achievements.

Houston may have quit serious climbing early, but he did not turn his back on one of the great perils of high mountains. In the second half of his life, settled into teaching medicine at the University of Vermont, he became one of the great authorities on altitude sickness. He had made earlier studies of 'thin air' during World War II. Entering the Navy as lieutenant in 1941, after interning at the Presbyterian Hospital in New York, he trained pilots in the effects of *hypoxia* at combat altitudes. Pilots had died as a lack of oxygen caused them to black out or make fatal errors. Immediately after the war Houston persuaded the Navy to let him do further research on volunteers in a decompression chamber. Called Operation Everest, the tests were ostensibly about gaining air combat superiority, though more interestingly to mountaineers they showed that, with acclimatisation, humans would be able to survive briefly at the top of the world. Twenty years later, Houston returned to the subject, directing physiology studies at a laboratory at 5300m on Mount Logan, in the Yukon, each year from 1967 to 1975 and rerunning a more ambitious version of Operation Everest in 1985. He was also the co-organiser, with John Sutton, of the biannual Hypoxia Symposia in Banff or Lake Louise, which began in 1979 and provides a stimulating get-together for mountain medicine specialists.

Most relevant to the growing numbers of climbers and trekkers heading for the greater ranges however, was the publication in 1980 of *Going Higher: Oxygen, Man and Mountains*, most recently updated in 2005. Houston explained why the majority of us suffer headaches on our first days above three or four thousand metres and detailed the more serious forms of altitude sickness, notably High Altitude Cerebral Edema (HACE), a swelling of the brain, and High Altitude Pulmonary Edema (HAPE) a build-up of fluid in the lungs. Each year these sicknesses continue to kill those who rush to altitude or do not acknowledge the symptoms, but after Houston there is not much excuse for ignorance. *Going Higher* is no dry tome.

Houston was a moral mountaineer. The loss of life on Everest in the highly publicised tragedies of 1996 and 2006 appalled him even though the victims were on the kind of big money peak-bagging trips he deplored. Commercialism wasn't evil, he said, 'but somehow it is unseemly for mountaineering.' He believed that on Everest and elsewhere *hypoxia* had eroded not only climbers' judgement but also their ethics and morality. Erstwhile strangers on a commercial trip did not have the 'sense of brotherhood' essential to pull through in extreme situations. That 'brotherhood of the rope' was at the core of his philosophy. And while he had not been able to save Art Gilkey on K2, Houston's own survival and subsequent work on mountain sickness surely saved the lives of many more.

Stephen Goodwin

Arne Naess 1912-2009

When Arne Naess addressed the Alpine Club on 4 December 1950, describing the first ascent of Tirich Mir, he concluded by affirming something with which he presumed all his listeners would agree, namely:

...that large scale mountain exploits are not of value to us climbers primarily for the opportunities of conquering great obstacles which they offer, but for those of arousing genuine enthusiasm for mountains, their grandeur and their beauty.

Whether all his listeners actually did 'agree' with the statement is a moot point, even in the AC. Naess certainly came to recognise baser motives among others, particularly those who climbed mountains to enhance their reputation. 'They want all the name, fame and cake for themselves, often at the expense of others,' he said. It was the cult of 'self-seeking', whereas at the heart of Naess's philosophy was the very different notion of 'self-realisation'.

Arne Naess 1912-2009
(Johan Brun)

For most of us, the physical terrain of Tirich Mir is easier to comprehend than the Norwegian philosopher's concept of deep ecology and the expansion of self to embrace the whole planetary ecosystem. But to label him simply as the genial leader of the first ascent of Tirich Mir would be to ignore most of his full life's work. He was the author of more than 30 books and hundreds of essays and articles. Very few of them were on climbing *per se*, but one in *Mountain* in September 1971 touched a few nerves as he argued against conventional notions of measuring 'success' as a climber.

Only a minority of climbers experienced mountains as he did, Naess wrote, but he went on: 'there are more of us than is generally assumed. Our numbers are distorted by the pressure towards conformity, and the need of young climbers to secure reputations in order to be voted on to expeditions by their fiercely competitive and status seeking elders.'

Arne Dekke Eide Naess was born in 1912 and was brought up at the family home at Vettakollen, near Oslo. His elder brother, Erling, became a shipping magnate. Nephew of both was that other Arne Naess, leader of the Norwegian 1985 Everest expedition (which put 17 climbers including Chris Bonington on the summit) and sometime husband of Diana Ross.

After graduating from the University of Oslo in 1933, Naess continued his education in Paris and then Vienna – where, naturally, he underwent psychoanalysis and also acquired a talent for 'pitonry'. An attempt on the test piece of the day, the Comici route on the Cima Grande north face, ended when his rope mate took a serious fall. Returning to Norway, Naess practised this dark art in the Jotunheimen and on Stetind, much to the distaste of the establishment of Norsk Tindeklub who took the same dim view of pitons as the gentleman of the AC.

In 1939, at the remarkably young age of 27, Naess was appointed professor of philosophy at the University of Oslo and continued teaching there until 1970. Within Norway, he was renowned for his face climb to the seventh floor of the university building where he had his office at the Institute of Philosophy. But if the university was his academic home, his spiritual, and very real home, was Tvergastein, the cabin Naess built above the treeline on the flank of his beloved Hallingskarvet mountain in southern Norway.

Naess's friend Nils Faarlund says visiting colleagues and mountaineers were told that a year with less than 90 days at Tvergastein was counted as a year of 'dissatisfaction':

'From this simple dwelling he had the option of leaving for varied (mountain!) face climbs, kilometres of solo traverses on the lower reaches of Hallingskarvet, ski mountaineering in the steep gullies, long cross country ski excursions, canalising spring melt water, visits to his nearest neighbours – the tiny, alpine plants and flowers, reinforcing the solid rock wall around the cottage to protect it from the often ferocious winds – and so forth, and so forth…

'But did he do any *useful* work here? His numerous publications testify to his hard working life style. In the *Festschrift* edited on the occasion of his 85th birthday, Arne leaves no doubt that a normal working day was at least 10 hours. Only then might he allow for a couple of hours of mountain recreation. Arne was 'bouldering' a generation before the word was coined.

'The library at Tvergastein is vivid proof of the breadth of his intellectual inquiry. It surpasses any normal expectation of a private library. Arrayed on self-constructed bookshelves in all rooms are books, every one of them carried in a rucksack for hours to the cabin at 1503m: generous coverage of philosophy world wide – of course – but also dictionaries *en masse* (Latin,

Greek, Sanskrit...) textbooks and biographies covering the social sciences, psychoanalysis and an impressive collection of literature covering the natural sciences as well as technology.

'Of course he also had literature on mountaineering at Tvergastein, even including Japanese texts. But in his life as a mountaineer he was a do-er and not a reader of fireside books.'

In 1950 Naess led the Norwegian expedition to Tirich Mir (King Tirich) at 7706m, the highest summit in the Hindu Kush. They approached by the south face. Per Kvernberg reached the summit on 21 July after a 10 hour push and the following morning Naess, with Henry Berg and Tony Streather, set out from their small snow cave on the summit ridge, reaching the top at 6pm (*AJ* LVIII, 6-15). Naess recalled it thus:

We were not far from getting frostbitten, a fact we only discovered later, as for some weeks thereafter we did not walk well, but otherwise we experienced no mishap. At 25,000ft we enjoyed immensely – in spite of our fatigue – the wide views given by our outstanding position of our mountain.

Even at such a moment, Naess subtly gives credit for the view not to the expedition's weeks of toil but as a gift from the mountain. And by the time he returned to the Hindu Kush in 1964 with an expedition from the technical university in Trondheim to attempt Tirich Mir East (7692m), Naess's reverential approach to mountaineering had evolved further.

Nils Faarlund takes up the story again:

'Arne set out to renew the philosophy of high altitude mountaineering, introducing the key concepts of *Thriving* and *Zest.* Thanks to his leadership, a team of youngsters from the university mountaineering club reached the summit of Tirich Mir East *thriving*. The motto for this first great face climb in Himalayan mountaineering to reach the summit of an untrodden peak was: 'A toe is more important than reaching the top.' Still in his analytical mode, Arne set up an algorithm for high altitude expeditions:

T = Z *divided by* (Pphysical + Pmental)

(T: Thriving, Z: Zest, P: Pain)

'Continuing his dialogue with the technical university mountaineers, who were the age of his sons, Arne's most radical move came 1971: An *anti*-expedition to Tseringma (7134m) on the Tibet-Nepal border, holy to Buddhists and Hindus. The concept had been thoroughly worked out at Tvergastein over more than 30 years. It was then adapted for 'expedition' use for a light-weight, three-man group who would live for weeks in high camps, making acquaintance with high altitude Nature and climbing Alpine style at between 5000m and 6000m using nature-friendly equipment – certainly no pitons on rock.

'By inviting two Sherpas to join us as ropemates and staying over in a nearby Sherpa village, an acquaintanceship with the local culture was also assured. Based on this example, the Tseringma *Faerd* (a journey cum pilgrimage) members appealed to the Nepali authorities to protect the summits of holy mountains against being 'conquered' by groups with an army-like approach. It was an appeal for an approach to mountaineering as if the mountain matters, as too does the local culture.

'The eco-philosophy concept for the 1971 Tseringma *Faerd* had been developed during the 1966 Stetind 'colloquium'. As the 'foreman' of the Alpine group of the TU at Trondheim, I had invited Arne to pitch his tent for a fortnight under the south wall to continue his explorations with us in this paradise of granite. He came with his second wife Siri, daughter Lotte and assistant Sigmund Kvaloey (later Setreng) – and a rucksack full of books. Roping up with 'the local' Arne, we made a total traverse, 'circumambulating' the eagle's wings and head of the 3km-wide, 1000m-high face. Enjoying the midnight sun we climbed continuously for 24 hours.

'At such a weather-exposed corner of the world sunny days do not occur often. Arne knew this well, yet still refused to climb on two consecutive days, commenting: 'I am a professional philosopher – I have to keep in shape for thinking.' I had already had many conversations with Arne on the demanding question of *why?* Here under Stetind the situation was ideal for working in depth on this important question, for though we lived in a country with more mountains than inhabitants, we were heavily attacked for risking our life for the 'useless pastime' of mountaineering.

'After an 'introductory course' in symbolic logics (Arne was still in his positivistic mode) we were soon deeply immersed in Spinoza's philosophy of self and Self. We took advantage of the professor's profound and recent studies of the master from Delft. Thus we found the best support for our mountaineering ventures. But Sigmund and I were also eager to work out ways of protecting our beloved mountains against aggressive engineers. Again we were lucky, as Arne, during a post-war UN-project on handling conflicts, had studied the philosophy of Mahatma Gandhi: Harmonize ends and means and if necessary, go for non-violent action. But would this suffice to change the pragmatic policies of a technocratic society united in rebuilding the country after the Second World War? Hardly!

'Fortunately the answer was at hand – ecology. During a year's alpine apprenticeship in Germany 1958-59, enjoying a fellowship at the Technical University of Hannover, I had, by chance, come upon this, at the time, rather unknown subject among the natural sciences. We set out to merge descriptive ecology with normative philosphy. *Eco-philosophy* was born.

'Sigmund (becoming a non-violent activist) and I (establishing The Norwegian School of Mountaineering/*Friluftsliv*) chose to follow Gandhi's approach right away. Arne, being an established professional philosopher, took six years to work out his philosophy for the Deep Ecology movement. Since 1972 the Deep Ecology has caught on internationally, finding its strongest support in North America and Australia. Arne would have loved to have read a statement of the French government in a 2009 spring issue of *Le Monde*, where the new green politics are presented as a follow up of Professor Naess's concept of 'deep ecology'.

'During the 1970s and 80s, Arne concentrated more and more on his personal *oikos*-wisdom: *Ecosophy*T (T refers to Tvergastein).

His mountaineering life was certainly a foundation for his work as a philosopher. From the 1980s the mountaineer and the philosopher merged, leaving us with a thoroughly worked out concept for a nature friendly future. Identification with nature is not the goal, it is the way!'

Arne Naess was made an honorary member of the AC in 1991. He died on 12 January 2009, aged 96. He was married three times, first to Else Hertzberg with whom he had two children, later to Siri with whom he had a daughter, Lotte, and lastly to Kit Fai, a Chinese student many years his junior.

Stephen Goodwin and Nils Faarlund

John Noble 1942 - 2008

John Noble was born in Edgbaston in 1942 and died of cancer in St John's Hospice, Lancaster on 31 October 2008. His mother died when he was a small boy and he was brought up by his Aunt Eileen. Dick Stroud and I have been close friends of John's since the late 1960s and he was in effect a member of both our families. He was at first an uncle and later a friend to our children, always showing an interest in their welfare, and we were all very fond of him.

While at school, the Duke of Edinburgh's Award Scheme stirred his interest in the outdoors and he was selected, as one of a group of six Gold Award holders, to be flown to Australia by the RAF to help promote the Scheme there. He started climbing and by his late teens had hitched to the Dolomites and climbed a number of classic routes, including the Dibona on the Cima Grande. He went on to climb in the Valais and Chamonix areas, the Himalaya, Colorado and the UK.

John was employed by the British Antarctic Survey from late 1963 to early 1968, including three winters and two return voyages aboard the *RRS Shackleton*. He first of all accepted a vacancy as cook at Signy Station in the South Orkney Islands, arriving in December 1963. When the promised move to a sledging base did not materialize he returned to the UK early in 1965 and, with characteristic determination, reapplied. The same year he returned south arriving in January 1966 at Stonington Island Station, the main sledging base in Marguerite Bay. Here John was employed as a general assistant, a man experienced in field craft who supported scientists involved in exploration and mapping. Each field worker had a team of nine dogs and John's were called the Vikings. During two years he spent 318 days in the field and sledged 1560 miles. As part of a four-man team, his main journey was to extend the topographic and geological survey of an area east of the Eternity Range to include the Bingham Glacier and as far as 71 degrees S. Having laid depots, they set out on 12 September 1966 and returned on 19 January 1967 after 130 continuous days in the field. He told me of a memorable winter journey he made to an emperor penguin rookery on the Dion Islands, some 60 miles NW of Stonington, across the

John Noble 1942 - 2008

notoriously unpredictable sea ice in that area. As well as making ascents of peaks during the course of his work, when time allowed, he climbed with friends in the mountains within reach of Base. John was in his element and these were truly formative years.

Soon after returning from the Antarctic in 1968, he went to work for the Colorado Outward Bound School, where he was involved in leading groups on extended backpacking courses in the serious alpine terrain of the Collegiate and Elk mountains, often being away from base for a month at a time. In his free time, as well as leading climbs himself, he gained valuable experience by partnering other notable climbers who were working there at that time, including Des Hadlum, Bob Godfrey, Howie Richardson and Rusty Baillie, on what were then high-grade climbs in Eldorado and Boulder Canyons and the Tetons. In 1969 he did similar work at Prescott College, Arizona, before returning home in September 1970 to enrol on a course in Youth Work at Leicester Polytechnic.

John was an instructor at Plas y Brenin from 1971 to 78, during which time he added to his professional qualifications in mountaineering, skiing and canoeing. He was a valued member of staff and benefited from the family atmosphere of the place at that time under the inspirational leadership of John Jackson and later Bill March. John led some of the first alpine ski-mountaineering courses for PyB and the two of us, with Fred Harper and Peter Cliff, made up the 1976 Deo Tiba expedition. It was organised and led by Peter and was one of the earliest Himalayan expeditions dedicated to ski-mountaineering. John was elected to the Alpine Club in 1972.

He married Sheila in 1976 and that year they bought a VW campervan in New York and drove it to Vancouver where John worked at Lester Pearson United World College. On their return the following year they started two complementary companies, Travellers and Wilderness Photographic Library. The former, in the years to come, involved John in leading ski-mountaineering groups, sledging journeys in Sweden and Greenland, voyages to the Arctic and travel in Australia, Africa and South America. His hallmark in this work was to provide personally vetted, environmentally sensitive adventure holidays for small groups. Testimony to the quality of the product was that so many of his clients became friends. During this time he also led treks in Nepal and, in May 1979, with Dick Isherwood, led a Mountain Travel climbing group on the first ascent of the north-east ridge of 6200m Chulu East, now a notable 'trekking peak'. For five years, from 1984 to their divorce in '89, he and Sheila ran Moor and Mountain, an outdoor shop in Kendal. He was elected a Fellow of the Royal Geographical Society in 1981.

Dick Stroud and I have fond memories of the times we spent on the hill with John. Highlights were ski- tours in the Alps and arctic Sweden. Also, for a number of Whitsun holidays we cruised the single malts on the west coast of Scotland, enjoying the spectacular sailing and beautiful remote anchorages. John and I, and another mutual friend, Ernie Phillips (first ascent of *Spectre* on Clogwyn y Grochan with Peter Harding), were keen sea canoeists and on one occasion, John capsized and came out of his boat in rough water near the Longships lighthouse off Lands End. Ernie still finds it amusing, claiming that 'Noble was treading water so fast that his waist was well above the waterline'. There was often mischief in John's humour too; on one occasion when walking over Dow Crag, we saw in the distance a long line of people coming towards us and he set himself up, very convincingly and much to their puzzlement, as a ticket collector. He was also a magician as I witnessed when, on the Haute Route and delayed by bad weather in the Vignettes hut, we were getting seriously hungry. John took our remaining food, a packet of thin spring vegetable soup, to the guardian at the crowded kitchen counter and, to our amazement and gratitude, was able to return with three bowls of very wholesome meat stew that carried us through to Zermatt. Our adventures were always a healthy balance of purpose, a lively sense of humour and rewarding companionship that made reminiscence almost as much fun as the actual events.

John was a good friend, a kind and gentle man, with not an ounce of malice. I never saw him outwardly angry. In later life he lived alone but had a wide circle of friends around the world who will remember him with affection. He was discreetly religious and if there is a path to a good place he will surely be on it, travelling, as he would so often say, 'Onwards and Upwards'.

Dave Penlington

William 'Bill' Percival Packard 1925 - 2009

Bill Packard was born in April 1925 at Palmerston North, New Zealand. His father owned a small newspaper and later was employed by the Christchurch Press as business editor. Bill's association with mountains began while he was studying for a degree at Canterbury University College in Christchurch. Very soon his enthusiasm and leadership ability emerged and he became involved with two local mountaineering clubs. In the latter stages of World War II he was lecturing in geography and working on his Master's thesis.

Bill graduated MA with first class honours in late 1948. This, combined with his fine sporting record in cross-country running and mountaineering, earned him a Rhodes Scholarship. He worked his passage to England shoveling coal in a very sluggish ship. (He once remarked to the current *AJ* editor: 'I was the only undergraduate to arrive at Oxford with coal dust in his hair.') He joined the OUMC and was soon on that Club's committee. Bill Tilman lectured there one evening and afterwards he was introduced to the committee. When Tilman was told that Packard was a New Zealander, he asked, 'Do you know Dan Bryant?' Bill answered, 'Yes.'

'Can you use a photo-theodolite?' The answer was, 'Yes.'

A week later Packard received a telegram inviting him to attempt Annapurna IV. This was in 1950, the first year Nepal partially opened access for western climbers. Dan Bryant had been a much admired member of the 1935 Mount Everest expedition and Packard, when a teacher trainee, had once heard Bryant, an accomplished schoolmaster, lecturing to admiring students.

Bill had watched me operating a theodolite while mapping his thesis country but he had never used one. At Oxford he had some brief tuition on an instrument, then just prior to embarking on the ship Tilman was told that the only theodolite owned by the RGS was away already with another party.

Some 150m below the summit of Annapurna IV, Packard's companion, Charles Evans, became too ill to continue and Bill was unwilling to try the steep ice ridge alone. The other climbers were also unwell. Bill's opinion was that the minimal food on the expedition contributed greatly to the poor performances.

The party separated for the return journey. Bill became infected with poliomyelitis soon after the walk-out had begun. His one Sherpa carried him all the way to Kathmandu and escorted him by train to Bombay where the ship's doctor refused to accept him. The New Zealand trade commissioner rang the Rhodes authorities in England and they agreed to fly him back.

Bill had many months of quality physiotherapy and made a gradual partial recovery, but with the time lost on treatment and on the expedition he abandoned his studies for a doctorate. He married Geraldine Ulrich, a New Zealand geography graduate. By this time I too was living in England.

For two years my wife and I rented a large, cold Georgian house near Bromley, Kent, and we invited the Packards to share it with us.

It had six bedrooms and an acre of bomb-damaged land. Bill was wasted in his arms and could not raise them above his shoulders. He was unable to assist me in outside work, however he was a brilliant and imaginative cook. In spite of the rationing we were soon entertaining numerous visitors, frequently on a residential basis. Among the mountaineers, I recall Evans, Noyce, the Hunts, Bourdillon, Westmacott, Viney, Rawlinson and of course the main New Zealanders.

Bill took a lecturing appointment at University College London and he was soon on the committee of the Alpine Club. This lasted until 1955 when he was offered a desirable lecturing position back in New Zealand. Soon he was on the New Zealand Alpine Club committee and the Mount Cook National Park Board. Along with all these commitments and a young family he also became the warden of Rolleston House. This was an all-male students' boarding establishment that had an unruly reputation. He brought some order into the hostel and found this type of work quite suited him.

In 1961 Bill was appointed as warden to the new, mixed, senior students' hostel, Bruce Hall, in Canberra, along with part-time lecturing in geography at the university. He occupied these positions until his retirement in 1987. He was involved with many voluntary groups in conservation and hospice work and was awarded the Order of Australia medal in 1987.

In retirement, Bill continued his voluntary work but also went on about eight treks. Although weak in the arms and no longer a mountaineer, he was still a very fit walker. He went back to Annapurna and other parts of Nepal, then to Tibet and Russia. In 1995 I invited him to join me on the Kangchenjunga 40th anniversary trek to the two base camps and in 2000 he came on the Silver Hut forty years reunion in Sikkim. Both occasions were enriched by Bill's wit and wisdom on mountain history as we talked for hours about those early expeditions and the affairs of the Alpine Club.

At the Rhodes Scholars' centennial dinner, Bill, being the oldest, was placed at the head table. Beside him was Bob Hawke, the ex prime minister of Australia, and also at the table was another illustrious Bill – Clinton.

Had Bill not become limited by polio, I believe he could have been among the New Zealanders invited to join British Himalayan expeditions in the 1952 to 1955 period. His friendship, particularly with Charles Evans, eased the way for some who were invited and was a big factor in my inclusion as Evans' deputy in the 1955 Kangchenjunga expedition.

When I e-mailed George Band that Bill had died, George replied, 'No longer will he turn up on the doorstep, even though it might be freezing weather, wearing his very brief shorts and humping a large rucksack. He will be sorely missed.'

Norman Hardie

Sir Edward Heywood Peck GCMG 1915-2009

Throughout a distinguished diplomatic career, which often placed him at the turbulent centre of European and world events, Edward Peck confessed an abiding passion for mountains. Memories of past expeditions and relishing the prospect of explorations still to come were keystones to a life spent in the lofty corridors of power. Although always modest about his abilities as a mountaineer, he was a sound navigator and stalwart partner on a climb and few would derive more pleasure from simply being among mountains.

'Ted' Peck died on 24 July 2009, aged 93. He was one of the AC's longest surviving members, having been elected in 1944. He served on the Club committee in the early 1970s and was a regular and valued contributor to the *Alpine Journal*. He also devoted much time to the Mount Everest Foundation, serving on the management committee from 1974 to 1980 and also for a time on the screening committee.

Peck was born in Hove on 5 October 1915, the son of a doctor in the Indian medical service, and spent summer holidays with his family in Switzerland. Aged nine he was taken to the summit of the Haute Cime of the Dents du Midi where he encountered General Bruce, at the time leader of British assaults on Everest and an heroic figure in the eyes of a boy who was already showing a strong enthusiasm for climbing. Peck described the meeting as inspirational. He was not, however, a natural sportsman. When he was sent aged 14 to the 'cold misery' of Clifton College, Bristol, the public school where Pecks had been educated since 1868, he judged his own efforts to play the game as deplorable. Deep fold on the cricket field was cover to read a book, on the rugger field major efforts were made to avoid any contact with the ball, his first and only boxing bout was mercifully stopped by the house master and on the shooting range he nearly shot the sergeant major.

His introduction to the Devon and Somerset Staghounds was equally unsuccessful. 'I have never been more than a passenger on a horse' he dryly recalled, whilst the tyranny of two full-scale compulsory Anglican services on Sundays, reinforced by the penalty of four to six strokes of the cane for non-attendance, gave him a life-long aversion to all forms of organised religion. He was even penalised for trying to improve his German during the tedious service by reading Luther's bible in the original. Holidays with his parents in Switzerland were a blessed relief, allowing him escape to the mountains to walk or ski and at an early age make a solo ascent of the Weissmies (4023m) by its south-west rock ridge.

In 1934 Peck went up to The Queen's College, Oxford, where he won a first in German and French. He was also awarded a travelling fellowship that took him to Vienna, coinciding with the time of the *Anschluss* and Adolph Hitler's triumphal drive down the Mariahilferstrasse. A career in diplomacy was already being forged but because the Diplomatic Service at the time required a private income of £400 a year, Peck was obliged to sit

Ted Peck on Ben Nevis in 1990

for the humbler Consular Service.

At Oxford he climbed in the Alps with the university mountaineering club and after acceptance into the Consular Service he was posted to Spain, where he watched Franco's troops march into Barcelona. As H M vice-consul, he was involved in helping British volunteers of the International Brigade to escape but the experience of twice being present in major European cities as they yielded to pressure from fascist forces gave Peck a profound abhorrence of fascism, whose influence he was to spend the war years combating.

The consular service was classed as a reserved occupation and Peck fought his diplomatic war in a short consular posting in Bulgaria and long ones in Turkey, where he served as private secretary to an ambassador who won notoriety after incautiously employing the German spy 'Cicero'.

Peck's early exploration of the Turkish hills, ostensibly to spot possible spies who had been parachuted in, led to more major accomplishments in the little known Ala Dağ region. He made the second ascent of Demirkazık (3756m) with Robin Hodgkin via what became known as the Hodgkin-Peck couloir. Reaching the summit they removed a swastika flag left by German climbers, replacing it with a sedate calling card. The descent ended with a full speed 400m glissade during which Hodgkin's ancient boots started to disintegrate. Peck acknowledged Hodgkin to be the bolder, more skilled rock climber – even though Hodgkin had lost all his toes and fingers, save his right thumb and forefinger, to frostbite in the Karakoram – but after two hours of hobbling, Peck exchanged boots with his companion and completed the 16-hour day 'more or less on tiptoe'. The following year Peck returned to the Ala Dağ and spent 10 days adding yet more first ascents.

At the end of the war Peck was transferred to Salonika as vice-consul and was soon engaged in combating another totalitarian menace, serving with distinction on a United Nations committee reporting on guerrilla infiltration into the country from its communist neighbours. By 1948 he was due for another move and the Foreign Office destined him for Moscow, an appointment resisted by the KGB who had found Peck a thorn in their side in the Greek mountains. They accused him of involvement in 'falsified elections' in Greece and blocked the appointment.

Peck was dispatched to Delhi instead and by now attitudes had changed within the foreign service as men like Peck had shown that the consular arm could hold its own in every way intellectually and socially. Throughout his middle years he continued to build his reputation and a well-rounded career. By the time he was 40, with the world engaged in Cold War and nuclear menace, Peck became the civilian deputy to the British general commanding in Berlin, and six years later he became, via a posting to the staff of the British Commissioner General in South-East Asia, the assistant under-secretary in the Foreign Office in London dealing with that corner of the globe. He served there until 1965, preoccupied on the one hand with developments in Vietnam, over which Anglo-US relations were becoming often embittered, and on the other with Malaysia's confrontation with Indonesia.

This conflict absorbed much of Britain's diplomatic authority and military strength amid accusations of 'post-imperial overstretch' but Peck's successful handling of so delicate an issue crowned his reputation in military, political and diplomatic circles. In 1965 Peck was knighted and sent as High Commissioner to Kenya where he added to his formal duties mountaineering ambitions on Kilimanjaro, Ol Doinyo Lengai, Mount Kenya itself and the distant Ruwenzori on the Uganda-Congo border. Three years later he was back in London on further promotion as deputy under-secretary of state dealing in the Foreign and Commonwealth Office with military and intelligence matters. Attached to this job was the chairmanship of the Joint Intelligence Committee, again a position requiring a delicate touch in dealing with the various military and political views and demands.

Peck moved to his last Diplomatic Service appointment in 1970 as the British representative to NATO in Brussels as Cold War warriors were still regarding one another with suspicion and politicians on both sides were seeking ways to reduce East-West tensions. Once more Peck's calm negotiating skills were invaluable in the search for a safe transition from nuclear confrontation. He devoted five years to the job, respected both by foreign colleagues and by British ministers, generals, air marshals and his own diplomatic staff. His work was rewarded by promotion to GCMG – which he wryly translated as 'God calls me God'.

In his early thirties Peck had met Alison Mary MacInnes, an administrative-grade member of the Colonial Service and they were married in 1948. When Peck's 60th birthday brought retirement they converted a steading in the Cairngorms into a permanent home and they spent the next 25 years there or travelling the world, often to places with mountains to explore. He wrote two well-received guides to the area as well as a carefully researched monograph on the 16th century battle of Glenlivet. He involved himself in the work of the National Trust for Scotland and the University of Aberdeen as a visiting fellow. Alison Peck died early this year and they are survived by two daughters and a son. Another daughter died young.

Ronald Faux

Bill Ruthven adds: My first meeting with Ted – as he preferred to be known – was some 25 years ago when I attended my very first meeting of the Mount Everest Foundation Screening Committee. The interviewees applying for grants were a typical bunch, mostly young 'hards' who thought that they knew it all. I remember one of them in particular, who after outlining his plans to visit some extremely remote area, was brought up short when the bespectacled gentleman sitting at the end of the table innocently asked where he intended to place his base camp. In a rather off-hand manner the leader trotted out the name of a village (probably the only one marked on any local maps) but was somewhat taken aback when Ted – for that is who the questioner was – warned him that the water supply in that village tended to be suspect, and suggested that he should trek a couple of miles further up the valley. By doing so he would find a spot where not only was the water safe, but a level patch of grass provided an ideal campsite. It was a somewhat chastened expeditioner who left the interview. Maybe he wasn't going where no man had been before! As well as many years' invaluable service on the Screening Committee, up until 1993 Ted also produced the MEF's annual summary of expedition results for the *Alpine Journal*.

For many years I always spent Christmas week in Nethy Bridge with a group of mountaineering friends, and although Ted and Alison usually travelled to Oxford for the festive period, one year, when they stayed at home, after a good day on the hill I took up Ted's long standing invitation to visit him at his remote home above Tomintoul. As we sat in his study drinking tea, he showed me wonderful aerial pictures of Mount Kenya, a peak that I had climbed a few years earlier, and which was one of Ted's favourites from the days when he had been High Commissioner to Kenya. He was proud of his claim to have climbed the highest mountain in each of the countries to which his diplomatic career had taken him.

Elizabeth Jennifer 'Jen' Solt (née Howard) 1921 - 2009

Jen's love of mountain sports was inherited from her grandfather Joseph Fox and her great-uncle F F Tuckett, pioneer alpinists in the Alps in the 1850s. (By coincidence the Swiss celebrated the 150th anniversary of Tuckett's first ascent of the Aletschhorn this July). Since that time, her family has had uninterrupted membership in the Alpine Club.

No surprise, then, that Jen started skiing and mountaineering in about 1934. After that she climbed in the summer and skied in the winter every year until the war and in the years following it. Mostly from her

Jen Solt 1921-2009

family's chalet in Grindelwald, she climbed many of the Bernese Oberland peaks – the list includes the Wetterhorn, Schreckhorn, Mönch, Jungfrau, Finsteraarhorn, Hinter and Kleines Fiescherhorn, Eiger (Mittelegi Ridge), and Tschingelhorn. Probably her finest climbs were made in the Pennine Alps in 1938, which included the Zinalrothorn and the traverse of the Dom and Täschhorn. (At that time she was a semi-professional photographer and has left a particularly fine picture of the Zinalrothorn.) Unfortunately she suffered from altitude sickness even at these relatively low levels, so there was no prospect of her trying anything like the Himalaya. At this time she was a member of the LAC.

In between visits to the Alps she climbed regularly in North Wales, and when the war restricted travel, she also turned to climbing in Skye.

Marriage in 1953 and then raising a family caused a second interruption, but she returned to the high Alps in 1974 (with her husband and her brother-in-law Ashley Greenwood AC) to climb Mont Blanc. She then climbed one 4000m peak in the Alps every summer, as well as many lesser mountains. The list of these 4000m mountains includes the Dôme de Neige des Ecrins, the Gran Paradiso, the Matterhorn, the Alphubel (by the Rotgrat), Piz Bernina, the Finsteraarhorn (again) and finally another return visit in 1991, to the Mönch to celebrate her 70th birthday. With the exception of the Finsteraarhorn, these were all unguided. She ended her mountaineering career on the Via Ferrata of the Brenta Dolomites in 2001 when she spent her 80th birthday in the Rifugio Tuckett.

She was also a passionate skier, and had been selected for the British Olympic Team for the 1947/48 games, but an accident (concussion and broken nose) kept her out of the games. That was one of 10 bone-breaking accidents, all suffered in climbing and winter sports. Ski tours included ascent of the Grossvenediger, Grosser Geiger, Östlicher Simonyspitz and Mönchjoch. She continued to ski regularly until the age of 84, often ski touring with the Eagles Ski Club. Lesser mountaineering and skiing events included the hills of Norway, the Caucasus (Georgia), Mt Etna, the Rockies (both in Canada and the USA), the Southern Alps, Mount Olympus, the mountains of the Sinai Desert, and Finnish Lapland.

Jen passed on the love of mountains to her three children, one of whom is an AC member. She had an ambition that her family should achieve 200 years' uninterrupted membership of the Club, which at present looks entirely possible.

George Solt

George Watkins 1926 - 2008

George Watkins who died on 22 September 2008 at the age of 82 will be remembered for his scholarly demeanour, his courtesy and his impish humour. He made a significant contribution in several areas, notably the affairs of the Fell and Rock Climbing Club.

George grew up in St Helens where he attended Cowley Grammar School. He won a scholarship to Cambridge but delayed his entrance to Gonville and Caius for about 12 months in order to join the RAF as a Communications Officer. After taking his degree in English Literature he taught in Liverpool before becoming English Master at Lancaster Royal Grammar School. For some time he was House Master for the boys who boarded at the school but later, after the death of his father, he made a home for his elderly mother and his niece, who was then a child of five.

He became Head of the English Department but he never sought a Headship as he preferred to stay at the 'chalk face' with the pupils whose interests he had very much at heart. Throughout his teaching career he involved himself in all aspects of school life and even postponed his retirement by two years to design and implement the new school library.

He was a skilful oarsman, was Master of the LRGS Boat Club from 1953 to 1962 and continued to coach for the Club for the next 20 years or so. Until the age of 70 he was Senior Umpire at the Chester, Liverpool and Shrewsbury Regattas. In 1970 he was invited by St Johns College Cambridge to undertake a six-month research project and while there he involved himself in College activities and coached its crews to great success in the 'Bumps' races.

A Freemason for almost 35 years, George was provincial Grand Master on two occasions. He became a member of the Manchester Masonic Research Lodge and in 2007 became the Worshipful Master and President of the Association. Unfortunately the research he was undertaking on Scottish poetry was never completed due to his illness and quick death.

George loved the mountains. He joined the FRCC in 1961 and played a prominent part in all aspects of the life of the Club. In addition to the days he spent on the crags and fells he was involved in the conversion of Beetham Cottage in 1965 and served jointly as Club Librarian and Archivist from 1988 to '98. He became Vice-President in 2000 and was elected President in 2002. He was always ready to don overalls for maintenance meets, while social occasions were much enhanced by his readings of prose and poetry, some of it his own composition. He was concerned that young people should be introduced sensibly to the hills and any he accompanied on the fells were certain of sound training in mountain craft and hut behaviour.

He was a keen alpinist and in 1963 joined ABMSAC where he was a popular and long-standing member. He attended virtually every Alpine Meet over many years, often assisting his alpine companion Harry Archer in the organisation of the meet. It was entertaining to listen to them reminiscing about their mountain adventures and occasional misadventures. With Harry he trekked and climbed in New Zealand. Later, after Harry's accident, they enjoyed a lively Quad Biking holiday around Aviemore. He was a good speaker too and gave some interesting talks to the club, particularly about the Abraham brothers.

George joined the Alpine Club in 1990 and valued his membership. When he attended the 150th Anniversary celebrations in Zermatt he was clearly reliving memories of past climbs as well as appreciating the actual occasion. He also very much enjoyed renewing acquaintance with other members at the Lincoln's Inn dinner later in 2007.

When George was told the prognosis of his illness he remarked to a friend 'Well never mind, it could be worse. I've had a good life.' He was a quietly courageous man who will be remembered with both affection and respect.

Maureen Linton

John Wilks 1922-2007, Eileen Wilks 1921-2008

John Wilks was an eminent low temperature physicist who also studied the First World War Dolomites campaign and was a campaigner for the preservation of footpaths in the Lake District.

He was one of the group of eminent Oxford physicists who, during the 1950s and '60s, worked on the properties of matter at low temperatures. He performed experiments to investigate liquid and solid helium, experiments which were very difficult in view of the low temperatures required. Most textbooks on solid-state physics will show his results for the thermal resistivity of helium demonstrating the mechanism of heat conduction in solids. His important measurements on liquid helium involved its sound absorption and viscosity. He wrote the authoritative textbook on the properties of helium at low temperatures (*The Properties* of *Liquid and Solid Helium,* 1967), another on the third law of thermodynamics (The *Third Law of Thermodynamics,* 1961*)* and a textbook (*Introduction to Liquid Helium,* with D Betts, 1987).

In the late 1960s he changed his field of interest and then, until his retirement, worked with his wife, Eileen, on the mechanical properties of diamonds. This work, together with the general properties of diamonds, was described in their book (*Properties and Applications of Diamonds, with E Wilks,* 1991). The excellence of all of his scientific achievements was recognised when Oxford awarded him the degree of D.Sc.

John's interests extended beyond the field of physics. He and Eileen wrote two books on the largely forgotten, but substantial, World War I campaign in the Dolomites involving the armies of Britain, Italy and Germany (*The British Army in Italy, 1917-1918*, with E Wilks, 1998*: Rommel and Caporetto*, with E Wilks, 2001).

Born on 21 June 1922 in Levenshulme, Manchester, he gained a scholarship to William Hulme Grammar School and then studied Natural Science at Brasenose College, Oxford with a State Scholarship. The War interrupted his undergraduate studies when he was seconded to Farnborough, possibly working on radar, although he took the Official Secrets Act so seriously that his friends and family were never told. Returning to Oxford, he graduated in 1948 with a first class degree. After taking his doctorate, he worked at the Clarendon Laboratory in Oxford until his retirement in 1989.

He was elected a Fellow of Pembroke College, Oxford in 1956. He was regarded as a good tutor and students soon learned that he was highly intolerant of slackness. Although reluctant to take College posts because he regarded himself first and foremost as a scientist, he campaigned for more scientists to be appointed and to take responsibilities in College. He was particularly pleased when a scientist, Sir George Pickering, was appointed Master of Pembroke.

John was an able and enthusiastic mountaineer. Elected to the Alpine

John Wilks 1922-2007

Club in 1950, he climbed throughout the Alps and the UK with many colleagues some of whom went to join John Hunt's successful expedition to Everest. His climbing friends included Anthony Rawlinson, who was his best man, Dick Viney, John Hartog and Tom Bourdillon.

He met his wife to be, Eileen Austin, also an eminent physicist and enthusiastic mountaineer, while climbing on the Cuillin Hills of Skye and together they spent their holidays climbing and later walking on the mountains of Europe. A year older than John, Eileen was an active member of the Midlands Association of Mountaineers and was elected to the Ladies' Alpine Club in 1949. Climbs together included La Luette, a traverse of the Pigne d'Arolla, Monte Rosa, the Jägigrat, Weissmies by the north ridge, and the Nadelhorn-Lenzspitze.

On an unguided ascent of the Matterhorn, John and Eileen saw two people fall to their death, an incident that persuaded them that with a young family they should stick to walking rather than more demanding climbs. High on the Dolomites they came across evidence of the World War I campaign there and this led to their books on this topic.

John and Eileen had one daughter and three sons, one of whom, Bernard, was born with Down's Syndrome. As a consequence of the lack of help and advice they received, they felt that they should write a book (*Bernard*, with E Wilks, 1974) to help other parents in similar circumstances.

John's main love in the UK was the Lake District, substantial parts of which are owned by the National Trust. In the 1980s John was concerned at the Trust's lack of effort to control erosion. He engaged in a long campaign to persuade the Trust to raise funds to reconstruct footpaths and to regenerate fell sides. The campaign took years and included motions at AGMs, articles in newspapers and visits to workers mending paths high up in the hills but it led to success. Wilks received a generous acknowledgement of his campaigning from Dame Jennifer Jenkins in her book telling the history of the National Trust. If you walk in the Lake District today, you should see the maintained paths and fells, in part at least, as a memorial to John Wilks.

John died on 27 September 2007 and Eileen a year later on 20 September 2008.

Ray Rook

Edward Addison Wrangham OBE 1928-2009

I first met Ted Wrangham at Cambridge where he was an undergraduate at Magdalene. His memories were of a very sybaritic three years, ostensibly reading English. He attended all the relevant lectures he could in the first two weeks, but never attended another, finding them a waste of time; other aspects of university life were too entrancing. He discovered mountaineering and made life-long friends in both the CUMC and OUMC, keeping fit by playing squash and real tennis.

He was born on 6 February 1928 under the sign of Aquarius and grew up mostly in Yorkshire but sadly lost his mother when only five, whereupon he inherited a 12,000 acre estate with five farms.

His father, Sir Geoffrey Wrangham QC, who later became a County Court Judge, signed on when war broke out in 1939 and was sent to India serving in the King's Own Yorkshire Light Infantry. So his Aunt Theresa looked after Ted, his elder sister Frances and two cousins, together with three babies of her own. This varied upbringing without too much cosseting gave him financial sufficiency and, by the time I met him, an acquired confidence, an independent spirit, and a love of fast cars. After Eton, in 1946 he did National Service, joining his father's regiment. While serving in the Mediterranean he taught himself to drive, writing his own driving licence, but rectified this later by passing the Advanced Driving Test.

In the early 1950s he climbed on CUMC Meets in Britain and the Alps, and made several first ascents on an enterprising Christmas visit to the sandstone monoliths of the Hoggar in the Sahara. By now he was one of the group of Oxbridge climbers, inspired by Tom Bourdillon and Hamish Nicol, who helped to raise the standard of British post-war climbing in the Alps. He was interviewed for the 1953 Everest Expedition but, not being chosen, had an excellent alpine season instead with quality routes like the Grandes Jorasses by the Tronchey ridge, the Charmoz north-west ridge (*Allain-Schatz* route), the Gugliermina south face, the Géant south face, and Mont Blanc by *Route Major*, these last four routes with Hamish Nicol. Another good route was the Peuterey ridge of Mont Blanc climbed with Roger Chorley in 1955. Ted was a founding member of the Alpine Climbing Group, becoming Secretary and Editor of their Bulletin

Ted Wrangham on Rakaposhi in 1954
(George Band)

and, most importantly, of the guidebooks of selected climbs from the French Vallot guides, but translated into English for the benefit of those with a less than classical education. This brought the Oxbridge dominance in the Alps to an abrupt end.

Back in the UK, there were occasional expeditions of note, for example, the first ascent of *Bloody Slab* on the West Buttress of Clogwyn D'ur Arddu in 1952 by John Streetly where Ted acquired the reputation of being a forceful second. When Streetly was poised *in extremis* on the first crux section, Wrangham shouted, 'Foot out to the left!' and sure enough there was a miniscule foothold which allowed John a moment's respite, and eventually to complete the climb solo after he had run out all the brand new 200-foot rope. I should have been in the party, but was delayed by a broken chain on my motorcycle. This was perhaps just as well because, had I been there, I would surely have tried to dissuade John from even starting such a demanding climb with the very inadequate safety gear they had with them.

Another time, in 1953, a party of six squeezed into Ted's spacious Jaguar. From Helyg they drove to Fort William, climbed Ben Nevis, back to the Lakes, climbed Scafell, enjoyed dinner in Lancaster, then on to Pen y Pass and up Snowdon comfortably within 24 hours from departing Ben Nevis, the first party to achieve this. As a keen driver Ted competed twice in the Monte Carlo Rally, the second time with Chris Brasher in a works car.

Ted also enjoyed long traverses: the Welsh and Lakeland three thousanders and the Scottish four thousanders, all in winter conditions. Perhaps the most notable was a solo traverse of the Greater Cuillin Ridge from Gars-bheinn to Bla Bheinn in May 1953, a feat first accomplished by the redoubtable J Menlove Edwards in June 1944.

After Cambridge, the Greater Ranges beckoned and six of us formed the 1954 CUMC Karakoram Expedition to Rakaposhi. We were lucky to get the very first grant from the newly formed Mount Everest Foundation. To make the trip more interesting, Ted agreed to purchase a new Bedford Dormobile so that three of us could drive overland to Pakistan and the other three drive back. The vehicle, more suited as a baker's delivery van, was not sufficiently robust to handle both the outward and return journey

Ted Wrangham jumping a crevasse on the Täschorn, 1952.
(Roger Chorley)

over the unmetalled, washboard roads of Pakistan and Iran so we had several serious breakdowns on the return, eventually shipping it from Beirut to Genoa. While we were away, the UK government had slapped an extra £200 purchase tax on that model, so Ted was able to sell it at a modest profit. For the buyer it seemed a snip: under six months old with only 14,000 miles on the clock, but he never knew what kind of miles!

On Rakaposhi, we had a lucky escape while traversing the heavily corniced south-west spur. A large section collapsed, precipitating Ted and one porter plus tons of snow into the void, leaving them dangling on the rope with their waists taking the strain, in the days before climbing harnesses. I was roped next to Ted and intuitively plunged down the opposite slope to try to counterbalance their fall. Fortunately, the rope bit into the crest and held, so we were eventually able to extricate ourselves, but Ted wisely descended for a medical check-up which, happily, he passed.

The Rakaposhi adventure concluded Wrangham's excellent list of expeditions in his application form to join the Alpine Club in 1955, in which he recorded his profession simply as 'Landlord'. Two other mountaineering expeditions followed: to Ama Dablam in 1959, and with the Russians to the Pamirs in 1961. Sadly two friends died on each of these: Mike Harris and George Fraser, then Wilfrid Noyce and Robin Smith. He became concerned that the Himalaya was too risky for a family man. He had married Anne Jackson in 1955 and an occupation became essential, for eventually they were to have four children, Mary, John, Geoffrey and Carole.

Ted turned to agriculture and, after a year at Cirencester, came north to Harehope Hall, which he had inherited, to help develop the farms on his Northumberland estate. With good farm managers, he was able to take on additional voluntary tasks as District Commissioner for Scouts and Assistant Liaison Officer for the North-East of the Duke of Edinburgh's Award scheme. He joined the Glendale District Council and the Northumberland River Authority where he was designated Chairman of Water Resources and Land Drainage. After numerous planning meetings, the concept of Kielder Water was invented. It took 23 years from 1959 to 1982, involving a special Parliamentary Bill and two public enquiries before the dream was realised. 'Kielder Water and Forest Park' became northern Europe's largest man-made lake within England's largest forest, the Park's remoteness and clean air and water offering a fresh outdoor experience. In 1988 he served as High Sheriff of Northumberland and in 1995 his work in the water industry and for outdoor activities was deservedly recognised with an OBE.

In mature years, despite increasing weight, Ted continued playing squash, both lawn and real tennis, and was a devil at croquet. He enjoyed country pursuits and spent many happy days with Anne on the grouse moors, becoming a good shot. A further interest in which he became internationally known was as a scholar of Japanese art. He started as a boy of eight, getting a netsuke from his grandfather, Stephen Winkworth. His Uncle Willie Winkworth, also a scholar in the Oriental field, guided him as an adult. He collected first netsuke, then sword furniture, followed by Inro and Lacquer work. (Inro are beautifully crafted stacks of tiny nested boxes held together by a cord secured by a netsuke to hang, in lieu of pockets, from the wearer's obi or sash. They were most popular during the Edo period in Japan, around 1615 -1868.) He compiled a much needed book, *An Index of Inro Artists*, copies of which have entered libraries all over the world, and contributed many articles to art magazines and mountaineering journals. These foreign connections brought many friends and visitors, including two from Japan, two Germans, and two from France in the month before he died on 23 June. He gave freely of his time with no financial recompense.

Having not seen Ted myself for several years, my wife Susan and I had the good fortune to spend a delightful evening with Ted and Anne, and daughter Mary, at his London Club just seven weeks before he died. Although no longer sylphlike and moving slowly, he was the same Ted I remembered as an undergraduate, enjoying good conversation, fine wine, and still liberally sprinkling salt all over his main course, in defiance of well meant medical advice!

George Band

Alpine Club Notes

Honorary membership of the AC has been accorded to Riccardo Cassin and Hamish MacInnes.

Riccardo Cassin died in August 2009, seven months after celebrating his 100th birthday. Cassin's centenary jogged the Club's memory that the Italian legend had never been accorded AC honorary membership and amends were quickly made. A certificate according Cassin honorary membership was presented to his son, Guido Cassin, by President Paul Braithwaite at a gala dinner in the Majestic Hotel, Chamonix, during the *Piolets d'Or* ceremonies in May.

There could hardly have been a more appropriate situation, with the scene of Cassin's greatest masterpiece, the Walker Spur on the Grande Jorasses, so close at hand. Writing in the *AC Newsletter*, Paul speculated on the Italians' journey after making the first ascent in 1938.

'Imagine arriving in Chamonix from Lecco then asking a local a farmer 'did he know how to get to the Grandes Jorasses' and showing him a picture of the face on a postcard… And can you imagine the joy of having climbed one of the greatest classics of all time, possibly the hardest and certainly the finest and most elegant route of its type – they must have had one hell of a good time on the journey back to Lecco!'

MacInnes, a mere stripling at 22 years Cassin's junior, accepted Paul's invitation to honorary membership with the minimum of fuss, simply replying on a compliments slip: 'Aye that'll be fine thanks!'

* A full obituary of Cassin is included in this *AJ*.

CHAMONIX SALUTES HILLARY AND HERZOG

Martin Scott writes:

One year Zermatt – the next Chamonix! Following the AC's 150th party in Zermatt in 2007, a year later (July 2008) we were at that other 'home of alpinism', Chamonix, where the *Mairie* hosted an event billed as *Rencontres aux Sommets* celebrating the first ascents of Everest and Annapurna.

Before the event, some of us went climbing in rather indifferent weather and in the evening the mayor, Eric Fournier, kindly hosted a dinner for various Club people and our President Paul Braithwaite made a short speech and presentation of the Club history to the mayor.

As regards the event itself, despite extra chairs being brought in, the lecture room was packed out with 400-500 people and many standing at the back. First we had a satellite link to Christian Trommsdorff and Yannick Graziani on K2, preparing for an attempt on the south-west face (later called off just before the major tragedy with 11 deaths). This was followed by the speakers – George Band paid tribute to Ed Hillary and Maurice Herzog talked and showed slides from Annapurna. Henry Day presented Herzog with a photo from his own second ascent as "a gift to the first ascentionist from the second'. Doug Scott recounted the 1975 ascent of the south-west face of Everest and Norman Croucher introduced the AC's Spirit of Mountaineering initiative to recognise and encourage selfless behaviour on the mountains.

The next day we were shown round by Claude Marin from the Mairie and in the evening had a large Alpine Club party – or rather a 'Françoise Call party' as the Club contributed wine and Françoise and husband Mark prepared everything else and hosted us all at their splendid chalet with *tartiflette* and other tasty food. The following day was glorious and some went climbing in the Aiguilles Rouges. Very many thanks to our Hon Sec Françoise Call for organising the AC end and to Claude Marin and the Chamonix *Mairie* for their hospitality.

HIMALAYAN CLUB 80TH ANNIVERSARY

Martin Scott writes:

I was privileged to be a guest at the Himalayan Club's 80th Anniversary events in India in March 2008.

On the first day in Delhi there was an interesting art exhibition followed by an enjoyable dinner. The following day the main function was held with the President Suman Dubey in the chair. The chief guest was Sonja Gandhi who is chairperson of the ruling coalition in India, with Mani Shankar Aiyar, the Sports Minister, and Sir Chris Bonington as other leading guests. A delightful film, *80 Years on the Top*, specially made for the occasion, was premiered (review p362) following which came presentations by Sonja Gandhi, then the sports minister, and lastly Sir Chris. The day ended with a relaxed rooftop dinner under the stars.

Next morning about 30 members made an early start on the Shatabki Express up to Haridwar, just before Dehra Dun, where 4x4s were waiting at the station to take us to the Nehru Institute of Mountaineering. Later the 4x4s took us into the Garhwal hills and we trekked up to the beautiful meadows of Dayara Bugyal.

On returning from Dayara Bugyal, most of the party took the 4x4s back south and rafted down the Ganges to Rishikesh. Meanwhile AC Hon Member Harish Kapadia took a small group of friends, including my wife and myself, on a long drive further into the Garhwal up to the Tons river. We then trekked for a week up the Mautar valley, round and down another valley back to the Tons. The Mautar feeds into the Ton's right bank about seven miles from where the Obra also feeds in on the same side (see article

'Temples and Mountains', p13).

All the events were most enjoyable and impeccably organised, and I was left with a warm impression of the close links between our two Clubs.

ALPINE CLUB LIBRARY – ANNUAL REPORT 2008

This has been the year when the Library has taken on a new look both metaphorically and physically. Metaphorically; because lots of issues, usually out-of-sight, have been addressed; for example, the master book catalogue system has been expanded and expedition reports are now on the Club website. Physically; because major cleaning has taken place, shelves reorganised, and a new set of mountain guidebooks has been established. Overall, it looks much the same Library but many volunteers have worked hard to make it provide a better service for Club members.

Whilst we sought a new Librarian, Barbara Grigor-Taylor, ably assisted by Ian Smith, took on the temporary role of running the Library. At the same time, Barbara took a hard look at the internal systems and many improvements were made; some will be further improved as we move into 2009. Meanwhile, Jerry Lovatt, our Hon Librarian, was searching for the right new Librarian. This culminated with the appointment of Tadeusz Hudowski to the post. He comes from the Polish Library in London so he knows about care of books; he is also a keen climber who knows his mountains. Tadeusz has taken up the role of our Librarian with enthusiasm.

The Library is now open for certain (or as certain as we can make it) every Tuesday and Wednesday from 10am to 5.30pm. On those Tuesdays, when there is a lecture meeting in the evening, it is open until 7pm. It is closed, as tradition, for the month of August and during the Christmas to New Year week. In addition, it is also open by appointment on many Thursdays – call 0207 613 0745.

As an initiative, we have run a number of afternoon 'open day' expositions to show books that describe 18th century visits to Chamonix and early ascents of Mont Blanc. Jerry Lovatt explained the context and members were able to examine the historic volumes. Numbers have to be limited but if you would like an invitation to attend a future exposition, please contact us.

The work to conserve the Club's collection of photographs continues, though it is clear that this is a Herculean size task. Anna Lawford has done really well but she needs more help. If you would be interested to work with the 40,000 historic photos, we would love to hear from you.

Financially, the year started reasonably but went from bad to worse from the summer onwards. The Library receives contributions from the Club but we pay rent and rates on the space we occupy, which costs more than we receive from the Club. The income from the Library endowment fund has to bridge this gap and pay for our professional Librarian. But our fund has now lost significant value – not good news. So, very careful money management has been necessary. We are grateful to our Hon Treasurer, Richard Coatsworth, who has kept the situation under control.

Early in the year, Margaret Clennett, our Hon Secretary who is also the Charity Company Secretary, retired after many years of service to the Library. We thank her and wish her a happy retreat to the Welsh border country. Mike Hewson has kindly stepped into the Hon Secretary role in addition to his work organising the second-hand book sales.

We have the duty to care for the Alpine Club's splendid collection of mountaineering books, the most important English language collection anywhere. Every member must be proud of this Club heritage.

Hywel Lloyd
Chairman of the Council of Trustees of the Alpine Club Library

DEDICATION OF THE BINER PLAQUE: ST PETER'S ZERMATT 12 OCTOBER 2008

Michael Baker writes:

Paula Biner of the Bahnhof Hotel in Zermatt died in 2007 not very long after the AC's 150th anniversary celebrations in June that year. She was present on that happy occasion and in good spirit, although very frail. Her death marked the end of a chapter both in the resort of Zermatt and in the annals of alpinism. In recognition of the debt owed by English-speaking mountaineers both to her and her brother Bernard, the legendary Swiss guide, a plaque has been placed in St Peter's, the English Church in Zermatt, and a substantial donation made in their memory for the upkeep of the Church fabric. Paula Biner held the English Church in great affection and the AC Committee was happy to support this project, to which many members subscribed.

The following is an edited version of the address I gave at the Service of Dedication of the plaque conducted by the Archdeacon of Switzerland, the Ven Arthur Siddall on 12 October 2008:

We are here to celebrate the lives of two well-known and much cherished natives of Zermatt – Bernard and Paula Biner. And perhaps more important, we are here to recognise the debt that English-speaking climbers owe them and to give thanks for their friendship and kindness to us, and to those who came before us, over a period of close to one hundred years.

Bernard Biner was born in 1900, the second and oldest surviving son of Alois Biner, himself a mountain guide of the Seiler Hotels and Chief Guide of Zermatt. Bernard's professional introduction to the mountains seems to have started young. According to what he told Paula – who was some 16 years younger than him – he would carry the coats of his father's clients to the Riffelalp Gornergrat or Schwarzee when he was only 12, though they were often too heavy for him. He first climbed the Matterhorn when he was 16 and, according to his führerbuch, was taking clients from 1918 onwards.

He was one of the most active of the Zermatt guides between the wars.

Among his favourite routes was the Younggrat on the Breithorn – of which more shortly. Such was the warmth of his personality as well as his prowess as a guide that many of his clients, particularly the international ones, came back to Zermatt year after year.

Perhaps the best measure of a man is the esteem in which he is held by his peers. Bernard was elected President of the Zermatt Guides in 1926 and held that office for five three-year terms, though not all consecutively, until 1956. He was for 24 years a member of the village's seven-man *Gemeinderat*. For many years too he was also President of the Ski Club of Zermatt, doing much to build up Zermatt as a winter resort. In recognition of his service he was made its Honorary President in 1961. Had he been well enough he would have served as President at the Matterhorn Centenary Celebrations.

A heart attack in 1945 caused Bernard to reduce his mountaineering, though he continued to climb on a restricted basis. Then in 1951 he was immediately behind his close friend, the guide Otto Furrer, when a fixed rope broke on the Italian ridge of the Matterhorn and Otto fell to his death. Bernard rendered first-aid to Furrer's client and probably saved her life, but the death of his friend profoundly affected him and virtually spelt the end of his own active guiding.

It was however at that point that the Hotel Bahnhof was opened by Bernard and Paula. It had been built by their father and for many years had been rented to the Seilers. But in 1951 the hotel was closed, being in need of modernisation. The story goes that a party of French schoolboys in the charge of a priest enquired about cheap accommodation. Someone suggested to Bernard that he might allow them to use the disused Bahnhof Hotel. He agreed, then forgot about it. Time passed. They arrived. Consternation. Bernard and Paula were found. The building was hastily unlocked. It was the beginning of a new life both for the Biners and for the hotel.

For the next 13 years Bernard and Paula made the Bahnhof a cheap informal lodging and a real home for young climbers. It has been said that no genuine climber was ever turned away. And during that time Bernard kept a fatherly eye on all who passed its doors. He was a shrewd judge of character and could divine after the briefest of talk and observation both a man's personality and his climbing ability. He was full of encouragement to the properly enterprising, however modest their attainments. He became synonymous with the Bahnhof and many are those who to this day recall his willingness to advise on mountain expeditions and his pleasure in their fruition. And so it continued.

Although Bernard had been seriously ill in 1964 his actual death in April the following year was both unexpected and sudden. When I made my first visit to the Bahnhof a year later in 1966, people still spoke of him as the doyen of Swiss guides and the friend of the British. He was a sort of unseen presence in the entrance corridor of the hotel.

In 1966 the snow lay late. I was a very inexperienced alpinist, my companion only slightly less so. We had aspirations somewhat in excess of our ability and all the impatience of (in my case) the 23-year old. We had set our sights on the Breithorn by the Younggrat. It was not in condition. We had to wait to for several days. Bernard was no longer there to provide advice. With the presumption of youth, we turned to Paula instead, pestering her for advice about the weather and the route and when it would become climbable. We had no idea at the time of the burden this placed upon her for she patiently tried to answer our questions and did not reveal how difficult it was for her to do this.

Eventually the time came when she said that the conditions had improved enough to make the route viable – or at any rate we construed her answers to our questions in that way. So off we went. We walked up to the Gandegg hut and on; we bivouacked at the foot of the route, started off before dawn and made our way up. It was a protracted business, the ridge being heavily snowed up. I recall only one true rock pitch, the crux, and that principally because there was a plaque at its foot commemorating a fatal accident. We were, I suspect, very slow but we made it in the end reaching the summit quite late in the day and then descended, eventually getting to the Trockenersteg lift far too late to avoid a very long walk down in the dark. We reached the Bahnhof very late indeed, but I said to my companion that I was confident Paula would not have locked us out. And so it proved. I was more than right. We crept in through the door into the lobby and there she was, in the little receptionist's cubicle that the hotel used to have, having waited patiently for our return. She told us then how she had spent her day. She had been worried about us. She had taken the earliest train up in the morning to Rotenboden. She had taken with her Bernard's powerful binoculars. From the other side of the Gornergletscher she had watched us through them as we climbed. She had watched anxiously until we reached the very top. Then, she said, we disappeared on the summit slope, and she felt her responsibility for us was over and she had come down. She was, she said, so pleased for us, for this was Bernard's favourite route. I realise now that she must also have been mightily relieved.

For me that was the start of an enduring friendship. It illustrates how Paula took on Bernard's mantle and hints at the cost. However, it is but one example of the kindness she displayed to scores, perhaps hundreds of British mountaineers, kindnesses which perhaps in our youth we took for granted but which in later life we have come to recognise more fully for what they are and how much they mean.

When I first met Paula she must have been 50. She was an established, if modest, personality in Zermatt. She had been a keen skier long before the days of chair lifts and cable cars. Among her skiing companions was Cicely Williams (author of *Zermatt Saga*) who to judge from Paula's conversation had been a close companion before and after the Second World War. Also she had climbed with Bernard. Paula had worked in the tourist office, among other things, but perhaps most importantly for her she was a member of her Church choir. This endured well into her old age.

But from the early 1950s it is for the Hotel Bahnhof that she will most be remembered, especially by English-speaking climbers, though in reality many nationalities stayed at the Bahnhof and were made welcome.

At the 150th anniversary of the foundation of the Alpine Club, Paula was invited as an honoured guest to the Sunday Service of celebration held in this Church. Frail as she was, she was determined to attend and was collected from St Theodul's Altersheim. A special place had been reserved for her in the front pew of the crowded Church. It was typical of her, however, that she found herself a seat near the back, and there she stayed. The place where she sat on that happy day is almost exactly beside the plaque that is about to be dedicated in her and Bernard's memory. How fitting that is. May this plaque speak to generations yet to come not only of the gratitude we feel for their deeds but also of our respect and love for the memory of two of Zermatt's, indeed of Switzerland's, finest mountaineering ambassadors.

OFFICERS AND COMMITEE FOR 2009

PRESIDENT	Paul Braithwaite
VICE PRESIDENTS	R M Scott
	D R Buckle
HONORARY SECRETARY	F Call
HONORARYTREASURER	R N K Baron
HONORARY LIBRARIAN	D J Lovatt
HONORARY EDITOR OF THE *Alpine Journal*	S J Goodwin
COMMITTEE	D R Buckle
	F E R Cannings, J S Cleare
	M W H Day, S V Hunt, M G Mortimer
	J E Porter (co-opted), A Stockwell, G Thurston
	S A Worsfold, D O Wynne-Jones

OFFICE BEARERS

LECTURES	D R Buckle
MEETS	D O Wynne-Jones
MEMBERSHIP	S V Hunt
WINTER DINNER	W A C Newsom
LIBRARIAN EMERITUS	R Lawford (died 11.10.09)
HONORARY ARCHIVIST	G D Hughes
HONORARY KEEPER OF THE CLUB'S PICTURES	P Mallalieu
HONORARY KEEPER OF THE CLUB'S ARTEFACTS	D J Lovatt
HONORARY KEEPER OF THE CLUB'S MONUMENTS	W A C Newsom
CHAIRMAN OF THE FINANCE COMMITTEE	R F Morgan
CHAIRMAN OF THE HOUSE COMMITTEE	F Call
CHAIRMAN OF THE ALPINE CLUB LIBRARY COUNCIL	H R Lloyd
CHAIRMAN OF THE MEMBERSHIP COMMITTEE	S V Hunt
CHAIRMAN OF THE COMPUTER WORKING GROUP	D N Baldock
ASSISTANT EDITOR OF THE *Alpine Journal*	P Knott
PRODUCTION EDITOR OF THE *Alpine Journal*	B C Newman
NEWSLETTER EDITOR	R Turnbull
WEBSITE EDITORS	D N Baldock, R B Quine
TRUSTEES	M F Baker
	J G R Harding
	S N Beare
HONORARY SOLICITOR	B M Wragg
AUDITORS	Dixon Wilson
CLIMBING FUND	D R Buckle, T A Gronlund
	P Knott, R M Scott, C Watts

Contributors

WILLY BLASER is a Swiss freelance journalist living in the Philippines and specialising in travel and mountaineering. While researching for a paper on Swiss mountaineers in the Himalaya he became interested in the story of Boss and Kaufmann who accompanied W W Graham to Kabru. He became convinced their claims were valid and in 2005 travelled to Sikkim to gain first-hand experience of the mountain and its neighbours.

ANTONIO GÓMEZ BOHÓRQUEZ lives in Murcia, Spain. A librarian and documentalist (information scientist), he specialises in ascents in the north Peruvian ranges. He has written two books: *La Cordillera Blanca de los Andes, selección de ascensiones, excursiones* and *Cordillera Blanca, Escaladas, Parte Norte.*He has climbed since 1967, with first ascents including *Spanish Direct* on the north face of Cima Grande di Lavaredo, Italy (1977), Pilar del Cantábrico del Naranjo de Bulnes, Spain (1980), east face of Cerro Parón (La Esfinge, 5325m), Peru (1985) and the south-east face (1988).

KESTER BROWN is the managing editor/designer of publications for the New Zealand Alpine Club. He produces the club's quarterly magazine *The Climber* and the annual *NZ Alpine Journal*. He is a rock climber and mountaineer of 17 years standing and lives in Lyttelton, NZ.

DEREK BUCKLE is a retired medicinal chemist now acting part-time as a consultant to the pharmaceutical industry. With plenty of free time he spends much of this rock-climbing, ski-touring and mountaineering in various parts of the world. Despite climbing, his greatest challenges are finding time to accompany his wife on more traditional holidays and the filling of his passport with exotic and expensive visas.

ROB COLLISTER lives in North Wales and earns his living as a mountain guide. He continues to derive enormous pleasure as well as profit from all aspects of mountains and mountaineering.

KELLY CORDES lives in Estes Park, Colorado, near the entrance to Rocky Mountain National Park, where he regularly chases windmills to prepare for bigger ventures abroad. He's established difficult new lines in alpine style in Alaska, Peru, Pakistan, and Patagonia. He works as the senior editor for the *American Alpine Journal*.

JIM CURRAN, formerly a lecturer at the University of the West of England, is a painter, freelance writer and film-maker. He has taken part in 16 expeditions to the Himalaya and South America. Books include *K2, Triumph and Tragedy*, *Suspended Sentences* and *The Middle-Aged Mountaineer*. Several years ago now he returned to his original discipline of landscape painting.

EVELIO ECHEVARRÍA was born in Santiago, Chile, and teaches Hispanic Literature at Colorado State University. He has climbed in North and South America, and has contributed numerous articles to Andean, North American and European journals.

PATRICE GLAIRON-RAPPAZ works as a mountain guide in the mountain rescue service. He and Stéphane Benoist have formed a strong unit in high-end alpinism. Patrice has climbed many routes on the north face of Grandes Jorasses, including the first solo ascent of *No Siesta*, while further afield he has done several routes on El Capitan, repeated the Fowler-Watts route on Taullijaru (2002), pioneered *One Way Ticket* on Thalay Sagar (2004), *Unforgiven* on Chomo Lonzo north summit (2005) and finally *Are You Experienced?* on Nuptse (2008), his finest high-altitude achievement.

KAZUYA HIRAIDE works in ICI-Ishii Sports, one of Japan's biggest mountain gear shops, in Tokyo. He is also a professional video cameraman and photographer. Born May 1979, he is a graduate of Tokai University Alpine Club. In 2001 he summited the east peak of Kula Kangri (a first ascent) and Cho Oyu. In July 2009 he summited Gasherbrum I with Veikka Gustafsson from Finland.

GLYN HUGHES is an ex Hon Secretary of the Alpine Club, but is feeling much better now. He accepts that he is somewhat past his prime as far as mountaineering is concerned and now occupies the two equally important and apparently synergistic roles of Hon Archivist and barman.

DEREK FORDHAM, when not dreaming of the Arctic, practises as an architect and runs an Arctic photographic library. He is secretary of the Arctic Club and has led 21 expeditions to the Canadian Arctic, Greenland and Svalbard to ski, climb or share the life of the Inuit.

MICK FOWLER works for Her Majesty's Revenue and Customs and, by way of contrast, likes to inject as much memorable adventure and excitement into his climbing ventures. He has climbed extensively in the UK and has regularly led expeditions to the greater ranges for more than 25 years. He has written two books, *Vertical Pleasure* (1995) and *On Thin Ice* (2005).

JOHN GIMBLETT is a teacher and poet living in South Wales. He has travelled widely in India and Asia, and spent time in the western Himalaya region of India. His new book *Monkey – Selected India Poems* was published in January 2009, by Cinnamon Press (**www.johngimblett.com**)

STEPHEN GOODWIN renounced daily newspaper journalism on *The Independent* for a freelance existence in Cumbria, mixing writing and climbing. A precarious balance was maintained until 2003 when he was persuaded to take on the editorship of the *Alpine Journal* and 'getting out' became elusive again.

LINDSAY GRIFFIN is currently serving what he hopes will be only a temporary sentence as an armchair mountaineer. However, he is still keeping up to speed on international affairs through his work with *Mountain* INFO and as Chairman of the MEF Screening and BMC International committees.

ELIZABETH 'LIZZY' HAWKER is passionate about mountains, wilderness and the Antarctic – and deeply committed to our responsibility of working towards both environmental and social sustainability. An environmental scientist, with a PhD in Polar Oceanography, she is now trying to balance freelance writing with her mountaineering and ski-mountaineering aspirations, and her career as an endurance runner. Her achievements include Gold at the 2006 100km World Championships.

MARK HAWORTH-BOOTH served as a curator at the Victoria and Albert Museum from 1970-2004 and helped to build up its great collection of photography. He is now Visiting Professor of Photography at the University of the Arts London.

DICK ISHERWOOD has been a member of the Alpine Club since 1970. His climbing record includes various buildings in Cambridge, lots of old-fashioned routes on Cloggy, a number of obscure Himalayan peaks, and a new route on the Piz Badile (in 1968). He now follows Tilman's dictum about old men on high mountains and limits his efforts to summits just a little under 20,000 feet.

HARISH KAPADIA has climbed in the Himalaya since 1960, with ascents up to 6800m. He is Hon Editor of both the *Himalayan Journal* and the *HC Newsletter*. In 1993 he was awarded the IMF's Gold Medal and in 1996 he was made an Hon Member of the Alpine Club. He has written several books including *High Himalaya Unknown Valleys*, *Spiti: Adventures in the Trans-Himalaya* and, with Soli Mehta, *Exploring the Hidden Himalaya*. In 2003 he was awarded the Patron's Gold Medal by the Royal Geographical Society.

PAUL KNOTT is a lecturer in business strategy at the University of Canterbury, New Zealand. He previously lived in the UK. He enjoys exploratory climbing in remote mountains and since 1990 has undertaken 13 expeditions to Russia, Central Asia, Alaska and the Yukon. He has also climbed new routes in the Southern Alps and on desert rock in Oman and Morocco.

HYWEL LLOYD has been a keen mountaineer for many years. Apart from the Alps where he has climbed and ski-toured, often with Ingram, his wife, Hywel's enthusiasm for more far-flung places has taken him to Iceland, Iran, the Garhwal, Joshua Tree (USA), Karakoram, Morocco, Norway, Peru, Slovakia and, recently, Mongolia. Hywel is Chairman of the Trustees of the Alpine Club Library.

JEFFREY MATHES McCARTHY is chair of Environmental Studies and associate professor of English at Westminster College in Utah. He is an active climber with first ascents in Alaska and the Pacific North-west. His writing is published in both academic and climbing journals. He edited *Contact: mountain climbing and environmental thinking* (2008).

JIM MILLEDGE has been involved in high-altitude medicine and physiology since 1960 when he was a member of the 'Silver Hut' scientific and mountaineering expedition, Nepal. A general and respiratory physician, he retired from the NHS in 1995.

MIKE MORTIMER started climbing regularly whilst at Leeds University in the early sixties. He first visited the Alps in 1966 and has been a devotee ever since. He has particularly favoured the Kaisergebirge and the Dolomites where he has made many ascents of the classics with his wife Marjorie. He was introduced to the delights of Jebel El Kest by Chris Bonington and now regards this as an essential venue at least twice a year.

TAMOTSU NAKAMURA has been climbing new routes in the greater ranges since his first successes in the Cordillera Blanca of Peru in 1961. He has lived in Pakistan, Mexico, New Zealand and Hong Kong and has made 30 trips to the 'Alps of Tibet' – the least-known mountains in East Tibet and the Hengduan mountains of Yunnan, Sichuan, East Tibet and Qinghai. He recently retired as editor of the *Japanese Alpine News* but continues as contributing editor. He received the RGS Busk Medal in 2008 and has recently been awarded the 4th Japan Sports Prize.

BERNARD NEWMAN started climbing the day England won the World Cup, so you'd think he'd be better at it by now. He joined the Leeds University Union Climbing Club in 1968 when Mike Mortimer was President, and was closely associated with that exceptional group of rock climbers and super-alpinists which included Syrett, MacIntyre, Baxter-Jones, Porter and Hall, without any of their talent rubbing off. One-time geologist, editor of *Mountain* and *Climber*, Bernard is now a 'freelance' writer, editor and photographer.

ANDY PARKIN is still pushing at frontiers as both an artist and mountaineer. Active on the UK rock-climbing scene in the 1970s, he settled in the Chamonix valley, gaining a reputation for his painting and sculpting, along with hard routes such as *Beyond Good and Evil* on the Aiguilles des

Pèlerins. Andy is commited to exploratory mountaineering: Patagonia, Tierra del Fuego and now Nepal have become favourite locations.

ROGER PAYNE has undertaken more than 25 lightweight trips to remote and difficult high-altitude peaks. He has served as the National Officer then General Secretary of the BMC, then Development Director of the UIAA. Originally from west London, Payne lives in Leysin, Switzerland, from where he pursues his enjoyment of climbing and mountaineering, and also his interests in mountain development and organisational leadership. He is currently president of the British Association of Mountain Guides.

SIMON PIERSE is a painter and art historian based in mid-Wales, where he lectures at Aberystwyth University. He is interested in mountain landscape, art and identity and wrote *Kangchenjunga: Imaging a Himalayan Mountain* to accompany the exhibition held at the AC in May 2005, to mark the 50th anniversary of the first ascents. He is a member of the Royal Watercolour Society and an AC artist associate. **(www.simonpierse.co.uk)**

SIMON RICHARDSON is a petroleum engineer based in Aberdeen. Experience gained in the Alps, Andes, Patagonia, Canada, the Himalaya, Alaska and the Yukon is put to good use most winter weekends whilst exploring and climbing in the Scottish Highlands.

ANDREW ROSS studied mathematics at Christ Church College Oxford from 2001 to 2005, but really he spent four years climbing and mountaineering. He was President of the Oxford University Mountaineering Club, 2003-2004, co-edited the 2005 edition of *Oxford Mountaineering*, and was on the OUMC Centenary Committee, primarily spending time researching the history of the club.

C A RUSSELL, who formerly worked with a City bank, devotes much of his time to mountaineering and related activities. He has climbed in many regions of the Alps, in the Pyrenees, East Africa, North America and the Himalaya.

BILL RUTHVEN, an Honorary Member of the Alpine Club, has been confined to a wheelchair for some 12 years, so relishes the opportunity that being Hon Secretary of the Mount Everest Foundation gives him to 'put something back' into the sport that dominated his life for the previous half century. If you are planning an exploratory trip to a high/remote area, why not find out from him whether it is likely to be eligible for MEF support?

YUSUKE SATO is the most active member of the Giri-Giri Boys and has participated in most of their expeditions to Alaska and the Himalaya. He has been climbing for more than 10 years and in July 2009 repeated Mick

Fowler's Golden Pillar of Spantik route with the same partners as on the 2008 Kalanka success. Sato lives in Yamanashi, Japan, with his wife and daughter and works as an engineer.

VICTOR SAUNDERS was born in Lossiemouth and grew up in Peninsular Malaysia. He started climbing in the Alps in 1978 and has climbed in the Andes, Antarctica, Papua, Rockies, Caucasus, India, Pakistan, Nepal and Bhutan. Formerly a London-based architect, he is now a UIAGM guide based in Chamonix. When not working he likes to relax on steep bits of rock and ice. His first book, *Elusive Summits*, won the Boardman Tasker prize. In 2007 he received an honorary MA from the University of Stirling for services to Scottish mountaineering and between 2004 and 2008 has successfully guided Everest four times.

MARCELO SCANU is an Argentine climber, born in 1970, who lives in Buenos Aires. He specialises in ascending virgin mountains and volcanoes in the Central Andes. His articles and photographs about alpinism, trekking, and mountain history, archaeology and ecology appear in prominent magazines in Europe and America. When not climbing, he works for a workers' union.

MARTIN SCOTT has lived and worked in many countries as an exploration geophysicist and later in computing. Now that he is retired, he has more time to pursue his great interest in first ascents of obscure remote peaks, in pursuit of which he has climbed in Tibet, Sichuan, India, Greenland, Nepal, Bolivia, Ecuador, Indonesia, Peru, Pakistan and Alaska.

UELI STECK was born in Emmental in October 1976 and worked as a carpenter before becoming a professional alpinist. Just taking his diary for the first seven months of 2009: in January he climbed the *Schmid Route* on the Matterhorn in 1hr 56mins, April he shared in *Piolets d'Or* for his ascent with Simon Anthamatten of the NW face of Teng Kangpoche, May he free-climbed *Golden Gate* on El Cap, and in July he summited Gasherbrum II by the normal route, taking 14.5hrs from camp 2 at 6500m to the top (8035m) and back to camp 2.

KEI TANIGUCHI works in Tokyo as a facilitator for outdoor activities. Born in July 1972, she has devoted herself to adventure racing, trail running and mountain biking as well as climbing. Her first high mountain was Denali in 2001 and she was a member of clean-up expeditions to Mount Everest in 2002 and 2003. In June-July 2009 she made an unsuccessful attempt at a first ascent of Khinyang Chhish East, Karakoram.

JOHN TOWN is a retired university administrator. He has climbed in the Alps, Caucasus, Altai, Andes, Turkey and Kamchatka, and explored little-known mountain areas of Mongolia, Yunnan and Tibet. He is old enough to remember the days without satellite photos and GPS.

DAVE TURNER spent his 26th birthday on Cerro Escudo in the Torres del Paine. Based in northern California, he has made more than a dozen solo ascents of El Capitan, including three solo new routes, and has completed five expeditions to South America. In 2009 he switched his attention to Baffin Island and climbed a new route (VI 5.10 A3 M5 60°) solo on the 1400m north face of Broad Peak in a 39-hour round push.

DAVE WYNNE-JONES used to teach before he learnt his lesson. He has spent over 30 years exploring the hills and crags of Britain and climbed all the Alpine 4000m peaks. By the 1990s annual alpine seasons had given way to explorative climbing further afield, including Jordan, Morocco, Russia and Ecuador, though ski-mountaineering took him back to the Alps in winter. Expedition destinations have included Pakistan, Peru, Alaska, the Yukon, Kyrgyzstan, Nepal, India and China with a respectable tally of first ascents.

SIMON YATES has, over the last 25 years, climbed and travelled from Alaska in the west to New Zealand in the east, from the Canadian Arctic in the north to the tip of South America. He is the author of two books, *Against The Wall* and *The Flame of Adventure*. As well as writing, Simon runs his own commercial expedition company (**www.mountaindream.co.uk**) and is a popular lecturer.

KATSUTAKA YOKOYAMA is a founding figure of the Giri-Giri Boys. He and fellow member Fumitaka Ichimura have climbed together in Alaska, the Andes and Himalaya as well as their native mountains. Their enchaînement on Denali with Yusuke Sato was an application of link-up games played in Japanese winter climbing to the highest mountain of North America. Yokoyama participated in the BMC International Winter Meet in 2007 and was so impressed he started a Japanese version of the event in 2008.

Index 2009

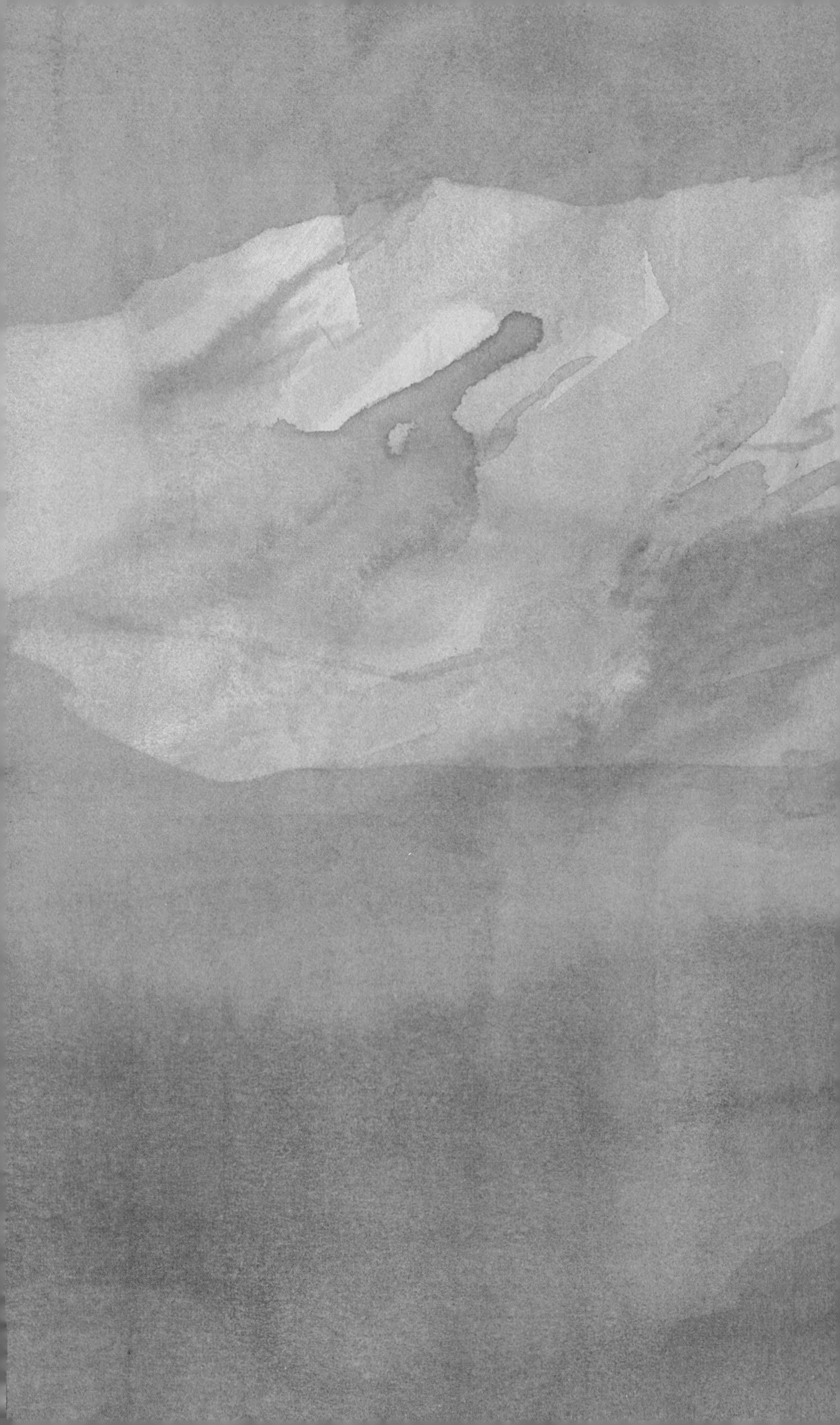